KEEPER

and

KID

ALSO BY EDWARD HARDY

Geyser Life

Edward Hardy

KEEPER

and

KID

THOMAS DUNNE BOOKS
ST. MARTIN'S GRIFFIN
NEW YORK

THOMAS DUNNE BOOKS.
An imprint of St. Martin's Press.

KEEPER AND KID. Copyright © 2007 by Edward Hardy. All rights reserved. Printed in the United States of America. For information, address St. Martin's Press, 175 Fifth Avenue, New York, N.Y. 10010.

www.thomasdunnebooks.com
www.stmartins.com

The Library of Congress has catalogued the hardcover edition as follows:

Hardy, Edward, 1957–
    Keeper and kid / Edward Hardy.—1st ed.
        p. cm.
    ISBN-13: 978-0-312-37524-9
    ISBN-10: 0-312-37524-7
    1. Single men—Fiction. 2. Parent and child—Fiction. I. Title.
    PS3558.A62373K44 2008
    813'.54—dc22

                                                                    2007039351

ISBN-13: 978-0-312-57376-8 (pbk.)
ISBN-10: 0-312-57376-6 (pbk.)

First St. Martin's Griffin Edition: August 2009

10 9 8 7 6 5 4 3 2 1

For Tamar

ACKNOWLEDGMENTS

Many thanks to my agent, the ingenious and farsighted Sara Crowe; to my editor, John Parsley, for his keen eye and excellent advice; to the wise readers and friends who helped this project along, especially Paul Cody, George Estreich, Jane Hardy, Kathleen Hughes, Tamar Katz, and Dana Kinstler; to the Rhode Island State Council on the Arts for their support; and most of all to Nat and Will, for taking me there.

ONE

If dogs, rats, and pigs can all sense a looming earthquake and make plans, how come all I can manage is a quick stare at the phone just before it rings? I was at work, wishing for another cup of coffee. It was 9:32 and they were playing Big Maybell on WRIU's Hard Boiled Jazz show, at some other Cynthia's request, so her name was already in the air. There was no one else in the shop. Just me, searching the Web to gauge how much the prewar Lionel trains and rolling stock in the box at my feet might be worth.

On the second ring I picked up and said, "Love and Death," as that's the shop's name. It's one half of this antique store salvage yard empire that my middle-school buddy Tim asked me to come down to Providence and help run. That was four years ago, shortly after everything in Boston spun apart.

"Jimmy?" It was Joan, Cynthia's mom and my ex-mother-in-law. My shoulders hiked because everybody here calls me something else. To Tim, I'm Keeper, my last name. Leah, my girlfriend, calls me Keeper, too, but she's working on making the switch to James.

"Joan? How did—"

"I called Tim at home, which was Cynthia's idea." Usually Joan sounded like the high school vice principal she used to be, but right then her voice felt thin, as if it were pushing out from under a rock. "Did you move?" she asked. "Would a forwarding message have been so hard?" Her tongue made a click. "This will be a shock," she said, "but Cynthia really is quite sick and I am not using that term lightly. She would like to see you. Today."

My first thought, which I knew had to be wrong, was that Cynthia had a cold or bronchitis, pneumonia at the worst. Something you could solve with soup. Cynthia never got sick. She was one of those healthy-as-a-horse exemptions you'd expect to read about in some study. I used to think it was all that adrenaline, knocking off viruses right and left before they could get a toehold. "What do you mean sick?" I asked.

"Exactly what I said." Joan's tongue clicked again. "We're at Mass General and she would like you to visit. Early afternoon is generally a good time for her."

A heating oil truck downshifted on Wickenden Street. I closed my eyes.

"Jimmy," Joan said, "Cynthia would like to ask a favor." Even from an hour away I could tell that Joan didn't like the idea of this.

I said, "What room?"

She hung up. I stared at the phone, examining the holes in the red handset the way everyone always does in the movies.

Mass General, I thought. Okay, I can find the room. And yes, it annoyed me that Joan wouldn't say what had happened, but it wasn't a surprise. I had already decided that whatever it was couldn't be that bad. Cynthia was tough. Tougher than me by a factor of ten. Cynthia. All those days, and a lot of them, most of them, good enough to be scary. Even then, in certain moments it still felt like I had done something wrong.

The snow-amplified sun kept pushing through the windows, reflecting off the hairdressing shop's plate glass across the street. Big Maybell kept on singing. I needed coffee. I still had the phone in my hand. It was still red. It felt like that night when I was ten, staring out my bedroom window when I should have been asleep, watching as the sky turned white because a meteor landed three states away and not knowing until the next morning what it was I'd seen.

TWO

I put the phone down and circled the long green table, thinking, shit, shit, shit. Cynthia. On the third lap I found myself at the door. I pulled on my leather jacket, put up the "Be Back In Ten" sign, and stepped into the sun.

I had to stop and pat myself down until I found my sunglasses in the right front pocket. I took a breath and turned left. It was 27 or 28 degrees out. I could tell. It's this weird skill I picked up from skiing a lot as a kid. I can smell how cold it is. Twenty smells colder than thirty. It's hollower. I watched my breath curl off as I waited on the curb. It felt like I'd stepped through some sort of window. As if by simply hearing Joan's narrow voice everything had changed. But it hadn't. You live here, I told myself. Right here. Now.

My cell phone waited in my coat, at the bottom of my chest pocket. When it goes off it vibrates and plays the theme from *Gilligan's Island,* which always startles me. But that's good, because when I'm lost in work, looking things up or writing yet another eBay description, it can get hard to pull away. That time it felt like I had a gerbil in there, headbutting my chest.

"Whatchadoing?" Leah's calls always start this way. She was checking in from North Carolina, where she'd been for the last three days. Leah's an architect, the newest partner in a three-person firm that's found a happy niche creating interesting, nonoppressive office and sometimes residential space out of beat-up factory buildings. She was in Durham, converting a hundred-and-fifty-year-old tobacco warehouse into a corporate headquarters. Leah has always put in a ton of hours and this could have been an issue, relationshipwise, only I understood. She didn't decide to be an architect until later on, and finding out what you want at that point in life always makes you feel a little behind. Besides, space in a relationship is good. It keeps the rust off.

"What am I doing? Walking down Wickenden. I'm next to the aquarium store because I didn't get enough coffee."

"Coffee Exchange?" Leah has this low voice. Horses and babies always respond to it.

"That'll work. I'm already pointing downhill."

"Get a hot chocolate," she said. "They make the best hot chocolate but nobody thinks to buy it."

Leah. An inch taller than me, dark-haired, straight bangs, with a gleam, an actual gleam, in her eye. At that point we had been together for two years and I would still look across sometimes and not believe it. I tried to think of what she might have on without resorting to: What are you wearing?

"We're just hanging out," Leah said and sighed. When things are going well on a trip Leah will check in. If they're not, she won't. "Jon's reading the paper. They wanted to have breakfast and talk about the teaming area. Which is another way of saying we'd like a room with a table. Then they changed their collective mind at the last minute. I'm in this shiny diner. Everyone here eats grits, for breakfast. Ever had grits?"

I tried to imagine Leah staring into a bowl of grits but couldn't remember what they looked like, so it turned into a picture of Leah wincing at a bowl of steam. "Nope," I said. "What does this company make? You told me—"

"But it bounced off." I heard the smile. "Satellite things. Geopositioning receivers. They need a lot of meetings to do that, I guess. It's warm, which got me thinking about our yard. I'm liking the idea of a yard."

"It's too cold to think about the yard," I said. "Our yard is frozen. You could park on it. I think I need to think about paint before I can think about the yard." We had just moved from an apartment on the East Side of Providence to a tiny, nineteenth-century house in Pawtuxet Village, down in Cranston, a few yards from Narragansett Bay.

"Any news from Fred?"

Fred is Leah's big orange cat. He's a dog-sized cat. He's a ten-year-old footstool with legs, only he gets ideas. The second time we let Fred out he didn't come back and this was February. I had fliers up all through the village. "Nobody's called," I said.

"Cecilia's still putting food out at the apartment," she said. Cecilia is Leah's high school friend from Syracuse who somehow also ended up in Providence. Her loft on the edge of the Jewelry District is so big you can rollerblade there.

"She's going all the way over to do that?"

"Yeah. Ow, dropped my glasses. Hang on." Leah has these red-framed architect glasses, which she takes off and twirls. Some North Carolina dishes clanked in the background, reminding me that I had to get groceries before Leah got home, because you can only go just so far on toaster waffles and nachos. "What were you doing before you needed coffee?" she asked.

It was weird. I heard Joan again and saw Cynthia in a bed with lights going across the bottom. It seemed suddenly important to keep all that separate. "Trains," I said. "I was going through a box of model trains. They're all Lionel and prewar. Some of them still have the orange inner box and the cardboard sleeve, which is so rare. It's rolling stock and one stunning Hudson locomotive and tender. It's gunmetal glossy and still sealed." My voice kept ramping up. But that is the amazing thing about what I do. It looks like life has flattened out and presto, some completely cool object pops up right in front of you.

"Did you open it?" Leah asked.

"Oh no. God no."

"You didn't peek? How do you know what it is if you didn't open it?"

"The number," I said. "It has a number on the box."

She giggled. "I'm not laughing at you, dear, I'm laughing near you."

"It's worth a couple thousand dollars, at least. Less if I tear the paper. I'm pretty sure Neil Young is a part owner of Lionel Trains."

"Is that so?" Leah thinks what I do is infinitely amusing and maybe it is, but it's my job. I make saves. I find new homes for interesting objects. Sometimes it's salvage stuff at the yard, stained glass and mantels, pieces that should fit into some house somewhere. And with the Web and ads in the right magazines, I can keep a lot of that out of the landfill. Or else it's straight antiques, Mission chairs, and French mirrors, the smaller things we sell all over the world. It's strange, if the dollar goes down people in Japan and Sweden suddenly start buying more of our stuff on eBay. Or we haunt auctions. Two months ago I bought a wooden canteen in a lot for $150. The guy who sold it said the canteen was a fake, but it wasn't. It came from the Revolutionary War. The inside still smelled like smoke. I got a rush just holding it. We sold it later at an auction in New York for $7,000. Every day amazing objects float to the surface, all from the strangest corners.

"Did Tim find the trains?" Leah asked.

"Yep. They're rolled up in old *Boston Globe*s, from 1963."

Tim finds everything. He has this sense. He's always had that, even when we were kids checking out the dump. In college we used to buy truckloads of stuff at farm auctions in Iowa, where Tim spent summers, and take them to California. That first trip we sold a whole load at this flea market in Pasadena outside the Rose Bowl. We were thousandaires. So when Tim asked me to come down I thought, Okay, for a while, until it turned into another life. You know how for a long time it seems like there's this big ramp and you're only supposed to be heading up? Then you gain a little altitude and finally realize, it's actually a big plateau. Once you're up there you can drive all over the place.

It wasn't a normal life, I knew that, but I was happy. I had great mountain biking twenty minutes away. I had the ocean. I had a kayak. I had Card Night. I had restaurants to explore, the Providence Bruins to see for almost nothing, music to check out that I'd probably not bother with if I had the endless choice of Boston, I had antique shows to do, stuff to learn. Plus I had friends. Okay, a lot of them were Tim's friends, but they took me in. And Leah, I had Leah. A good life, everywhere I looked.

"I forgot," Leah said. "I'm coming back Sunday night not Saturday."

"I wish you were back now."

"Me too, but it's Card Night. Is Card Night at Tim's?"

"Indeed."

"Good. I'll get Jon to drop me. His car's at the airport already. Oops, we have to go. Miss you much." She hung up. Leah hates to actually say good-bye.

THREE

It felt good to drive. I'd done that hop up I-95 to Boston maybe seven or eight million times by then. It's usually under an hour, unless it rains or you run into commuters, but I always see things. That afternoon it was a bald guy in a blue minivan with an unknown number of kids in the back, talking on two cell phones at once. At first he had one in each hand, so he must have been steering with his thighs, then he moved them both to his left, like he was palming a basketball. I started to pass only I slowed down to watch. Sad bastard, I thought. See, I know I'm not set up to be a lot of things. I don't have the eyesight to land an F-14 on a carrier at night, I can't wrap presents, I don't have the patience to decorate cakes, the lung capacity you need to be a long distance runner or the oversized heart. And I can live with that. No one has to do everything. So every time I see a baggy-eyed dad at the grocery store with five kids draped over the cart, I have to look away. I could never get that good at herding. I don't have the peripheral vision.

I called the yard and told Tim I was closing the store and had to go to Boston, but I didn't say why. It wasn't like I didn't want to tell him or that scooting up there wasn't entirely justified, it was just that old life—new life thing. It felt important not to cross the streams. I also probably didn't want to admit that this had to be serious if Cynthia was calling me back from the dead for a visit. Was I still annoyed that Joan couldn't just tell me what had happened? Yes, but Cynthia's entire family has a nearly comical history of secrecy. Some of it tended to be absentminded and some of it wasn't, but all major announcements were saved for the nearest holiday or the camp reunion in New Hampshire. That way they could be delivered in person, thereby doubling or tripling their dramatic value. You had an operation on what? They fired you when? You bought a silver car without telling me? My family does a low-key version of this too, so I understood, which I'm sure is one of the reasons Cynthia and I did so well together, for a while.

Here's what happened: Eight years ago I married my upstairs neighbor. That's not how you expect it to go, the girl next door, the girl upstairs, but that's how it went. We were living in Somerville, on different floors of an up-down two-family and in wildly different worlds, but that June Cynthia and I started hanging out on the front porch. I was editing at an info tech magazine, which seemed to double in size or spin something off every nine months. I even had the word "Executive" in my title there at the end. Cynthia used to say: "Would the Executive Whatever Editor either take Arrow for a walk or find me some cilantro?" She had finished a pastry program at the French Culinary Institute in New York, followed by a year as an assistant pastry chef in Manhattan, before picking up nearly the same job at a restaurant in Boston, in the South End. Before that she taught English in China (I did it in Japan) and filed a fistful of years in the sad corridors of social work, until that all felt too hopeless. She used to come home and bake out her frustrations anyway, so pastry chef? Better hours than a regular chef. It made a kind of sense.

A lot of things with us never did make sense. That's what I say now. Like our schedules, they never matched, since pastry chefs go in around dawn and are done in the afternoon, while I could never figure out how to make it home before eight. Cynthia would grab my arm on the stairs and say: "How come we're never both in bed and awake at the same time?" We'd forget to tell each other things. We kept secrets. We put off all the big discussions. Together, we couldn't plan our way out of a well-lit paper bag. But we were smitten, actually smitten, and that never exactly wore off. Here was this funny, optimistic, almost fierce do-it-yourself girl with bright gray eyes, waves of sandy, fly-away hair, and a thing for sparkling scarves. It always felt like we were getting away with something, just by being together. I knew how rare that was.

Things never fall apart the way you think they will. This time it was real estate. I'd been making great money for a while and Cynthia decided that since this was Boston, we should buy houses. And at that point you still could, in spots, so we bought the duplex in Somerville we were living in and a pair of nearly dubious two-families at the edge of Jamaica Plain, which we let a management company run. Everything appreciated. We couldn't believe it. Some months the buildings made more than we did. Cynthia went from restaurant to restaurant and started baking these tall, tipsy-looking *Alice in Wonderland* wedding cakes on the side, which people would order months in advance. Then one afternoon she got a take-it-or-leave-it chance to buy a European, all-butter-and-cream bakery on Concord Avenue in Cambridge. She had a partner, Fay, but to actually purchase the building Cynthia sold the Jamaica Plain houses. There was a little left over, which she plowed into three stocks, a nano-something company, a pharmaceutical start-up, and some other one. A restaurant friend said these were all about to go straight to the moon and she could make up the difference overnight. Only for various strange reasons all three crashed.

I didn't find out she sold the houses until eight months later, after the fire at the bakery. It was electrical, at night, and no one got hurt, but the building was wildly underinsured. Next a San Jose company bought the magazine and I got laid off. Fay started hearing voices and retreated to Maine and somewhere in there Cynthia and I unraveled. We never had a big blow-out. If we had that might have saved it. But neither of us is remotely good at any kind of confrontation. The lengths we'd travel to avoid that stuff. Instead we just got furious and stayed that way. We stopped talking and started sniping. Doors slammed. We moved in wary circles. It never occurred to us to get help and our groceries ended up on separate sides of the refrigerator. Then one Friday night I came in and found her taking all the CDs out of their jewel boxes and smashing the cases with a hiking boot. "I hate fucking jewel boxes," she said without looking up. "These are all going in plastic sleeves." The next morning Tim called asking for help, and running off to Providence seemed like an excellent idea.

I couldn't stop feeling burned. I kept thinking: How could this happen? These were secrets the size of—buildings! You're in a relationship and stuff that huge is going on and nobody tells you? Yeah, I know, I was there. How could I not know? But I had a job that ate my brain. I thought it was all going fine. It's like stocks: You never pay attention as long as you're making money. It's also true that even though it was my money, the two-families were in Cynthia's name. I don't remember why we did that. We were married. Joint assets. Who cares whose name is on what line?

From here, at times, it almost seems amusing. They were only buildings. It was only money. Except I tossed off what remained of my sense of humor, scrunched down, and got bitter. We never actually called lawyers, but we did end up in mediation. I guess it was civil. We sat in a conference room and then drove home to divide up the stuff. I'm taking the chair made of sticks. You take those stupid sky paintings. And no, that potato masher never belonged to your grandfather. It's amazing how love turns into things and things can only turn into money. I am never divorcing anybody again. Ever.

Cynthia and I did keep in touch, but faintly. A few e-mail probes, nothing more. It felt safer to just pretend we lived on other planets. The last time I actually saw her was four years ago. It was July and her grandfather Will's one hundredth birthday, so they sprang him from the nursing home while the family convened at their camp in New Hampshire. They have a cluster of cottages at the north end of Lake Sunapee that's been in the family on Cynthia's mom's side since before the Depression. Cynthia and I used to go up for overnights and her grandfather still asked about me. He would always shoot the fish with a pellet gun after we caught them. I never understood that. The thing was nobody told Grandpa Will that Cynthia and I weren't together anymore, so I went along to act the part. Everyone pretended, some better than others and Cynthia's sister Grace not at all, that they weren't disgusted with me for running off. That was okay; I understood.

It stayed hot the entire weekend, even at night. You could hear the heat. Then Cynthia and I were on the dock after midnight, drinking white wine mixed with crushed ice from tall plastic beach glasses. A faint breeze kept the bugs away and you could see the stars. They were muted but there. I sat back, leaning on my elbows, feeling buzzed and happy. It felt strange being with her, but strange in the best way. Familiar and surprising, yet not exactly real. I turned my head when someone laughed back at the house. The sound crossed the water and I remembered that I was still playing a part. It did no good at all to think about the consequences of anything here, I thought. I smelled cedar. I heard a loon, and then a zipper as Cynthia took off her clothes. It was both a surprise and not. She said, "Come on," and pointed off the edge, before slipping into the water with a smooth sound. "Oh, hurry," she said. I remember the embrace of air across my back. The slight coolness of the water. We swam silently out to the float and made love, surrounded by that lake smell, the stony taste of it on her skin, as we spun slowly under the fuzzy stars. We spent the night in her brother's one-room cabin that he built around a tree. There were bird bones on the ledges, a fox skull tacked to the post over my head. Even when we woke up, it still didn't feel like a big deal.

Later that morning, driving down through Boston and the forest of cranes surrounding the Big Dig, I got scared, because it was all still there. It felt like we had jumped back to before and that frightened me, because before was wonderful. Only I knew what came next and I couldn't live there with all those secrets, or things that looked like secrets, hanging on the walls. I also knew that if I'd stayed another four hours, if I'd stayed for lunch, we'd have been back together.

I parked and crossed the street and thought, Mass General is huge, this has to be bad. It's a warren of tall connecting buildings and Cynthia was in Ellison 8, the Cardiac Surgery Step Down Unit. I blinked when the tall guy at the desk told me. I found the right bank of elevators. I found the room and knocked lightly. It was a double but there was nobody in the first half. I stepped around the curtain. The bed with a yellow light flashing at the bottom, the chair you could sleep in, and another that looked even less comfortable. The drapes were open. You could see a square of faint blue sky.

Cynthia was asleep, curled up on her side and facing me. She had on blue flannel pajamas and a red fleece ski hat that made her look a little elfin. The IV went into her left wrist. I couldn't move. It was that weird time-jump moment when you see somebody you used to love. That strange second or two where you fall back into the echo of that other life. I can never tell if it's a wish or a reflex.

Joan sat in the chair at the end of the bed. "Jimmy," she said and stood. "Hello." Her long fingers folded around my wrist. Her straight, blunt hair seemed to be a brighter white. She looked both happy and dismayed that I was actually there. She pulled me over to the empty side of the room.

I always tried to brace myself for head-on encounters with Cynthia's mom. I had to remind myself that yes, this woman is selfish and unpredictable, that she suffers from a kind of tunnel vision that's only sometimes admirable. I needed that bit of distance.

"Cynthia made me promise not to tell you over the phone," Joan said. "I don't know why but— Aortic aneurysm." It sounded like the title of a play. "This is rare, but it happens. On Monday Cynthia was at work and having back pains. They got her to an emergency room in time, then here, but her heart stopped twice. The surgery was successful. It was a large one, seven centimeters. There was leakage and had it ruptured, she would have died in five seconds. We were in the ICU until yesterday."

"Mom?"

Joan's empty ring finger touched her lips. "It's Jimmy." She rattled the pink-striped curtain.

Cynthia smiled. It hurt. I put my hand on the white blanket and squeezed her knee. I reached behind for the chair and it felt like one of those times when even lifting your arm seems scripted. The back of her hand felt cool. She looked pale and puffy. "What are you doing here?" I asked.

Her lips tightened. I saw a faint smile. She seemed to be thinking, I don't know how this happened either. "It's good to see you," she said.

"I'll be down the hall," Joan said.

Cynthia stared. Her eyes seemed bigger. "I'm so tired. Mom told you—"

"Yeah."

"I thought I'd hurt my back." She smiled again. "I was lifting a cake and I dropped it. Then it went from my back to my chest. The pain was amazing. I thought I could be having a heart attack, but the EKG was fine. They thought I had gallstones, then they did a CAT scan and some other tests and found it. It was like a balloon on the—"

"Aorta?"

"Yeah, it ballooned out below my heart. They replaced part of it with a tube. Most people don't get this far. A lot of people. I am going to be okay." She nodded, a faint, swift piece of punctuation.

I nodded back. But something about that felt strange, as if this would be the moment I'd remember later on. Stop, I thought, you're being overly dramatic. She had a close call. The world looks different after a close call. "How long will you be in—"

"Some more days. Last night they let me take a shower. I climbed four stairs yesterday. It hurts," she said. "I have fluid in my lungs, which they're worried about. The nurses keep asking me where the pain is on a scale of zero to ten. It's hard to put a number on."

"Are they giving you enough, so you're not—"

She nodded. "I wanted to see you," she said. "It's good to see you. It gets sad in here." She blinked, twice. "I never meant for it to get this long—"

"I know," I said. "It's what happens, you get lost in your own life."

"I never meant," she said. "I really didn't. How are you?" She squinted, as if she were piecing together a suspicion. "How is your life?"

My life. My other life. "Good," I said and felt instantly awful.

"Tell me. How's the job and Tim—how's Tim?"

"Good," I said. "He's good." I told her how working at the yard was still surprising. How it's strange and interesting and hardly ever feels like work. How it's kind of living by your wits. How nothing can happen for a long time and you can sort of lose faith, then all of a sudden, you catch a lot of fish. I wasn't making anywhere near the same kind of money, but I didn't dread Sunday nights. "I'm amazed I did what I used to do for so long."

Cynthia smiled. "How's Leah?"

"I feel bad telling you."

"Don't. I've never even seen a picture. What does she look like?"

"She's . . . tall. She wears bracelets, kind of jangles when she walks."

I thought of all the other things I could say. How Leah keeps me balanced. How she checks up. How we just bought this tiny house and she wants a basketball hoop in the driveway. How she used to play in college. How we went on a roller-coaster tour last fall: Coney Island, Six Flags. How I never would have thought of that.

"Do you ever fight?"

"We quibble about stuff, like the best way to peel a kiwi."

"But you tell each other things. You don't let them sit, like we did."

"No. That doesn't happen."

"Does she want kids?"

I didn't expect that. I finally said, "I guess. Someday." I pretty much knew that was a lie, but I didn't want to make Leah sound hard, which she's not. Or maybe someday was the thing I wanted to think about myself. But mostly that felt like a part of the world I knew existed, only I couldn't see the need to actually explore. Like Antarctica. My dad's been there twice on nature tours. It just sounds cold to me. I did sometimes wonder what it would be like to be old and not have kids, if I'd regret it and pathetically latch on to someone else's, like my brother's. Only the last time I was there his boys were running around in football helmets firing Lincoln Logs at each other. I mean, you're thirty-six. You settle into who you are.

"Send me a picture," Cynthia said.

"Sure," I said, but I knew I never would. Then I wondered about the favor. "Your mom said—"

She nodded. Another slight, familiar, that's-what-we're-here-for head shake. It made me feel very much on the outside, as if I were only one of many on a list. But that was the place I'd built for myself. Cynthia watched, as if she were thinking about something entirely different, as if she were deciding between two paths, or two things to tell me. "It's Arrow," she said.

Arrow. We nearly had a custody battle over Arrow.

"He knows you. He's not at the house now, but at Sally's in Acton. I need you to take him. For good."

Arrow, half husky and half German shepherd, black with one blue eye. I used to pile up snow in the backyard to build him a hill and he'd smile and bob his head, saying: You get it! You know what I need! But I couldn't take Arrow because of Fred. Then Fred ran away. That was pretty much official. Right?

"Sure," I said. The roof of my mouth prickled.

Cynthia gave me that look—sad, piercing, and deadly serious. "I've been thinking about it for a while. I can't handle him anymore," she said. "Even before this and I'm—" She closed her eyes. "He'll be home next Wednesday. I could be home by then, too. Grace will be there, so call her. Or I'll have her call. He's on a natural diet now. Raw food. Mostly chicken backs and necks."

I nodded. I couldn't think of what to say.

"We just screwed up," she said. "You know that. It never really changed anything between us."

I had to blink and bite my tongue.

"There are other things we need to talk about. We really do. I've been working on telling you some things."

"What things?"

"I can't. I'm so tired. I'll see you, then, so?" She closed her eyes. "Don't go until I'm asleep."

I held her little finger and rubbed it. It was a thing I used to do. I sat back in the chair. I watched the blinking yellow light at the end of the bed. I kept thinking, she was almost not here. Almost.

After a while Joan came in. She touched my shoulder and told me to give her all my phone numbers. "We'll call," she said, "if there's a change."

Cynthia's breathing settled and I slipped out into the blinding bright of Boston, where everything felt overquick but somehow in the distance. Then I did a funny thing. I forgot where I lived. I got in the truck and veered up through Cambridge. I drove to Somerville, almost to Davis Square, before I turned around.

FOUR

I came home, sidestepped some boxes, and glided around the house. I reheated the leftover chicken masala and drank three pale ales, but sleep was hard. I kept twisting in the blankets and seeing Cynthia in that room. I kept wondering about the scar. Then with everything else I could have worried about I started obsessing about the house. I don't know why. All those boxes to unpack, each one holding a thousand layered decisions. I also meant to start priming the dining room, since there were some big color discussions coming up with Leah. I'm a neutral-toned guy and Leah goes for richness. I wanted to clear some of that away before she got back, but I kept ending up staring at the floor and forgetting to move my feet.

Saturday appeared and disappeared and I didn't go to the yard or talk to anybody. Leah even called with her flight numbers and to tell me about North Carolina barbeque and contractors who make things up and I let the machine take it. I kept thinking about Cynthia. Five seconds, her mom said. If they hadn't caught it, Cynthia would have been gone in five seconds. I kept seeing the arc of her neck when she got out of the shower or that tiny smile she'd flash when someone gave her a compliment. She always got the hiccups when she laughed too hard. She always brought up the big questions when she was brushing her teeth. It dawned on me that had it happened, if she hadn't made it through the surgery, only I would know those things.

By Sunday it started to feel like I'd made some kind of adjustment. I got out to the grocery store. I watched the Bruins beat Tampa Bay on NESN. I left a message for Leah, but I couldn't fight this lingering suspicion, the way the air smells before it snows, that if Cynthia and I hadn't blown apart, maybe this wouldn't have happened to her. I knew that didn't line up or really make sense, but the idea kept following me around.

Eventually I started thinking about Arrow. The quick black dog with the optimistic soul. I went on the Web to look up dog house plans. I started wondering about that raw diet. I even made a run to PETCO and picked up two chrome bowls and a leash. I still had them in the truck Sunday night when I drove up to the East Side, because in spite of everything it was still Card Night.

Tim and Julie own a tall two-family off Hope near Rochambeau. They have the top floors and Justin, the astronomer they never see, lives downstairs. It's a narrow, turn-of-the-century house with lots of porches and they've painted it a deep blue that looks black during the day but purple by evening. The kitchen is crisp and minimal, but the dining and living rooms are part of Tim-world. There's a Victorian fainting couch, an Eames chair, and two white department store fixtures that look like spaceships but make great end tables for the zebra-striped couch. The shelves are full of patent models, eighty-year-old stuffed birds, and wind-up toys from the 1930s. There are two ancient manhole covers up on the plate rail and above the dining room arch there's a yellow and red Pennzoil sign. Tim loves objects. When we were kids he used to bring stuff back from the dump, gears, long pieces of metal, things we couldn't identify, simply because we loved the shapes. Before he got to Providence Tim did time as a grad student in New York in museum studies and covered part of his rent Dumpster-picking for copper. I mostly hang on to old things you can still use: tools, kitchen stuff, a generally functioning answering machine from the 1970s. It's good to keep the objects in circulation.

I came upstairs with a twelve-pack of Sam Adams and a tub of oil-cured olives. Tim sat at the oak table, loading slides into a carousel tray. He had on his blue SPAM baseball hat, which hides the bald spot.

"Hey," I said. "How was that house?" On Saturday Tim went to northern Connecticut to look over an ornate 1920s four-square that we could have bought the salvage rights to.

Tim picked his glasses up off the table. They're silver-framed and small. "Far away," he said. "There are some nice panels, but not enough to make it worth it. And when I got back to the yard somebody bought three columns. We never sell columns. How is it that we sell more when I'm not around?"

I landed the beer and Tim caught the falling tub of olives. "You don't look so good," he said. "What happened with Boston?"

Usually I talk all the time, but I can't stand telling people bad news. Back when I worked for the magazine, at the end, I had to lay off a bunch of people. You don't ever want to be fired by me. It takes a week and then I buy you lunch.

I sat in the ladder-back chair. "Remember Cynthia?" Tim gave me that "of course" look and I told him.

He stopped loading slides. Historically, I'm the one who comes in all twisted out of shape and Tim has to talk me down from the tree. This time he didn't have anything to say.

"I'm still in that deer-in-the-headlights phase," I said. "It's like I'm walking into the room but I can't believe the room actually exists."

"You sure you're good for Card Night?"

"Remember Arrow?"

Tim opened a beer with the shark-shaped opener on his key chain and handed it across. "The snow dog."

"I'm bringing him down. Next week."

He took a long breath. "How'd Leah take it? The news."

I was going to tell her. I just didn't want to call back and lay it all out on voice mail. Then I thought: Why would Tim care what Leah thought? But of course Tim cared. I met Leah at Card Night. These guys have known Leah longer than I have. Leah would be fine, I decided. Arrow's a great dog.

"You are going to tell her," Tim said. "No sign of Fred?"

Fred wasn't coming back. I knew that. "Not yet."

"How are you going to manage that? Cat, dog, the proverbial—"

"Arrow's an outdoor dog."

"Outdoor dogs are never all that outdoor." He smiled. "You'll be getting up on dog time. Six-thirty comes quick."

This had not occurred to me.

Julie climbed the stairs with two brown paper bags of snacks. I saw cheese doodles, a baguette, and a container of mung beans. I love mung beans. Tim gave me the should-I-tell-her glance. I shook my head. I mean Julie's great. She's smart, kind, perky, but with a dark sense of humor. It was just, I didn't think I could explain it all over again so soon.

"The people from Planet Child are falling like flies." Julie's hair snapped as she turned around. "Rory's sitter is sick and Jill's kid has a fever. Sam has the flu but he could have made it yesterday. Is Leah coming?"

"From the airport, but late," I said. "Jon is dropping her."

"She's a trouper," Tim said.

"It's Card Night," I said.

Card Night has been around for longer than I've been in Providence. Usually it's the second Sunday of the month and everybody puts in ten bucks, which is a complete entertainment-dollar bargain. It's poker, it's just not very intense poker. We play the regular games and some that only exist in this particular universe, like Caveman (clubs are wild) or Jackson Five (jacks and fives are wild) or Elevator to Bosnia. That night it was only the four of us: me, Tim, Julie, and Phil Reynolds, a burly mountain bike buddy who loves Tom Waits and designs action figures for a toy company.

Phil is actually hard to play against because he doesn't say any-thing. Tim talks. Julie talks. Leah talks, bets small, goes for a huge pot when she has nothing and thinks it's hilarious if she wins. I talk too much and bet big in the wrong places. You'd think after a while I'd notice a pattern.

For the first hour I played pretty well. I split a nice hi-lo and actually remembered to fold before I went too deep on a couple of others. But I kept seeing Cynthia. Conspiratorial glances from long-ago dinner tables. That glimmer-look she used to give me. You never wanted to play cards with Cynthia. She could bluff. She used to tell people on planes she was a twin and go on in de-tail about the strangeness of it all or explain that her dad was a semi-famous folk singer from Texas. My parents couldn't always sift for the joke, which left Cynthia surrounded by a small cloud of constant misinformation. She liked that.

At 9:30 I started wondering if Leah's flight was late. At 10:02 I wanted to hop on Julie's computer and check one of those flight trackers on the Web. Then I heard the door and Leah's boots on the stairs.

"Leah," they all said and it sounded like an exhalation. Then it was "Heys" and kisses all around.

Leah's black coat flew across the zebra-striped couch. She kissed me with the metallic scent of airplanes and travel. She had on those caramel-colored Bakelite earrings and her bracelets rattled. I felt her gray-sweatered arm drape across my shoulder. I never like it when couples go in for public displays and at Card Night we al-most try to pretend that we're not involved. It's better for the game, but right then, just sitting next to her left me kind of ecstatic. The lucky guy, I thought. I am the lucky guy.

"I'm so glad to be here," Leah said. "Are those olives?"

"I brought 'em," I said.

"Why, thank you." She smiled.

"How was North Carolina?" Julie asked. "Is that right?"

"Warm, and next week we're going to Phoenix to pitch a new

project. I think these are way too far away, but I'm in the minority. I left my bag at the bottom of the stairs. Is that okay?"

"That way when I trip over it I'll know who to sue," Tim said.

"They'd still be your stairs." Leah turned to me with one of those looks that makes you believe there is no one else alive in the universe. "Any word from Fred? Is he back?"

I shook my head and realized I had to decide exactly when I was going to tell her about Arrow, and Cynthia.

"Fred, the cat of another species?" Phil asked. "The cat who needs a saddle? How could anybody lose a cat that big?"

"I don't think it's a question of losing the cat," Tim said. "I think it's more the cat gets an idea."

"I had a dream last night," Leah said, "and Fred knew how to drive. But he had to sit on this woman's lap to reach the wheel. She was skinny but I couldn't see her face."

"He's always been a smart cat," Tim said. "For his size."

I opened Leah's beer. "Only he hisses whenever he sees himself in the mirror. Sometimes his reflection doesn't even fit in the mirror."

Leah squeezed the back of my neck. "Stop."

I smiled. I liked being possessed.

"Pets are overrated," Phil said.

"Keeper and I used to have a pet trout," Tim said. People laughed and Leah turned to stare at me. It was kind of amazing to still be at that point in a relationship where the stories haven't all been told.

"It was in a river in Lincoln, where we grew up," I said.

"You guys grew up in Nebraska?" Phil asked.

"Massachusetts," Tim said. "It hung out in this same hole and we used to go touch its back."

"How old were you?" Julie asked.

"Eleven," I said.

"I don't think regularly visiting an animal in the same location in the wild makes it a pet," Phil said.

"I had these friends," Julie said, "in Cambridge, who were trying to get two cats to live together, so they put the same perfume on them."

Tim kept counting out Leah's chips. "Would that work with a dog *and* a cat?" He actually winked. Did he think I was going to tell Leah right then? At Card Night? I'm never very good when people tell me what to do, even if I know they're right.

The game went on for another hour until Julie ran out of chips and asked if it was time to watch the Wilsons. The Wilsons are a recent, secondary element of Card Night. A few months ago Tim bought a locked maple chest at an auction, which turned out to be full of slides, hundreds of those tiny yellow Kodak boxes. And given that Tim is the kind of guy who already had a slide projector and a screen in his hall closet, we started watching. Mostly it's a series of well-documented vacations from the 1960s. There's a mom, a skinny boy with curly blond hair, and his younger also blond wide-eyed sister. The dad apparently takes most of the pictures, as so far we've only seen him twice. At first we were kind of in it for the irony and the time travel, but then everybody got interested. It feels like this strange, found documentary. The gas prices are absurdly low, the cars all have square edges, the milk bottles are glass, and the women wear white blouses and head scarves. We've spied on the Wilsons at Disneyland, in the Grand Canyon, in the Florida Keys. This year the boy must be seven or eight, which today I guess would make him a bit older than most of us, except Phil. We don't know their real names, but they look like Wilsons—Ray, Susan, Stevie, and Karen.

That night the Wilsons were in South Dakota. They had a pop-up tent trailer, which was a departure since on other trips we'd meet them at drive-in motels. The slides changed with that familiar hum and clunk. They were in the Badlands. I watched the kids wave from their black Chevy station wagon and realized that no future generation will ever know the long-trip freedom of rolling around in the vast back of a station wagon with the seats folded down. We went to Rapid City, Mount Rushmore, a rodeo in Deadwood, then back to the campground in the Ponderosa pines. Campfire sparks streaked and blurry kids waved sharp sticks armed with burning marshmallows.

I loved the Wilsons. They looked comfortable, nuclear in a way that had always seemed deeply dubious to me. But sometimes there were shots we couldn't understand: ten or twelve in a row of a burned-out house in a field, police cars, and an angry crowd outside a San Francisco bar, a flipped cigarette boat in Florida. It kept us watching and we wondered if the father was a news photographer or if he wanted to be. That night we came across five pictures of a motorcycle accident. A red pickup and a Harley on a curve in the fading evening light. At first there wasn't even an ambulance, only a cluster of people in short-sleeved shirts and the motorcycle driver lying on the asphalt across the yellow line. No helmet, a light blue sweater covering his head, the blood pooling underneath.

Leah squeezed my elbow. "Promise me you'll never ride a motorcycle."

"I already have."

She exhaled and puffed her bangs. "Never again."

This was something we did, the list of promises. I'd promised that I wouldn't be in World War II, turn into a corrupt bond trader, join the Mafia, become a nineteenth-century hit man or sign up for the crew of Apollo 13. But I still wouldn't allow myself to get married. Not again. It was a question with Leah that I kept thinking would one day fade from view. It never did.

I hate missing Card Night," Leah said, falling into the black flannel sheets. "It's so hard when I'm away and I don't get to come home and jump you immediately."

That's the best thing about business travel. When Leah gets back it's a blur, arms and legs and lips, still.

"Wait." She looked over the side of the bed. "I had something for you. Hey, did we leave my bag?" She laughed. "Fuck, it's at Tim's."

"Tomorrow." I pulled her back on top and hiked the covers. Her shoulder looked so white against the dark sheet.

"I had a different dream about Fred on the plane," Leah said and kissed my neck. "He was in the woods, living in a barn, but it all looked like a scene from a children's book. This guy in the seat next to me kept talking about coyotes and house cats, how they're moving into Rhode Island."

"House cats?"

"The coyotes. They eat the house cats."

"In this neighborhood?"

Leah sat up. "You don't seem that worried about Fred. And what was that dog-cat stuff where Tim winked?" She tapped my nose. "James."

So I told her. I started with Cynthia and how I hadn't seen her in four years and how it all felt beyond surreal. How at the end I felt a little dismissed and that, too, seemed weird. "Is it strange, me telling you all that?"

Leah gave me a wide look and asked why I hadn't told her sooner? But there was more to it. Leah had never met Cynthia and I knew she wondered about her. It wasn't jealousy exactly, but the way you can worry about someone's former life: if they were happier in some ways, if they compare at all, if they're still in love with a certain part of what they had. The other person can always say no, no, this is a zillion times better, but you wonder. You want to see the whole story. I wonder about Gary, the guy Leah almost followed to minivan land, until she got scared and swerved to grad school. Those two were together for seven years. They're friendly now. Gary sends Christmas cards of his kids and Leah gets this look, like she's both fascinated and reliving a near-death experience.

I kept talking about the hospital and Cynthia's mom and the aneurysm stuff I found on the Web and by the time I finished

Leah had on her silk pajamas, the ones with the small, dark moons.

"I'm sorry," she said. "That's really hard."

"There's this favor, too. There's a dog. Arrow."

Leah looked at the spot on the bed where her toes made a bump under the quilt. "The dog you two used to have? But Fred?"

I didn't think there was going to be any more Fred, but I was sharp enough to respond with only a series of um-like noises.

"What kind of dog?"

"Husky, part shepherd. Blue eyes. Well, one blue eye."

"Is this the dog that brought back the neighbors' stuffed animals?"

"They were always intact. Never shredded."

"Fred could still come home. I've had Fred longer than—I was going to say you but that doesn't sound right."

How did I end up on the losing end of a comparison to an obese cat?

"You waited to tell me this until after we'd made love?"

"Well, yeah," I said. "I am a guy."

"Great."

Leah has limits. There's a horizon and it usually only stretches so far. But sometimes you can make a deal and the horizon will loop out a little more. It's like buying extra innings and I respect that. Making this move, getting this house, that was a kind of deal, a commitment. A semi-substitute for the marriage question? Almost. And I understood, Leah has considerable family pressures. She has long weekly phone calls from her mom. I used to always tell Leah that if she died first she could come back and haunt me all she wanted. But mainly I kept thinking, if I don't get married, I won't have to get divorced, ever again.

"When are you going to go get him?" she asked.

"Next week, I think."

She gave me a kind of sad look. "I don't understand pack animals," she said. "They seem so needy. Can we talk about this again?"

"Sure," I said, only I knew there would be conditions.

"I don't know. I mean, what happens when Fred comes back? Really. But I have to sleep. I have to go in tomorrow."

I turned out the light and slid my chin in against Leah's long back. I could feel her breathing. This was far from okay, even I could see.

FIVE

Days passed, an entire week. I kept thinking about Cynthia, only it stayed in the background, like a shadow. I assumed things there were okay, or getting better, or else they would have called. Then it came to be Friday night and I was up on the ladder. My butt hurt and I was on the second coat in the pantry. I'd almost reached the point where I could begin to tolerate the radioactive canary yellow I was touching up around the cabinets.

Leah kept smiling and smiling. The potential clients called and postponed her Phoenix trip until the next Monday, but she was already prepped, which gave her this bubble of time to work on the house. I got a break because Tim found Maggie, a grad student, to take over the Wickenden Street shop three afternoons a week. The plan was to give me more time to find buyers. Instead, I stayed home with Leah to work on the house. Work guilt is a constant feature in the land of the nearly self-employed.

The result: a tiny bonus, a sort of vacation. We slept in, saw Yo La Tengo at Lupo's, slept in again, took down wallpaper, had dinner at the Red Fez, had lunch at Olga's, and picked up coffee and scones every morning at the bakery around the corner. Plus, I got a new drill. I was in the Home Depot, trying to decide between the six-volt and the more expensive twelve-volt version, when this guy in Carharts walked by and said: "Buy the big one. Don't even think about it. Spend the money, buy the big one."

Sometimes I need the nudge to do the right thing. I understand this. Just as I understood that as soon as I told Leah about Arrow I'd eventually have to make a deal. And I knew this was a hard spot for Leah to reach, because even thinking about a deal meant admitting that we'd lost Fred. So in the end I consigned full interior paint control to Leah. It pained me, but I needed my dog.

Pre-deal the plan was to divide up the spaces, given that Leah likes big statements and I'll go for a wheat tone if you push me. The fights we were going to have? Monsters. You could have watched them on the Weather Channel. But color is like that. It goes right to the core. You have to live with the result, every day. Leah would have been waving her slappy wand of paint shades. I'd have been shouting, "Stop with the periwinkle!" All of which would have been followed by a little light stomping.

Except I caved. I said yes and in return got this week of domestic bliss and industry. I avoided the slip into the long unnecessary negotiation, I just caved. Even at this late date there's room for advancement. Only up on the ladder I kept wondering what it was I'd actually signed on for. We had deep and different tones in every room: a hazy gray front hall, the spruce green living room, a cranberry dining room, the canary yellow pantry, a cerebral blue ceiling over the kitchen cabinets. But when you looked from one room to the next, the colors did kind of work, like frames. It added up, only I couldn't understand why. And Leah makes these picks off the top of her head.

The thing I kept forgetting was that with Leah, once you made the deal everything was great. There was no lingering animosity. No grudges lurking under the bed. It's an amazing capacity because it allows you to keep going. There's no psychic mud to get stuck in. And all week unexpected things kept spilling out. We were sitting on the couch eating leftover Strange Flavor Chicken and scanning the channels when Leah said, "Aren't the Bruins on tonight?" I was stunned. How did she know that? She must have looked it up. I watch hockey all the time now, only I'm not quite sure why. I played wing as a kid but moved over to soccer when the checking started. There I ended up as a goalie, which my grandmother, who was from Edinburgh, would chalk up to destiny, given my last name. I played goal all through high school and beyond, and it's great, once you get past the idea that you can't save everything. Except I kept getting hurt—ribs, a shoulder, concussions—so I stopped. I took control of the remote and we shot to NESN, Bruins and Rangers, no score, halfway through the first.

I had just finished with the yellow paint when Leah came by to put on some Donna the Buffalo. They're rootsy and Cajun-sounding, a little funky. Leah loves jam bands. She likes Phish, String Cheese Incident, even the Dead. She always wants to dance until we slide way on out to that spot where you can't think anymore. It is only another religion-trance substitute, I know that, but it works.

Just before, Leah was on the phone with her mom in Syracuse and those are usually tough calls. She stopped in the pantry and put her hand on her hip. She kept kind of looking past me.

"How was it?" I asked.

"Oh." Her eyebrows did that little pop. "She was talking and talking about Becca and the kids. Things sound better with Richard."

Becca lives in Brooklyn and is the sibling that Leah actually gets along with. Richard and Becca have been shaky for a long stretch but every time they get to the border of calling it quits, they pull back because of the kids. I don't know how happy that makes you in the long run, but then I don't have kids.

"She kept complaining about Becca's complaints about Andrew's school. I was sticking up for Becca. It doesn't even matter if Mom and I disagree because whatever I say never even registers. It's the not listening part that's getting worse." Leah stopped peeling blue paint off her wrist. "And I was thinking about doing a new cottage for them. I started drawing."

"Do they want a new cottage?" Leah's parents have an ancient cottage in the Thousand Islands. It does have a large lot.

Her index finger circled. "They wouldn't say so, but a lot of things could be better. Becca thinks we could get Ben to pay for it."

Ben is the older brother/lawyer with far too much income. He is a generous guy but he's never come up with an idea on his own. "That's a good use for him," I said.

Leah puffed a little air into her left cheek. She glanced back through the dining room to the living room. She watched the walls and turned and slowly smiled. She peered into the kitchen and reached for my ankle. "Look at this," she said, "I'm happy. I'm actually happy. It's always such a shock." Her sneaker squeaked on the floor. "Come down. Let's go to bed."

Leah left for Phoenix on Sunday afternoon and after that the world felt strange, almost lopsided. I had to remember how to get my balance again as a single person. This always happens and I hate it. We'd painted the whole downstairs but the furniture was still in the wrong spots. So I ordered a pizza, took the tarps off the couch, and pushed the pieces around until they seemed to fit. When the pizza showed up I sat in the spruce green living room, taking in the view. All those colors and it worked. But the house felt empty, as if it had been done up for a canceled party.

I started thinking about Arrow, only more layers of Cynthia stuff came back, wave after wave of it, setting off the metallic twist in my stomach. That entire week had felt awkward because I kept pushing all that to the side. Leah asked a couple of times but I didn't explain. Then I'd be in the shower and see the constellation of freckles on Cynthia's back. The IV coming out of her wrist. I didn't want to think about it. Things felt so much better simply falling into the minutes with Leah. I even forgot until Leah left that I hadn't heard from Grace.

It began to bug me that I couldn't remember what day I was

supposed to call. I checked my date book. Arrow should have been in Somerville on Wednesday. Four days ago, a fact that led to a completely new line of questions. How was I going to get Arrow down here? When I had the station wagon he used to just lie across the back seat, but I wasn't sure the jump seats in the truck were wide enough and he was too tall for the front. I could get a kennel cage but he'd freeze in the back of the truck. Stop, just make the call.

I couldn't. The problem was, actually bringing Arrow into the house made me nervous. I'd be introducing a dog into the equation. A good dog, a trustworthy soul, but a dog. What if Arrow and Leah took an instinctual dislike to each other? I mean I used to have this very tall friend Don and every time he came over Arrow would get low and growl. I never found out why. But would this feel like such a risk if Leah and I were actually married? I wasn't sure. Come on, he's your dog. If you're going to spend these next years in a yellow pantry, you should at least get your dog back.

Some phone numbers get embedded. They feel that good coming off your tongue: 617-555-6886. Cynthia never had it changed. Thus began the whole phone stare-down sequence, which went on longer than usual because I knew Grace would answer. I like Grace. She's blunt and wry and six years older than Cynthia. They look sort of the same, only Grace is taller and her face is a little more filled out, but they have identical gray eyes. Grace is a public school music teacher near Pittsburgh. She runs choirs, teaches voice, composes, plays violin, and introduces elementary school kids to the wonders of bluegrass. It's a completely noble life. Her own kids are both in high school, since she had them ridiculously early. The thing is, Grace and I get along so much better in the abstract. Live, we're good for about forty-five minutes. She's intense and a little grumpy, and grumpy people can be interesting, as long as you have a sense of humor. We seem to expect too much of each other and I'm not sure why. Grace is loyal. It's that thick-and-thin, engraved in stone, all-weather family commitment and I knew she was still mad at me for walking out.

One ring later Grace and I were breathing at each other. "Jimmy," she said as if another layer of some vast problem had just uncovered itself. "Oh."

"I was calling, to see how things were?"

"Cynthia died."

I looked at the floor and saw two green spots. I looked through the too-bright rooms. "What?" It felt hard to breathe.

"Things went—there was a blood clot and she had a stroke. At least they think it was a blood clot. It got into the bloodstream and she had a stroke and went into respiratory failure. It happened Sunday, in the morning."

There seemed to be wavy lines around everything. It felt like I was leaning downhill. "Shit."

"There was a service yesterday."

"A service?" A car stopped out front and drove on. "What kind of service?"

"Small. She wanted—"

"You mean you—"

"Jimmy, I'm sorry. We called. I know we called. Mom left a message on your machine. She said there was a woman's voice on the tape."

"I didn't get any—wait, *my* voice is on the tape."

Grace took a long breath. "I don't know, maybe she called the wrong . . ." Her voice backed off. "There were so many."

"She died last week and you didn't fucking get through to me?"

"Come on. Mom's pushing to do everything really quick and we have—issues to sort out. There's a time pressure."

"I don't fucking believe this." I walked from one end of the rug to the other and did it again. "You didn't fucking call me?"

Grace didn't answer. I heard a TV or a radio on her end. I was still in that free-fall moment, bouncing again and again against the fact that the thing you couldn't imagine has already happened. "Wait," I said eventually, as if it had just dawned on me. "There's still Arrow?"

"Arrow?"

"The dog."

Something thumped behind her. "Not now," Grace said. "Okay." She sounded weary. "Sure. The dog. Come here tomorrow. At one." She hung up.

I sat on the dining room floor and stared over at the answering machine. For a few minutes I actually thought if I hadn't made the call, Cynthia wouldn't be dead.

SIX

How did I give away my dog? It's weird and hard to believe, but that's what I kept thinking Monday afternoon, all the way up to Boston. Then again, I hadn't stopped feeling stunned. Late Sunday night, when I was still kind of speechless, Leah called to say she got to Phoenix okay and I told her about Cynthia. The first thing she said was, Do you want me to come back? And I said, No. And she said, Are you sure? And I said, Yes. I should have been thinking about how lucky I was to even have someone who thinks that way, among other things. But there I was on I-93, passing all cars and beating up on myself for giving away my dog.

Arrow started out as Cynthia's dog. She nabbed him from the pound and named him and always said that once you saved a dog from the pound there was no need to feel guilty about anything that happened after that—ever. I met Arrow when Cynthia and I first started hanging out on the porch. He became a fixture in our conversations, a kind of glue. Then Cynthia began working longer hours and I missed having a dog, so I started walking Arrow after work. The true ownership slide only began once Cynthia moved downstairs. It kept on like that until everything fell apart.

When that happened Arrow was the last piece. He was going to be the big custody battle, I knew that. Only by then I was exhausted and one day I got up and said: You keep him. I sacrificed my dog to get out of town. That's what I kept thinking the next foggy morning, driving the truck down to Providence. Did it bother me, knowing that I made a whoppingly bad decision under pressure? Sure. What kind of person gives away his dog?

It was suspiciously warm. One of those fake February afternoons where you begin to believe that everything really is going to keep on melting until spring and I was late. Grace said one and it would probably be two, but I got behind at work. Take a week off and two million things stack up and fall right over.

The fuzziness only began to clear once I got off Alewife and turned in on Broadway. I still couldn't wrap my head around the fact that Cynthia wasn't going to be there. I didn't even try. A left on Packard, a right on Electric Avenue, and I started wondering if my neighborhood parking karma still had any zing left.

Grace's midnight blue Saab filled the concrete driveway, so I parked across the street. Grace loves fast cars, which I've never been able to square with the whole music educator thing, but there you have it. When I saw the Steelers sticker on the bumper I thought, how did Tom convince Grace to put that on her car? Lumpy Tom, that's what Cynthia called him. Tom is thirteen years older than Grace. He's a communications lawyer who makes pots of money, but aside from being a chronic Steelers fan, he's as bland as a mirror.

You would think being late wouldn't matter, but little things can set Grace off. Then I could always lie about the traffic. That's the power of traffic. And how could Grace be mad? They didn't even get through to tell me what happened, which made it pretty clear where I stood on the great runway of friends and relations.

I set the parking brake and glanced at the chrome leash on the other seat. Should I bring it in or just say hello to Arrow first. Get reacquainted, I thought.

The house is a white, up-down two-family like plenty of others in the neighborhood. It has vinyl siding and a deep porch. At the end of the porch I saw a bright yellow tricycle, which didn't make sense, and there weren't any tennis balls. That used to be

Arrow's game. I'd sit on the floor with a beer, even in winter, and bounce them off the low walls, while he would spin and dive and make catch after catch. Just watching him felt somehow therapeutic.

At the storm door that twitchy feeling started up inside my knees. A small line of sweat bloomed along my hairline. I looked across the street and took a long breath. I kept trying to calm myself down but this strange thing happened. It felt like an afternoon from long ago. Cynthia and I were heading out for a walk or to get coffee and she had gone back inside with Arrow to find her wallet or sunglasses or a thicker scarf. She was always making last-minute adjustments. I stood there until it went away.

I rang the bell and heard Grace cross the living room. I could tell her head was down just by the sound of her shoes.

The royal blue front door opened a crack. Grace is taller than Cynthia and it always surprises me when our eyes meet. "Oh," she said. "Jimmy." She looked down as if she were listening for something.

"Sorry I'm late," I said.

"No, no. It's not that." Grace squinted. "Let's be outside." She stepped past me as the storm door rattled. She had on a light green sweater made of thick yarn, brown wide-wale corduroys and black Doc Martens. She positioned herself on the top step. "It's almost warm," she said, but sadly. Her eyes were still red. "I need sunglasses."

I'd left mine in the truck. I sat and we peered into the street.

"There is no dog," Grace said.

I turned, expecting to see the words go by again. "What do you mean there's no dog?"

"There is no dog." She reached for her elbows.

"What?"

"Jimmy." She frowned as if I were stuck on something that really couldn't matter. "He was on the long leash and he chased a squirrel in front of a recycling truck. The leash broke. It kept spooling out."

"When? When was this?"

"I don't know. Last week. When did you see Cynthia?"

I suddenly couldn't remember. Then I didn't want to count back. "Friday," I said.

"That afternoon. He saw the squirrel and kept going. I yelled and everything."

A week. He'd been roaming a week. The odds were not good. "Was he wearing his collar? His tags?"

"What tags?"

"Shit." I almost said something else, a sentence that concluded with the phrase "fucking clueless." I thought about the leash on the truck seat. I saw the chrome water bowl on the pantry floor. It came right back, that lifting sensation in my shoulders, the one I used to get with Cynthia, every time I learned some small but crucial bit of news a few months behind the fact. I began to stand. "And we talked yesterday?"

Grace caught my knee. "So—I lied." She pointed at the truck. "Is that yours?"

"Yeah." I sat back down. "It's good for work."

Her lips pressed together. She spread her fingers and looked at them for a second. She glanced at my shoes, then up at me, as if she couldn't remember why we were sitting here on these front steps, in Somerville.

"Why are you looking at me like that?" I asked.

Grace's hands ran along her thighs. The nap of her corduroys went from dark to shiny and back. She shook her head. "Sorry. I only just remembered what it is you do."

I was about to say: What the fuck am I doing here if you've lost my fucking dog?

Inside a high, distant voice called: "Gracie. Graaaaaace?"

She checked her watch. "Shit."

"Somebody?" said the voice.

Grace's hand went to the storm door. She stared back with a look that clearly said: Come on.

It felt odd stepping inside, just reentering the space. The living

room was still a big square with an arch in the middle leading to
the dining room. After that it went kitchen, bedroom, bath, bedroom, with a small officelike space beside the back door. The rug
with the green squares still covered the floor in front of the
poufy, rose-colored couch. A much larger TV waited in the corner and a rocking chair I didn't recognize sat across from it. But
everything was covered by a scrim of toys. There were bins of
wooden train tracks and lines of tiny dump trucks and cranes.
A wicker basket of kid videos sat beside the TV.

I kept thinking about Arrow. He'd been gone for a week and
nobody told me?

Grace went back through the kitchen while I peered into the
peach-colored dining room. White moving company boxes lined
the floor. Some were taped shut, but pots and baking trays poked
out of the others. Everything looked half-started. I turned to the
living room. A Cat-In-The-Hat doll had its head stuck between
the couch pillows. It looked like a rock slide victim.

"Hey," I called, "did you and Tom have another—"

"No." Her voice came from the small bedroom. "Don't move,"
she said.

I stopped beneath the arch. The dining room table was covered with cookbooks. I went back to the living room and considered taking off my coat. I don't know why I turned when I did
because I didn't hear them come in. It felt like the moment when
you look up to answer a stare.

She had a kid beside her. A sleepy kid with wild, shimmering
dark blond hair, like Cynthia's. His yellow, long-sleeved shirt
had a plate-sized green-and-black soccer ball on the front. He
winced when he reached behind to pull up his purple sweatpants.
I watched his toes curl against the wooden floor. I watched his
chin, the way he rounded his shoulders as his head pressed into
Grace's leg. A spot of red from a marker on the side of his right
index finger. He licked his lips and pulled the top one in. It was
eerie, only I couldn't understand why. He did look like Cynthia,
more in the eyes and the narrow forehead, except his chin squared

off in a familiar way that hers didn't. I couldn't stop staring at it. My tongue pressed against the ridge at the roof of my mouth.

"He didn't have much of a nap," Grace said, her fingers disappearing into his hair. "We're starting to use a big-boy bed, aren't we?" She shook her head as if she had said something out of order. "So," Grace said, "Leo." Her hands went to his shoulders. Her eyes looked shiny. "This is—" She stopped as if she couldn't think of how to introduce me. "Somebody your mommy loved very much."

Leo's hands wrapped around her legs. I watched his fingers. They seemed long. Grace's bottom lip crinkled. It looked like a moment she had rehearsed but still couldn't approve of, even as it continued to unfold. "He's yours," she whispered.

I blinked. My tongue seemed too large to move. I felt a metallic thump in my chest. My lips formed the "wh" of "what" but nothing more.

"Noooo," Leo said. "I don't want SpongeBob."

Grace nodded.

My feet felt huge. I remember thinking it would be impossible to ever lift them again. I remember not being able to take my eyes off the kid's face. The squared chin, the high cheeks, the gray eyes. The way he crossed his legs as he stood. My forehead felt strange, as if it had started to expand. I suppose I should have been feeling a list of things—fear, despair, some kind of distant joy—but it all seemed practically unimaginable. Baffling and nearly rehearsed, the way it sometimes feels inside the most surprising moments. My mouth tasted like pennies, just like it does when a cop's red-and-blue lights appear in my rearview mirror.

Leo crossed in front of me, moving slowly toward the blank TV. The room began to seem bigger, but that's because I was backing toward the door.

"SpongeBob is too scary," Leo said. "I want a drink."

"What kind?" Grace's hands went to her hips. "Milk? How would you ask for that nicely?"

She turned toward the kitchen as Leo said, "Please."

I thought: You're not leaving me here. My teeth pressed against my top lip. I stared at the still open blue door.

"Juice," Leo shouted. The back of his hand slid over his eyes and into his hair. He looked up as if he had just noticed me. "I want Kipper," he said.

"What's a Kipper?" I asked.

The refrigerator door closed with a familiar slurp and Grace appeared to hand Leo a bright pink cup with a yellow lid. "It's a video," she said. "He's a cartoon dog." She put her hands against my shoulders and aimed me toward the porch. I went out and tried to take a few deep breaths. It didn't help. I looked in through the front window and saw Grace on her knees, fishing in the video basket. I reoccupied the top step. Across the street the sun gleamed in a slippery way on the truck's windshield. My hands folded until my fingers covered my mouth. Mine.

Grace sat next to me on the top step. "So," she said.

"What do you mean mine?" It sounded like I was shouting. "Mine in what sense?"

She closed her eyes, exhaling quickly as if that could change something. She looked at me in a sad, completely frustrated way I'd never seen before. "The usual ones," she said. "Biological, legal. You're on the birth certificate. You're in the will, as the surviving parent and legal guardian. I'm second in line. That's how she set it up. She only did that a few months ago, and we were trying to figure out how to take care of Leo, and I found it, the will, in this folded-up yellow envelope. I mean, I didn't even think she had a will. I'd yelled at her about that, because with a kid you have to, and so I'm glad she did it, but—I'm the executrix."

My jacket felt heavy. The air seemed thick. "Jesus." I started chewing my index finger. "She just did it? Why would she do that? Does he know who I am?"

Grace nodded. "We've talked about you. Or around you. Only recently."

I stood up and sat down again. "Why are you so fucking calm?"

"I don't know," she said. "Because I'm exhausted? Because . . ." She tapped the step. "You can think of when it happened, right?"

My tongue pushed against my teeth. The air seemed warmer.

"He's a little more than three," she said. "Count back."

"July?" I said. "You knew about that?" Of course she knew.

I got up to peer through the window. Leo sat on the couch with his feet straight out and crossed at the ankles. I sit like that when I watch TV. I use the ottoman, but I sit like that. My hand got stuck on my ear. Then that strange voice behind my head kept coming up, moving in like a very large person to put an arm around my shoulder. *You have a kid,* it said.

Grace looked like she was expecting me to answer a question. It felt teacherly and that bugged me.

I sat and banged my heels into the step. "No one told me? You? Cynthia? Why am I even surprised?"

"I wasn't going to tell you. I threatened to once, but—she was going to tell you. She was going to tell you a thousand times. She meant to tell you when she saw you last. She told me she would."

"I can't believe she went through this and never said—"

"You can't? Cynthia?"

"Okay, if I thought long enough. Maybe. But like, she doesn't want me in the kid's life and then—"

"No, no. It wasn't that. It was never that. This has been a long thing. I mean, I almost got her to fax you the sonogram once, at the beginning." Grace's hand folded under her chin and she smiled. "I can't remember, but, I think it went like—when she first found out, she was going to do everything herself. I could have told her that was nuts, but then it went on and she realized she did need people and she wanted to tell you. She wanted you to be a part of it. But, you know how you can only be stubborn for so long before it turns into something else? Then the longer this went on, it got more complicated. It got to be a bigger and bigger deal and she didn't know how to tell you. She wasn't sure how you'd react and how that would be for Leo. She thought you'd feel tricked. She also knew about Leah and she didn't want to wreck things there. Then Leo got older and she kept deciding, over and over, that it would be too dramatic to introduce you into his life like that. You know, everybody got busy."

"Busy? Everybody got busy?"

"Well, yeah, time is different with kids. Look, she was going to tell you when she saw you or when she got home." Grace covered her eyes for a second then looked across the street. "I found her datebook, it has all these 'tell Jimmy' countdowns in it. Every few months. I really think she made out the will only a while ago because once she did that, she had to tell you. She just never imagined she was going to die first."

I stood up again. Somehow it felt better to be standing up. I mean it did make a weird sort of sense. Even with everything, it sounded like Cynthia. I could almost hear her thinking like that, but I still had no place to go. "You lied about my dog," I said. "Why did you lie about my dog?"

"Yeah," Grace said. "That was me. Go ahead, shoot. I don't know. Jimmy, everything's happened at once. We know you. If I'd called and said what this was over the phone—and you've always been so good with surprises. What would you have done? Planned a trip? World cruise? New Zealand, after all?"

"I am going to New Zealand."

"Jimmy, what would you have done?"

"I don't know. Fold, probably."

"That's the thing. You can't fold. I knew that if you met Leo . . ." She rubbed her forehead. "You always do the right thing, eventually. Cynthia knew that." Her eyes watered. "She knew you'd be fine at it, that's why—I don't want this to be any worse than it already is."

Larger chunks of panic fluttered under my jaw and bounced into the backs of my knees. Of course she was right. I'd met the kid. I'd had the eerie moment. Where was I going to go?

"I don't even know him." I closed my eyes. "He knows you. How can I, you're the one who should be—"

"It has to be you." Her left knee began to bounce. Her socks didn't match. They had the same vinelike pattern but one was red and the other blue. Her chin dimpled. She started to cry. "Look, Mom can't take him. She can barely take him to the library. I—can't. That's what I decided. I feel awful, but Tom is entirely against it. He says he's too old and he's right and we did that once already. I've already got the boys. Yes, they're in high school, but they do need me. Tom says there isn't room in the house for another personality and—I'm going to grad school, in the fall."

"You are? For what?"

"Composition. At Pitt." She waved over her shoulder. "Look, this is all awful, I know, but it would be worse for me to take him and then bring him back. Jimmy, he's your kid and all this has gone on long enough. Yeah, he doesn't know you but what was I going to do? Raise your kid and not tell you?"

I felt her arm on my shoulder. I tried not to move.

"He's your kid. It's a gift. People should raise their own kids."

I was somewhere between mad and overwhelmed when the ache in my throat, the one I'd been pretending wouldn't come, spread again. Grace's arm slid down my back. It made a soft sound against my jacket.

"People should," I said. "But they at least know they have kids." I rearranged my fingers. "I don't know kids. I mean if I take him, he'll be totally traumatized. You're running out and I'm going to bring him some place he's never been? We're all traumatizing the kid."

"That's Mom," Grace said. "Mom is running out. That's how she's dealing with this. I can't stay. Mom can't handle him. She already canceled his daycare. He loses his spot on Friday."

"Lose your spot and you can't get it back?"

"Something like that. This is awful but I want it to be one move instead of a string. You're the parent." She smiled, softly.

I tapped my knee. I was coming up on a bad moment. I could tell. With that smile I decided I was being paid back in some skewed sense. "You're still pissed off," I said. "Long term, because of Cynthia and—"

"I was." She turned.

"But you tell me, what should I have done? Smile and say, 'Oh sure, that's okay, honey, you sold the houses? It's only money.' I didn't decide to open a fucking bakery. I didn't disappear into that. That's all we talked about, that and the health inspector. It got to where I couldn't trust a thing she said. If I'd stayed that wouldn't have changed anything that happened—after."

"I *was* angry," Grace said, making sure I caught the tense. "I didn't approve of what she did. But I didn't like the way you handled it. I didn't expect that, of you."

I watched her socks. She missed an eyelet on her left shoe. It was an awful afternoon and what was I doing yelling? Her eyes were red. "Sorry," I said, "I don't know what I'm doing—"

"I was jealous of you two. It got hard to see you together. You had a lot."

"I know."

"So why did you do it? They were only buildings. She embezzled with the best intentions. So what?"

"I don't know. Panic? You reach a point?"

Grace laughed and the circular sound of it surprised me. "But you like difficult women. You told me that at some Christmas thing when I was drunk."

"Challenging," I said. "That was challenging."

"I'm challenging."

I stared at my boots. "Why did she do that?" I pointed back to the window, to Leo.

"She always liked you."

"Like is not a reason. Was getting me up to the camp for Grandpa Will's—"

"No." Grace shook her head. "Never. It wasn't planned. She was as shocked as anyone, but she wasn't sad it was you." Grace rubbed her cheek and tried to look brave. "Besides, no one in this family has ever had the slightest trouble getting pregnant."

"I don't remember knowing that," I said. "It might have helped if I'd remembered knowing that."

"She had no idea." Grace tapped the step with her first two fingers. One-two-three. One-two-three. A waltz. "I think she decided, eventually, that it did make sense in some zigzag cosmic way. That Leo should have happened, but you ran off and the timing got—confused."

I stared at the street. I couldn't think.

"When I'm packing up the house it feels like this has to be done, that you have to take Leo now, like there's no choice," Grace said. "But Leo has friends. He has routines. He loves his routines. He's lost his fucking mom and I'm uprooting him. I'm like some monster from Dickens."

"Yup," I said. "So why are we doing it again?" It only faintly began to dawn on me in some subterranean way that I would need to have answers for things. "Where did you tell him Cynthia is?"

"In the clouds." Grace folded her arms. "Honestly, I couldn't think of what to say and Leo doesn't understand forever. He doesn't understand why there's a Monday and a Tuesday. He wants to go on an airplane to see her."

An old black Jaguar with a dent in the rear quarter panel pulled in behind the truck. Joan got out, slammed the door, and crossed the street without looking up. When she reached the steps I saw the dark circles under her eyes.

"Jimmy." Joan's hand appeared in an entirely businesslike way.

I shook it. "I'm sorry," I said, and a second later I felt like yelling at her.

Joan let go. "It has been a very sad time. You've met—"

I nodded. I couldn't remember his name. The kid, I thought. The kid.

"Well, it's a surprise to us, too. Where he's going, I mean. But Cynthia has surprised us like this before. You, for instance. When I first met you, I had no idea how long you two had been together. Six months, right? You just appeared."

I nodded. "Yeah."

"Is that your truck?" She pointed. "Does it have an air bag?" The red nail polish on her thumb had chipped at the base. "You'll need to get it disconnected or find another car before you take Leo home. You cannot have a child in the front seat with an air bag."

"Mom." Grace reached for Joan's elbow. "If you're taking Leo to the library he needs a snack first. The videos on top of the television have to go back."

Joan stepped loudly around me and went inside. "How long has he been watching?" she asked as the storm door closed.

"I could kill my mother." Grace sat down and something lifted between us. It felt like the power grid had shifted. "She wants to do everything immediately and Leo's still—" She rubbed her lips. "The other problem is we have to be out of here on the fifteenth."

"Why? This was Cynthia's. I folded and ran on that one."

"She sold it to Roy. From upstairs?"

"Roy," I said slowly. "How is Roy?"

"Roy married this girl from Amsterdam and moved there. He sold it a year ago to a landlord in Medford. On Friday, Mom called and said we'd be out on the fifteenth so he canceled the lease."

"Why did Cynthia do that? The upstairs apartment paid the mortgage."

"She needed the money?"

"Don't look at me like I'm a complete moron," I said.

Grace shook her head in that slow way. "You have no idea. There was, what do they say on TV? A mountain of credit card debt? All from the bakery. She redid the kitchen. She wanted to stay, but she needed the cash to live on."

This bothered me. Maybe because when I gave in on the house I thought, here I am for once actually doing the right thing in a bad moment, and Cynthia didn't even keep it? I stared at my glistening deep green truck. I felt the keys against my thigh. I heard a bird. I shook my head. "How long have you been here?"

Grace seemed surprised. "Two weeks? I forget. I came right when it happened. Somebody had to take care of Leo. I mean,

Cynthia has some other single mom friends but . . ." She pointed at Joan's car. "Mom's not even taking the time to sort. She's dumping all of Cynthia's things into storage."

Leo shouted: "Noooo. I have to watch."

"He's normally in daycare. He goes four days a week. This is his day off. That's what he calls them."

"Leo. Stop." It was Joan's assistant principal's voice.

Grace rubbed her eyes. She pressed her wrist against her cheek. "We have to make plans for when you pick him up," she said quietly. "Go back and think. Get used to it. I'll call you in a day or tonight. It would be better if you two—"

"Leo. Now," Joan said.

I followed Grace inside but stopped as she took her mother's arm. "Mom—" Joan looked back from the dining room and her hand slapped the wall beside the kitchen door.

My eyes closed. I couldn't think. I took another deep breath.

Leo sat on the couch, still watching the video that Joan never turned off. His purple legs fell back into their grooves across the cushion.

I didn't know what to do. I just went forward. I sat beside him and thought: This used to be my couch. The cushions still seemed to know my shape. I looked at Leo and my tongue felt funny again. I'm sitting next to my DNA. My DNA. He has my chin. My toes. It was getting hard to breathe.

"Don't sit close," Leo said.

I moved over until there were a few inches between us. On the screen an orange and white dog and a gray Scottie were on top of a slide, looking for a rocket with bright green binoculars. They had English accents and there was plucky cocktail music in the background.

"If you can't make the decisions, you need to go home," Joan said from behind the kitchen door.

"You're right," Grace told her. "I need to get the fuck out of here, but if I leave everything to you—" The back door rattled.

The dogs went down the slide and walked over to talk to a pair of pigs sitting on the edge of a swimming pool. "What are we watching?" I asked.

Leo stared at me, as if now it would take him a full second to fall back into the story. "Kipper," he said.

But somehow I didn't get it. "Keeper?" I said. "That's my last name."

"No. Kipper."

"No," I said, elongating the vowel, invoking patience. "My name is Keeper. My last name."

"Kipper." Leo looked over and uncrossed his ankles. "I'm Leo," he said and pointed at my chin. "Gracie told me who you are. You're the dog."

SEVEN

The next day around noon I pointed my brand-new-to-me dark green Subaru wagon toward the yard. I was feeling kind of good about the car at least, the sun being out and all. I even imagined it would last. I know, I should have been at work earlier, as Tim and I were set to have another of our meetings, where we stare at all the stuff on the tables and wonder why we're not making more money. I should have also been thinking about calling Leah, or thinking about the consequences of not calling Leah, but I was blocking, big time. I kept pretending that nothing had changed, which was entirely ridiculous. Then somehow in the middle of that, getting the car seemed crucial. It was the only thing I could imagine that felt like progress.

The Love & Death yard is a big piece of old mill space up in Pawtucket. It's half a salvage yard, half an antiques warehouse. From Warren Avenue the first thing you see is a long rectangle of double high chain-link fence surrounding all the stuff that's too heavy to steal—claw-foot tubs, odd bits of statuary, a lot of cast-iron fence. Under the awning we've got columns and rows of theater seats that we'll never sell but Tim liked the look of. In through the big swinging doors are more doors, all sorted by age and size and resting comfortably in racks against the white brick walls. We have wainscoting, chair rail, soapstone counters, two church pulpits with spiral stairs, and five school blackboards I should be able to get some restaurant to buy. Beyond that are the mantels. We probably have eighty of them hanging on chains, all sorted by size. We have tables of porcelain doorknobs, thumb latches, transom lights, featherboards, and on and on. Up front there's about a thousand square feet of furniture, Mission rockers, Empire sideboards, and oak cases that still smell like the law books they used to hold. That all rotates through the Wickenden Street shop. I love the yard. It's an entire world of saved parts and second chances.

When I pulled in, the gravel lot was empty, except for Tim's long white van. He peered out from the office window and the sun flashed off the rims of his glasses. He probably thought I was a customer, since I didn't have the truck. Inside he had some Afro Celt Sound System lilting down from the speakers. Tim can occasionally be a little too pleased by his world-beat tastes and I'm never sure how great an idea it is to go around singing songs in languages you don't understand, but Tim hears more than I do. He finds all these spaces between the beats. I found him sitting on the floor, surrounded by parts of an oak pedestal table. "Two bolts short," he said. "That'll be my epitaph. 'Tim: He was two bolts short.'"

"Where'd that come from?"

"Patrick. I bought it for eighty-seven dollars."

"You bought from Patrick?" Patrick is in his seventies and owns a marine salvage yard in Jamestown. I'm never sure where he gets his pieces but Tim likes talking up the old guys.

"I shouldn't have." Tim patted the large bare oval at the top of his head. "But Patrick told me my haircut is known as a horseshoe." He tugged the sleeve of his black fisherman's sweater to check at his watch. "Where've you been? We're in a state of total chaos here."

I couldn't figure out how to start. You'd think that wouldn't be a problem, given that I've known Tim longer than anyone I still speak to, except my actual family. "Why are you checking your watch?" I asked.

"I ordered a pizza. Prosciutto and roasted eggplant." Tim

nodded carefully. He's that way, a little hangdog but solid, like a rising tide. "Want the rest of the good news or the bad?"

"Bad," I said.

"The good news is I found three tulip chairs in a Dumpster over by the hospitals. They're the real thing, from the 1950s and in okay shape. Get them recovered and we're good for at least $1,500. They're in the van."

"Actually in a Dumpster?" That's what people always say when they show up trying to sell us dubious pieces.

Tim showed me his palms. He has an amazing knack for spotting things—sleepers in consignment shops, ceramics at yard sales. It's like owning a ninth sense and he already has a memory with extra rooms. What Tim's not good at is keeping the boat afloat. The details roll up and take him out at the ankles and the only way we make any money is if we stay organized.

"Too bad there weren't four," I said. "What's on the other list?"

Tim gazed into the chandeliers. "Something's wrong with the digital camera. This contractor called with a barn full of nineteenth-century house parts he wants to sell for $5,000, only I lost his number. We're behind on eBay and the Web page. I'm still wondering if we need auction services or if there should be a coupon on the Web page. We've got to figure out better weekend schedules, since Julie's getting grumpy. And you and I have to pick a day to ski in New Hampshire. We should go to Cannon." He folded his arms. "We're out of bubble wrap. The little kind."

I kept watching his lips and thinking, this is important, this is my life. Then no, this doesn't matter at all. "We don't need auction services," I said. "A coupon maybe and Cannon's too cold, until April."

The doorbell chimed and a guy with no hair and white eyebrows smiled as he swung the pizza box out of its red insulated carrier.

"Mr. Wizard," Tim said, "got any money?"

I paid and tipped and Tim carried the pizza into the office proper. It's a long room with chest-high windows on all sides.

We have desks, a computer, a refrigerator from the 1950s with copper shelves that spin out, and a wall of reference books with titles like *Know Your Old Radios* and *What's It Worth?*, only these days eBay turns out to be pretty much the best price guide. I sat in a yellow box seat from the old Boston Garden and took a slice. Eggplant and prosciutto isn't bad.

"Are you okay?" Tim asked. "You look a little . . . weird."

"You mean the sudden fuck-up that is my life?"

He gazed out the window. "Where's the truck?"

When something strange or deeply weird happens, I wish I was the kind of guy who could just go home and tell everybody all about it. The guy who unloads on the nearest passerby with no second thoughts. That woman sitting next to you on the train— she'll do fine. I mean I talk, a lot, but when the big things happen I go into the cave. I never want to be a burden.

Tim's hand stopped at the refrigerator's handle. "Where's the dog?"

"The dog didn't work out."

"What do you mean the dog didn't work out?"

"Yesterday?" I said. "Last night really, I got on the Web and did the research, and something with a backseat is a lot safer, since with the truck, because of how old it is, I'd have to disable the air bags and what's the point of that? I wanted an air bag and all-wheel drive so I did it."

"Did what?"

"Traded the truck. I went to that Subaru place on 146 and I got a 2000 with only forty-four k on it. They did the plates and registration while I cleaned out the truck. It wasn't an even trade but it could have been worse. Have you ever bought a car that way? It's weird. You show up, dig out all the maps and stuff, and pile it into this other car. It feels like I'm subletting."

Tim sat on the desk. "You traded the truck for a wagon with a backseat for a dog you knew you didn't have?"

"The dog's lost," I said. "I have a kid." The words sounded strange, like the announcement of a terminal condition.

"Whose kid?"

"My kid." I felt my voice getting watery again. "I made the trade because of the kid and the air bag. The truck had an air bag. You can't have a kid in the front seat with—"

"You don't have a dog, you have a kid?" Tim stared and stared, as if if he did that hard enough he might be able to see what forced me to come up with a fabrication of this magnitude. He pulled a six-pack of Harpoon from the refrigerator and popped four of them with the shark opener on his key chain. "Being two bolts short is starting not to seem like a problem. Tell me everything. Go."

So I did. I told him how Grace was so nonchalant about Arrow it made me want to leave her there on the steps. How I went up to the lake in New Hampshire three and whatever years ago. How I met Leo, how I sat next to him on the couch and got swamped by the surreal sense of it all. "After that I went home, watched some old Stanley Cup games on tape, and listened to a lot of Cowboy Junkies with headphones on. Then last night I had this dream where they were fitting me for a spacesuit, but no one could say where I was going."

"You find out you have a kid and your first response is to buy a station wagon?"

"At least it's a response." My breathing sped up and that tug at the back of my throat returned. "I'm not equipped. I don't have the capacity for this. I can have a dog. I'm allowed to have a dog."

"We'll take the kid."

"No you won't," I said and that felt strange, like discovering a reflex I didn't know I owned. Then again Tim and Julie had been trying to have a kid for ages. I could never even joke with Tim about that.

"I'm kidding," Tim said. "You're sure he's yours? Did you think about a test? Do you want to?"

I shook my head. "I saw him and I knew. It's the same chin. He has my fingers, exactly. He has Cynthia's eyes. It's just, obvious. You know last night, maybe this morning, after I got depressed,

I got pissed off. I mean completely. Like how the fuck could they do that to me? I even had this moment of thinking, where could I go? Brazil? But I don't speak Portuguese. It has to be somewhere they speak English."

"Canada's closer."

"You're right. I could *be* Canadian. But this—this is never going to fucking end. I'm going to have an adolescent driving around with his buddies, using a baseball bat to pick off mailboxes out the passenger side window." My knee started again. "This isn't the future I had planned."

"You had one planned?"

"How am I going to find the income to—"

Tim waved. "Stop. All this does you absolutely no good."

"What's tuition going to be in fifteen years? A million? Two?"

"You're not listening." He pushed another beer into my hand. "How can you tell if a man's preparing for the future?"

"Don't know."

"He buys a second case of beer."

I stared. That's what I needed. Tim the steadfast, talking me down from the tree. That's what we signed up for here, long ago.

Tim looked around like he was still getting used to some strange smell. "You just met the kid and they're dumping him on you?"

"It's a handoff," I said. "Joan keeps calling it the handoff. Grace is upset about it, but legally I'm the guy. It's in the will. Cynthia put it in the will. There's probably some paper to sign but I'm the guy, anyway."

We ate more pizza. I kept chewing until Tim picked up that middle distance stare, like he'd just remembered something but couldn't decide if this was the moment to bring it up. "You're going to have to find a pediatrician," he said. "There's daycare. Weekend baby-sitters so we can keep paddling here. He's three? Is he potty trained? Do you know what he eats? A lot of kids only eat certain things. Have you got life insurance? You're going to need a will. Something happens you don't want the state raising your kid. Where is he going to sleep?"

"Why are you doing this? You told me to shut up about all that."

"You got me thinking."

"Stop." I almost got up to open a window but it seemed too far away. "I knew I had too much money in my checking account." I drank the second beer. "How do you know all that?"

"I was a kid. You were."

"I don't remember."

"Come on, I have twin sisters. I was fourteen when my parents had them. You were there."

"I want my dog back," I said. "I want Cynthia." Then as I said it I thought, probably for the first time in a while, about Leah. I could see her across the table in some restaurant. I heard that bracelet jingle as she raised her wrist. "I mean I want Cynthia," I said, "not with me, but—back."

Tim put down his beer. "Leah's away?"

I took a new slice.

"You called her?"

I shook my head. "She was okay with the dog so—"

"Dude, you have to call her. Do you know any kids?"

"You just called me dude?"

"Okay, I didn't mean it."

"My brother Mark has kids."

"Right, and you see them what, once a year?" The CD stopped and the office felt suddenly bigger. "Have you and Leah ever talked about kids?"

"Not really," I said. "Maybe in the abstract? I can't remember. We just made it to buying the house."

"How long did you stay? All afternoon?"

"Almost. Joan and Grace had a fight. Grace went for a walk while Joan packed and pretended I wasn't there so Leo and I watched videos. They have to be out of the house next week. I go up on Wednesday."

"That's tomorrow? Does he know?"

"I think so," I said. "It'll be okay, right?" Here it was years later, so you'd expect that asking Tim for help wouldn't feel like a problem, but I hate asking anybody for anything. I always think that whatever I sign up for I should be able to chew through on my own. Or maybe that's something my dad would say, but I still think it. "I need help. There's a lot of—gear."

"I'll come," Tim said.

"You will?"

"Of course. What'd you think? Keeper, you only ask for help when something's too heavy to lift and that would be after you've hurt your back. We'll close at noon and take the van, but you have to call Leah." He nodded toward the phone as if I'd forgotten where it was. Then he took out his cell. "She's on speed dial."

"Tonight," I said. "I'll call tonight." I looked at the floor. It seemed like I was getting a lot closer to the floor. I closed my eyes. Then I thought, you can't have that conversation on the phone. We'll have the conversation, but it has to be in person. I mean what's the hurry? Leah will be fine with this. She already said yes to the dog.

EIGHT

No, I did not call Leah. I meant to, and she even left a little check-in message on the machine, but every time I got close that other voice would roll up over my shoulder and say: *Pal, think about it. How's that conversation going to go? Hi, I'm bringing home a kid? Or better: I'm bringing home the bastard love child from my first marriage, the relationship you thought I'd never really gotten over?* I kept telling myself there had to be a right and a wrong way to handle this and with a little more time I'd come up with the proper way to break the news.

I thought Tim was going to call me on it, all the way to Somerville, but he never did. He didn't even say anything about the fact that it was the middle of the afternoon before we got going, and that was all my fault. I slept in, which I never do, but I kept lying there thinking about Cynthia, and it would just drape down, that disgusting lumbering sadness you can taste. Then I started going on about how many years you think you have, versus how many there really are, which left me circling the suspicion that I was probably wasting my life one errand at a time.

At work we were swamped and people kept calling and we still had to clean out the van to make room for Leo's things. Then right before lunch Tim decided he absolutely had to get the van's left headlight fixed before we could go. The van is this older, white Econoline with a roof rack and windows all around, and Tim had to drive to Warwick to find the right bulb.

Eventually we were up on I-93 North, at that spot where you can look across the harbor and just see the JFK Library. I had my palm against the window and I started nattering away about the cold and how I always forget my long underwear. I went on about this woman in Tokyo who e-mailed with a huge list of questions about some Santa chocolate molds I put up on the Web. "The world market is a mysterious thing," I said.

Tim kept adjusting his SPAM hat and looking over as if it had just dawned on him, again, how absurd this all was. That got annoying, but I was in no position to complain. I put some Radiohead on the CD player and hunched down in my puffy gray coat. Tim loves Radiohead.

We made it to the Mass Pike and were speeding past Fenway when Tim said: "Have you thought about how this is going to play out? Every day?"

"Sure," I said. "There'll be an adjustment, but me and Leo—we'll be pals. He'll be my little buddy. We'll stay up late, watch horror movies in our pajamas, eat popcorn, drink root beer."

"You don't wear pajamas."

"I'll teach him soccer. How to ride a bike. How to skate." The words jumped from my mouth like fish.

"He's three."

"So, it'll be a trike instead of a bike."

Tim rubbed his chin. "Did you tell your parents?"

The silver car in front of us swerved to another lane. That had never occurred to me. I knew I'd have to tell them some day but— I chewed my lip. I tried to guess how my dad would take the news. He'd be in his study, reading something new about Mark Antony at Actium. He's a professor, ancient military history. He's retired but that hasn't changed a thing. He would look up, blink twice, and be puzzled for half an hour before going back to work. My mom's voice? That I could hear: "How nice. What size will he be?"

"This is all kind of unimaginable," Tim said. "You know, the way things happen, then they happen?"

When I saw the house again the tightness under my tongue reappeared. It's as if my reptilian brain had jumped to life and said: Oh yeah, that's where the problem lies. Grace's car still sat in the driveway and I realized I didn't even know if Leo was going to be there. I hoped he was still in daycare. This was all awful enough, but to make the kid watch while we loaded out his things?

Tim nabbed the space out front. But as he set the brake I started to wonder about Cynthia's car. She used to have this spunky red Toyota wagon and I just wanted to know where it was. Then it all came in, another quick washdown of sadness. I pulled on my gloves. "This is going to suck," I said.

Tim nodded. He looked like he'd been thinking that all day, only he hoped he wouldn't have to explain it to me. He zipped up his black jacket.

Grace had the door open before I could get the slush off my boots. "Hi," she said with a sad, can-you-believe-this wave. She rubbed both hands on her purple sweatshirt. She had on Cynthia's black Converse high tops. "I lost my boots," she said. "Mom threw them in with Cynthia's stuff and they're gone. Those were great boots."

Her eyes looked a little less red but as she shook hands with Tim I could tell she hadn't slept much. I turned on my heels. The living room furniture had been replaced by random towers of boxes.

"Five-thirty," Grace said. "I've been up since five-thirty. They took the couch this morning, but the dining room table was covered and we forgot it. I wanted to do everything today so it would be less hard on Leo." She laughed, as if that was clearly impossible. Her hands came back to her hips. "So, how are you?"

"Okay, I guess." But I hadn't seen the dining room.

"I thought you were coming earlier because Leo and Mom

will be back——" She looked at her watch. "Shit. In an hour. Except for the porch, Leo's things are in there."

Tim stepped under the arch and his head went back. "Whoa."

I peered. The dining room was full.

"I don't know how you'll want to pack this," Grace said. "But you'll need to get the big-boy bed out first, for tonight. So, pack that last?"

"Last." Tim pointed to make sure I'd remember.

I stared. It was a mountain of gear. "I had no idea."

Grace laughed again, this time as if I had no idea in general.

I couldn't take my eyes off the pile. Some of it made sense but there were objects I couldn't begin to identify, like two tan, knee-high, robotlike plastic things, which I later learned were old containers for toxic diapers. Or the pair of white potties, which looked like hinged footstools with outsized blue handles. I saw a tall gray kid seat for a bike, a three-foot-high plastic castle, a purple-and-orange basketball hoop, a folded blue plaid stroller with curved green handles, a jogging stroller. There were bins of wooden train tracks, a bin of engines and rolling stock, red bins of Legos, green bins of Legos, and clear bins filled with all kinds of plastic objects. Against the one wall I saw a bookcase, a dresser with silver star knobs, a night table, a rocking chair, a floor lamp with cows flying across the shade, a plastic kitchen that came up to my chest. Cartons crammed with dump trucks, cement mixers, and front loaders, all sized for sandbox work, ran along the other wall. A four-foot-tall plastic house with a slide, all in pieces, a yellow porch swing, a tricycle. Then an armada of boxes that said things like "old art" and "plastic food" on the sides in Grace's lowercase handwriting. The others had some kind of code: "3T winter," "4T summer," "5T future," "totally 2T."

"He has a crib, too?" I asked. The parts were up against the red headboard.

"Yes," Grace said. "I'm sending both in case there's regression."

"Regression?"

"You know about the rails for the big-boy bed? They have Elmo on them? So he won't fall out? Leo is a wild sleeper."

"A wild sleeper." I stared at the headboard but couldn't spot the rails.

"On top," Grace said. "You do know who Elmo is?"

"Yes, I know who Elmo is." I closed my eyes. "He's the red one. Right?"

Grace gave me another look, only I unzipped my coat and fell into the rhythm of loading: lift, walk, what fits where. I was okay, for most of it. I kept pretending that all this stuff had nothing to do with me, until I went to get a drink in the kitchen and saw a stack of Cynthia's coats on the counter. Her scarred leather one with the shearling lining was on top. I opened it and found two silk scarves inside, a sky blue one and the other a gauzy green with silver threads in the weave. I twisted them together and put them in my coat pocket.

The van continued to fill and forty-five minutes later you could see the dining room table. There were still some huge plastic objects on the porch, a blue kiddy pool, a frog-shaped sandbox that I didn't think would fit, but Tim said he'd strap them to the roof. It all seemed to be going on just beyond reach. It was that near out-of-body sensation I get when I've had too much coffee, only I wasn't sure why it was happening. I decided it had to be all the gear. Before, I'd been thinking of picking up Leo as a discrete event. A thing I'd do and get through, like a morning with Martha, the mean dental hygienist. I wasn't thinking of Leo as someone I'd have. All the time.

Grace stood across the living room, stuffing sheets into black garbage bags. "So, did you know Leo was a preemie?" The question had a weird edge.

I stopped in midstride. "How could I have known that?"

"He was a month early. There's a book that Cynthia kept. It's one of those black-and-white marble-covered journals. It has all the baby pictures. She kept lists of what he liked or didn't like at certain ages. All the foods. You should know that. It's in a box."

"Which box? Any box?"

Grace took a heavy yellow envelope from the mantel. "I found this."

It had all of Leo's papers: his immunization records, a passport, his Social Security card, then a birth certificate with my name, James C. Keeper, in the father's box. I unfolded the packet with the will and scanned down to Article X: Guardian. "If I leave a minor child surviving me I appoint as guardian of the person and property of my minor child the birth father James C. Keeper." I stared at it again. My name looked so long.

"There's life insurance, too," Grace said. "You're the beneficiary. Because she knew with Leo, if something happened. I can't remember how much."

"Is this it?" I shook the will. "We don't have to talk to a court or anything?"

"I don't know. What county is this?"

It took me a minute to remember. "Middlesex?"

"I'll call, in case we have to sign something. But remind me. I found the datebook again," she said. "Do you want to see it?"

Grace looked out the window. The light was dusky. It had to be after four. I heard a muffled thump on the porch. "Shit," Grace said. "They're here."

I tracked Joan's shoulder past the living room window. She turned and stopped. Her long black coat made her face seem even paler. She had a canvas beach bag under her arm and pieces of painted construction paper flopped over the edges. Grace opened the door. Joan took three steps in, looked around, and paused, as if now that everything had been set in motion she was less certain that this was the right thing to do.

Leo stopped in her shadow. He held the back of her coat with his purple mittens and spread the coattails to make a screen. When he lowered his head I felt like a kidnapper.

"Leo?" Grace said. "Did you bring everything home from school?"

"Yes. From my cubby." He sounded tired. Joan slid him out

and pulled back his red hood. He twirled once, his hair splaying, then he ran to the dining room and stopped. "Where are all my things?" His bottom lip folded over.

Joan handed me her keys. "Leo's seat is still in my car. Go get it. Don't forget the locking clip. You know about the locking clip?"

Tim appeared and took the keys. "I'll get it."

Joan gave Tim the beach bag, too. "His blanket and sheet from daycare are in there. No nap," she announced. "The child has had no nap. And last night he was up until all hours."

This is awful. I kept thinking that, but there wasn't any way to stop it.

Grace's hands circled Leo's arms. "You remember how we talked about this? How we said going with Jimmy would be a good place for you?"

Leo nodded. "I don't want to go."

"So, you'll go with Jimmy and Tim. That was Tim."

"You'll come, too," Leo said.

"I can't now, but I will. Soon." She started to cry.

"How much soon?" Leo stamped his feet. The yellow lights in the dump trucks on the sides of his sneakers flashed. "Soon," he said. "Very soon like now. They have a trampoline? Like you said?"

Grace nodded. "Yes." She rubbed her eyes.

"A castle fort in the backyard? Like we did draw on the map that time?"

"Yes."

"Behind the sandbox?"

Grace kept nodding.

"You'll come, we'll play in the castle?"

It began to feel like I could speak again. "Hi, Leo," I said.

Leo pressed his head against Grace's shoulder. "Does the trampoline work in winter?" he asked.

"I don't know."

"Mr. Kipper?" He wiped the back of his hand across his eyes.

"No, I'm—"

Leo turned back. "Gracie?" She put her hands on the sides of his face. "How will my friends know where to find me?"

"We'll call them."

I needed to sit down. But the only place left was the floor. The van keys felt huge in my coat pocket.

Joan said: "Leo, come. I'll buckle you in."

"Why can't you come?" He pulled Grace's arm.

"Not today," she said and rubbed her eyes. "But I will. This is my phone number." She took a green Post-it from her pocket and snapped her fingers until Joan found a marker. "You can call me. Jimmy will dial it for you."

Leo folded the Post-it but dropped it before Joan turned him toward the porch. "Let's go see what all your things look like in a van," she said.

"Van. Van," Leo said. "Va-van."

I picked up the Post-it and looked at Grace as Joan and Leo walked down the steps. "What trampoline? I don't have a trampoline."

"Get one," Grace said.

"There's no castle sandbox."

"So, I made some things up. Sue me."

"How many things?"

"I don't remember."

"Now he'll get there, none of that will exist and I won't even know what he's looking for?"

"That's it," Grace said. "That'll be the worst of it."

A tingling ran down my arms. "If this counts as being helpful—"

"He's ours, too," Grace said. "He'll always be ours. Don't forget that."

"Then why the fuck are you giving him away?"

"I'm not," she said. "I can't have him. I want him and I'm not sure you do. If you screw up I'm—"

"Stop this." I pointed at her chest and went to the porch. It was dark and the temperature had dropped. I watched Tim try to bungee cord the kiddie pool to the van's roof. I ran down the steps and got in the driver's side. I looked in the rearview mirror and saw a blue car seat with a kid in it. I blinked. Leo's head rolled to the side. "Blankie," he said. "I need red-blankie."

Joan handed it through the other window.

"I'm driving," I said. "I need to drive."

Tim got in. "Right, chief."

I had the key between my thumb and index finger when Grace tapped on the glass. I rolled down the window.

"He loves Burger King onion rings," she said. "He calls them onion rungs. And Oreos. He's very, very verbal. He'll tell you things if you ask, but you have to listen. He only drinks milk and apple juice. He is very afraid of cats, except his Sleeping Cat. It's the Cat-In-The-Hat doll and you'll need to find that before bed. Bed is seven-thirty. He always falls asleep in the car."

I watched the instructions float off with her breath.

"Round food," Grace said. "He likes round food."

"Round food? Why are you telling me this when I'm too wired to remember? Why can't you tell me what I need when I need to know it?"

"Not here." Tim tapped the wheel. "Start the van."

We pulled out. I heard the thwonk of a bungee cord letting loose. The kiddie pool rolled off the roof at the end of Electric Avenue.

Nobody said anything for a very long time. Leo fell asleep almost immediately and we made it unscathed through Cambridge, onto the Pike, through downtown, and out to I-93 South, where people were bumpered-up in the breakdown lane and still driving at sixty miles an hour. We were close to the I-95 split when Leo woke up and said, "I'm thirsty."

"You're what?" I asked the mirror.

"Thirsty. I need a drink, please."

I looked at Tim. We had nothing to drink in the van. We didn't even have a cup. A wave of brake lights came on before me.

On 93, a scrap of wood in the road or a big puddle can accordion everything to a crawl.

"I'm really thirsty." Leo's voice went up. "Please."

Shit, I thought, this is it, my first test as a provider and I can't even find the kid water. "How long can I drive around looking for a Burger King?"

"Next exit," Tim said.

"You sure?"

"Guys," Leo said, sounding like a weary captive.

"What?" we both said.

"I did ask for a drink. I'm really thirsty."

"I'm working on it," I said. "We'll see if we can solve the problem. We are working on the problem and we will solve it." That's no way to talk to a kid, I thought. You've got to be definite, the way you'd speak to a dog, but that idea sounded awful the instant it appeared.

"You sure he's three?" Tim asked. "He sounds like he's four."

"He's three," I said. "Grace says it's all the words. He's like an old person in a small person's body. She even forgets how old he is."

Tim pointed and I scooted down the exit ramp. Tim has an amazing geographical memory. We found the Burger King, even though Tim was sure he hadn't been there in nine or ten years, and they had onion rings! Leo also drank a carton of milk and ate all the onion rings. It seemed like a good omen or maybe he was just hungry.

"Remember," Tim told him, "if you have to go to the bathroom, you tell us. We'll find you one."

I asked Leo why he liked round food.

"No edges," he said and nodded.

"You mean corners?"

"Edges." He made a circle with our leftover French fries but wouldn't answer any more questions. For each minute that passed I felt more and more like a sanctioned kidnapper.

Back in the van everything was too loud for Leo. We had to turn down the music and it was only Emmylou Harris. We went to all classical and that still hurt his ears. "It's prickly," Leo said. Then with nothing on Leo told us the road noise was "too rumply." I watched in the mirror. He began to squirm. I had no idea what to do.

"Well," Tim said, "he's strapped in. He can't go anywhere. I'm just amazed he's not crying his eyes out."

"Amazed?" I said. "I don't have time to be amazed." I sped into the left-hand lane when Leo began shouting out names.

"There's Clarabel!" he said. "We're passing Henry! I see Diesel 10!"

"Who's he talking to?" Tim asked.

"I think he's hallucinating. I think it's the onset of—"

"That's Thomas." Leo pointed as we passed a blue contractor's van.

"Thomas?" I rubbed my forehead. I started sweating again.

"The *tank* engine," Leo said.

"It's the train set," Tim said. "Those wooden trains in the bins? He's pretending the cars have the same names as his engines. The engines are all characters."

"How do you know this?"

"They're collectable. But I don't know who buys them. British railroad geeks?"

Leo's hands were in his hair. The blanket slipped to the floor. He squeezed his eyes shut and started to cry.

Tim unbuckled and went back. He retrieved the blanket and sat beside Leo as my cell phone rang.

"Whatchadoing?" It was Leah.

My face flushed. "I'm, I'm—we're bringing some stuff back to the yard."

"Sounds like you're on the highway."

"We are. What's up?" I kept switching the phone from ear to ear.

"Just saying hi. I'm in a bookstore. It's weird here. We keep meeting with more and different people. Then they ask us to wait another day so we can meet again, but I'm still coming back Friday. There's another group here, too."

"Huh," I said and closed my eyes for a second. Friday. "That's strange, the other group I mean." I made a little static sound in my throat and felt like an idiot. I did it again. "Can you hear me? I think we're breaking up. Okay. Bye." I folded the phone back into my pocket.

"Who was that?" Tim asked.

"Just, ah, I don't know." I couldn't even think of how to lie.

Tim gave me a dubious look and went back to murmuring with Leo. I heard him explain that his name was short for Timothy. I watched in the mirror and thought, shit, he already knows how to do this. It didn't seem fair.

Tim's hand stayed on Leo's knee and the kid stayed asleep the rest of the way home. I let him sleep in the van while we unpacked. Then I discovered that his bed would only fit in the room that was supposed to be Leah's office. We were screwing the rails to the headboard when a high voice spiraled up from the driveway. "Somebody?" Leo was still strapped in and crying.

"Carry me," Leo said. I brought him inside and positioned him on the couch. Tim, the wise man, had already unloaded the basket of videos. I cut off the packing tape with the Swiss Army knife on my key chain and said, "Kipper?"

Leo stared, as if he wasn't sure what an answer here would mean. He nodded. The video bought me half an hour and by the time we got the bed set up Leo was asleep on the couch. I gave Tim my car keys so he could pick up the wagon from the yard. He called Julie, who had been visiting a friend farther up in Edgewood, and she swooped in to pick him up while I was still upstairs.

I closed up the van and fell into the couch. The cushion was still warm. It felt strange, having another person asleep in the house.

NINE

5:47 A.M. The first day and Leo's voice cranked up like a siren in the dark, flattening out on the "wahhhh." In the dream I am floating atop a warm wave and trying to teach a group of obese cats to swim. They keep bobbing around in orange life jackets while I keep yelling, trying to loop them all together, before an even larger wave launches me into a small courtyard. I've just landed on my side, on something hard, when I hear the siren.

I opened my eyes but couldn't figure out the sound. The wind? The return of Fred? I kicked off the blanket and stood barefoot in the cold hall.

"Someboooody." It came from Leah's office. I went in and found Leo rolled up on floor. He had fallen out of bed.

I picked him up. "Are you okay?"

"I'm wet," he announced, as if I had something to do with it. A dark circle covered the crotch of his purple sweatpants. I sat him on the edge of the bed, pulled off the pants and his Thomas the Tank Engine underwear, balled everything up and threw it into the corner.

"I need new clothes," Leo said. "I did leak." He started to cry.

"Okay," I said. "It's okay. You're okay."

"No I'm not. I fell *out* of bed."

It took me a minute to remember that I was the one who put Leo to bed in his clothes. Weren't there supposed to be special night diapers? Grace said something about bed rails, too. Those were still in the van.

"Wait here." I covered Leo's legs with the Bob-the-Builder fleece blanket and headed for the stairs. Halfway down the crying went up a notch and I decided it would all end sooner if I just ran for the door.

Last night after everyone left, I gave up. I sat on the couch and stared at the TV. I should have been emptying the van, building a home, but I couldn't face it. I could face *The Simpsons* and as the hours rolled together leaving the van packed began to feel like a minor act of rebellion.

I hopped down the front steps. I wasn't even wearing socks, only sweats and my black, long-sleeved, Pretenders shirt. The sidewalk ice hurt, but not enough to cancel out the panic. I had a kid upstairs sitting on a bed and not wearing underwear. I jumped from foot to foot until I got the back of the van open. All those boxes and Grace never gave me the code. I grabbed a few with numbers, "Totally 2T," "5T future," and made it back upstairs. I stumbled on the top step and banged the front of my knee. The boxes tumbled into Leah's office.

"Stop it," Leo shouted. "You're hurting my ears."

The pain spread like a collar around my leg so I started to crawl. I can't do this, I thought. I can't do this without coffee. "Leo, calm down," I said. "I've got your clothes." I tore open the 2T box and the shirts in there all seemed small or maybe I was only looking down at them from a great height.

"Those are toddler clothes." Leo started to cry.

"Whose clothes?"

"I'm a kid."

I pushed that box off the bed and opened "5T future." I had to paw through layers of sweaters, but I eventually found a pair of longer-looking red sweatpants. "Here," I said. "You like red."

"They're too big."

"But I'm wearing sweatpants."

"I want *my* clothes. I need a nighttime diaper."

I remembered seeing a purple and white bag of those stuffed under the jogging stroller in the van. "Don't move," I said and ran outside.

When I made it back my feet burned from the cold but we got the diaper on. Then Leo told me his bed was wet. I pulled off the sheets and threw them into the hall. The Bob-the-Builder blanket seemed dry, so I spread that out in place of a sheet. I dragged the comforter in from my bed and added it to Leo's. This is work. I kept thinking that.

Leo watched from the floor with his legs crossed. "Crisscross applesauce," he said and yawned.

"Put on your sweatpants," I said.

"You help." He started to cry. Only then did I realize that Leo couldn't exactly dress himself. I got him into the sweatpants, we rolled up the cuffs, and I tried to convince him to lie down. "Be next to me," he said, so I climbed in. The digital clock on Leah's shelf said 6:21. I hate digital clocks. I closed my eyes and still saw the blue numbers. I remember thinking, maybe this is the dream.

7:13 A.M. Leo kicked me in the knee. "Mr. Kipper?" In the dream I am sleeping in the woods on a log and the log kicks me. "Time to go downstairs," Leo said in a very matter-of-fact voice. "I'm barely starving."

I put my hand over my eyes. "You're what?"

"Starving." He climbed across my knees.

I crawled off the bed. It was a little less dark but the heat hadn't kicked on. I got up to find a sweatshirt as Leo started to cry. "What?" I said.

"You didn't tell me where you were going."

"I have to tell you?"

Leo nodded as if that were another regulation I had chosen to ignore.

I explained and my destination seemed acceptable, but when

I came back Leo was still on the bed. "Come on," I said. "We can go now."

"You have to get me," he said. "*Get* me out of bed."

That turned out to only involve lifting Leo up and placing his feet on the floor. But as I took my hands away I had the frightening sense that this was just one of several thousand moves I would never correctly learn how to perform.

In the hall I said: "You go first. These are steep stairs—"

"No." Leo grabbed the tail of my sweatshirt. His forehead pressed into the back of my legs. "I don't know what's *down* there. Are there cats?"

"I don't think so. Do you like cats?" I couldn't remember if I'd told him about Fred, or the possible existence of Fred.

"Nooooo." Leo pulled on the back of my sweatshirt and the neck caught my throat. He hooked his chin over the banister. "Where are we?"

"My house."

He tugged at the sweatshirt as if he were steering a horse. "You have very many boxes," he said when we entered the living room. "Does your house have a kitchen?"

"It's back there."

"Do you eat food there?"

"Pretty much. Well, sometimes we eat on the couch. Nachos, mainly. Then there's the dining room, but we've been painting and—"

"Where's your TV?"

I pointed to the corner. It seemed hard to miss.

Leo peered around some boxes and let go. "Is *Sesame* on?"

"*Sesame* what? *Street*? I don't know." I went ahead into the kitchen.

Leo stopped in the yellow pantry. "Where's Gracie?"

My hand twitched. He knew Grace wasn't going to be here. Right? "Grace is in Pittsburgh," I said carefully, though I wasn't sure if she had left Somerville yet. "Have you been to her house, in Pittsburgh?"

Leo turned as if I'd asked him about going to Mars or what house he'd like to live in on *Sesame Street.* I explained that Grace's house was brick and had a wall in the backyard. I nattered. I thought I was buying time.

"I want to go to Gracie's house now," Leo said.

"But you're hungry. Shouldn't we eat first?"

"Oh." He followed me through the pantry and stopped at the square kitchen table. "Which side do I sit on?"

"There, there, there. Anywhere." Outside the sky was whiter with a slight orange streak. I turned on the hanging light.

Leo squinted. His lower lip curled down. "Where's my place mat?"

"I don't know," I said. "Later, we'll find it later. What do you eat for breakfast? Cereal? Toast?" Luckily, and this was the only lucky thing from that morning, the house always has a lot of breakfast food.

"Cereal," Leo said. "I did eat round cereal with milk, please."

I had the milk. "What kind of round cereal?"

"*Round.*" Leo slipped off his chair and his bare feet made a faint slapping sound. He looked up as if couldn't I make this all stop?

Cheerios, I thought. Cheerios are round. I poured some into a white bowl. They rattled and it sounded loud. I added an inch of milk and placed it before him.

"Where's the sugar, please?"

I added the sugar.

Leo shook his head until his hair splayed. "*I* put on the sugar."

The first bowl went back to the counter. I assembled a new one and let Leo weigh out a giant spoonful of sugar. "When do the servants eat?" I asked.

"When do I go to school?" Leo asked.

My leg began to twitch. Another thing to figure out and I hadn't even put it on the list. "This is a day off," I said, feeling temporarily clever because I had remembered Leo's word for it.

"Calvin goes to Preschool Community One."

"He certainly does." I brought over the original bowl of nearly soggy Cheerios and we ate. It was quiet, except for the crunching. It occurred to me that for this instant, at least, things weren't entirely awful. Then I had a horrifying thought. "Leo, when do you normally get out of bed?"

"When the sun's up." He sounded bright in a way I couldn't imagine.

"Oh," I said.

8:03 A.M. Once the coffee kicked in I could almost focus. Leo came back to the kitchen wanting to know if my TV had "PBS Kids in it." He waved. "Even if we drove all night to get here?"

"Yes," I said. "Thank all domestic gods for the invention of TV. We are going to watch as much TV as we can stand." I soon discovered that you could toggle between the Boston and Providence PBS stations and go through the whole lineup: *Clifford, Caillou, Zoboomafoo, Barney, Sesame Street, Dragon Tales, Boohbah,* and a bunch of other shows I'd never seen.

Leo seemed astounded. He sat completely still on the couch, asking, "Can I watch another?" Sure. Sure. Anything you want.

When life in the living room began to look somewhat solid I put on jeans and went to unload the van. I hauled the strollers and tricycles in past Leah's VW bug and our one-car garage suddenly looked like a closet. Boxes filled the edges of the living room and the walls moved in. Every few minutes Leo would spot a new plastic bin, take out an object and say something like, "Ahhh, my stringly." It was like watching an anthropology experiment where the person from another time is dropped back among the familiar artifacts. When I carried in the last cartons of clothes, the charcoal-colored living room rug had disappeared under a constellation of toys. Leo jumped on the couch holding his stuffed Cat-In-The-Hat doll. "Sleeping CAT!" he said and waved it in a circle.

"You bet," I said. "Wait, Leo, I thought you were afraid of cats?"

"No," he said and frowned, as if I'd made another mistake.

I climbed the stairs. I was up there for a while, stacking a tower of boxes on one side of Leah's office to make room for the dresser, and when I came down Leo was gone.

I checked the dining room. I looked under the table. I checked the kitchen. I checked the landing for the cellar stairs. I ran upstairs. How could he be upstairs? I was just upstairs. I checked the bedroom, the other closet, the bathroom, the tub, Leah's office, the tiny back room, under the bed. I ran down again and outside. But Leo didn't have shoes on. He wouldn't have gone out without shoes. In the kitchen I started opening the cupboards.

"You're hurting my ears." The voice came from under the table. Leo was curled up with his red-blankie, holding Sleeping Cat.

"Leo, where'd you go?"

"I'm right here."

"You have to answer when I call. You can't hide."

"I always hide." He crawled out and grabbed his crotch.

"Do you have to go the bathroom?"

Leo shook his head. "My penis hurts," he said as a dark stain appeared.

I carried him up to the bathroom. I never realized that endless peeing leads to endless laundry.

"Is this where you live?" Leo asked as we opened more boxes to find new clothes.

"Yeah." It stopped me. What did he think? "We used to live in an apartment," I said. "A duplex, over on the East Side. We almost bought a big loft space in Pawtucket, but I wanted a house. I wanted to own all the walls. Down here you can hear the tankers when they go up the bay. And tugboats. You can see tugboats. Have you ever seen a tugboat?"

"What's a duplex?"

"Two houses stuck together."

"Oh, with sticky tape?" Leo pointed into the hall. "You did sleep there and I slept here," he said. "When I'm asleep my eyes are awake."

I pulled up his green sweatpants. "They are?"

"But I live in Boston."

I couldn't finish the breath. He didn't get it. I was just realizing that. I didn't want to think about what would happen when he did. "You used to," I said. "Used to live in Boston."

Leo started down the stairs. "Where's the trampa-leen?"

"The what? Leo, I can't always understand you."

"Tramp-a-*leeeen*."

"There is no trampoline."

"Yes, there is." His bottom lip folded under. "Gracie said so."

"It's in the shop."

"What shop?"

"The fixing shop." We stood in the living room. "Leo, what's in this box? Trains?" I pried open the plastic bin and started handing out wooden engines.

"Oh, yeah." Leo took a red engine for each hand. "These are both James. Did you know that? Why do you keep bringing in my things?"

"Because we have to take the van back to Tim."

"Who's Tim?"

It was like living with someone from another planet. "Don't you know the customs here?" I said.

Leo gave me a twisted look and pulled a third red engine from the bin. He lined them up on the couch. "When is it a school day?"

"I have no idea," I said. "This is a day off. I told you."

"But what are my friends doing? What's Calvin doing?"

"Calvin? I have no idea."

"Where's Gracie?"

"Home. She's driving home, to Pittsburgh."

"What's Pittsburgh?"

"A city."

Leo stared. "When am I going home?"

"This is home."

He kneeled on the couch. He had a funny look, like he'd just seen something equal parts frightening and amazing. I thought he was going to cry, only he rose up and jammed his hands on his hips. "No it's not."

11:41 A.M. It was time for lunch except I was unaware of this. I needed to finish cleaning out the van, only Leo and I were stuck in another circular argument. I kept trying to explain that *Kipper* was on TV, too.

"No, it's a videoooooo," Leo said. "It's only a video and it's lost. Lost means you can't have it. Right?"

"*Kipper* is on TV."

Leo shook two fingers at me. "Kipper," he said. "That's your name."

For a second this seemed like a good sign. At least I had a name. But I was hungry and the cartoon dog comparison suddenly bugged me. "I'm your daddy," I said and the words felt shocking.

"My daddy's away on an island."

"He is?" I didn't know where to go with that. "Okay," I said, "then stay here and play. Don't hide. Okay?"

Leo gave me a snug little nod which reminded me of Cynthia. I had to catch my breath. He picked up his blanket and started to twirl. That was the first sign I should have caught; instead I went out to the van. For a few minutes there in the cold I even forgot that Leo was still in the house. But when I brought in the last dresser drawer the kid wasn't in the living room. I found him in the kitchen, standing on a counter. He'd pulled a chair over to climb up. "I'm Superhero Saves-the-Day," he said. "I never boil!"

I swung an arm around his middle and plucked him away. "My tummy hurts," he said and kicked.

"Leo, do you need to go to the bathroom?"

"Noooooo." I let him go and Leo thumped upstairs, pulling himself along by the balusters. I could tell by the stomping that he was in Leah's office. I made it into the living room and glanced up to see the tan diaper genie fly down the stairs. It looked like a small robot ejected from a spaceship. When it bounced off the front door the word "tantrum" unfolded in my mind like a piece of paper. I thought of that time in Iowa with Tim, at his grandparents' farm, when I saw my first funnel cloud: Oh, I thought, so that's what a tornado looks like.

"My tummy hurts," Leo shouted. "I told yooou."

"You sure are a mean drunk," I said. And only as I looked up at the top of the stairs to see Leo's folded arms did it occur to me that he might be hungry, too. "Leo, what do you eat for lunch?"

"Oreos."

"What else?"

"Celery. Oh, yeah, of course."

"Okay," I said. "We're going out."

There's a small grocery store, Lindsay's, around the corner. It's straight out of the 1950s and they have pretty much everything. I coaxed Leo into his coat, only out on the front steps he said: "You're really not taking very good care of me."

"I'm trying," I said. "I get points for trying."

"What's points?"

I zipped him up and remembered that they had pizza at the bakery. It was just up the street and Leo liked round food. Inside, the bakery was bright and yellow and warm. Jazzy guitar bits dangled from the speakers. We ordered slices and I got Leo a small milk with a straw. I felt like congratulating myself, or taking a nap, as soon as he started to sip. The slices arrived and I cut Leo's up, but he seemed perturbed. "This isn't round," he said. His bottom lip folded in.

Oh God, I thought, I can't handle insoluble crying in public. "See the top, by the crust," I said. "That's round. That's an arc."

"No, that's the handle."

"Yeah, I guess. Sure."

Leo surveyed the situation. He blinked three times and I thought, those are Cynthia's eyes. He really does look like both of us. My leg started to shake and as Leo began to eat, I got sad.

Even after two slices of pepperoni the big hand of hopelessness stayed clamped on my shoulder.

There was a couple at another table. They were taking little sideways, smiling glances at us, no doubt thinking, that's cute, a dad and a kid on a Thursday. They looked nice enough, in their late thirties, rings, jeans and hiking boots, woodsy but hip, sometimes glancing around in that quiet, isn't-it-amazing-to-have-a-day-off way. I thought: See this kid, the one you're smiling at? He's cute, but—I can't do it. You two look nice enough. You're good people. I can tell. Won't you take him? Please?

12:17 P.M. Back at the house I was stunned by how much better Leo was with food. He wanted to know if we could watch more videos, but when I said we had to take the van to the yard, he looked up as if I'd suggested something deeply dangerous. "No we don't."

I sensed the arrival of another rhetorical spiral. Every time we had to do something new that seemed to be a problem. Leo hadn't unzipped his coat so I scooped him up and stuffed him under my arm.

"Nooooo," he shouted. "Red-blankie. I need red-blankie." He started waving like someone trying to stop a bus. "Get it. Please."

I stationed Leo on the stairs, grabbed the blankie from the couch, and when I got back he was crying. "What's the matter?" He gave me this look, like everything was the matter and I thought, you're right, everything is the matter. I picked him up. His fists pressed against his eyes.

"You're supposed to say when."

"When what?"

"When we're going. You're supposed to say ten minutes. Then we go."

"Oh." I thought, yeah, that makes sense, you need a warning. I carried him to the van and strapped him into the car seat. He was still staring at the foggy window as we backed out. "Leo, are you okay?"

Leo blew a circle of mist on the glass. "I'm sad. I want Mommy."

"I know," I said. "I do, too."

I watched him lean forward in the mirror, as if he couldn't believe that I knew who Cynthia was. I had to find some pictures of us, I told myself. Do it tonight, after dinner. I turned on NPR. It was a story about Israeli pilots and Leo said: "Pirates? They talking about pirates?"

"I don't think so," I said, as the word "killed" came out of the speakers.

"Killed," Leo said. "Killed means dead and dead means flat. Right?"

I hummed. I didn't know what to think, except that now I had to be careful of the radio. I took a left on Narragansett and watched the gray bay slide by. A few side streets later Leo was asleep. That's right, I thought, checking the mirror, the kid needs a nap. The kid always needs a nap. How come I can't remember any of this?

1:43 P.M. I took the long way to the Love & Death yard, trying to think of as many drive-through errands as I could, but that only amounted to stopping at the bank and getting some Krispy Kreme donuts farther over in Cranston by the prison. When I did get to Pawtucket and saw my new-to-me station wagon dusted with snow I just sat there. Everything felt freshly wrong, like I'd been hijacked, only I hadn't gone anywhere. I had this new, entirely unfamiliar life on completely familiar ground. After a while Tim came out and tapped on the window.

Leo woke up when I opened the door. He seemed to recognize Tim but the wind was sharp and he wanted to be carried. When we got inside he pressed his head into my shoulder and wouldn't even look around. I guess if you're three, seeing the yard for the first time might be a little overwhelming. Or maybe he was always like that after a nap. I didn't know.

Tim stopped beneath the overhead heater. "I never thought about childproofing this place." He laughed.

"Stop laughing."

"How's it going? Much crying?"

"Much? Yeah, much."

Tim's hands went up as if I'd shown a weapon.

I don't quite know what I was thinking bringing Leo to work, but I had all these chores to finish, which was the only way to keep the place afloat. Leo finally perked up and we got him some water, but we had to convince him that it was okay to drink it from a coffee mug. Finally I said: "Leo, why don't you go play?"

Leo stared. I could have been speaking French, Hindi, Spanish, German.

"Well," Tim said, "that worked."

I kneeled and tried again. Leo folded his arms. I had things to do and I could feel the edge coming. For me frustration always rises in these sharp, bright peaks and when you go over, it feels like sticking your finger in a socket. "Leo," I said, but far too loud.

Leo covered his ears and ducked. "I want Calvin."

"Hey," Tim said, "look." He handed Leo a green, glass door-knob.

Leo turned it over in his fingers. "Heavy," he said. "What is this?"

"A doorknob," Tim said.

"No it's not. It's a dono."

"Yeah, I guess. Come on," Tim said. "I have more." He led Leo to a table full of door sets and I went to do e-mail, only I couldn't. I came back to watch from the office door, as Tim kept collecting boxes of things for Leo to sort—knobs, drawer pulls, little hinges. He brought them out to a clear spot on the floor beneath the cloud of chandeliers and Leo started taking out the parts, looking them over, wiping them off, and lining them up in rows. He clicked his tongue. Cynthia used to do that when she worked. I leaned against the doorframe. It's a strange sensation, knowing that someone is related to you simply by watching them across a room. He's from another world, I thought. One I used to live in.

"That kid has an amazingly long attention span," Tim said a few minutes later. "He locks in. Like you."

"I shouldn't have yelled."

"He's three."

"I should put that on a Post-it. Can you tattoo that on my forehead? He's three and I just uprooted him."

"Naw," Tim said. "You caught him. There's a difference. I have lots of Post-its. How'd Leah take this? She's back, right?"

I noticed my breath against the roof of my mouth. I could feel the molecules. "Not yet." Then I blinked and turned down the friendly path of least resistance. I lied. "She took it okay," I said. "It's a surprise and all and there's going to be some working out, but I think it went—okay."

Tim gave me this skeptical look. He nodded, as if he really didn't mean to call me on it but he had obligations. I went back to my overflowing inbox.

Leo stayed happy for almost an hour, which I realize now, in kid terms, is an incredibly spacious amount of time. Eventually he wanted a snack and after we couldn't find one he started to twirl beneath the chandeliers. I finally remembered the donuts in the van. That worked, but when Leo said he had to pee I forgot about the stuffed crow next to the bathroom door. Leo saw it and screamed. "Pick me," he shouted. I picked him up and his arms went around my neck as something warm spread across my stomach. He wet his pants. It left a volleyball-sized stain on my sweatshirt. We had to go home because I didn't bring extra clothes for anybody.

As we wrestled the car seat out of the van Tim said: "The kid's going to need a bath tonight, you think?"

"I need a bath," I said. The circle under the stain was chilly. "Wait, I have to give the kid a bath?"

Tim seemed amused.

I shook my head. "This isn't going to end, is it?"

6:23 P.M. For dinner I got Leo to eat some pasta, but only after I convinced him that penne were tubes and tubes were round, so it really was round food. Then while Leo watched the further adventures of Kipper, I found some pictures of me and Cynthia—one of us in the kitchen, a little drunk with our arms around each other in front of the black refrigerator, and another from that first summer, at her birthday on the porch.

"That's my porch." Leo looked at me strangely, as if he couldn't add up the information. "Gracie did say these are my getting-used-to-it days. This is getting-used-to-it day number fifty-hundred." He slipped quietly off the couch.

Brave kid, I thought. Braver than me.

I finally finished cleaning up the kitchen when the phone rang. At first I thought it might be Grace, then I thought I should call Grace, then I thought, no, just keep going. Figure it out. When I picked up it was Julie, who wanted to know when she could meet Leo? I hummed. "He's not big on the meet-and-greet right now," I said. "You know, he only eats round pasta? We had a long conversation about the meaning of round. Does this make sense?"

"I know kids Leo's age who are complete pastatarians," she said.

"You know kids Leo's age?" It never occurred to me that my friends knew people with kids. "Huh." I tapped the sink with a wooden spoon. "You know that PBS show in England where everybody goes off to be a servant at a manor house? That's me. I'm down to nothing but a nub."

"Keeper, it's only been a day."

"I know. I am very aware of that." Then Julie had to go because someone was at the door so we hung up. But it was true, every time I sat down to congratulate myself, to think that for thirty seconds here it looked like we were actually sailing the ship, something else would go wrong. I'd forget to ask if Leo had to go to the bathroom, so he'd just go. I wouldn't understand that "spagley" meant spaghetti and there'd be a meltdown. Then I remembered about the bath. The kid needed a bath. I went up to unpack the "bath box."

When I came downstairs Leo had built a railway that went all the way into the dining room, but I forgot the rules of engagement, the ten-minute warning. "Bath time," I said.

Leo rose on the couch in a way that had started to look familiar. He spread his fingers and shouted: "Nooooo."

"You're a kid. Kids take baths. I took baths."

He jumped up and fell into the cushions. "I don't."

"How about a shower?"

"Nooooo. What's a shower?"

I moved in to scoop him up, since that worked the last time, but he ran. "No thank you. No thank you." I tried to corner him in the pantry but he went between my legs. "Get away. Mommy does it. Not you. Never you." He climbed the stairs.

I let him go. I stopped on the third step and sat. When I heard Leo jumping on my bed I understood that I was too tired to stand.

8:09 P.M. I decided to skip the bath; that was a plus. Then I made a few strategic errors. I knew bedtime was coming, only I didn't know when exactly bedtime was supposed to be. Grace told me, but I forgot. I knew it was in that notebook of Cynthia's, the one with all the answers, that Grace couldn't find. The problem was I kept asking Leo and the answer was always "Noooooo." Finally he said: "I go to bed at past o'clock."

Fine. Leo seemed happy enough playing with his Bob-the-Builder trucks: Scoop, Muck, and Dizzy, and somebody else, so I started unpacking the boxes of books. "Leo, which of these do we read at bed?"

"We have to play Superhero Hides."

"Superhero who?"

"Superhero Saves-the-Day. You say 'Saves-the-Day.'" Leo's red blanket went around his shoulders. He started to twirl.

"Which book? Tell me."

He stopped to shake his head, staggered, and started again.

The first carton was full of Dr. Seuss, Little Bear, and Corduroy, books about cranes and dump trucks, Mike Mulligan, and Mary Anne. Then at the bottom I saw it—a black-and-white marble notebook with "Leo" on the front in Cynthia's large loopy handwriting.

"Mom's book," Leo said. "About me." He pointed to his stomach.

Overhead something crashed in Leah's office. The floor shook as if a 300-pound person had fallen out of bed. Leo covered his ears and ran to the kitchen while I went upstairs. The tower of boxes had toppled. I shouldn't have stacked them that high, but I was tired and the heavy ones ended up on top. I gathered the tiny boots and sneakers up off the floor and realized that Cynthia had never thrown out any of Leo's shoes.

When I got downstairs the notebook wasn't on the couch. Leo said: "I hid it in a very secret place."

I could feel the fuses going. "Well, find it fucking fast," I said. "That's all about you. That has the answers. That's how we're going to *learn to get along*."

"No." The arms stayed folded.

"If I give you an Oreo?"

"Two."

I got them. Leo took both, laughed, and ran back to the kitchen. "Thank you, thank you, thank you," he screamed.

Why did I think that would work? I was on my knees with my head under the couch. "Will you tell me tomorrow?" I shouted.

"Noooo." Leo reappeared with a cookie mustache.

"Fine. Let's pick books. What do you read before bed?"

"I'm not telling yooou."

Somewhere around nine and an armful of books later I got Leo upstairs, into the bathroom, and into a nighttime diaper. Since I couldn't find any pajamas I decided that sleeping in your clothes was the new official policy. I sat in the rocking chair and Leo grabbed Sleeping Cat and climbed into my lap, as if finally I had done something the way it was meant to be done. We read four or five books until Leo explained I wasn't reading them right. "Say *all* the words," he told me. Every time I tried to put him to bed he said he needed to sit on my lap again or else he was hungry and thirsty. I got him a piece of bread, but I had to peel off the crust. I got him water in a cup with a lid, but he needed ice. A few minutes later I said I was going downstairs. "Come check on me," Leo said and I agreed. Only every time I'd make it downstairs he'd call nine seconds later. Or I'd come up to find him quietly crying, and quiet crying is the worst. Once a plane went over and Leo covered his ears and said: "Why do you live near thunder?" I heard, "This is not my favorite place," again and again. The shadows on the wall were "coming off." He needed a "noogly," which I eventually figured out was a pacifier, only I had to hunt through the kitchen for the right box. In the end I wound up sitting next to him for half an hour at a time, trapped in the rocking chair, thinking: I need to find that notebook or make a list of questions for Grace. Then thirty seconds later it'd be: No, I'm an adult, I went to college. This isn't rocket science. I can do this without the stupid notebook. And every time I thought Leo was asleep I would stand in slow motion and try to sneak out of the room. I never made it to the hall. When we got to "I want Mommy," what could I say?

10:58 P.M. I watched Leo's eyelids flutter as the phone rang downstairs. I leaned forward but the instant my hands moved Leo's eyes snapped open. The machine picked up. It was Leah.

"Hey," she said, her low voice winding around the furniture. For a second it all felt suspended, like that moment on a mountain bike, on a steep trail, when you know you're about to crash and you're already airborne. It's almost exhilarating, but there's no way to reel any of it back. "Your cell hasn't been on," she said. "Anyway, I'll still be back Friday, tomorrow, honey. Don't worry about picking me up. Love you."

The machine clicked and whirred.

TEN

Yeah, I'm an idiot. I should know better but I get caught up and then I get caught. Leah actually came home from Phoenix on Saturday, after dinner. She was supposed to be back Friday, but a snowstorm wandered up the East Coast Thursday night, leaving thirteen inches in our driveway and planes on the wrong runways all over the country.

Was I worried? Petrified. That's a good word. Leah did check in to say that she'd be there some time after dinner. But I couldn't call and tell her about all this while she stared out at an empty runway from some airport lounge. She wouldn't have believed me. I wouldn't have believed me.

Then it came to pass. Saturday, day three, a little before eight, and I knew by then we had entered Leo's bedtime zone. He had been pretty good all day, except for a few rough moments here and there. Well, more than a few, as it had become clear to Leo that he might be staying here for a while, even if we certainly hadn't made it to the idea of forever. But Leo kept saying things like: "In days and days will you *still* be here?" Of course, I'd say. "Will I?" Yes, I'd say. Completely convincing. But all this wasn't helping life in the present.

The snow helped. It turned out to be a big quiet distraction. We watched the plows go by with their winking yellow lights. We heard a snowmobile in the distance. We dug out the driveway and dug it out again after we got plowed in. We carved a fort into the pile at the sidewalk's edge. After dinner we drove to the grocery store to test out the wagon's four-wheel drive. But Leo seemed to think this was a completely exotic adventure. Or maybe he was just happy to be outside again after dinner. I had no way to know.

When Jon dropped Leah off I had a brown paper grocery bag on my head. I didn't even hear the car. Actually, Leo and I both had bags over our heads. We were bumping into each other in the dining room while I tried to explain the difference between visible and invisible.

"Now," I said, pulling the bag over my eyes, "I'm invisible."

Leo pulled his bag down. "No, I'm indivisible. See—told ya." He lifted the bag's bottom corner. "Is this indivisible?"

"Now you're visible to me and I'm visible to you."

The front door rattled. We stared. Leo's bag snapped down.

"Hey." Leah's voice rolled across the space. "Whose car is in the driveway? It has your plate but—" Three steps in she stopped. She had her black travel bag over one shoulder and cream-colored roses wrapped in clear cellophane in her left hand. Her red-rimmed glasses began to fog and the flowers went down slowly, until they pointed at the floor.

Leo slipped behind and held on to my sweater. "Woo," he said and faded into a corner.

My bag stayed up on my head like some vagrant chef's hat. "Hi." I stepped over a flock of yellow dump trucks. They seemed extraordinarily bright against the gray carpet.

Leah looked around as if she were trying to remember the space. The longer it went on the lower the ceiling seemed. Her bag landed. I felt the vibration. The glasses came off and she held them in her left hand. She kept scanning, past the plastic bins of Hot Wheels and over the wooden trains. "Oh," she said. "Who?" She tried to look into the dining room. "Is—that?"

"Ah." I took off the bag and began to fold it. "Leo," I said, looking toward the kitchen. "This is Leah."

"Noooo." Leo stamped his feet in a tiny, make-this-be-over dance.

"Leo." I knew he wanted me to pick him up, but I couldn't move. I felt like that thin strip of metal in a junior high science experiment, wavering between the magnetic fields.

Leah squinted and made a small wave. "Hi, Leo?"

"How was your trip?" I asked.

She blinked. "My trip? Awful. I spent the night in Denver, in the airport, on the floor. You knew that. I left a message."

"You did? I didn't get that."

"The rest of it—where's the dog?"

"The dog," I said. "The dog didn't—work out."

"The dog didn't what?" Her eyebrows went down.

I felt a tug at my sweater. "Leo is, kind of, instead—"

"I have to go to bed," Leo said from inside the bag. "I have to go to the bathroom. I have to pee right now."

Leah stopped unbuttoning her coat. Her arms slowly crossed. "Instead?"

I picked Leo up and held him at my side like a football. "I'll be back. Right back. Don't go anywhere. Just don't."

Leah gave me a slow, complicated, largely incredulous stare that followed us upstairs. I didn't dare to look back over the banister.

Yeah, I never should have left Leah standing in the living room. That was bad. But I could see the Leo meltdown coming, right around the corner. And how was introducing Leah to that particular scenario going to improve the situation? I got Leo to the bathroom, into a nighttime diaper and into his purple sweatpants. He wanted to wear his long-sleeved Bob-the-Builder shirt to bed so I said, fine. I kicked the camping pad back into the closet while he worked to put on the shirt. I had spent most of the last night sort of sleeping on the pad, since Leo kept waking up every time I tried to crawl out of the room. It's a strange thing, camping in your own house. It's practically exotic. I kept lying on the floor thinking: How did I end up here?

As Leo brushed his teeth I sensed Leah moving through the downstairs. She would pause in the living room, take a step into the dining room, cross the pantry, turn into the kitchen, and go back to the living room. I heard the TV and it sounded like she was watching basketball on TNT. That seemed to be an excellent sign.

I sat in the rocking chair and Leo picked the books: some bears go to the moon, some wooden people live on the edge of a tub, the kid with the purple crayon. I edited as I read until he caught on in the middle of *The Cat In The Hat Comes Back*. He banged my knee and told me to read *all* the words. I had to retreat and start again. Then I handed him Sleeping Cat and we rocked.

The TV went off and Leah came upstairs. She left her bag in the bedroom and stopped outside Leo's door. Later I figured out that was the moment when she realized she no longer had an office. Her foot tapped twice before she went back downstairs. It was entirely nerve-racking.

"It's bright in here," Leo said.

"It's the night light." I kept on tucking him in.

"No—some of it's the sun."

"The sun is on the other side of the earth right now."

"The sun's over there." He pointed out the window. "And the earth's here and the grocery store is there. Are we spinning?"

"Yes," I said, figuring out that this all came from the *Blue's Clues* episode about day and night we watched on tape that afternoon.

"Spinning around the sun?"

"Yeah."

"Why not the moon?"

"It isn't big enough."

"Oh." Leo put his fist against his cheek. "It's been a long time since we haven't gone to space," he said. "We need a little spaceship to find that moon." He sat up. "Hey, I just had a big idea. One, two, three, seven, nine. We're going up to Mars and blasting up!

We need to go past that moon and we need to get our schedules to tell us when to get there and we need our special routines. Off the start! We're going up to the dark!"

"Leo," I said, "sleep."

"I'm not talking to you. I'm telling a story." The front door opened and closed. I bit my tongue. "I don't like that person downstairs. He scared me."

"That person is a she. Leah is very, very nice."

"Oh." Leo crumpled his red blanket. "Would a ghost eat a moose?"

"I don't know."

"Okay, thanks."

I heard a scraping sound in the driveway as Leah cleaned off her car. Why didn't I think to clear off her car? Leo pushed his head into his pillow and squirmed. That meant he was on the edge of going out. His right arm flailed around for Sleeping Cat and I slid it closer. Come on, I thought, as his breathing settled.

I stood carefully and made it to the door without alerting the guard. At the bottom of the stairs I stuffed the monitor in the front of my jeans and remembered to put on boots, but I wasn't wearing a coat. It was so cold out. The stars felt like they were sitting on my head.

The broom Leah used to clear off the back third of her Volkswagen bug stuck out of the snowbank at a low angle. The line where she stopped was crisp. I saw the quarter moon reflected in the round black fender.

"Sorry," I said. "I forgot to clean off your car."

Leah's red mittens were caked with snow. She stopped scraping the driver's side window and waved the ice scraper at me. My eyes kept blurring, maybe from the cold. The ice scraper seemed to leave streaks in the dark. "Is he yours?" she asked.

This was the moment I should have planned for. This was where I could have used the flow charts. This was why I should have gone through the decision tree and come up with all the options, all the best ways to break the news. I'm usually good at that. But every time I started, this looked so much like a thing you could never plan for that—what was the point?

The ice scraper kept moving. I thought, now I know what it must feel like when you're waiting for an execution. That moment right before you see the bullets leave the rifles. "Yes," I said.

A breeze curled snow off the roof of Leah's car.

"Cynthia is the mother?"

"How did you know that?"

"He looks like you—you idiot. He has your face. It's your chin. That's why I thought he was one of your brother's, then I realized he was too—"

"He looks like me? Nobody's said that. Well, no. Tim did."

"Tim knows? Do other people know?" She looked at the stars. "James, did you know from the beginning there wasn't a dog?"

"No."

"In bed, when you told me, did you know there was a kid? Did you make up the dog because you didn't dare tell—"

"I did not make up the dog. The dog disappeared two fucking weeks ago and nobody told me. Arrow was the dog." I made a box in the air showing how big Arrow used to be. I started to hop. My calves were that cold.

Leah bit her lip. "When?"

"When what? Did I get him? Leo? Two days ago."

"When did you know?"

"Before that, a little."

"Did you know when you told me about Cynthia? Yesterday, when I left that message? When?"

"I think the machine ate that message."

"Before that? Did you know when I called and you and Tim were in the van? Was he there? Was he? Why the fuck didn't you tell me? How could you not tell me? How can we be together and you decide to not tell me?"

"I'm sorry. I didn't—decide."

"And I was feeling awful because of what you must have been feeling about Cynthia and I bought you stupid airport flowers the day *after* Valentine's."

"Valentine's." It's such a funny-sounding word. Why does Valentine's Day exist simply so I can forget it?

"Imagine what I was expecting when I came in—"

"I did. I imagined you'd be looking for—"

"A dog. I was looking for a stupid dog. I didn't want there to be a dog, but I was prepared to look for a dog. I didn't know if he was going to be one of those dogs who jumps on you or what. Dogs scared me as a kid."

"They did?"

"I kept wondering if Fred came back and you'd forgotten to mention it because of the dog. He didn't, right? Fred? I worried that the yellow in the pantry might be too bright. I kept thinking that my job is turning into a complete mess. I even brought you homemade fucking dog biscuits. Some person made them—at home. Who has time to make fucking dog biscuits?"

"That was a wonderful good faith offering. I appreciate—"

She waved a snowy mitten at the station wagon. "What is that?"

I explained about the truck and the air bags and the lack of a backseat.

"James, you had time to buy a car but you couldn't figure out how to tell me? You didn't even want my opinion? Like it didn't matter?"

At first I assumed she was talking about the car. Then I realized she meant Leo. Maybe I was wrong, but my first thought was: No, in a way it didn't matter. Because what could I do? I couldn't not take him.

My front pocket began to howl. I took out the monitor and saw the red lights arc across the face of it. I tugged the blue antenna but my fingers were cold and I dropped the whole thing into a knee-high drift. "Shit," I said as Leo yelled on, muffled a little by the snow.

"I'm really upset." Leah waved the ice scraper in a circle until it flew into a snowbank. It left a hole the width of an envelope. I'd never seen Leah throw anything before.

"This will work out," I said. "It will." I grabbed for the monitor but the snow hurt my hand. It was in too deep. I folded my fists under my arms. "I have to fix this," I said and ran for the front door.

Yeah, I know, I should not have left Leah out in the driveway. If I'd even faintly understood how important that would be, I would have thought of something else. I don't know what, but something. By the time I got to Leo he was all ramped up and sobbing and an hour later I was still in his room. He'd had a bad dream. He wanted to talk to Mommy and someone wouldn't let him. I heard Leah come in and take a shower. I heard her pad to the bedroom. I heard drawers opening. The bed creaked as she got in.

"Is he asleep?" Leah sat up when I opened the door in the dark. I closed it and the hall light left an outline, as our bedroom door doesn't actually latch, another charming nineteenth-century effect that comes with sloping floors.

"I think, yeah."

"Good," she said, her voice dropping. "You don't even know about all the awful things that happened."

"Well, that's because on work trips you climb into the bubble and don't always tell me stuff until the very end." I sat on the edge of the bed.

"I don't tell you—okay. This afternoon we flew through a thunderstorm and I thought I was going to die. There were laptops bouncing off the ceiling. And I realized I didn't want to die not sitting next to you. It was awful. The only good thing was we didn't get the project, so I don't have to go back. They called on Jon's cell to tell us while we were in line to go through security. They didn't even wait until we got back. It was a complete waste of time. Jon and I got into a fight about these long-distance things. We don't know the builders, it's harder to check up. Of course we weren't going to get the project. Then he said he and Phoebe are separating, which came as a surprise, but not, and I started to wonder what that had to do with all this silly travel. Jon has not been acting at all like a functioning person and this is who I pick to work with?"

"I'm glad you're back."

"Why the fuck did you do this?"

"I didn't do anything," I said, even though that sounded wrong.

"Yes, you did."

"I did what, exactly?"

"You had a life," she said.

I knew she meant Cynthia.

"I don't want to know the details," she said. "Or the timing, I don't—"

"It was before us. Not a lot, but before. It was. You had a life, too. And I didn't know. Cynthia didn't tell me. She never told me. How could it be a life if I didn't know it was happening?"

"What happens if—okay, let's say you die, you get hit by—your choice."

"A recycling truck."

"Right. Then what happens? Where does that put me?"

"What happens to what? I'm not getting hit by anybody," I said. "I've decided. I'm living to one hundred fourteen. That's the plan. No more white bread."

Leah pulled a pillow in front of her and squished it. "I'm not ready, to begin with. Kids scare me. There isn't room in—and I'm certainly not ready to be a stepparent. That's me, the wicked fucking stepmother. This house fits two. It's small for two and a dog. With a kid—we just got here."

"I'm not ready either." I took a long breath. I glanced around the room. I could see a little better in the dark. "It could work. We have two bedrooms."

Leah shook her head as if a point the size of an ocean liner had passed me by, again. "I need an office. I don't want to have to live at work. We have a bedroom and an office and a closet." She covered her eyes. "How are you going to afford it? You don't make very much. Together it's one thing, but—"

That should have been a sign, if I'd been sharp enough to pick it up. "I could go do something like what I used to do," I said. "That would make more. No, wait, there is life insurance."

"Oh," Leah said.

"I have to find out about it but, anyway, I can't strand Tim. And you like what I do. You're always basking in my reflective alternative glory."

She laughed. A small laugh but still. "Stop. I'm really upset." Leah stared and it went on and on. "Let's stop talking and make love," she said. "Let's pretend this isn't happening. I need that. Now."

She pulled her red flannel pajama top over her head and it startled me. After a few seconds I reached over to rub her shoulder, but I didn't know where to go next. Eventually, we fell into a rhythm. It was better without our clothes on or maybe it was deciding not to talk about it that helped, but by that point I was tired enough to pretend that this alone was all that mattered. Leah's hair still had that traveler's smell, the metallic unfamiliarness of the familiar.

I heard the door. Doors in old houses always creak. "Mr. Kipper?"

"Oh God," Leah said and pulled the covers over her head. "Of course, we're naked."

"I did have a new bad dream," Leo said.

"You did?" I sat up. "Leo, you got out of bed. You never get out of bed. Go back to bed. What was your dream about?"

He stood on the threshold, small and backlit. "That bird? At where your office is? It's frozen, right? It can't fly anymore."

"Yes, it's stuffed."

"What's stuffed?"

"It used to be a bird."

"What's it now?"

"Stuffed. It's like the outline of a bird. Like it used to have a life but something happened and now it doesn't."

"Oh," Leo said. "Where's that person?"

"Leah's asleep. Under the covers."

"Can I see?"

"No."

"Did you know our names both start with leee?"

I reached over the edge, trying to find my sweatpants on the floor. "He's never done this," I whispered to the mounded quilt. "Got out of bed on his own." I pulled on the sweats.

"This is sweet," Leah said. "Complete lack of privacy. Another new development."

I aimed Leo across the hall. "We're going to bed."

"If you insist," Leo said.

"Where's that from?"

"*The Grouchy Ladybug.*" Leo made a fist and opened it. He wiggled his fingers. "Want to see me blink my hand?"

Leah and I both woke up at eight, while Leo kept on sleeping. I had finally gotten him settled again around 3:30 in the morning, so the fact that he slept in shouldn't have been such a shock. The big surprise was that I woke up bathed in adrenaline. "I'm going to make you French toast," I announced and hopped out of bed. Even I knew this was ludicrous, as if French toast could make up for wrecking her life, but Leah at least smiled.

In the living room I saw the baby monitor on the coffee table, as Leah must have brought it in from the snow. That, too, seemed like a good sign. I turned it on and carried it to the kitchen so I could keep an ear out for Leo. Last night, after we were all back in bed, Leah told me that when she walked in it felt like the house had been invaded. I agreed. Having Leo was like developing a new chronic condition. I was only beginning to understand that. I added extra cinnamon and nutmeg to the batter and made Leah Irish Breakfast tea. When she came down ten minutes later she wasn't in her bathrobe and sweats but jeans and a purple turtle-neck sweater.

"I have to go in," she said.

"You do?"

"There's all this North Carolina work that didn't get done."

We ate. We traded sections of the Sunday *Times*.

"I need your keys," Leah said. "So I can get out."

"Are we breaking up?" I asked. Then I thought, shit we are. Why did I ask?

She paused. She took a sip of tea. "No," she said. "The French toast was good." She poured the rest of her tea into a travel mug. "I'll call."

At first I thought, that's fine. That's as much as anyone has a right to expect, given the situation. Then I listened as my station wagon crunched out onto the street and my keys came in through the mail slot with a hard metallic ring. When I heard Leah's engine rev before she backed down the driveway, I wasn't so sure.

ELEVEN

I'm thirty-six. And every time I come up on a birthday I start worrying about it a whole year ahead of time. I spent all of thirty-five running around going: I'm almost thirty-six, I'm almost thirty-six! That's the top of the slope! After that things fall off! So when I finally turned, it merely felt familiar, which is all strange. Some days I spend so many hours imagining the next room that when I get there I already know my way around.

Tuesday was the day after President's Day, when the whole wide world struggled back to work and I wanted to go, too. Work by then was a problem. Tim kept giving me a pass on pretty much all of it, which is what I would have done, but pieces weren't getting sold or shipped and everything on the Web had to be updated. I couldn't keep letting it pile up.

This was also day six of life with Leo, only by that point I'd learned a few things. Like that Leo and I shared a fondness for toaster waffles, even if he mainly liked them because they were round. That Leo would eat red and green grapes, but only if they were seedless so they could explode in your mouth. That Leo woke up every morning between three-thirty and four and it took an hour, minimum, to get him back to sleep. That his clothes couldn't be too prickly or too slippery, so they had to be cotton or fleece. That Leo was scared of floods. He found a book with pictures of the neighborhood after the Hurricane of 1938 and one showed a sailboat sitting on top of the Pawtuxet River bridge, which is about a block away. That was good for a nightmare. It's tough explaining the concept of a more than 100-year-old flood to a three-year-old whose idea of time extends to about the day after tomorrow. I'd also learned that I would never get to finish anything again as long as I lived. And, if you shampoo with Mr. Bubble by mistake, it takes a half an hour to defoam yourself, plus you smell like watermelons all day.

I picked all that up on my own because I still hadn't found Cynthia's notebook, the one with all the answers. I kept asking and Leo kept saying "Nooo" until I wasn't sure he even remembered what we were talking about. Twice, after Leo was in bed and before Leah got home, I found myself crawling across the living room looking for it under chairs. Once I even rolled up the carpet. At that point actually giving in to the idea that I needed an instruction manual began to feel kind of pathetic. Couldn't I simply keep a list of questions and call Grace? I could, I guess. And why hadn't Grace called me? Even to check in? But maybe she had and the machine ate that one, too. Anyway, it drove me nuts to think that the Leo answers were all there, somewhere in the house.

What hadn't I figured out? Who Leo's friend Calvin was. What to say the four times a day when he cried for Mommy. How to get Leo to take a bath. I'd tried air-lifting him to the tub before bed, luring him with Thomas engines, Oreos, grapes, and it all ended with Leo naked and shrieking, "No thank you! No thank you!" as he ran for the stairs.

How was Leah through all this? Hard to say because she wasn't around much. Mostly she stayed at work and edged back in once I had Leo in bed, about when I could only sit on the couch and prop my eyes open for another twenty minutes. She seemed cheerful enough, at times, but it felt strange, almost eerie. She said she was getting things done and I couldn't fault her for hiding out at work. It takes balls to be an architect. You go up there and say: I've thought this building up and it's staying up until someone knocks it down.

But we weren't talking about Leo, which wasn't right for us, because day-to-day Leah has always been a talk-it-out kind of girl. I was too exhausted to bring it up and she seemed to be pretending it hadn't happened. It felt like we were walking around with a hand grenade sitting on the coffee table, which we were. But I couldn't ask her about it. Well, I could have and I thought about it, sometimes. Other times that low voice behind my ear kept saying: *No, no, give her space. Let her get used to the idea. Let her puzzle this out. Leah's always like this when she's working on a puzzle.* I could never decide if that advice was wise or just cowardly. We were living in a pause. I knew that. Only how long can you exist in a pause?

I had my radar up. I kept looking for hints that this silence might mean actual trouble. I'd examine the depth of Leah's frown as she stepped between long lines of wooden train track on the rug and wonder if she sounded happier on the phone talking to Jon than she did a few seconds earlier talking to me. I'd try to gauge the tone of her footsteps while she looked for something in what used to be her office. Mostly I couldn't tell. Then I realized I didn't really know how Leah broke up with people. Was she a final dustup and a walk-out kind of girl? Or did she do the distance thing? A little more space, a little more space until you reach the long slow fade. I never thought I'd need that information. Gary would know. Maybe I should call, but I couldn't even remember what state he lived in.

Sometimes, usually after midnight, when I was trapped in the rocking chair beside Leo's bed, the dark fascination of looking directly over the breakup cliff would swirl up to snare me. Sometimes I could already sense it. That twisted fist of a stomach that never unwinds. Feeling torn for months at a time. How your throat aches every morning when you wake up and realize you're still in the same spot. Listening as the line from that Police song, "The bed's too big without you," winds into your DNA. It all happened with Cynthia, too, only that breakup was on me.

Then there were other moments when it felt like I was still in my life but already looking at it through a new frame. Tiny things, like the way Leah fingered her bracelets while we watched our Netflix episodes of *Six Feet Under* would seem amazingly poignant. Or I'd roll over in bed, wind my arm in across her warm stomach, then remember where we were and miss her already.

Tim assigned himself to the Wickenden Street store so it was my day to run the yard. I even had a plan to get to work—employ a baby-sitter. I found Daisy, yes that was her name, on a flier at the drugstore in the village. We talked Monday night and she sounded great, even if she laughed at almost everything I said. Daisy was in her twenties, a former preschool teacher between jobs and going back to grad school in the fall. Perfect. But should she meet Leo first? No, just have her come over in the morning.

Daisy appeared on our front steps at ten minutes after nine. She was short with short blond hair and wrapped in a puffy blue coat. She had two scarves, each a different shade of orange, and when she began to unwind the first scarf Leo immediately retreated with red-blankie and Sleeping Cat to the cave under the kitchen table. I showed Daisy around, listed the things Leo would agree to eat, the things he liked to do. I left her my library card so she could restock the videos. "He's like this at first," I said, waving under the table. "But eventually . . ." Then the lies started. I went on about what a calm, reliable, and charming kid Leo was, the total pleasure he could be. I knew that was wrong, but I had to get to work.

I told Leo I'd see him at two, after his nap, as Daisy peered under the table and pretended to play peek-a-boo. Leo scooted out across the floor until he reached the corner where he gave me a suspicious look.

I handed Daisy my cell number and said: "Okay, I'm off to work." I waved and didn't look back.

Free at last. It's true, those were the words in my head. I put *Stop Making Sense* into the CD player and slid down the driveway, out along Narragansett Boulevard, past the tank farm on Allen's Avenue, and up onto I-95. No one drives a getaway car better than me.

Eleven minutes later my phone went off. It was Daisy. "Mr. Keeper?" In the background I heard a wail and a clank, then a deeper wail. "I really don't know about this." She sounded cornered. "He's been basically hysterical since you left. Normally I wouldn't call and I know you have to get to work, but he's asking for his mother and Calvin and—how long do you want me to give this?"

"Ah." I chewed my lip. I coasted over to the State House exit. "Okay, I'm coming back."

Leo was still wound up when I got there. Tears, red eyes, heaving, "I want Mommy," all of which made me feel awful in seventeen new directions. I paid Daisy for the full five hours and said we should try it again, someday. She smiled quickly and waved over her shoulder.

"You did leave me all by myself." Leo clawed at my arm.

"You weren't alone. Daisy was here."

"I don't *know* her," he said. "I don't want you. I want Calvin."

"Who is Calvin?"

Leo paused and did his you're-not-listening dance. "Calvin is my friend," he said. "You're not. Ever. You're not anything."

I stared. "Okay, whatever you say."

I changed Leo's wet pants and undies and planted him in front of the television, watching an endless video loop of Mr. Rogers episodes. He seemed transfixed enough so I went to the back porch without a coat and stood there feeling trapped and dumbfounded. I can't do this, I thought. I'm shackled and marooned and the world is getting smaller by the second. It's like living under house arrest. I wake up every morning, lie there feeling sad, and reach down to see if the ankle bracelet is still attached.

I took out my phone and called Tim at the shop but Maggie answered. She said Tim had gone to look at furniture in Warren and he'd left his cell phone behind. Lucky guy. I leaned against the corner post and wished I smoked. It seemed like that kind of minute, then something turned and I started missing Cynthia. It was another wave. It hurt. I looked through the kitchen window and saw Leo's legs on the couch and thought, how wrong is this? It's two halves of something that can never line up.

Eventually I got cold and when I went inside I found Mr. Rogers talking about death. And he seemed to have been talking about it for a while. "Toys don't die," he said. "But people are part of life and in life things die." I couldn't believe it. I mean, I don't want to think about this, so how could Leo? Then I decided we needed to trade that life lesson for more time with Bob the Builder (Can we fix it? Yes, we can!) and went back to unpacking. Because if everything else falls apart at least the house can be neat.

Around 11:30, I made Leo lunch and piled him into the car, hoping that might lead us to a nap. "I want to do errands," he said as I slid the car seat straps over his thin shoulders. He seemed to have semiforgiven me for the morning. But what choice did he have? All prisoners make deals with the guards.

"What kind of errands?"

"Errands!" Leo said, as if the category qualified as a destination.

"Sure, sure. These days I'll agree to anything."

On the way into town Leo informed me that *Where the Wild Things Are* was "so too scary." Then he wanted to know when the next flood was coming? I said not for a while, because it's winter and too cold for floods. "Oh," he said. "And I love cold." As we passed the hospitals he asked about the buildings. I explained and he shook his head. "Bah," he said. "I say bah to hospitals. Mommy did get tired in a hospital." A backhoe rolled toward us as we wove through the highway construction near the hurricane barrier. "A pirate's driving that," Leo said. "Pirates bury treasure with front loaders all the time."

At the edge of downtown I saw Leo getting that glassy stare in the rearview mirror, so I turned up the heat. Five minutes later he fell asleep. I kept driving, out 146, up into Cumberland, all over and around until an hour and a half later I circled back to the yard. The lot was crisscrossed with fresh tracks, no doubt left by people who wanted to pay us thousands of dollars for old objects, if only I'd been there to catch them. I felt completely wayward again. Then I thought, wait, this is a salvage yard. If people want something that bad they'll come back. It's not like we're brain surgeons or public defenders. They're not exactly in trouble when they get here.

I sat for another forty minutes, just worrying, until Leo woke up. When I carried him inside it was so cold we could see our breath. I got the heaters going, then I turned on the computer and discovered a PBS Kids Web site. "That's lovely," Leo said and took the mouse.

The upside? I had Leo occupied, but he also controlled the computer and everything I had to take care of was on the computer. So I packed some pieces to ship, returned a dozen calls, and when I couldn't stand up anymore, fell into the red leather couch in the office and let my eyes close. Forty-five minutes later I woke to a long ringing crash.

I found Leo out in the warehouse, standing on a folding table covered with hinges. The end of the table next to him had collapsed and there were door sets all over the floor. He stared back at the mess like a cartoon character who had leapt to the canyon's edge, just as the suspension bridge behind him fell away.

"Leo, get down." I stumbled closer. Only when he saw that I was upset did he start to get upset. I grabbed him around the middle and he kicked. I thought: I can't do this. I'm not awake enough to do this. Leo cried and pressed his left fist into his cheek.

"What are you doing?"

"Mommy's talking to me." He nodded, as if to say of course.

"What's she saying?"

"It's secret. I'm not telling you—ever."

We were good at the yard for another hour. Mostly I spent the time herding Leo, then at four I called Leah, just to check in, but when I only got her voice mail the knot in my stomach tightened right up. I called to order a pizza in the village and we drove home in the semidark. The good thing about being exhausted is that sometimes you're too tired to be sad.

I was out of cash so I pulled around to the bank's drivethrough ATM. I rolled down the window and the wind had a bite to it. I hit the sixty-dollar button and when the bills came out a gust pried them away. They made a brief flapping sound and vanished. I'd never seen that before. I tried to open the door but I was too close to the machine. I rolled up the window, inched the car forward and got out to track down the cash.

"Don't leave me!" Leo shouted.

"I have to get the money. The money blew away."

"Can I see the lobster?"

My key chain has a small plastic lobster on it, as well as the remote to lock the doors. Leo's hands kept moving back and forth making little clamping motions. "What are you doing?" I asked.

"Lobstering around," he said.

I handed him the keys and closed the door.

I found the first two twenties plastered to the side of the left front tire. I stood up just as Leo pushed the big button on the remote and the door locks clicked.

My hand slapped against the driver's window. "Leo, what'd you do?" I pulled on the handle. I pounded on the next window back. The thump startled him and Leo threw the keys into the front seat. He was still strapped in and his fingers weren't strong enough to undo the car-seat latch.

I lost it. I gave the car a push. More of a nudge, at best, only I'd left the car in neutral and the drive-through happened to be at the top of a slight incline, something you'd barely notice walking up.

Leo wailed and the tires crunched on the snow. I tried to hold it back but the car kept inching down. The driveway ended at Broad Street, complete with traffic and parked cars. I grabbed the side mirror and held on before the hinge worked. It folded in and my fingers slid off. More car went past. I reached for the roof rack and dug my heels in like Fred Flintstone.

With the keys out of the ignition the steering locked and the car veered to the left. I ran along, hanging on as the car crossed the sidewalk, crunching ever so slowly to a stop beside a planter and a phone pole.

"I'll get you. I'll get you," I said.

Leo wailed. "Get me now." He kicked the seat.

Sweat popped around my neck. I thought, shit, my car is blocking the sidewalk. I don't know why this seemed so important, but it did. I had to get in. I had to break a window. I looked down at the base of the phone pole and saw it—a shoveled-off, cracked, palm-sized chunk of sidewalk. It was roughly the shape of Wisconsin and it came right up.

"Leo, cover your eyes."

For some reason I went for the window behind the backseats. It took two hits but I got a spider web, then I punched the rest of the way in, only I couldn't get my arm far enough forward to flip the lock.

"Oh fuck." I moved up to the next window shouting: "Leo, keep your eyes covered." That one went pretty quickly, but I covered the inside of the car with small squares of green tinted glass.

I flipped the lock, unstrapped Leo, and held him as the lanky guy with glasses from the Sunoco station next door came over holding a valise full of tools. He could have unlocked any car in the universe. He waved at the broken windows. "Ah man, you didn't have to do all that." He saw Leo. "Or maybe you did. Everybody all right?"

"Yeah," I said. "More or less."

Leo kept hitting my shoulder. "You're not taking very good care of me." He hit me again.

After our pizza (pepperoni because they're round), Leo and I dressed for the cold and sat on the front steps watching the bearded man in the jumpsuit from FirstGlass use suction cups to put two new windows in the station wagon. Leo leaned against my knee and made clouds with his breath. He seemed better. He kept trying to maneuver his head into a cloud so he could smell it. "If we're pirates," he said, "when we smell bad, we just don't care." His red-mittened hands flipped out to the side.

The cell phone in my pocket sang again and I expected it to be Grace. For a second I knew she had caught the psychic vibrations of this latest fuck-up and decided to zoom in and call me on it.

It was Leah. "Hi," she said and took a breath. "Listen, I came by this afternoon and picked up some things." Her voice sounded incredibly close.

"What?" I knew what she was going to say next.

"I just . . ." A pencil tapped in the background. "I'm still freaked out by everything and we don't seem to be talking about it. You don't seem to want to and I've been toying with the idea since I got back."

"The idea of what?"

"I'm staying at Cecilia's, for a while."

"You are? No you're not," I said, as if simple contradiction ever solved anything. "What's a while?"

"I don't know."

"You said we weren't breaking up."

"That doesn't mean this is fine."

"Then what are we doing? Breaking up for now?"

"I don't know. I have all this work. I'm tired and I don't think I'm in a particularly good spot to make any lasting decisions."

"Oh." Then I understood. This is how Leah breaks up with people. It's the long slow fade. The underside of my jaw felt cold.

"I'll call," Leah said. "You should get some sleep."

I looked at the cell phone's purple screen. "Call duration: 1:26," it said, as the windshield guy walked up with a receipt for me to sign.

TWELVE

I sat at the bar, still in my long wool coat, watching the Bruins while away the second period against Detroit, when Julie materialized next to me. "What did you think was going to happen?" She didn't even take off her gloves.

I pulled up my collar. "Hey."

"Keeper, you're the most confrontationally challenged person I know. Except—"

Tim slid in beside us and pursed his lips at the grove of beer taps. He unzipped his ancient bomber jacket but left the black fisherman's cap on. "You're not talking about me," he said.

Julie pulled off a glove. "Your kind of stubborn is different. Keeper's is . . ." She made a face as if I couldn't be described. It felt like a compliment of sorts.

This all came to pass two nights later, on Thursday. We were in the bar at the front of the restaurant just down Broad Street. It's two hundred yards and an alley away from my front step, at most. When Tim had called at dinner to check in, since I hadn't really seen him at work, I explained what was up with Leah and heard a great big gap on the other end of the line. I thought, maybe we could just go have a beer. Get out of the house, make a big list of all the things that weren't getting done at work and—pretend. I needed that. I needed to pretend that my life wasn't what it seemed to have turned into. It was a wish you could taste.

When I dared to look over again I saw that Julie really was mad. But who wasn't mad at me? Tim had to be, given how things were at work; Leo was, just given the situation; and Leah— Leah hadn't been home since Tuesday morning. I was still too shocked by that to remember that I was supposed to be heading into a swoon. I'd walk through the house, turn a corner, and there it was, that big, damp sheet of a fact, hanging there for me to step into again. Leah wasn't home and I had no idea when that might end. I woke up that morning, like the day before, and remembered that Leo and I were the only souls in the house. A finite set.

Julie stared at my full pint and asked the tall woman behind the bar: "Can I have a cider? Just that size?" Tim got the same thing. "Wait," Julie said, "I'm hungry after all. Can we order a pizza at the bar?"

"Good to see you, too," I said. Lack of sleep can make me snarky. I glanced at the neon in the fogged-over windows. "I remember this," I said, "going out, having fun."

Tim kept looking around. "How come we're here?" he asked. It is a strange little bar, stuffed into a storefront that in another life could have housed a Laundromat. The restaurant part is in the back.

"It's close?" I stared into the foam on top of my IPA and realized that it looked exactly like Block Island, a teardrop with a hole in it.

"You have a sitter?" Tim nodded, answering the question. "We could go anywhere."

"I like to walk," I said. "Walking is underrated. Besides, sticking close to base camp in times of turmoil is always good policy."

"Keeper." Julie unzipped her parka. The fabric made a slippery sound when she took it off. As a rule you never want to have Julie mad at you. She can be fierce. But if Julie's mad and on your side, that is an excellent combination. She popped off the red fleece hat and I don't know why, but the way she dropped it on the bar made me think they had been talking to Leah. Of course, they'd been talking to Leah. We used to joke about what would happen to the rest of the universe if Leah and I ever split up. Julie shook out her hair. It looked almost amber in the light. "Answer the question," she said, "or I take away your beer."

"Which question?"

"The what-were-you-thinking one."

"Oh," I said. "I don't know what I was thinking. I mean, I couldn't figure out how to explain it to her ahead of time in a way that wouldn't turn this into a complete train wreck."

"She really thought there was a dog," Julie said.

"You've talked?"

Tim nodded. I wasn't sure if he was answering the question or happy to see their drinks. He put a ten on the bar.

"You're not supposed to know," Julie said. "But that's where we are."

"Stuck in the middleland," Tim said.

"Is that from a song?" I asked.

Tim looked confused and shook his head. He ordered a small pizza with goat cheese and sweet potatoes.

On TV they lined up for another defensive end face-off. The Bruins lost the draw and Detroit scored from the point. "I might have thought I don't have any choice in the matter so maybe neither should anyone else."

"That's a clever negotiating strategy," Julie said.

The word *negotiating* surprised me. It sounded foreign.

"How's Leo?" Tim took a long sip. "This is good."

"Okay, I guess. We made it into work for an hour on Tuesday. I forgot to tell you."

Tim smiled.

I looked at them. They're here. They came out. They're my friends. Julie's mad but that's because she wants to put this all back together. "It's scary," I said. "With Leo, I'm not used to being needed all the time. It freaks me out. I don't know how you're supposed to get used to it. The other night when it sort of got through to me that Leah was gone, I started having these thoughts, like what if I left, too? Complete escape fantasies. It's sick but I could see Leo waking up, sitting in his bed for a long time, finally making his way downstairs and opening the refrigerator. Climbing up on something to get the Cheerios. It's awful, even to pretend to think about. What does it mean when running away doesn't even make a good morbid fantasy?" I took a sip and knew I'd need another beer. "Why did I tell you guys that?"

"Keeper," Julie said and stopped it with a sigh.

"He's better than when we brought him down," I said. "He's a brave little kid."

"Have you told him that?" Julie asked.

"No," I said and realized that it might be a good idea.

"He's a brave little kid in denial," she said.

"I've figured out more stuff he'll eat. I know the videos he likes. He still does the I-want-Mommy and I don't know what to do there. He has nightmares. He keeps asking how long he's going to stay. He's started carrying red-blankie and Sleeping Cat in this black canvas bag he pulled out of Leah's stuff. He goes: 'All my things are RIGHT HERE!' "

"It's like living in a foreign country," Tim said. "You don't know the language. You don't know the customs. You stay packed in case they yank your visa."

"Anyway," I said, as Tim gave me a look like I wasn't listening, "he's still up in the middle of every night for at least an hour. I will never again sleep for more than four hours in a row."

"That was bound to happen," Tim said. "Like in ten years when you're up every ninety minutes to take a piss?"

"I had no idea how hard this was going to be."

They stared. I couldn't tell if they were thinking: Sure, of course, it's hard. Or maybe they really didn't understand. It felt impossible to explain, the dailyness of it, the way there's always something else you have to do, right now. It's like running a restaurant on a leaky boat—trim the sail, fill the catsup bottles, fix the rudder, tie yourself to the mast, and do it all again fifteen minutes from now.

"It feels like I'm under house arrest," I said. "Like if my life got any smaller the whole thing would simply fold down into a black hole. There's this *Teletubbies* tape Leo wants when he's sad and I'm starting to wonder, what's beyond the berm? I can see trees. They look real."

They nodded, but slowly.

"The sleep stuff is hard," I said. "Yesterday I fell asleep on the back porch while Leo was out in the yard."

Julie looked puzzled. "You did?"

"On *Car Talk,*" Tim said, "they were saying the only way to deal with having kids is total self-denial."

"I can't do that much denial," I said. "Nobody can. It's a stunning lack of liberty. You know where you used to be, you can see the shadow of how you used to live, but you can't get there. It's like owning a phantom limb."

They gave me these pained looks that finally slid away. I felt bad. For a minute at least. I mean here I was complaining and look at them. They'd be great at this. They're ready. They think they're prepared to make the jump. They don't know what's on the other side, but the idea of the jump is fine. I've been jumped and I can't get back.

"Leo's a stubborn kid," I said. "I think he was stubborn even before. It would be good to know that, only I don't have the instruction book."

"The instruction book?" Julie angled her head.

"Yeah," I said. "I mean a certain kind of stubborn is good. Except we confront all the time. I can't get his teeth brushed."

"Baby teeth," Tim waved. "He's going to lose them all anyway. Feed him carrots."

"I can't get him to watch SpongeBob, either. Too scary. Only *I* need to watch SpongeBob."

Julie gave me the change-the-subject look. "When do I get to meet him?"

"Anytime."

"The poor kid," she said. "That's what I can't get over. All these losses—his mom, his house, his school, his friends, Grace."

It was an awful list. I was afraid she would keep going. "Something's up with Grace," I said. "We keep playing phone tag. I don't get it. You'd think she'd be worried."

"She's probably still torn up about having to do this," Tim said. I hadn't thought about that. "I also can't get Leo to take a bath."

Tim's eyes widened. I'm not sure why that fact pushed him over. "You mean he hasn't had one since we brought him down?"

"Nope. Every time I bring it up he yells. He says 'Mommy does it.'"

"Don't bring it up," Tim said. "Take him."

"Yeah well, I've been folding on that."

"He's got to have a bath," Tim said. "D.S.S.? Department of Social Services? They're got these vans with special sensors roaming the neighborhood. They'll be by your house to sniff it out."

"Stop," I said.

"Some of this stuff is like being a lawyer," he said. "Never ask a question you don't already know the answer to. That and you can only give a kid two choices: A or B."

"I still don't know how you know this."

"It's like having a dog. You anticipate." He took a long drink. "You had a dog. Okay, I was off about the bath. You're right. It is only a bath. You should relax, float on your back, let the water do the work."

"What water?"

"The water." Tim smiled.

"Mr. Aphorism, stop being so cryptic."

"Take deep breaths. Come on, he's still alive. You should drink heavily whenever you can."

It was between periods and an ad for a doll shop in Warwick came on. They panned across a table full of ceramic Wizard of Oz figures and the camera zoomed in on the Tin Man. Julie tapped Tim's arm. When Tim was in grad school, around the time he met Julie, he used to get wrapped in duct tape, stand on corners in Manhattan, and pretend he had rusted into place. He could make fifty bucks an hour doing that. "I was a good Tin Man," Tim said.

"Some days I had the exact right personality." They smiled at each other.

"Wait." Tim shook his head. "I didn't tell you about the aprons. I bought a box of aprons at that estate thing in Warren."

"But I don't know anything about aprons."

Tim shrugged, as if wasn't that supposed to be the fun part? "Only I found an 1860 Lincoln campaign flag in the middle of them."

"You're kidding."

"Not about that. It was laid out flat. They're up at the shop. I have no idea what it's worth." He did his isn't-that-amazing smile. "Did you get any baby-sitting ideas?"

I heard the itch in his voice so I told them about the Daisy fiasco. "I've got to do something about daycare," I said. "But it's one more thing. Every time I walk by the Yellow Pages I have to leave the room."

"Keeper," Julie said, "there's one across the street from your house."

"One what?"

She laughed. "A daycare."

She could have told me a comet had just rolled down the street. That glow? Out the window? I kept staring. I wanted to see if her lips could make that shape again.

"Yeah," she said. "That big gold Victorian with the rowboat in the yard? The plastic things behind the fence? The slides? The picnic tables?"

"I only thought they had a lot of kids. Like they were grandparents or something."

"Who had a kid there?" she asked. "Someone we know."

"Jess and Eric," Tim said. "They loved it. Wait, isn't it a preschool?"

"I think it's both," Julie said.

It all felt hopeless. This was more than I could ever absorb or figure out. I covered my eyes and tried to will the third period to begin. "Where did you guys learn all this?"

"Keeper?" Julie's hand slid out along the bar. She has very small hands. "I'm sorry. This is all awful. Are you okay?"

If I'd been more drunk the question might have seemed hilarious. Only I kept thinking, of the last two people I've been in love with, one's dead and the other's disappeared. I was tired enough and buzzed enough so I said that out loud. They looked sympathetic but I could see their thoughts: There goes Keeper singing "Poor, poor, pitiful me." The problem is Tim and Julie together are like this optimistic cloud. They reinforce each other's goodwill. Sure, you can do it. We'll just hike to the top. At times this can be desperately annoying.

"You guys really talked to Leah? I need to know."

"Of course," Julie said. "But I can't—"

"Yeah you can," Tim said.

"Every time I do I get in trouble and feel really awful afterward."

"We're on the back channel here," I said. "I have to know where—"

"She is with you and Leo?" Julie finished her drink. "A, you could ask her. And B . . ." She watched me as if she couldn't figure out how to start. "She's really pissed at you for not telling her. She's thinking, even if she wasn't so mad, there's no way she can do it. That it's your ex-wife's kid. She doesn't want to think that way and she feels bad about it, but it's a huge commitment, it's twenty years, it's more than that, and you're not talking, and she can't imagine it. Why do you think she broke up with Gary?"

I was still stuck on "there's no way she can do it." I frowned. "I've never met Gary," I said, as if I'd been mulling it over.

"The guy wanted a million kids," Tim said. "He was nice enough and everything only he suddenly wanted to repopulate most of southern New England. He had the complete vision. The mini-mansion on the cul-de-sac. The tree-fort complex in the backyard."

"You should meet him," Julie said.

"Do I have to?"

"You'd kind of see," her lower lip folded in, "why she's with you."

I had something in my eye. "Leah's not particularly with me now."

The third period hadn't started so they jumped to highlights of the Celtics-Nuggets game, which had just ended.

"She's started playing basketball again," Julie said.

This seemed hard to imagine, since I'd been nagging her to do that for a while. "She's only been gone three days," I said.

"But she found this early morning game at Brown," Julie said. "Twice a week. That's the only good thing."

Julie said something else only I wasn't listening. I kept hearing: There's no way she can do it. Leo shows up and takes me through a barrier where Leah can't go. Just like that.

"Leah does the right thing," Tim said. "Eventually."

"Depends on the meaning of right." Julie waved. "I'm sorry, I mean—"

"Don't be," I said. "It's not clear that life with me now is the right thing for anybody. Me, even."

Tim said: "She's tough. She needs to get something for it."

I still hadn't figured out quite what he meant when I heard a dog bark. It surprised me because the sound came from my coat pocket. I shook my head and it happened again. I peered into the black wool tunnel and the baby monitor's red lights glowed back. "Shit."

"They let a dog behind the bar?" Tim stood to look over.

Julie looked into my pocket. "Keeper. You don't have a sitter?"

My neck prickled. "It's just, I'm half a block away. This has a quarter mile range."

"Leo's in bed?" Tim leaned in to check my pocket. "Look at that glow."

"He's fine. He doesn't wake up for another four hours." My throat got tight.

Tim grabbed the blue plastic antenna and dragged the monitor from my pocket. "You idiot," he said. "You can't do this. Go home." He tapped the monitor and it barked again. "Wait, you don't have a dog."

The red lights zipped back and forth. The tall woman behind the bar came over as if she had never seen something like that up close.

"You don't think a dog got—" Julie's hand covered her mouth.

Tim slid the switch on the front from channel A to D and the dog vanished. He turned up the volume. I heard Leo's breathing. I heard the creak as he rolled over.

"If there's another one of these in the neighborhood on the same channel you'll pick that house up, too," Julie said. "This happens to my sister constantly."

Tim squeezed my arm. "Keeper," he said, "go home now."

And like a good dog, I did as I was told.

THIRTEEN

The monitor thing turned out okay, eventually. Tim and Julie sent me home and then came over with the rest of the pizza. They yelled, justifiably so, until I got on my knees and begged. But I picked up points once I decided to introduced Leo to Julie while he was asleep. "He's beautiful," she said softly, leaning over the Elmo bed rail. "All that angelic hair." It surprised me, almost as if I hadn't noticed. I didn't know what to say.

The next part came two days later, on Saturday, and by then Tim and Julie were on vacation, wandering around Vancouver before spending the rest of the week skiing at Whistler. This left me piloting the ship at work, which I'd completely forgotten about. It was on the calendar and all, but stuff kept slipping by. Plus, the whole idea of anybody actually being allowed to go anywhere completely depressed me. Every night after Leo was in bed I'd get stuck on the Travel Channel. Florence? Never going there. Bali? Nope. Iceland? Nope again.

That would have been a bad Keeper moment, the total self-pity bath, which is how it went: Good Keeper, Bad Keeper, an okay moment, then another awful one. Like the next morning, when Leo was getting dressed and wanted to wear his green and turquoise pajama top with the red sweatpants. I said, "No," just like that. It looked awful and since when is it a good idea to wear pajamas out of the house? "Absolutely not," I said, sounding like my mom thirty years ago. We always fought over things like that, though I now know that's not what we were fighting about. Leo started watching me with this extra bit of distance, like he was appraising something he couldn't quite figure out. Finally his chin dimpled and he began to cry. "Don't be mad at me," he said and stamped his feet. I thought, you idiot, what are you doing yelling at an orphan? Then I realized, wait, he's not an orphan, he has me. Besides, who cares what a three-year-old wears? Just keep the kid warm and shut up. Only later, when we were out the front door, did it dawn on me that for Leo my being mad at him was probably one of the worst things that could happen. Bad Keeper.

Two cinnamon buns later Leo and I were at the library, restocking our supply of three-day kid videos. Leo kept telling me this wasn't his library. I kept saying, "No, it is. Now it is."

"Stop talking that," he said. "I'm sad and you're mad with me."

I sat next to him on the deep blue kid-section rug. "That's not it. I'm grumpy about the situation and I get sad, too, but I'm not mad at you."

He turned and stared. "The situation?"

"You know. Where we are." Leo still looked puzzled, then I remembered that thing Julie reminded me to do, so I told Leo I was proud of him yesterday for going to visit the daycare across the street. And that had gone okay, a moment of Good Keeper. All the furniture there was surprisingly small and bright; they played classical music on the stereo; the teachers seemed nice; I couldn't find any kids off crying in the corners, and Leo liked the toys, especially the art area. I had a brisk chat with Mrs. Green. She's skinny with bright white hair and reminded me of a very intent bird. She seemed like the kind of distanced, determined woman who would never be anything but a Mrs. Green. She asked if Leo was toilet trained and I said sure, mostly. They had space and I was too frazzled to have reservations, so I wrote a check for three days a week, to start.

On the rug I told Leo he'd had a lot of getting-used-to-it days and that was hard. I promised there'd be no more baby-sitters.

"Maybe when I'm older. Like seven?"

"Sure. Seven."

"You won't get mad at me for getting sad?"

"Nope." And for a second, sitting there, it felt all right, completely unfamiliar but not entirely awful.

Leo leaned against my leg. "Mommy did go on a trip," he said. "Calvin knows where. I think Gracie's coming back, soon. I know that beforehand."

I wasn't sure about Grace and I still didn't know who Calvin was. That had started to depress me, too, but I kept my mouth shut. Good Keeper.

With Leah I took Julie's advice, again, and e-mailed early that morning to ask what was going on? I had no choice since Leah was clearly screening her calls. I asked not if she wanted to talk about things, but when, making it sound like I had a jump on the world. I got an answer when we got home: "not now."

I watched those words until the fireworks screen saver wiped them out. I heard Leo down in the kitchen, smashing his fist into big balls of yellow Play-Doh. Thump. Thump. It alarmed me at first, but the more I thought about it, the more appropriate it seemed. I stood up too quickly and that jittery anger, the kind that makes you walk circles in the rug, came right back. I stared into the yard and wished for Arrow. I jumped in place four times, shouting "Fuck." A minute later I banged into the kitchen to find Leo some crackers and he thought I was mad at him. Bad Keeper.

At work there was still too much to do and now I was sailing the ship, actually me and grad student Maggie were in there hanging on to the rudder together. I figured I'd finish what I could but mostly I'd end up leaving the "Open by appointment or chance" card in the front door at the yard and letting Maggie do whatever she wanted up at Wickenden Street. I knew all of that hands-off stuff would not help with the books, but what could I do? I still had to go in and take Leo with me, which had become a battle. He kept saying, "That not my favorite place." The yard was too dark, too loud, too windy. Only I needed to figure out a

way to do things with Leo there. Because that's what I do. I
work. I even work Saturdays. The new plan was to simply not tell
Leo where we were going and let the trip fall under the already
approved category of errands.

As I buckled Leo back into the car seat he asked if I knew how
to cook.

"Yeah, well enough," I said. "You can always learn to cook."

"Will you teach me how to cook?"

"Sure."

"Do you know how to drive?"

"I'm about to start driving now," I said, buckling in.

"You're not going to make me learn to drive until I very
much bigger." Leo folded his arms. "That driver is too hard."

"No, I'm not going to make you learn how to drive."

"Oh, okay."

I backed out only I kept watching Leo in the mirror. I mean
those are the things he's worried about? But at that age how
would you know that somebody wouldn't try to make you drive?

Leo took the red mitten out of his mouth. "The world lets
you die," he said, "but you stay yourself longer than you think."

"Where'd you hear that?" I asked.

"I just know it."

"You do?"

"There's fur on my tongue," Leo said.

"Wipe it off with your fingers."

"Okay. Thank you."

I stayed stuck at the stop sign, staring at Leo in the mirror until someone honked.

Leo conked out as soon as we got up on the highway, which
gave me a little space to think. I should have used that time to try
and slow down, take a few deep breaths. I could have tried that
floating idea, just let the water provide the support, or whatever-
it-was Tim told me to do. Instead that other thing, the one Julie

said, about how I was the most confrontationally challenged person she could imagine, kept popping up. It turned into one of those moments where you pick a fight with someone in your head and keep it going far longer than could ever be healthy because the rebuttals feel so good. This one with Julie wouldn't stop. I was being confrontational as hell.

When we got to the yard I set Leo up on the computer. For a second I couldn't think of what to do, then I remembered to check the answering machine, where I found about a dozen messages.

One was from Stanley. He's a contractor in that loop of people here who only work on old houses. Something from 1920 would feel brand-new to Stanley. The message was from three days ago. "You haven't heard it from me, but there's a nice, late-Victorian going down in Elmwood and nobody's taken a thing out of it. Call me." This is the kind of message that Tim and I live for. This is what we pay finder's fees for. When it all works we just have to go in and say save us that and that and hand over a reasonable amount of cash and get to work. Only I didn't get the message. I called Stanley's cell. "Keeper," he said. "It's gone."

I sat and watched the phone awhile longer. It's awful when a house goes down and nobody saves anything. It really is. Then I thought, what were you thinking? You couldn't have gone anyway. I watched Leo's head bob in time to some repetitive *Boohbah* tune. I can't do this, I thought. It's been days now and I still can't do this. Sometimes at night I'd find myself watching those nature shows, and you always see prides of lions, or crows taking care of other crows, whole flocks of penguins, elephants traveling in herds, only in herds, happily in herds. Everybody takes care of the baby elephants. This is what I don't get, we're a social species, so how come we've gone to such elaborate lengths to set it up so everybody spends all their time raising kids by themselves?

Then Leo started peeing in his pants. It happened twice in fifteen minutes. He didn't tell me he needed to go, either time. I had to put a paper bag over the stuffed crow up on the office wall to get him into the bathroom. We were on the last pair of sweats when the electric doorbell chimed and this guy came in.

He was in his fifties, leather jacket, a crimson wool scarf on the outside, black corduroys, running shoes, a broad face with curly gray hair. His nose seemed outrageously red but it was cold out. He had ear buds and an iPod in his jacket. I recognized the cord. People wearing headphones move differently than the rest of us. A little slow, a little underwater, and they're always directly in front of me in line. This guy nodded and started walking around, but something in the exchange didn't seem polite. If you're going to look at our stuff, I thought, at least take those stupid things out of your ears.

I eventually wandered over. "What are you listening to?"

He took out one ear. "Jimmy Buffett."

There's nothing wrong with Jimmy Buffett or Parrotheads in general, but it seemed to fit a whole picture and that bugged me. I thought okay, this guy retired young, he's got way too much money and he's wandering around my store listening to Jimmy Buffett and making me keep an eye on him, which takes up my precious kid-free work time. I can count my hours of kid-free work time on half of one hand.

"How much do you want for the pulpit?" he asked.

I peered. The pulpit had been leaning up against our back wall since the beginning of time. It came out of a church in eastern Connecticut that two designers were converting into a house. It was oak, dark with winding stairs, some carving, but nothing amazing. "Depends on what you have in mind."

The guy's look translated as: You're-kidding/What's-wrong-with-you?

I was being a jerk. And why? Just to prove that I could confront somebody? It did feel nice. Surprisingly loose.

He laughed. "No, really."

"Thirty-five hundred."

He shook me off. I'd just made that number up. Nobody had ever looked at the pulpit as if they were remotely thinking of buying it. On a better day I would have taken five hundred. Half that. "Three thousand, five hundred, that's it." I finished off with a small I've-got-all-the-cash-in-the-universe smile.

The guy frowned and took a slow look around, as if to say: How could I even pay the overhead with that kind of attitude? He started to go, then he reached in his coat pocket and came back with a business card.

"I have this funny job," he said. "Once upon a time I set up a chain of micro pubs in the Pacific Northwest. Around Portland?"

"I've heard of Portland."

"Eaton's." He tapped the card. "We go into old theaters, abandoned churches, spaces no one can figure out how to use. We fix them up, show movies, serve burgers and pints." He nodded as if that all still sounded like an excellent idea. "But I had to move to Boston, because of my daughter, so I'm starting over." He looked around. "I buy big things. Those blackboards? I'm always looking for big things—only not here."

I took the card. The edges were sharp. I started to say something but the guy put Jimmy Buffett back in his other ear and waved.

I walked the aisles a few times and still felt like an asshole. I had his card. Maybe I'd give it to Tim, tell him what an asshole I was and see if he could make the save. I sat down next to Leo.

"Know what, buddy?"

Leo shook his head but didn't look away from the screen.

"I'm an idiot."

"What's an id-dot?"

"No, idiot."

"Does that mean you're tall?"

I leaned back in the chair, only then noticing that Leo was no longer at PBS Kids. He was navigating some maze on the Bob-the-Builder site. I had no idea how he got there. Did I bookmark that? Did he Google it? No, he can't spell. Scoop, the yellow front loader, trolled along, picking up packages while Leo directed him with the cursor. Finally Scoop reached a dead end and I helped

Leo back out. What was I doing here, teaching a toddler to play video games?

I'd left this Web station, Radio Paradise, on in the background. I listen to them a lot and that R.E.M. song, "Man on the Moon," came up. I flicked the toggle under the table to turn on the warehouse speakers. Tim demanded that we have speakers in all the corners. At the time I thought it was silly but I like the open, rumpled sound of it.

"Mommy likes this." Leo pointed up. "That moon song is on my sleeping tape."

"You listen to music when you sleep?"

"Oh, of course."

The chords rolled off the walls. Then I remembered, he was right, Cynthia used to sing little snatches of this when she was doing things. "Yeah, yeah, yeah." I started to think of her as somewhere behind us, leaning against a wall and watching, as if in some parallel universe this configuration could have existed after all.

How many longest days of your life can you have in a row? This part happened later, in Shaw's, the grocery store. I had pushed us past the tomatoes and pointed the cart to the already-peeled baby carrots, the ones with the bunny on the bag, since the last time I learned that Leo liked those, and then we could snack and shop. Good Keeper. Except all the way across the parking lot Leo kept telling me what he wanted for dinner, only I couldn't figure out what he was saying. He started doing it again. Bad Keeper could see the edge coming closer.

My phone went off. I saw the number on the screen and blinked. Leah. I held it in my palm and let the *Gilligan's Island* theme go on a little longer. At first it felt like this moment of massive relief, yes—finally, then I got pissed off. Why was she calling now when I had to shop? Wait, if she's actually calling after that e-mail, something has to be wrong. I pressed the green button and pretended I didn't know I was about to hear her voice.

"Whatchadoing?" she asked.

"Buying carrots. I'm in the vegetable aisle. Where *are* you?"

"Oh." She sounded half-astonished. "What store?"

"Shaw's."

"Huh. I'm in Whole Foods." She was fifteen minutes away, up on the East Side. "For a second I thought we were in the same store."

"Yeah, well, how do your carrots look?"

Leah hummed that little waiting song of hers. "Not bad actually. I'm by the red onions now, but the carrots were nicely presented, as always." This used to be one of our jokes. How the vegetables there always looked so perfect that you felt bad breaking up the display just to buy a potato. Leah used to call it the Food Museum.

"Shit," I said and clawed through another pocket. "I forgot the list." I opened the bag of carrots and gave Leo two. I wheeled us one-handed toward the green apples. "Leo keeps saying he wants Indiana food. What do people eat in Indiana?"

Something clattered on Leah's end. Why did I launch into that?

"Does he mean Indian food?"

I stopped the cart. "Whoa, Leo. Do you mean Indian food?"

"Yes, of course. Sure."

"Yes," I said. "Takeout. I can get takeout. How did you know that?"

"A guess." Her voice went flat.

"Everybody knows more about this than I do. You know there's an instruction book and I can't find it because Leo hid it."

Leo shook his head. "No I didn't."

"Wait," I said. "Why'd you call?" There was a longer pause and I thought: Stop talking about Leo. You're talking too much about Leo. But what was I going to do? Pretend he wasn't there?

"Ah—I don't know. Habit? I forgot, for a second. No, really, I couldn't remember, what's the name of that pancake mix you get? She has a cornbread mix, too."

"Sylvia's. It's in a turquoise bag. I don't think they have it. I got it here."

"Oh."

"That's it? That's why you called?"

"Ah—yeah."

"When are you coming home?" It just flew out. "Come on. I love you." There, that's the new no-longer-confrontationally-challenged Keeper. I felt a small twist under my tongue. No, this is going to turn out badly.

"Don't say that. Please."

I stopped in front of the bins of coffee beans. "Why? Because it makes it harder? It's true."

A sound like a cart nudging a wall of glass bottles came through the phone, then Leah's surprised, distant voice saying, "Oh, sorry." She coughed. "Keeper, shit. I'm bumping into things. Okay, tell me why I should do this? Because you love me? That doesn't change a thing. That's not, I can't—"

"What do you mean can't?"

"I feel bad but—I can't do it."

"You can too. You always say you can't do stuff. Everybody in your family says they can't do stuff. What is it about people that makes them think they can't do things? Your family, they're like, you'll never finish that dessert. It's too big."

Of course there was a pause. I could hear people over there ordering chops at the meat counter.

"No," Leah said, as if enunciation alone could solve something. "My family has nothing to do with this. Hold on. Now I'm sitting on the floor of this stupid grocery store because I can't talk while I'm pushing a cart. I keep thinking I should be able to do this, but I can't. With a kid, there isn't room for us anymore. There won't be. It's like when Ruby adopted from China? That was the end of Ruby and Gail. It's too much work, and everybody has to agree to start with and—I can't. I can't do this just because you love me. If you love me so much, if I'm that big a deal, why haven't we done the other thing? The word that starts with M, which you no longer know how to pronounce."

"No," I said, just like that. Pure reflex. "That has nothing to do with this. That doesn't have anything to do with—it's a fucking ceremony with tax consequences and I'm not getting divorced again. Ever. Any time you—"

"I knew he was yours," Leah said. "As soon as I saw him, when I came into the room. I don't know how but I knew. I thought this is what I gave up with Gary. This is exactly where that would have gone and I wasn't sad about giving that up. It wasn't easy but then, there it was, with you, right in front of me. Like we'd skipped all these steps and nobody even asked. Or bothered to tell me—that's how it felt."

I started fiddling with a coffee bag. Multitasking at the exact wrong time. It occurred to me that maybe life as a confrontationally challenged person might not be so bad. I shook open the bag with my left hand. "You knew?"

"Yeah, of course. When I was shoveling off my car and you came out? You went back in before I could even finish a fucking sentence and I thought, oh God, this is it, this is the future. This is the whole future. No more—"

"What? The monitor thing? He howled. I went in. I came back out."

"I—I'm not big enough to do this, now."

"Now?"

"Don't jump on that. I don't know that I want to do it. This sounds awful and I'm embarrassed to say it, but—"

"But what?" I had the phone under my chin while I lifted the plastic thing on the bin with the Kenyan beans. I got the bag in and the beans streamed down, but the plastic thing that cuts them off got stuck and they wouldn't stop. I kept trying to pull the thing down with one hand. "You don't want to do this? You think I want to do this? I'm out on a fucking limb minute by minute. I want my old life back. I can taste it but I can't get it."

The beans kept hitting the floor. It sounded like rain. I went to the cart and pushed, while Leo waved. "Spilling?" he said. "Spilling! Spilling?"

We were in that pause. The pause that always pops up in

phone arguments, where you can't think but you can't hang up. The wheels on the cart squealed, like they were trying to go in a bunch of directions at once.

Leah took a breath. "Okay," she said. "Let's—"

"When are you coming home?"

"I'm not," she said, as if she had decided this weeks ago. "Only to get my things." I heard a click.

I stared at the phone even after she hung up. Call duration: 4:11. The twist in my stomach came back. I looked around and people kept on shopping. I couldn't understand how they could do that.

"See," Leo said, offering me a carrot. "Now you don't have to be grumpy anymore."

FOURTEEN

I let the rudder go. I fed and showered myself, I kept Leo in clean
underwear and supplied him with French fries, which he'd now
decided were okay, but I let the rudder go. That whole week I
never made it into work. I'd try but things kept happening or
somehow they wouldn't. And I couldn't even use Leo as an ex-
cuse, since after a rough beginning he'd settled suspiciously easily
into the daycare across the street. He went Tuesday, half of
Wednesday, Thursday, all of Friday, and seemed to like it, once I
got out of the room. These were his "other getting used to it"
days, he told me. He was being brave and I knew it. I even told
him that. But the fact of daycare itself was both miraculous and
awful—awful in that it left me an actual minute to slow down
and see where I was. And the instant it all came into focus I'd slip
on the self-pity wings and jump over the cliff. It takes time and
space to go into a proper swoon. You need the right altitude to
notice the sad pleasure of falling.

Mainly I slept. I'd be up, acting semifunctional, and at some
point, either in the late morning or early afternoon, the exhaus-
tion would swell and seven kinds of hurt would sweep right in.
I'd pass out on the couch or the rug, the bed, the chair, only to
wake up two hours later, sadly surprised to find I was still in my
life. Sometimes I wouldn't wake up until Mrs. Green called from
across the street to remind me to pick up my son. My son.

Sure, depression, you could say that was a factor, but sleep debt weighed in, too. Leo had started this thing where after every bad dream he would wake up shouting: "Help, help," until I appeared. "Sit next to me," he'd say. I'd start out in the rocking chair but wake up cold in the morning, curled in the fetal position on the camping pad, shaking off more dreams about nights in open boats. Every time I'd think: Why can't I find myself a blanket? Or a pillow?

When I was awake the moments of self-pity, actually entire afternoons of it, were always followed by sharp intervals of throwing-soft-stuff-around-the-living-room rage. Not that it ever does a tremendous amount of good to shout: "How the fuck did this happen?" seven or eight thousand times, but I still felt like the victim of some divine conspiracy. I mean, how could Cynthia not be? I'd think of being in her car. A silver light on her cheek. That twisty thing she did with her wrist. How she blinked so slowly.

And having time to think about the future only made me feel more confined. I'd wake up, put my feet on the maroon rug by the edge of the bed, Leah's rug, and feel for the ankle bracelet. Leah. How could I have lost Leah? That remained concretely unimaginable. Except I knew it happened because I felt so completely unmoored. Then sometimes it felt like it wasn't anything I'd done, more like I'd been duped into losing Leah. I wrote her a bunch of desperate sounding e-mails and never sent them. I tried not to call her cell and whenever I called Cecilia's apartment the machine always picked up. I'd think about leaving a message, but as soon as I imagined my voice on the other end, streaming out all thin and depressed from the machine, it never seemed like the wisest idea. I kept thinking, give her space. She'll miss us. It'll add up and something will happen. That was the extent of the plan.

But the usual dumped-guy symptoms were out in force. I'd accidentally find myself in the Jewelry District driving by Cecilia's apartment three or four times in an afternoon, scanning for Leah's black bug in the long slanted parking lot across the street.

Or while Leo was in daycare I'd spend far too much time at the Wild Colonial, a basement bar in an ancient warehouse on North Main, mainly because Leah's office was on the third floor. I'd be there nursing a stout, watching CNN, accidentally prepared in case she walked out to her car or popped in to pick up a *Phoenix*. I'd sit telling myself there had to be a way to convince Leah to come back. There had to be a route, it existed and all I needed to do was imagine myself into the plan. If the sun was out and I'd had even some sleep, that sometimes felt doable. But at home, with Leo, even I could sense how ridiculous a wish it was.

Saturday night around 9:30, after I got Leo to bed, I was back on the couch watching white-haired Germans talk about U-boats on the History Channel. I was tired and restless but I kept wandering to the kitchen and glancing across the yard and through my neighbor's picture window at the wall-sized TV where he had Spice on pay-per-view. I'd watch for a minute, a few minutes more, tell myself this is pathetic and return to World War II. I had just gone back to the living room when someone knocked twice on the front door. I thought: Leah? But why would she knock?

Tim appeared wearing that green Eisenhower jacket. He held a straining white plastic bag. "Did you eat? I got ribs."

"You're back," I said and fell into the couch. I was kind of stunned to see him. He seemed taller. His face had a ski-tan. Those pale raccoon-eyes.

"Indeed." Tim nodded, as if finding me out flat confirmed something. He walked to the dining room but his stride seemed a little too direct. He placed the bag on the table and gently removed the Styrofoam container. "They're from Wes's," he said. "I got the baby ribs. I was at the yard and I had an attack. Julie can't stand it when I get the little ones. I got a single order but it's always too big, which is why I'm here. You in?"

"I guess." I went to get beer, silverware, and a roll of paper towels.

"I know I'm going to animal hell for this," Tim said. "There'll be all these cows and pigs and little pigs sitting in a circle, staring at me. It'll go on like that forever."

The silverware sounded loud when it hit the table. "How was the trip?"

"Good. We got back this afternoon. The snow out there is always wet. Lots of corn. The bad thing was by day five I was worrying about work."

"You were?" I didn't want to talk about work.

Tim unloaded the sauce and the cornbread. He put a small rack of ribs on my plate. "I was on the Web at the hotel, it was one of those hotels, and I kept looking at other salvage sites. We've got to get bigger pieces. We've got to get stranger stuff to sell and raise prices. We have to get larger. That's the only way we're going to make more money. Seriously, some of those doors, the good two-light Victorians? People on the Web are getting eight to twelve hundred for those and we're selling them for two."

"Which people?"

"We can't be selling fifty-dollar stuff on the Web. It takes too much time. We have to go for big strikes. We'll charge a lot and give people free shipping, worldwide, like Amazon."

"How much do you think it costs to send a door to England?"

Tim gave me a look. It was all weird. Usually it takes Tim a very long time to get this wired and even then it's a measured response. He kept going and suddenly the entire problem of making more money began to sound deeply trivial. Given the scope of current events, who could possibly care?

Tim's hand circled the air. "We have to do ads. We have to do *Old-House Interiors* and *Traditional Home*. I was reading those on the plane. We need lists of architects all through the northeast. We want the ones who work on old houses. If we have a big strange piece, they all need to know about it."

I closed my eyes and saw the Parrothead guy with those micro pubs. I guessed this wasn't the time to bring that up.

"Buddy," Tim said, "when did you last make it in to work?"

Centuries ago, when Tim and I first started doing this, we agreed that if we ever wound up battling about how to do things I'd collect my stuff and head back to Boston, because none of this was worth trashing the friendship over. We actually shook hands. It was one of those moments you plan for knowing it'll never happen, like Leah telling me not to join the Mafia.

I shrugged. It felt like acting. "I haven't been."

Tim's lips did a kind of wince.

"Saturday," I said. "The other one." The question itself pissed me off.

Tim nodded as if that data point fit the scenario. I've always known that if you ever let Tim down in a big way he won't exactly hold a grudge, he just won't forget.

"Why are you so cranked?" I asked, as if that were the problem.

"What the fuck have you been doing all week?"

I picked up a small rib and shook it. What had I been doing? "I've been looking for things," I said. "All week. Did you know that when Leo's mad, and he's mad a lot, he hides stuff. My keys? In the train bin. The cell phone? In the oven. The liner for my snow boot? Under the couch. He likes to take the laces out of one shoe. When I ask where it might be? Leo says, 'It's gone hide-ish.' Plus, I can't find things because I haven't slept for more than three hours at a time in weeks. Before you got here? I couldn't find the remote because it was on the arm of the chair and they're both black. Or Leo hides and that freaks me out. Or I'm fending off meltdowns. Leo's carrots are too squishy. Meltdown. He can't find James? The red engine? Meltdown. The second day of day-care he—"

Tim waved. "You have daycare? You have daycare and you still couldn't go in? What the fuck?"

"Yeah," I said. "It's the second day of daycare—"

"Which daycare? The one across the street?"

"Yeah, and I can't find Leo's lunch box. It has to be his Bob-the-Builder box, the one from before, or he won't go. I told him a paper bag with a drawing on it would make a great lunch box and dragged him over anyway. He screamed. I felt like shit. I drove right to Toys R Us in Warwick and said, 'I'm the guy who needs a Bob-the-Builder lunch box' and the woman in the smock just said: 'Yes you are.' I got it to Leo but Leo melted down before lunch. Mrs. Green called and I had him all afternoon. I'm already in the bad parent column over there with Mrs. Green as it is. The first day? I'm supposed to pick up Leo and I oversleep. I'm having some strange intimate dream about Grace, and Mrs. Green calls at six. 'Isn't that funny,' she says, 'and you live right across the street.' What have I been doing? I've been lying in bed next to Leo listening to him tell me things his mommy can do when she's dead. She can fly, that makes sense. Be a tree? Float? Bake? I don't know what the fuck to say. The next day he's on the floor with a flashlight and he says, 'I am here to keep people safe.' And 'I can find Mom with this flashlight,' while he's shining it under the couch. Then he says: 'I want to stay real.' "

Tim put a bone on the pile. "You say 'fuck' a lot more now that you have a kid. Have you noticed that?"

"Poop," I said. "I say 'poop,' too. You ski, I deal in poop. Leo won't tell me when he has to go. He knows but—one night he pooped in his pants so bad it smelled like a dead animal in the house."

"Aw man." Tim pointed at his plate.

"It's awful. You get so tired and so pissed off you almost want to be mean to the kid. Like driving off somewhere while he's asleep. It's the worst temptation in the world."

"I'm still back on the dead animal."

"Know what else? All my socks are wearing out. Know how you buy ten pairs together in a bag, like you're going to save a ton of money doing that, then they all wear out at once and it's another errand. Got that? It's another fucking errand and I don't have time for another fucking errand." I was pacing. "And I keep shampooing with Mr. Bubble. I've done it twice, by accident. Have you ever shampooed with Mr. Bubble? It keeps on foaming. You turn into foam man in the shower. I am foam man."

Tim ate half his corn bread. It looked good so I took his other piece.

"Did you ever get Leo to take a bath?"

"Sponge bath. I got these big puffy sponges. Fifty cents at Building 19. I catch him when I'm getting him into a new pull-up. At first he screamed, now it's almost a game. I had to do something. He still won't go in the tub. Wednesday morning? I'm returning a video and I drop my keys down the return slot instead. That's how tired I was. It's at Acme and I have to wait until noon when they open. I tried to go to work. Wait, that day I did, I went to the store."

"Is that when you gave Maggie a raise?"

"Yeah, so what? She's a grad student. They don't make any money, ever. It's like being an indentured servant."

"We don't make any money as it is."

"When I couldn't get my keys I walked up Wickenden. I got there and she'd rearranged everything. She'd been coming in at night. It looked great. You could find stuff. That counts."

"You gave her a raise without telling me?"

"You hired her without telling me."

Tim glanced around the room to change the subject. He stopped at the big painting over the couch. It's all these textured, red and black triangles that look like they're dancing or swimming, depending on where you sit. "What's up with Leah?"

"She moved out."

His head bobbed. "But it's temporary, right? That's her painting."

"She says no. She says over." I pulled out a rib. It was sweet. Still warm.

"You say?"

"I say that's the last thing I want on earth."

It seemed to take Tim a long time to decide to close his mouth. He chewed a little. "This is going to sound hard, but does it have to be Leah?"

The question stunned me. I had never even thought that. It

was like someone asking: Do we have to breathe oxygen? Why not some other gas? Just for kicks. "Yeah," I said. "Yeah. Of course it has to be Leah. It works with Leah. All the negotiation? All the how you get through things with somebody?"

"You're not getting through this."

"Fuck you. Leah is great. Leah is who I want." I folded my arms. I didn't tell him how I was still unimaginably in love with Leah or how lonely it felt now. How flinging my arm across the bed at three in the morning kept waking me up. How I'd walk around this tiny house always expecting to find her in another room, still. How I had seven million things to tell her. How I'd decided I wasn't going to open anything addressed to her. Even the bills.

I also wasn't going to tell Tim the next part, but I did. How it is when you spend all this time imagining how you're going to face the awful new future you've been saddled with, which only makes it all worse. How when I couldn't sleep I'd end up scanning the personals at Yahoo or those Match.com places. How so many people have such pathetic requirements. Must have hazel eyes. Must be named Steven or Will. "People are so desperate and picky," I said. "You're scrolling down through line after line of hopeless desire. It's all selling. Then it dawned on me: I can't sell myself with a kid. I'll never be able to sell myself with a kid. Who in their right mind would sign on for that? Next you start looking at the pictures a second time and knocking people off for stuff like, oh look at that flowered shower curtain in the background. I could never live with that curtain."

"Have you seen Leah?" he asked.

I still had a rib in one hand. I started picking Hot Wheels cars up from the rug and plunking them into a bin with the others. "I can't do this alone."

"When was the last time you saw her?"

"A week ago. We talked Saturday on the phone. I was grocery shopping with Leo. She was at Whole Foods and called while I was at Shaw's. It was weird. She wanted to know about this pancake mix I used to buy and in fifteen seconds we went from there to it's over. She's saying she can't do it and Leo's yelling because I can't get the next carrot out of the bag."

"I don't think she is coming back," Tim said.

"Why are you saying that and who the fuck asked you? Her stuff's here. Most of it." I pointed the rib at the painting.

Tim's head wouldn't stop shaking. "Leo is a huge deal."

"I am aware that Leo is a huge—"

"The equation is not the same. I hate to say it but—I don't think she's coming back, except to get her stuff."

"Which is still here." I jumped in place on the rug, Leah's rug. "Every time I leave the house and come back her stuff is still here. Every fucking time. I get paranoid now whenever I see a moving van coming into the village. I have dreams about changing the locks so she'll have to talk to me. Or carting her things to the yard and holding them hostage, only I don't have time and that's probably not a great way to start a dialogue. Did you guys talk again?"

Tim shook his head, which was a relief, because if they'd talked and he hadn't told me—I took another rib and finished it. Then Tim's "ah-ha" look, the one that takes an incredibly long time to cross his face, began to seep in. "You two are kind of alike," he said. "You and Leah, reaction-wise."

"Alike how?"

He patted the air as he rolled into a long, useless explanation about how my reaction when Cynthia sold the buildings exactly paralleled Leah's reaction when she found out that Leo wasn't a dog. "You both bolted," he said. "You cut and ran. It took longer in her case but the pattern is eerie."

He might have been right only I didn't need it pointed out. So I picked that moment to tell Tim about the Parrothead guy and all the things he was never going to buy.

Tim crumpled the paper towel. "When was this?"

"Saturday," I said. "The first one."

"Did he give you a card?"

"It's trivial," I said. "It's all fucking trivial."

"What do you mean trivial? It's a job. All jobs are trivial but they're still fucking jobs." He flipped the balled-up paper towel over his shoulder. "If we're still doing this you have to come to work."

"Maybe I don't want to."

"Want to what?"

"Do this."

"What are you trying to say?"

"Trying? I'm saying I'm tired of you knowing everything and pointing everything out. I'm tired of you and your big fucking knowledge base."

"Shut up."

My arms folded. We stared. This was the moment we had planned for, only it felt both shocking and inevitable, the way it always does when you enter one of those spaces.

Tim began putting paper towels and chewed ribs and the little plastic containers of sauce back into the plastic bag. He had that dense you-just-let-me-down-in-an-irretrievable-way gaze, but it also felt like he wished we could go back a step. "What I came over to say, besides to see if you wanted ribs, was that Card Night has moved. It's next week but Thursday."

"Card Night can't be on a Thursday."

"What do you mean Card Night can't be on a Thursday? No one could make Sunday. It's still the first week of the month."

"Sunday night is Card Night. That's a constant. Anyway I'm not going. Fuck Card Night."

"Good," Tim said. "You know what? All this is about how you live it in the smallest moments, from minute to minute. Stuff happens and you deal or not." He took a new paper towel from the roll, wiped his hands a second time, and dropped it on the table. "So you're not going to Card Night. Fuck you." He got his coat from the couch and left without putting it on.

FIFTEEN

Sunday morning, almost ten thirty, and we were still hanging around the living room. Leo had been up since six, so he really needed another toaster waffle. If I had been able to figure that out what was about to happen could have been avoided, only I was too tired.

In the middle of the night Leo had a bad dream. He wouldn't tell me what it was except that he kept flying and falling and it was four when I finally got him back to sleep. I even escaped the camping pad and made it out of the room, only then I couldn't get back to sleep. It was windy and branches kept scraping the house. It started to snow and I started to float around out on the Web. I got caught, again, on that site about why it's a good idea to turn into a Canadian. (Reason number 6: Longer life span: 79.8 years in Canada, 77 years in the United States.) I even took the test on the official Canadian emigration page, to see if my work experience gave me enough points to get in. I only needed a 67, but I never finished because I got distracted and found someone who'd taken all these pictures of things that looked like small, liquid tornadoes suspended throughout his house. He thought they were the souls of the dead; I wasn't so sure. Then I got mad at everybody, again. I started with Cynthia for, well, dying. I kept thinking of that moment in the hospital, when she looked out from the bed and told me she was going to be all right. It was stupid but

I believed that. I got mad at Tim for his pompous "deal with it—it's only moments" speech; at Grace for the current situation and not checking in; at Leah for running away, which led to another grand vortex of self-pity. But is it really self-pity when all this stuff actually has gone wrong? That wound me into a fresh spiral of sleep panic, the one that goes: Look, it's 4:30. Now it's 4:31! Leo will be up in an hour! You have to GO TO SLEEP! YOU HAVE TO SLEEP NOW! That always works. When Leo called, "Somebody get me," at six, I'd been out for about twenty minutes.

We navigated the early morning well enough. Leo peed through two pairs of sweatpants but we survived. I stayed on the couch under a pile of bright fleece throws and let Leo watch as much television as he wanted, only there's never enough kid stuff on Sunday morning TV. There's the Disney Channel but PBS has all these stupid public affairs shows. This is not what the hung-over exhausted parents of America need. Does anybody understand that?

When Leo gets bored he also hides things. He'd already told me that the cell phone had gone "hideish" again. He said something was "in a rug" but I was dozing. Then Leo decided he didn't want to watch *JoJo's Circus*.

I started feeling around over my shoulder. "Where's the remote? It used to be next to my head. Leo?"

"Hideish in the rug," Leo sang. He still had on his fish pajama top and he hummed as he pawed through Leah's black canvas bag. He pulled out red-blankie and put it back. "Actually, no." He nodded like a hardware store owner. "Can you change that channel—again?"

"I need the remote," I said. "I have to have the remote." I was too tired to get off the couch and hiding the remote suddenly felt like a very big deal. "You hid it, didn't you?"

"I already told you."

"I'm not changing the channel if you can't find the remote."

"You always want to have an argue."

"I do not always want to have an argue."

"At my new school they don't have meeting." Leo crossed his legs. "You have to have meeting."

I had no idea what meeting was. "There are too many meetings in the world as it is. Why do preschools need meetings? It's like continued corporate—"

"You mean cooperate."

"No, it's—"

"I want my old school. Calvin says new school isn't nice."

"I don't care what Calvin says. Wait, how does Calvin know?"

"Can we call Calvin? But we don't have his number. Google will know the number. You did ask Google about the sharks? Remember that day?"

The whole Calvin thing depressed me. I didn't know who the kid was or how to get in touch with him. Grace must know. Why didn't she tell me?

"Can you call Calvin?" Leo bounced and his hair swayed. It looked like a move from a very slow tap dance. "Please?"

"I don't have his number."

"It's in Mommy's book. The one about meeeee." Leo leaned in and his breath smelled like milk. "Call him from the book!"

"I don't know where that is," I said. "Do you know why I don't know where that is? Because you hid it. I can't find things if you hide them." I probably needed a toaster waffle by then, too.

The kid folded his arms. He brought the inside of his elbow to his mouth. He was talking to Mommy. He used to do that by talking into his fist, but he discovered a new radio in his elbow. "I'm not talking to youuuu."

"Good. Don't move because I'm going to the bathroom."

Leo half stuck out his tongue. I grabbed *The New York Times Magazine* and climbed the stairs. It was all I could do to not make that left into the bedroom and collapse.

I sat on the toilet and read "The Ethicist." Someone was having a vexing but ultimately trivial problem with a locksmith. There are a lot of vexing but trivial problems in the world, I thought. I started in on a page of recipes that used red rice in

novel ways until it began to really annoy me that I still didn't have
Leo's notebook. If I'd actually lost it, if it had fallen into a river or
if I knew it was now in a landfill somewhere, that would have been
one thing, but it was in the house. It was within the sound of my
voice. I closed my eyes and tried to visualize. I could see the black-
and-white marble cover, except it kept spinning, or I could only
see it with Cynthia's freckled hand folded around the binding. If I
had a dog, a dog could sniff this out. If I had my dog. That got me
thinking about Arrow, at large and lost in greater Boston, if he was
even still alive. What if he went back to the house in Somerville
and no one was there? He wasn't even wearing his tags. I should
have found someone I still knew up there to keep an eye out.
Then how would that have worked? It was all too sad.

By the time I came downstairs I was back on the notebook. If
I could only get my hands on that one thing so many vexing
questions would vanish. What will Leo eat that isn't round? What
is the mystery bedtime song about the bear? What was Leo like as
a baby or has he always hated loud noises? The cloud would va-
porize. "Leo?"

I expected to find him sprawled across the rug or on the
couch but the living room was empty. I glanced into the dining
room. I looked under the table. I walked around the kitchen. I
looked under that table. Nothing. I stood in the canary yellow
pantry. If he had climbed the stairs I would have heard it, even up
in the bathroom. I thought, maybe he's gone? It was sick and I re-
gretted it but the thought did arrive with a flutter of relief, which
instantly flipped to panic.

"Leo, where are you?" I looked behind the wingback chair in
the living room and under the couch, places where no three-year-
old could actually fit. I ran upstairs. "Leo," I shouted to the bedroom. I checked under the bed. I went into the bathroom. I
checked the tub, behind the shower curtain. Into Leo's room. In
the closet. I went downstairs and out the front door in bare feet.
"Leo." There was an inch of snow from the night before, but I
only saw my tracks on the walk from when I went out to pick up

the papers. "Leo?" The bell in the white church tower across Broad Street began to clang. "Fuck."

In the house, I thought, he has to be inside the house. I stood in the living room with my hands in my hair. "Leeeee-oooo."

I heard it, a faint half-giggle from behind the moss green door that leads to the cellar stairs. I turned the white porcelain handle and there he was, with red-blankie across his shoulders like a cape.

"I was hideish," he said.

I squeezed Leo's arms and plucked him from the tiny landing. He'd never gone there before. It was always too scary. "What the fuck are you doing?"

"Mommy told me to go hideish there." Leo covered his mouth and giggled in that staged, annoying, frightening way those kids do on *Barney*.

"Why did your mommy tell you to go there? Why does your mommy talk to you and not me?"

"Because she's MY mommy."

"Yeah but—"

"My mommy listens to me." Leo squatted and got this look, as if he were trying to read a far-away road sign that happened to be in a different language.

"Are you pooping?"

"Nooooo."

"You are, you're—"

"Noooo I'm not."

The bell across the street kept ringing.

Leo put his hands over his ears. "Nooooooo."

I could feel the fuses going. They made small popping sounds, like Roman candles exploding a few streets away. I'm always surprised by the surge, that metallic wrinkle in my veins.

"Yes, you are." My hand, palm open, came around from behind my back. I slapped the door frame above Leo's head. I led with my pinkie and it stung, down the arm and into my ribs. I didn't know that was about to happen. I shook my hand as if I'd burned it. "Fuck. Fuck."

Leo sat the rest of the way down with a thump. His palms pressed against the floor.

I picked him up and lobbed him onto the couch. He kind of folded up as he flew, his blankie fluttering as it peeled back from his shoulders. He bounced in place on the cushions and stared, too shocked to be scared. The look began to narrow. It was one I'd never seen. Bewildered, with no place to go.

I fell on my knees and everything widened out. Oh god, I thought. I just threw my kid into the couch. I threw my kid.

The bell across the street stopped and quiet came over the room like a lid.

SIXTEEN

So I went home. And two hours later I found myself still stunned, but in Lincoln, Massachusetts, sitting in my parents' gravel driveway. Leo stayed asleep in the car seat behind me, the sun stayed out, and as the temperature climbed through the forties, everything began melting loudly. I knew that if I opened the car door Leo would wake up, so I just sat, waiting for the knot in my stomach to untwirl.

I kept getting stuck in that moment on the floor, the one right after I threw Leo into the couch, where everything widened out. It never occurred to me that I had the capacity to do a thing like that. I was slowly rounding the corner to realize that I wasn't the guy I'd always imagined myself to be.

The moments after that one on the floor only made everything worse. Leo hadn't pooped and I saw the remote, staring out like a stalled subway car from the end of a small tunnel in the carpet. "In the rug," that's what Leo said before, only I wasn't listening. Between the sobs Leo started shouting: "I want Mommy. It's not good without Mommy."

"I know," I said. I placed red-blankie on Leo's shoulders but he curled back into a ball. I stared at Leah's painting over the couch and felt infinitely helpless. I thought, maybe donuts would help? Then, it's true, I can't give you Mommy, but I can get you grandparents. Why didn't I think of that before? But it's hard to think when you're in the cave.

I eased away from the couch, put on a Kipper video, made the toaster waffles I should have made earlier and announced that we were going on an adventure. More crying. I promised Munchkins. "In the car?" Leo asked. "The place where they come from the window?" Yes, the drive-through and we can listen to the Bob-the-Builder CD in the car. We can rent three Thomas the Tank Engine videos on the way home. You can have Captain Crunch *before* Munchkins and drink apple juice from the green water bottle all the way there. What else could I pile on to make him forget? I stuffed extra clothes into the backpack, folded the kid into his big red coat, and we were gone.

I can't do this, I thought, as I buckled Leo in and handed out the first installment of Captain Crunch, which only slowed the crying. I can't do this alone, I thought, as I backed down the driveway, trying to unfold my sunglasses and hold the wheel with my knees. All the way up I-95 I kept thinking about that child abuse billboard with Karl Malone on it, or maybe it was a TV ad, but it said something like: *If I look big to you, think of how big you look to your kid.* I threw my kid. What the fuck is wrong with me?

My parents' place is a nineteenth-century farmhouse, ringed by fields that have been deeded to stay fields forever. The house is white and narrow with black shutters, almost the same age as the one Leah and I just bought. That didn't dawn on me until I'd been sitting there for fifteen minutes staring at it. There's a long side yard and the backboard is still up on the barn, but Mom wouldn't allow us to blacktop the strip in front of her studio, so we played on grass. Behind the barn is the falling apart soccer goal I made from two by sixes. A white fence that never stays painted runs across the front. It stops for no reason in the pines to the left. It all looks idyllic, and it was, sort of.

Mom's blue Wagoneer waited up by the barn and Dad's Volvo sat like a silver-green island in a lake of slush before the porch door. I checked the fence in the station wagon's mirror. I'd painted that fence maybe ten or twelve times all told, my dad's piecework substitute for an allowance. Five or six years ago I bought Dad a sprayer for Christmas, but I still came over and did it for them. Three foot icicles hung from the porch gutters, which no one had cleaned. When I lived in Boston I used to pop up more. Providence is just that much farther away.

I watched the living room windows, but no one seemed to be moving around. Even if Leo hadn't been asleep I'm not sure I would have jumped out and run right in. I felt spylike and I liked the distance. It helped with the reentry. From the tracks in the slush I guessed that Dad's car had been out and back. He might have gone to church, which he does a lot now. He was almost certainly in his study, a small bump-out at the end of the dining room. History professors never retire, they just keep reading. We knew everything about the Greeks and Sparta and what actually happened at Actium. It's odd growing up that way. There's always time for a lecture and you collect strange facts at the dinner table. ("I'll bet you didn't know the Chinese had ancient recipes for toxic smoke.") Or you can learn to build a catapult in your back-yard and lob pumpkins, which had its moments. But even when he was around it felt like my dad was only about 70 percent pres-ent. He never actually forgot our names but he used to mix my friends up with Charlie's, which seemed strange since Charlie was six years older.

I used to worry Dad a lot. When I moved to Providence he was completely opposed to my becoming a "junkman." Then again he didn't exactly pick a normal thing to do with his life ei-ther. He sort of relented when I pointed out that we both did the things we did because we were in it for the time travel. His eye-brows went up and he gave me a slight smile. The big worry with Dad has always been that we all had to be financially solid. He got that with Mark, who is technically my cousin, though I didn't find that out until I was nine. Mark sells boat insurance in Florida and makes surreal amounts of money. He's the one with the boys.

Charlie is a year and a half older than Mark. He's a bearded, perpetually bemused entomologist at Penn State. With Dad that still counts as solid. Me, I slipped around the corners. I'm still the mystery kid.

So what would happen when I finally got out and walked in with Leo? I'd deposit a soft knock on the study door. Dad would glance up and say, "Jimmer," but fondly, as if he had just recalled the feel of the word. Only I'd have Leo wrapped around me and my father's stare would go on forever.

My mom still calls me Jimmy. She'll always call me Jimmy. She taught high school art for years in the Concord-Carlisle system and then retired to do arts advocacy and her own stuff out in the barn. It's a big space piled with decades of parts that could turn into something someday. She goes through cycles: landscape painting, sculptures made from familiar objects, some soft sculpture, and back to landscapes. I couldn't see any new tracks to the barn but for some reason I couldn't guess what she might be doing in the house. Then I remembered, I hadn't actually returned any of her calls. I thought about it, I just never did.

I rolled down the window. It occurred to me that if either of my parents looked out they would have no idea why a green station wagon was sitting in their driveway. They wouldn't know about trading in the truck because they didn't know about Leo. The tight spot in my throat came back when I realized that I hadn't told them about Cynthia either. They liked Cynthia, or at least she seemed to amuse them. No, they liked her. They were actually furious with me for a while after I ran off to Providence. I also hadn't told them about Leah leaving and Mom would be upset about that. Those two had a connection, all that drawing, combined with a kind of practical view on things. The first time I brought Leah here it was summer and Charlie was putting mackerel in the smoker behind the barn. The light was orange and sideways in the trees. Nobody saw us drive in and Leah said, "Let's just sit." I liked that, lengthening out the moment before.

I took a slow breath. Some of throwing Leo into the couch, a lot of it really, probably had to do with Leah. Without Leo she'd still be here. I closed my eyes and saw Leah in the car, beside me, at night with blue all around. We were on a highway beneath some hills and there had to be lightning in the distance because her face turned white for an instant. But it was this car, the station wagon, and something about that felt both outlandish and hopeful.

Leo yelled, "Noooo." I looked in the mirror as his hands flapped in front of his face. He opened his eyes and strained against the straps. I got out and stepped in the edge of a cold puddle. "Bad dream," Leo said while I unbuckled him. "I did have a bad dream."

My hands stopped. I knew the dream was about me.

"I sat in my car seat," Leo said, "but somebody else was driving." He looked out and saw the house. "Cats?" He waved, "No cats."

"No cats here," I said and carried him to the porch.

The white storm door kept sticking. It would have surprised me if it hadn't. The porch floor made its traditional creak as I passed the bundled-up summer furniture. Leo seems to weigh more when he's not really awake and I had to concentrate on not dropping him. I turned the black knob on the real door and the iron knocker rattled as I pushed inside.

My parents' house has this smell, like scorched butter and apples with an undercurrent of wet dog. I only ever notice it for the first few seconds. I stood at the edge of the dining room, which seemed really dim until I pulled off my sunglasses. I stared at the floor, all newly painted in diagonal black and cream squares, as Mom appeared at the door of Dad's study. Her hair is gray and tightly curled. It seemed shorter. She had on a pale green, sweater, fleece pants, and those suede hiking moccasins that everybody wears. The Sunday *Globe* magazine hung in her hand and she peered as if she had just spotted me in an airport. "Jimmy," she said. Her reading glasses came off. "I'll get your father. Charles? Jimmy's here."

I tried lowering Leo to the floor but his arms tightened around my neck. He looked up as if I had tried to drop him into a river.

My father came out in a hurry. His white hair was slicked back, as always, and with the gray work pants and a yellow button-down under his tan cardigan he seemed even more sparrowlike than usual. "Jimmer," he said. Mom had stopped again but Dad got a little farther around the long newspaper-covered table before he saw Leo. "Who is—"

"Leo," I said and spun him around. "These are your grandparents."

It was blunt but I was tired. I don't know what I expected next. A gasp? Some fainting? But all the air stayed in the room, it just seemed to solidify.

I put Leo down and his feet moved to different squares. "Pick me," he said. His arms went up and I lifted him again. "Are they like Joan?"

"The same idea," I said.

"More of them?" Leo waved both hands as if erasing a chalkboard.

"Then he's—Cynthia's?" my mom asked carefully, her voice dropping.

"You know?"

"Yes, I know, about Cynthia—but not this. I called but—"

"I know."

"Jane Deutch told me." Jane Deutch was one of mom's art friends and Joan's cousin, which seemed like one of the world's strangest coincidences when Cynthia and I first figured it out.

"He's mine, too," I said and put him down.

"Oh." Mom pulled out a ladder-back chair. Her fingers covered her lips as she sat. It was a look of half-shock and half-thinking ahead.

Dad came closer and hummed. "Leo?" he said. "Leo. Leeeo."

"Why does he say my name?" Leo curled behind my legs.

Mom's fingers dropped. "I had a feeling."

"You had a what? Mom, you always say that after the fact."

"But I did. When I didn't hear and I didn't hear and I knew what had happened to Cynthia, I thought something, I was ready to—"

"Sorry," I said.

Dad's index finger slowly waved at Leo, then me. He pointed at his own chest as his lips moved through a frown to a sort of smile. "A surprise?"

"Yeah." Leo pushed at the backs of my knees.

Dad hummed again. "Well, I saw you out there and I didn't recognize the car, but you looked like you were waiting for something. I figured you'd come in when you were good and ready. I thought you had a dog with you."

"Leo?" Mom asked. "Are you hungry?"

A huge black, long-haired cat emerged from the kitchen. It stopped and regarded us with gold eyes as its tail lifted and twitched.

Leo yelped and punched my thighs.

"Buster," Dad called out, as if the cat knew its name.

"When did you get a cat?" I picked Leo up. "I told him there would be no cats. Come on, he's deathly afraid of cats."

"Fine. Fine." Dad scooped up the cat, who went instantly limp, and deposited him in the cellar.

"He's a Maine Coon cat," Mom said, "with double paws. Alice Little, our friends? They moved to Arizona, which I'm not at all happy about, and a long-haired cat was not going to thrive there. We took him in. He's an outdoor cat."

"Except when it's cold or dark." Dad pulled a chair out for me and I swung Leo around to my lap. This wasn't going like I expected. I was ready for hysterics. Wailing, running. This only felt surreal. I was getting used to surreal.

Leo and Dad watched each other. "Look at that hair," Dad said as his hands went flat on the table. "What does he call you?"

I didn't expect that. "Keeper," I said.

"It's a start." Dad seemed to squint at us a little. "You get a lot of gifts in this world, Sonny." He smiled in a bemused way. "Leo, do you like boats?"

Leo nodded.

"Boats with sails or oars?"

"Boats that floated."

"I have something to show you. It's wonderful. Come with me."

Leo simply slid off my lap. He took Dad's hand and they headed into the study. They were going to look at the models. My dad has always been good with little kids. I'd forgotten that.

"Oh my." Mom got up and put her hand on my shoulder as she passed. "Jimmy, Jimmy, Jimmy," she said. "Come. I'm making lunch."

When her fingers brushed my neck it felt like I was about to cry.

I sat on the yellow step stool while Mom opened a cupboard. It seemed miraculous that someone was about to make me lunch. It felt equally miraculous that my parents weren't more flustered by this. There was a fair amount of concern in the air but they looked almost happy. I didn't get it.

My mom is tall, about six feet, and her hand hung on the cupboard's white knob. "Does Leo like soup?"

"I've never tried him on it."

She licked her lips and I knew we were going into interrogation mode, which in my family is the second stage after a big news flash. "Honey," she said, "how are you?"

I felt the back of my head press against the small wall between the windows. "You mean Cynthia? I don't know," I said. "Sometimes I'm sort of used to it, which surprises me. Then I'll be in the car or waking up and it's this visceral shock all over again. I feel really guilty about before, like running out of Boston. I don't know why that's coming back now, because it wouldn't have changed—"

"Did you know about Leo?"

"Nope. I mean Cynthia and I—after I left we weren't exactly talking."

"You saw her in the hospital?"

"Yeah. Joan called, but they only told me about Leo after. It's been what, three weeks?"

"Cynthia never did?"

"No. That's—that was her, the stubborn, secret thing. I'll do it myself. Grace says she meant to but time went on and she wasn't sure how to do it."

"Three weeks is a very long time. You could have called."

"I know." My fingers crossed my jeans. "I think not being able to believe it myself made it hard to imagine explaining it to anyone else."

Mom rubbed her cheek. She seemed to be looking out the window but she smiled. "That is the thing with children," she said. "You still can't quite believe it's happened. It changes, but that never quite goes away." She took two cans of Progresso mine-strone to the electric can opener. Are electric can openers the one appliance that belongs entirely to my parents' generation?

"With Mark," Mom said, "that was a complete shock all around and Charlie was only eighteen months at the time. I didn't think I had room in a way, but there wasn't a choice and so we did. The shock does wear off. It's the dailyness of it. Not having time to think can be a very good thing."

"I feel like one big nerve cell," I said. "Just prod and I react. I'm a huge receptor for need. It's like, Leo's always taking out puzzles and after he goes to bed I'm on the floor putting them all back together. At this point my fine motor skills don't need that much brushing up."

"All right." She pulled a large translucent blue spoon from the drawer. "This is your mother making a pronouncement, but you're a captive audience. My Aunt Dot, who you never knew, would say that much of life is received rather than taken and your task is to receive it gracefully. I know that's probably not what you want to hear but . . ." She rinsed the empty cans. "I was go-ing to set out some cheese. Does Leo like—oh my, what about Leah?"

"Leah's not on board with this. We're not really speaking."

Mom stopped at the refrigerator. "She's not in the house?"

"No, not exactly. Well no, it's just no."

"Where is she?"

"At Cecilia's. It's been a while."

"I am so sorry to hear that. I am. Your father might say it's water under the bridge at this point, but I am sorry."

"Thanks." I got up and started setting the table.

"You should still talk. There need to be lines of communication."

I kept on collecting plates.

"Pumpernickel or baguette? What will Leo eat?"

"I don't know." I stacked the bowls. "Both?"

"He drinks milk, right? I only have one percent. Maybe I'll add some cream."

When I came back into the kitchen her arms had folded. "Did something happen this morning? With Leo?"

I knew she would get to that. I knew she was thinking: Why is Jimmy here now? "Yeah," I said and I felt it, a conscious move to try out the new, full disclosure Keeper. I returned to my stool, took a breath, and started in. I told her about life with Leo, about picking him up in Somerville, how it's lonely. Then I got to this morning and the lack of a toaster waffle at a crucial moment, the alleged poop, the lost remote, the toss. Out loud it sounded even worse.

"You tossed him onto the couch," she said. "Only the couch."

"I thought he was pooping, that's—he just goes in his pants. He didn't before, at least that's what they told me."

"Of course he does." Mom waved the spoon. "This is a huge trauma. It's regression. It makes perfect sense. Put him in pull-ups. Doesn't he wear those at night? They have them for daytime, too."

"Oh," I said.

"Your father will get some at the drugstore after lunch. How much does Leo weigh?"

My hands went out as if I were about to lift him. "Thirty? Thirty-five?"

"You have to not pay attention to this for a while," she said. "Things will settle down. He'll right himself. Kids are either in balance or something is out of whack. This is extreme, but you have to let everything balance again."

Balance. The entire concept felt laughable. I stood over the silverware drawer and stared at the pointy-handled forks. They'd been there for decades. It felt hard to imagine a life that stable.

"How's Tim?" she asked.

"I don't know. We had a monster fight. About work."

"Well, when it rains it pours."

"What was I like when I was three? Leo has to have things go certain ways. When we're shopping I have to look for round food. Did I do stuff like that? I'm just thinking, you know, genetics."

Mom peered at the soup. "This'll be in a round bowl," she said. "I don't know about genetics. You—you were a happy kid. You conducted to records. Those Brahms symphonies of your father's? It was a long time ago and things blur, but before you could talk you were very insistent and mysterious at the same time." She waved at the steam. "I've told you all this."

"How did you do it?"

"How what?" The question seemed to make her happy.

My hands floated up.

"I forget," she said. "You do, forget. You find shortcuts. You cut corners. You'll adjust."

"I'll adjust and not be the same person."

"Honey," she said, "you're not the same person now."

I was still on the stool with that when Leo and Dad clattered downstairs.

"There," Dad said, pointing to the cleared-off, set-up end of the dining room table. "This child needs to sit on a phone book."

"Nooo," Leo said.

I walked into the dining room. "Where were you?"

"The attic. We found the bins of blocks. We gazed at the ship models. There are three train sets up there." Dad went to get the Yellow Pages. "I don't remember how there happen to be three sets." He lifted Leo and placed him at the end of the table.

Leo tapped the phone book's sides as if he were fluffing a pillow. "A frigate has masts," he said gravely. "Masts."

Dad smiled to himself. "It's never over when you think it is. And imagine all the advice I can give you now."

"Dad, if I have to imagine, what's the point?"

"That never took with Mark, the advice part. He just used anything I said as a starting point for the next argument."

Leo frowned. "Does *he* want to have an argue?"

"No," I said.

Dad's finger circled. "Remember, you think you're steering the ship but in reality you're just holding on."

Leo folded his arms. "Don't let's have an argue. No argues."

Lunch was quietly stunning. First off, Leo ate soup. He was three spoonfuls in when I remembered to ask if he always ate soup? "Of course," Leo said. "I knew about this beforehand." We talked about a trip to Athens my parents had planned for December and Mom explained how they decided to repaint the dining room floor. Dad tried to butter Leo's pumpernickel, which caused a flare-up, and Leo covered his ears if anybody mentioned the cat, but it was a frighteningly civil lunch, only there were four of us.

"When I have a dog," Leo said, "he will eat cats and rocket to the moon. You have to wait until you get to countcast. Three-two-one. That's how to do the fine part." He showed us his palms.

Mom glanced over. "Cynthia did a good job," she said. "You can tell."

I was still watching Leo eat when Dad said: "Bet he runs you ragged. You know I can tell you now, but why do you think I had that big gin and tonic every night when I got home? You have to make it to bedtime somehow."

"What's a matunic?" Leo asked.

"A drink," Mom said. "For grown-ups."

"Oh, can I have another drink? Water, please?"

I got up to get some.

Leo said, "Thank you," as I handed back the purple plastic tumbler. "You never say you're welcome," he said. "You should say you're welcome."

My mom laughed. "Leo, do you like to draw? Would you like to see the place where I draw?"

"Oh sure." He seemed surprisingly comfortable here and that alone felt mysterious. Or did my parents just know how to talk to kids? "Do you have glue?" Leo asked.

"Yes."

"Is it school glue?"

"It's school glue." Mom got Leo's coat. "We'll go to the bathroom first."

"Okay." Leo checked the floor. "Will there be cats?"

She shook her head. "Jimmy, go take a nap. You should."

So I went. I felt like a kid, but who in the world is adult enough to do this anyway? I climbed the stairs to my room, a guest room now, but with a halo of tiny Celtics and Red Sox decals still stuck to the window by the bed. I pulled the orange afghan over my shoulder and went very far away.

It was gray out when I woke up and I had no idea where I was. Only as everything came back did I feel myself thinking: How late is it? Does Leo need food? Do I have enough underwear in the bag to get him home? I came down and found Leo quietly eating popcorn and doing puzzles I didn't know they'd kept on the living room rug.

Leo scrambled to the couch. "This is how a bear looks going off a dock," he said and jumped down.

It was early for dinner but Mom said: "Never put a hungry child in a car." We had penne with bacon and peas and ricotta and more amazingly mundane conversation, as if Leo and I dropped in every Sunday. I cleared the table, put the pillow-sized packet of pull-ups in the car and said good-bye. "We will see you soon," my mom said, pressing her hands into my shoulders.

Leo and I were only on Trapelo Road when he said, "I have the pee song. Where's that bathroom?"

I swerved for the shoulder. "We'll pee in the snow."

"You can do that?"

We stood in the headlights beside some pine trees, arched our backs, and drew things in the gray snow.

"Know what?" Leo shouted. "You have a hunormous penis."

"You shouldn't say that out loud."

He folded his arms over his chest. I pulled up his pants. "Can we do this again? That lady did call you Jimmy."

"Your grandmother."

"I can call you Jimmy."

"Okay," I said. "Maybe you should."

SEVENTEEN

Leo fell asleep on Route 128 and stayed out all the way to Providence. It was after nine when I turned up Sheldon Street and the lights in the house were all on. It glowed and I didn't expect that. My first thought, really a wish or more of a detour into the realm of magical thinking, was that Leah had come home. Only as I got closer I saw a salt-stained midnight blue Saab with Pennsylvania plates filling the driveway. It took me even longer to realize that the car belonged to Grace.

I kept shaking my head, as this appeared to be yet another astounding development I would never fully comprehend. Something close to the fact that light exists as both a wave and a particle or that we've been hanging out in space since the beginning of time on this large blue rock and nobody exactly knows where we are, even now.

Leo kicked my seat. "That's Gracie's car. Like she said when we telephoned."

"When you what?"

"Out. Out." He clawed at the car seat straps.

"Hang on." I stopped us at an angle on a snowbank and unbuckled the kid. Leo tumbled out and ran, pushing his shoulder into the front door while I thought: He knows how to dial the phone? Then: I left the house unlocked? Apparently so.

We found Grace ensconced at the far end of the couch, still in her yellow and black ski jacket, her red-socked feet draped across the cushions. She was watching *Monster Garage*. Her cigarette dove into the cereal bowl she had decided to use as an ashtray and her arms shot up. "Honey," she said, as Leo climbed over her gray bag and fell onto her chest. "Ufff," Grace said, wrapping him tight and drumming on his back.

My knees pressed against the couch. I'm not sure what I felt, happy for Leo, a bit excluded, some of that awe you only notice in the presence of the real thing.

Leo pulled back to spin. "You'll stay and stay and stay. Forever and stay."

Grace covered her mouth, as if the thought had just occurred to her.

"When did you call?" I asked.

"And hello to you too, Jimmy."

"Okay, okay." It was surreal, seeing her on Leah's couch. I couldn't believe she was actually in the house. And when I looked, I kept seeing Cynthia. The room felt suddenly smaller.

"I called," Grace said. "Didn't you get the message?"

"No, when?"

"You know, maybe a vintage answering machine isn't the best idea."

"I turned that knob." Leo pointed to the little table in the corner of the dining room with the machine. "So Gracie talked!"

"The second time I called Leo answered."

"He's never done that when I'm around," I said. "When did you start smoking?"

"It's again, Jimmy. It's when did I start smoking again?"

Leo's arms went wide. "Everybody be still." He pointed at me. "That other lady calls you Jimmy, too."

"Your grandmother." I waved at the window. "That's where we were. How'd you find us?"

"MapQuest. I Googled the phone number to get the address. Your door was unlocked." She sat up and laughed.

"Ah." My hand hovered over Leo's head. "We left in a rush.

They'd never met and it went really well, which I don't understand."

"There were boats," Leo said gravely. "Mo-del boats with masts."

Grace rubbed her knees. "Bringing them a little kid changes things."

"Yeah, but this is some price to pay for improved parental relations."

She hummed. "Where's Leah?"

It was odd hearing Leah's name in Grace's voice. "Not here," I said. "In a big way." The stomach twist came back and the thought that I would have to explain everything with Leah twice in one day pushed me onto the couch.

"No?" Grace looked around. She seemed shocked. "That's sporting of her. Then I guess this isn't for everyone."

The sporting line annoyed me. But I was too sad and tired to defend anybody. I also couldn't figure out how Grace knew about Leah.

"Cynthia told me," she said.

Leo's arms folded. "You mean Mommy."

You could almost see the gap in the air.

Grace reached across and unzipped her bag's side pocket. "Yes," she said. "Mommy. Know what I have for you?" she asked and pulled out a green Thomas engine.

"Percy," Leo shouted. "Open it."

She pried the plastic away and the engine fell to the rug. "He's another tank engine."

"I know he's a tank engine," Leo said. "Like Thomas. I have always wanted Percy from the first time I was ever in this land. Did you know that?" He flew the engine in circles.

"How'd you get so tan?" I asked.

Grace's hands draped around Leo's neck. "Day before yesterday I was in Utah." She still sounded amazed. "Skiing. It's school vacation week, only Tom is extending it for the boys. They ski together and I'd had enough of fending for myself. So—I was in a hot tub, alone, looking at the moon and thinking about Leo and it occurred to me: I don't have to be here. No one here needs me. So I got a plane home and drove. I told Tom I was going and he said, 'Okay.' That was it."

"Just okay?" The bit about Tom should have slowed me down, but I was really thinking: Why would anyone voluntarily leave Utah when they could be skiing? "Where were you?"

"Alta. Snowbird. We stayed at Snowbird." She rezipped the pocket. "I had a feeling this would be okay, even though I knew you'd never ask."

I hummed. Alta, another entry on the vast list of places I would never get to. Leo shrugged off his coat all by himself. A first. He seemed suddenly taller and calmer. He sat down to hook together a circle of track on the rug and a second later I had to close my eyes. I was that tired. I put my head back and thought: Grace is here, in the living room. It still sounded bizarre. I felt the spring holding my shoulders in loosen again. "I think," I said, "I think I have to go to bed."

"So go," she said. I opened my eyes and saw Grace's hand disappear into Leo's hair. "Leo," she asked, "honey, how about a bath?"

"Oh, yeah, sure. Of course."

"Can you show me where the bathroom is?" Grace undid her coat and I watched, stunned, as Leo took her wrist and led her to the stairs.

Monday. I woke up under the covers but still dressed. I wasn't sure how that happened, though I'd at least remembered to take off my shoes. It also felt like I'd slept straight through, which seemed impossible. I rolled over and the clock said: 9:46. I had. I took a breath. The air felt thicker, relaxed somehow, but with a hint of cigarette. I heard voices downstairs so I changed clothes and brushed my teeth.

"Yes," Grace said, as my hand cupped the newel post. "Good morning to you." It stopped me because Cynthia used to sound like that when I got up way after her.

"Jimmy." Leo almost shouted it. I wasn't used to that either.

Grace had on red sweatpants and a big blue sweater. Her hair was pulled back and she laughed, but not unkindly, as I staggered past. "I think there's coffee," she said. "That's a good bakery around the corner. Leo showed me. It's slippery out. One big plate of ice."

I stood at the window. "Huh," I said. Leo and Grace had been watching *Mr. Rogers* with the sound off. On the stereo the Tallis Scholars sang tunes from the fifteenth century. That had to be Grace's CD. Thomas trains, wooden track, and Hot Wheels cars dotted the gray rug. The couch and chairs were covered with mingled sections of *The New York Times* and the *Providence Journal*. It all felt exceedingly strange, as if the boat I'd been attempting to pilot had somehow sailed away on its own.

I sat as Grace brought me a cup of coffee with the half-and-half already in it. "Thanks." I sipped. It tasted wild and rich.

"Leo is having a stay-home day," Grace announced. "Is there someone to call at his school?"

"Yeah," I said slowly. "I can do it."

"Good. So—do you have work to go to?"

Work. The idea of it appeared like a word problem. Only I didn't feel like explaining that situation, too. I didn't really know what that situation was. "No," I said slowly. "It appears I'm taking my own personal day."

"Great, because there's lots here for us to do. Right, Leo?"

Leo stood up with two Hot Wheels cars I'd never seen before. "What?"

"Was he up last night?" I asked.

"Yeah," Grace said, as if I'd asked if it was dark. "I got him."

"Where'd you sleep?"

"On the twin. In Leo's room. For a kid's room that space needs serious—"

"How long are you staying?"

Grace smiled in an amused way that I should have wondered about.

Leo showed me the glittery dragsters. They had giant chrome engines. "This way." He banged them together. "These are the fronts."

Another present. One a day. That seemed to be the pattern. I drank more coffee and peered around. The room looked like it had been lived in hard for a hundred hours. Then the one time Cynthia and I stayed with Grace and Tom in Pittsburgh their house had the same whirlwind feel. I went to the kitchen for more half-and-half and found a gold-rimmed saucer that Grace had turned into an ashtray. The smoking was going to be a problem. But I slept the entire night. I could hardly remember how that felt.

I stuck my head out when Grace reminded Leo to use all his words. "Look at me so I can hear what you're saying," she said, and I thought, she's better at this than I am, already. When I got back they were both on the floor, lining the dragsters up for a race. I can't seem to play with Leo like that. I'm always setting him off on his own and wondering why he comes back with so many questions.

"I wanted to talk last night," Grace said, leaning against the front of the couch. "But you were—"

"I haven't been sleeping much. You know—those reasons."

"I'm sorry about the way all that happened, up there." She nodded toward the door and I knew she meant Somerville. "We all ran out and left you. I knew it was bad, but—I'm sorry about your dog, too. That's part of why I'm here."

For a whole day I had forgotten about Arrow. I didn't want to think about where he might be now. "It was awful all around."

"Mom." Grace sort of sighed. "I don't know. She's my mom."

I'm not sure why I thought of it then and I probably sounded a little desperate. "You know that book about Leo?" I asked. "Cynthia's instructions? I lost it. Or Leo hid it. You've read it. Can you tell me the bear song? He keeps asking."

"Leo?" Grace wiggled two fingers. "Do you remember Mommy's notebook? About you? Where is it?"

Leo jumped up with a dragster in each hand. "Oh sure. Of course." He handed the cars to Grace and ran to the cellar door.

"You just asked?" I got up to turn the knob for him. "How does this happen?"

Leo hopped down to the landing. He reached for the shelf and slid the black-and-white marbled notebook out from behind a can of WD-40. It was in plain sight. I'd walked past it every day when I went down to water the furnace. He carried the notebook to Grace, holding it flat with both hands as if it were a pillow.

"Here," she said, handing it across. "I've read it."

I squeezed the covers. It was fat with pictures and scraps of yellow paper. I placed the thing on the table, realizing that I was treating it like a relic.

"It started out as a folder and when she couldn't tell you . . ." Grace's hand rolled in the air. "She meant it for Leo, too, eventually."

Leo's name was on the cover in Cynthia's round handwriting. It had been traced over twice in red and blue ballpoint. I rubbed the indentation with my index finger. I suddenly wasn't sure I wanted to open it.

"Leo," Grace said. "*Sesame*'s on. Let's watch."

"With red-blankie?"

"Yes." She turned off the stereo and they clambered onto the couch.

"I always watch *Sesame*," Leo said. "I watch the Count."

I finished my coffee and finally began flipping pages. It turned out to be more of a scrapbook than a set of instructions. Some entries had dates, most didn't, and others were just taped-in pieces of paper. I thought of those scrapbooks from the twenties or teens that you see at auctions. Collectors hunt them for the postcards but that always seems wrong. It's a collection. It only means something if it's all together.

I couldn't look for long. It was harder to see Cynthia's handwriting than I thought. I saw the sonogram. The proofs of Leo's baby picture at the hospital. He's wrapped in a white blanket with red dogs on it. His face is pink and squished. He looks grumpy. I found a sheet with other names that could have been his: Julian LeMay, Jackson Keeper LeMay. My tongue pressed against my teeth. There were the foods Leo liked as a baby: applesauce with blueberries, squash, turkey dinner. A picture of Leo in the arms of Cynthia's restaurant friends. Leo in a giant industrial mixing bowl. Two pictures of Joan holding Leo. In the first she looks resigned, then she's a blur, dancing the baby around the kitchen. "Grandma!" it says.

"Are there more pictures somewhere?" I asked.

Grace looked over. "There should be. There's a box. I think Mom has it. You need to put pictures up in his room. The ones with Cynthia."

I flipped ahead. A word list from when Leo was fifteen months old: nana = banana, ca-ca = cracker, A-oh = Arrow, waaaa = go for a walk, oh-oh = anything that falls, arrrgn = I want, dis na woking = broken. There were thirty more. A list of songs Leo liked as a toddler: "Crash," by the Primitives, "Should I Stay or Should I Go," by the Clash, "Mockingbird," by James Taylor, "Ray of Light," by Madonna, "Turn, Turn, Turn," by the Byrds. A bunch of these were on a mix tape I made years ago and thought I'd lost. Sometimes there were single line descriptions with dates, like the one explaining that Leo always pressed his fists into his eyes when he napped. "6/20, I realized I've watched too much Teletubbies because now I need to know what's beyond the berm." I blinked. I'd had that same thought. I kept flipping and the density bewildered me. And that whole time I was here, with Leah, renting movies, going to restaurants, driving to work, answering e-mail, completely unaware.

Tuesday. I opened my eyes at 10:44. Yes, later than the day before, but at least I didn't sleep in my clothes. The fact of sleep still amazed me, only I sat up and entered a fog of hurt. I missed Leah. That's all. I wanted to run my hand across her shoulders. I wanted to hear her hair slide over the pillow. I flopped back and watched the newly painted ceiling for a while. Was having Grace around making me miss Leah more? Probably, if that were possible.

I came downstairs barefoot, in jeans, a Road Runner T-shirt, and my green fleece pullover, to find Leo and Grace doing some kind of art project in all corners of the dining room. It seemed to involve maps and a huge roll of white restaurant paper. They had already been to the art store and back, as yesterday Grace said: "This child needs an art box," making it sound like I'd forgotten to buy him boots.

Grace and Leo spent all yesterday together, playing or fixing up Leo's room. I spent it at the fringes, upstairs mostly, sometimes looking at the instruction book or getting the twin bed into the back room or sorting boxes that had been sitting for weeks. Leah's things I placed neatly in the corners or consolidated into smaller towers of boxes. I still expected all her stuff to simply disappear some morning.

Leo hopped off his seat. He seemed genuinely puzzled to see me. But that's the attention span thing. He locks in and everything outside becomes a surprise. Grace gave me a bright smile. Her hair was loose and her eyes flashed in a quietly startling way. She is happy to be here, I thought. I was happy, too. True, there was the mess and the smoking and I kept making compromises all over the place. And there were parts of this I wasn't ready to think about, the way her voice made me think of Cynthia, the strangeness of the three of us moving through the house, how it felt like a new configuration, but I'd slept in now for two days in a row.

I found the coffee maker still heating the empty carafe. I had to let it cool before I could make more, so I surveyed the kitchen—crumbs and butter across the counter (Grace would eat piece after piece of buttered oatmeal toast in the morning but she never seemed to use a plate), two half-filled milky bowls of Cheerios, three orange juice glasses, each holding a different amount, two purple and yellow sippy cups of milk, newspaper sections on top of the gas stove. I started collecting. It felt like cleaning up after a party. How does Tom live with this? Or do you just stop noticing? I emptied the gold-rimmed ashtray-saucer and re-membered that it belonged to a tea service that came from Leah's grandmother.

Back in the dining room Leo and Grace were mapping out their day.

"See," Leo said, holding up the paper and showing me a tangle of interconnected, multicolored circles. "We're going here."

"Me, too," I said.

"No, you're not," Grace said. "We're going to the Children's Museum, having lunch with onion rings at the mall, then grocery shopping."

"You know where all that is?"

"More or less. I've been on your computer."

"We saw you," Leo said.

"You're practically cute when you sleep like that with your arms over your head. Except the grocery store is—" Grace's fingers fluttered.

"Shaw's." I pointed out the dining room window. "Follow the right fork, up the Post Road, first right at the light."

Leo stood on a chair as Grace took his wrist. "No chair-standing. That's a rule."

"But what if—"

"No." She shook her head and Leo jumped down. Something about that bothered me, not the standing on chairs part but the way she cut him off.

"Isn't it going to be harder getting Leo used to daycare again?" I asked. "With all these stay-home days?"

Grace smiled as if I'd said something amusing. "No."

I sipped my coffee. I was in the shower when they left and it was almost noon by the time I got back down to the kitchen. I wasn't going to make it into work. I actually didn't know what to think about work. I was less mad at Tim, true, but I wasn't sure I still had work to go to. If I saw him we'd have to wrangle and I didn't feel like wrangling, where staying home meant I could sort the back room and move some boxes. That seemed doable.

Later that afternoon two strange things happened. First, I was up in the top of the garage and I'd left the back door open to air out the kitchen, so when the phone rang I heard it. By the third ring I was down the ladder as that ridiculous voice in the back of my head kept saying: "Get there. It's Leah!" I got there but didn't pick up because Tom was already on the machine.

"Grace? Grace?" His voice was gruff and windy, like he was outdoors, stopped by the side of some black diamond trail. "Did you get there? You should have called in. We need to talk about what you said. That and Jonah dislocated his thumb. Bad pole plant. He got a cast. We'll fly back tomorrow. I'm not one for ultimatums and I hope this is the right number."

The machine's red light flashed. Oh and by the way your kid dislocated his thumb? If I'd thought about that more it would have clued me in to why Grace seemed so happy here. But I went back to the garage.

The second thing happened upstairs, as I discovered again that the problem with unpacking is that you find stuff. All that unintended time travel takes a toll. Anyway, it was a box full of objects that had once been on my desk: a Peterson's bird guide, an Altoids tin full of pushpins, a black and orange Swatch in need of a battery. Only this box came straight from Boston. It had never been opened, even while Leah and I lived on the East Side, so of course I was curious. When I lifted out the bird book I found a check I'd been using as a bookmark. The check was from Cynthia, dated about a year before we broke up, and made out to me for nine million dollars. On the memo line it said "lost bet." It made me smile, at least. That was the difference with us, I would never think to write out a check that couldn't be cashed, even as a joke. I kept turning it over. I had to take a lot of deep breaths. I kept wishing I could remember the bet. I was an idiot. I was. I know that.

I left the check on my desk and hoped that a nap might make things seem less sad. I must have fallen asleep because it was dark when I heard Leo down in the living room say something about

his grandmother's barn. "Gracie," he called. "The TV is all mixie."
When I got downstairs Leo had two giant floor puzzles, one of a
barn and one of a construction site, spread across the rug. They
came from the Children's Museum, he said. Today's present. "Can
you fix the TV?" he asked.

I jiggled the cable as Grace went back and forth bringing in
groceries. It worked and I went out to collect the last few bags.
She'd bought a lot of things I never would: a big pump container
of natural moisturizing hand soap, orange marmalade, Bob-the-
Builder bubble bath, a dozen white tulips. How long is Grace
staying if she's buying natural moisturizing hand soap?

"Did you get Tom's message?" I asked, pulling out a tub of tofu.

"Yeeup."

"The part about Jonah?"

"Yes, and you can stop asking now."

"Are you cooking tofu?" I weighed the tub in my hand.

"No honey, you are."

I don't mind cooking but I won't do it on demand. "Not today I'm not."

"We'll see." The smile seemed to go around me. "You should
save these plastic bags and use them in your wastebaskets."

It was strange though, because we fell into a rhythm, gently
bouncing off each other in the domestic dance of putting things
away. At first I was surprised that Grace knew where it all went.
Then I realized she was just putting stuff anywhere.

Grace opened the doors for the long cupboard over the stove.
"Of course, you can't keep spices there," she said. "They dry
out." The jars formed a loose herd on the counter.

A small fist pounded my leg. "No hitting," I said, looking
down at the curled top of Leo's head.

"He was only getting your attention," Grace said.

"Where does metal come from?" Leo folded his arms.

Grace's hands went to her hips. "Ah, rocks, originally."

"Oh." Leo spun once and returned to the living room.

"That's what I miss," she said. "They get older and they don't do that. Can you cook these?" Her hip brushed against mine and stayed there. She put a tray of boneless chicken breasts on the counter. "Sweet potatoes and brussels sprouts?"

"Nobody likes sprouts."

"Leo does."

I gazed at the breasts and decided I could either make a scene or think of this as a puzzle. I was hungry. I opened a beer and found the sweet potatoes while Grace went to smoke on the porch.

After dinner, which came out nicely, thank you, I cleaned up room by room while Grace got Leo into bed. I made it to the couch maybe an hour later with a stout and the Bruins and the Canadiens on NESN, but one ear kept straying to the baby monitor on the end table. Just sitting there, by myself, felt deeply luxurious, only I could still hear Grace reading *Harold and the Purple Crayon* through the speaker. Her voice sounded like Cynthia's. I muted the TV. The monitor's red lights rose and fell and it turned into this weird time-trip moment. As if this were the parallel future, the one that didn't fork, the one where some version of this happened every night and I was in it and Leo was upstairs with his mom.

After a while Grace came down and settled into the couch. "Why do you like hockey?"

I sipped and licked stout off my lips. "It's fast, faster than soccer, beautiful in its way. Things line up for a second then they're gone. But they're there."

Her hand moved as if a bug had fluttered by and I remembered that Grace never liked the smell of beer. "It's also violent." She went to the kitchen and came back with a tumbler of scotch. I don't drink scotch. The cubes rattled as she sat.

We turned as Leo's voice came through the monitor. He sighed and began to sing a small song. "Moon, moon where are you? Gracie has my other shoe. Moon, boon where is soon? Gracie has my shoe." He sighed again.

"That's pretty good," I said.

Grace listened for a second more. "Yeah. He's got intervals.

Those are fourths." She kind of smiled. "Think we're still trau-matizing the kid?"

Wednesday. I woke up at 11:02, still missing Leah and feeling newly awful about everything. The rhythm of these mornings had started to scare me. Actually a lot of things had started to scare me. All these fresh routines and the fact that they felt like routines. Or that Leo was clearly happier than he'd been since I'd brought him here. That he seemed to be toilet-trained again, which I knew I'd screw up the instant Grace left. The long list of all the things I wasn't having to do to take care of Leo. And all of it, I knew, I shouldn't be getting used to.

I got dressed and stopped halfway down the stairs. Leo had an accordion. A small red one, with buttons instead of keys. Wednes-day's present. Grace had her fiddle out, which I didn't know she'd brought. She kept playing the same figure over and over. Da-de-dot-dot, de-de dut. A tiny syncopated Celtic-sounding run.

"Why you did play that same song?" Leo asked.

"I'm practicing," Grace said. "This is what you do. You play the same thing over and over. That's how you learn."

"Oh." Leo pulled on the accordion. "Like getting used to it? I think so."

I slid my hand along the banister. "Today's present?"

Grace squinted. "We've been up since 6:15 and know what? I can give Leo as many presents as I want."

"That's good because you are. When is the kid going back to daycare?"

"Good morning to you," Grace said. "And why don't you have some coffee?"

Leo pulled on the accordion.

"I'm paying for that," I said and pointed across the street. "Preschool. It's $185 a week, whether he goes or not."

"I'm glad." Grace played the phrase again. "He'll go. In a while."

"I wish you wouldn't smoke in here."

"That was hours back, but—I'll try. Don't you have some-where to go?"

I squeezed the railing. The fuses weren't going but I knew where they were. Maybe I do need to go to work, I thought. Go-ing to work meant facing Tim, but it would at least get me out of the domestic submarine. So I went.

Even the drive up was a relief and when I got to the yard the note on the door said: "Open by chance," so I knew Tim had stopped by and gone over to Wickenden Street. I turned on the office lights and felt like a ghost. Maggie called in right after that. She was home with pneumonia and had been for days. "Pneu-monia," I said. "How did that happen?"

"Some evil child breathed on me?" She sounded weary.

I had more than enough to do. There were objects to ship, ads to renew, e-mails to face, Web pages to update. A few live people even came in. I sold a Windsor chair and an eighteenth-century door to the same guy from Exeter. The hours flipped past and I was happy. I felt like an adult. At four I looked around and thought, there, this *is* better. And it occurred to me that at work all I do is chaos management. It's a life of disorder and maintenance. You prioritize, keep your head down, and off you go. If I can do it at work, why can't I do it with Leo?

Half an hour later I was back in the village, driving up our street. The light was white and coming from that funny early spring angle, when I almost ran into the black Volkswagen bug in front of me. I knew the plate: LZ 707. I blinked and Leah's brake lights went on, because right in front of her a woman in a yellow-and-black ski parka happened to be leading a little boy in a red hat across the street. Grace was taking Leo home from an after-noon at daycare. We waited while they climbed my front steps. Leah looked in the rearview mirror. We made eye contact, then she looked away and sped to the corner.

Leah drove by the house! Why would she do that? This can only mean one thing: The walls are breaking down. *Call her cell!*

At least that's what the large voice in my ear kept saying, until the silver pickup behind me honked.

I parked and ran in. Leo and Grace were already upstairs. The house smelled like cigarettes and latex paint. My bedroom had somehow magically filled with Leo's dresser and a new stack of boxes and when I crossed the hall, Leo's room had new blue walls covered with straggly clouds. The ceiling had turned dark purple. I spotted the masking tape outline of a crescent moon up in the corner. I saw the spots Grace missed and lots of purple dots on the pine floor. Would it have been so hard to use a drop cloth?

Leo jumped on the bed. "It's like outdooooors."

"Oh hi," Grace said. "The glow-in-the-dark stars are still in the car. We'll put those up after Leo's bath."

I would never think to paint a room like this. I would never pick these colors. What if in three months Leo wants something else?

Grace kept smiling as if this had all gone unexpectedly well.

"Just how long are you staying?" I asked.

Her smile got bigger.

I kept looking around, because what would Leah think? This was supposed to be her office. This was her space. The questions kept piling on until I finally realized that no, this really is Leo's room. The thought felt like a corner. It's weird, sometimes you can actually feel it when the center of gravity changes.

EIGHTEEN

I went to work, again. I'd made it to Thursday and by that point going in to the yard had started to feel somewhat normal, which meant I still worked there, no matter what I thought. I hadn't talked to Tim yet, but his Sierra Club daybook was on the desk so I knew what he was up to. That morning he was in Connecticut, scouting an eighteenth-century house for parts. But it also said "buy/move?" next to the address, which I didn't get. I had more than enough to do anyway, so much so that by five I didn't want to go home.

Last night, even at dinner, Grace refused to say when she was actually leaving, beyond the cryptic, perfectly enunciated: "Once-things-are-set." Then she got up and drove to Cambridge for an early music concert, pretty much without warning. I couldn't tell if she was mad or needed some space. It was kind of amazing, given all the weird unspoken tensions, that we'd gone that far without some kind of a blow-out. Leo went happily to bed, which also amazed me, and I cleaned up and cleaned up some more and sat on the couch, flipping between hockey and the History Channel. It should have been a relief, having the house to myself; instead it felt disturbingly lopsided.

So Thursday night after work I walked in and found Grace and Leo dancing on the rug to kid songs and kicking through a layer of sea green packing peanuts. It looked like the aftermath of a snow globe explosion. Leo's purple sweatshirt had stamps of the USS *Constellation* all across the front. Actual postage.

"What are those?" I asked.

Grace paused and leaned in. "Stamps," she said, sounding pleased. "Leo thinks they're stickers."

"Those are expensive stickers." I waved as Leo stomped through another low fog of ankle-high Styrofoam. "What happened?"

"Good day at work, honey?" Grace smiled like someone's older sister. "Want a beer? Wanna dance?"

"We did get a CDeee from the library," Leo said. "It's *Dragon Tales*. We used a CARD. Your card!"

"If the wallet's on the counter . . ." Grace circled away.

I glared. It all felt invasive and endless and made me want to stick up for something. Plus, I knew those peanuts were going to clog the vacuum cleaner no matter what. Leo went back to spinning, only every few seconds he'd stop and insert some sort of superhero martial arts move. Is that what he's learning across the street?

The crankiness kept piling up until I finally thought: Wait. Take a breath. Reset. Look at this, Leo's happy. So why are you thinking like a troll? I unfolded my arms and told everyone to keep on with what they were doing, while I went to the kitchen to find beer and something to invent for dinner.

I had the pasta water ready to boil. I had a big pile of shredded cheddar. I had the flour out and butter melting for the sauce when the phone rang.

"Jim?" It was Tom and he didn't sound like he was outdoors. He sounded annoyed. "Is Grace there, still?"

I checked the living room. "Yup. Dancing."

From the pause it seemed that the thought of Grace dancing had pissed Tom off anew. I heard something crumple. "Can I talk to her? Now?"

I brought the phone over and when I told Grace who it was she shook her head. I thought, no, I'm not getting sucked into this. So I left the receiver on the dining room table and got Leo to bring it to her. Eventually she took the phone, only to tell Tom she didn't feel like talking, right before she pushed the "End" button. It all seemed weird. I'd only been a parent for three weeks, but if my kid had his thumb in a cast I'd be all over it. I went back to whisking.

I had the oven preheated, the ziti drained, and I'd started to assemble it all when Grace told Leo to stop dancing and ask me how to set the table. This produced an immediate spasm of crying and I thought: Come on, he's three. "He doesn't have to set the table," I called out.

"He can help. It's time. He likes to."

"If he doesn't want to, fine. That's the rule. All this corrective stuff—"

Grace moved to the arch, arms folded. "What do you mean corrective?" she said. Then she whispered: "And not in front of Leo."

"Yeah, yeah, but he's my kid." The words felt sticky as they left.

"Mine, too," Grace said. "In case you forgot, I am always going to be his family, too. Hence the problem."

I held up the spatula as if I might soon decide to conduct something. Grace's arms stayed folded. She was right. I knew that. This was the question we were only starting to engage. I made a large humphing noise and went back to folding the ziti into the liquid cheese.

All through dinner Grace and I didn't exactly look at each other but Leo finished his ziti without complaint. He only wanted catsup. Actually Leo did most of the talking, mainly about the Mars Rover and how it crawls across the red plains of Mars smelling for rocks. I couldn't imagine how he knew all this.

"Can I have an Oreo?" Leo asked and Grace got him one. Leo slipped down and announced that I was going to watch him take a bath. He angled his head and pushed up his bottom lip. It's a thing Cynthia used to do. "I want a bath right now." He folded his arms.

"All right." I took my beer, Leo grabbed some plastic tubs

from the cupboard, and upstairs we went. Leo said his bath had to be "hottest" and since this was our first bath together I wasn't about to argue. "Bubbles," he said and I complied. Leo got in and I sat on the floor with my back to the wall, sipping my stout as the room steamed up. The beer tasted wonderful in the heat. I was so tired it felt like my arms were only attached to my shoulders with pins. I closed my eyes. It seemed like I'd slipped off the planet.

Grace found me. Leo kept on playing, happily, but apparently falling asleep with your kid in the tub is a big sin. "Look at this," Grace said, swinging the door back and forth to scatter the steam. "He's taking a bath! A child can drown in a cup of water! A cup!" She had on those furry moccasin things and she kicked the base of the tub. "Ow."

My hands covered my eyes. "A cup?"

"Come out here." Grace squeezed her fingers around her toes, then motioned me into the hall. I crawled across. "Two days," she said. "You've been at work two days and you're already back to your self-satisfied pre-child life. Two days. You have no interest in raising a child."

"No interest?" I stood and waved at the steam as it rolled into the hall. "This is nuts. Leo turned off the water just fine. I was tired. I dozed."

"Doze in bed."

I banged my palm into my forehead. "Why didn't I think of that?" Then probably as some reptilian brain defensive measure, I decided to remember that it was still Thursday, the new Card Night. "I am leaving this domestic submarine," I said. "I am going to Card Night. Tim's number is inside the cupboard door. The cupboard with the mugs. It's in pencil."

Leo splashed in the tub. "Bye," he said.

And I thought, shit, he heard all that? Grace just stared.

Card Night seemed like a good idea until I got in the car. I only made it to Broad Street before falling into another spasm of missing

Leah. It had been there all along, that morbid, swampy soundtrack looping through the edge of every hour, only this felt sharp. Card Night was part of what we did. It was one of the things we liked about us. A new episode in a quietly fascinating monthly play about not much at all. And Card Night always started with a detailed discussion of which treats we should pick up on the way there. I tried making a list, but without Leah there were all these moments when it felt like half of my mind was just gone.

I knew I didn't want to show up empty-handed and I thought I could still figure out how to buy beer. I turned left and stopped at the big drugstore in the village and came out with a case of Sierra Nevada Pale Ale. That would make Tim smile, but it had also dawned on me that appearing at Card Night meant we would actually have to talk to each other. The meeting was bound to happen, but all the way over I kept stabbing the radio's scan button, trying to find a decent song.

Then standing in the slush before Julie and Tim's dark blue three-story house it seemed completely obvious: I can't do this. I'm about to go up there and face a table full of people and most of them have no idea what's happened to me in these last weeks. The explaining alone will take hours. It suddenly didn't feel worth it, all that reliving in the telling. But I'd brought beer and the box was heavy. Where could I go? Home? To chat with Grace?

They had the front porch light on but I kept going down the driveway to the back stairs. It's the way I'd normally go in if I was coming over just to hang out. I climbed to the second-floor porch and saw Tim through the kitchen door window. He had on a black sweater and a green Red Sox cap but the rims of his silver glasses looked sharp in the fluorescent light. The bell inside the door jingled against the glass when I turned the handle. Tim peered and you could almost watch the information crawl across his face: Keeper's on the porch. What does this mean? Keeper's opening the door. Keeper has a case of Sierra Nevada. I like Sierra Nevada.

"Here." I handed across the beer. Tim looked surprised and dubious and I thought, shit, this isn't going to work. This is a far bigger rift than I imagined. If beer can't solve it I'm screwed. "Apologies all down the line," I said. "You know, the storms of life and all."

Tim hefted the case. "Look," he smiled down at it in a cautious way, "all my friends are here." He nodded. "I've felt your presence at work for days now. Could have been your evil twin."

"I keep misplacing my evil twin." I laughed, too loudly. "You could have called me."

"You could have called me, too."

"I made it here."

"Even on a Thursday." Tim slid the box onto the counter and undid the top. He took out two, opened them, and gave me one. We clinked necks. "Yesterday?" he said. "On my way back from Connecticut?"

"That house thing?"

"Yeah, but I found this tackle box in a guy's shop in Brooklyn. I paid him $150, so he was happy, but it's full of lures and reels. It's complete turn of the century." Tim's voice slowed down. "It's ten grand worth of stuff."

"Really?" It surprised me, not the tackle box so much, but that we could reset this quickly. Then this was Tim. I grew up with Tim.

"It's up at Wickenden. The other thing? We should think about buying whole houses and moving them."

"You mean taking them down?"

"Yeah, take them down gently, then put them back up somewhere else. This one I saw, it was in the middle of the woods. It's two hundred years old and no one's ever wired it or put in plumbing. Isn't that amazing? The guy who owns it said it used to be a stage stop."

"We don't know how to take down houses."

"We'll find people who do. Who's with Leo?"

"Grace."

"She's in town?"

"Been here for days. It's—interesting."

"Interesting good? Bad?"

"Both. It's confusing. It's like she and Tom are having some thing, too."

"How long is she staying?"

Julie appeared, but her hand stopped on the refrigerator's wide chrome handle. The smile took a second. "You're here," she said and Tim waved as if to say it wouldn't be a problem. I didn't know what they were talking about.

I helped Tim pull a half dozen beers from the box and deposit them in the rolling blue cooler that always comes to the table at Card Night. He poured in ice while I collected the purple opener from the counter. Out in the living room Phil loaded the Wilsons slides. Rory, Jill, Sam, and George sat at the dining room table opening tins of nuts, eating olives, or sorting poker chips into red, white, and blue ten-dollar piles.

It all pretty much stopped when they saw me. The collective gasp, the hole in the air, the second hands frozen in place on the clock. Rory's thumb plowed right through a nice stack of blue chips. Phil floated in with a little yellow Kodak box in his palm. I felt like a captured ghost.

"My." George pulled out the nearest Windsor chair. George is like that, always bouncing up to get things or open a door. He's a serious mandolin player, has CDs out and everything, but by day he designs Web sites for private schools. "We didn't think you'd be here. That you could."

"Keeper." Rory watched as if I had a curious disease. "How are you?" It took me until then to remember that Rory and Dave have kids. Rory's always talking about going into development meetings with pinkeye or Cheerios stuck in her sweater.

"I'm behind." Sam's fingers waved. "Since last time, you've become a parent?" It sounded like the name of a new species or a secret order. "Are you okay?" Sam and Kelly have twin boys. I think they're around four. Sam used to be more of an artist, big ceramic stuff, now he's an administrator at RISD. His Card Night winnings, he says, only go to feed the financial beast that is pre-school. This makes us feel better, as Sam wins a lot.

"I'm stunned," I said. "It doesn't seem to end."

"I'll bet." George tapped the table. "Keep talking."

So I did. I rolled out into the monologue woods. It wasn't hard once I started and I tried to keep from sounding too pathetic or angry, since by then it all felt more surreal than anything else, a condition I'd begun to realize was never going to wear off. "Grace has him tonight," I said and George pulled me another beer from the cooler.

Rory's hand stopped in her curly red hair. Her kids were what? I couldn't remember. Three and five? "Wow," she said, "do we have things to talk about. Like we have this extra Children's Museum pass because we got two by mistake and they never check. We need play dates. He's almost the same age as Lucinda, right? I've got bags of boy clothes in the attic that Nate's outgrown. It's really hard to find secondhand boy pants. They just wear them out."

"You know I can't buy orange juice with pulp anymore," I said. "Because it plugs up the sippy cup valves?"

Sam's head kept bobbing. "We knew that. You have to come over," he said gravely. "If he's three it'll work with the boys."

Jill's fingers pressed against her lips. She has a long face but I'd never seen her look that puzzled before. She runs a historic wallpaper company with her ex-husband. "I wish I still had things, but Suzie's ten."

I didn't know what to say. But as before, as I spieled on, the parents all got this look, as though they were trying to remember if they still had that blanket in the car to put out the brush fire they'd accidentally parked beside. "Thanks," I said. My throat tightened and I couldn't say it again.

"I'd help but I'm an awful baby-sitter." George kept slicing the dry salami.

"You were fine that one time," Sam said.

"Yeah, for an hour. No, I'm The Cat In The Hat's cousin. Chaos with dubious cleanup."

People smiled. Tim checked his watch. "Maybe we should play," he said. His hand floated above the three decks on the table.

We always play with cards from the 1940s or earlier. Tim says it's better because those cards have seen more. His index finger paused over the gold box of Cosmopolitans. I liked those. They had silver and black art deco swirls on their backs. Tim did a bridge shuffle and George cut.

Phil said: "Why do we play poker when we could just watch it on TV?"

I laughed and watched my hand slide a white chip toward the center of the table.

For the next hour I didn't think about much. I wasn't losing or winning, I was in a comfortable space. Phil had his iPod hooked to the stereo and we were in a long run of the Kinks. People were still humming along to "Apeman" when Rory and Julie went to huddle in the kitchen. Julie took her cell.

I had my back to the stairs as Tim called for Caveman. It's the game where all clubs are wild, only my cards kept coming up red. How can you play a game with three draws and thirteen wild cards and never get a single one? I know it's all statistics but the mysteries of timing still confound me. I folded and thought I heard someone say Leah's name in the kitchen. It occurred to me that all during the monologue nobody asked about Leah. I didn't offer any information, but nobody asked.

Tim and Phil entered a face-off over a seven-dollar pot. Phil had six eights, which in Caveman is nothing, and Tim won with seven kings. He was still pulling in chips when I heard Leah's boots on the stairs. My eyes closed, a three-year-old's quick route to invisibility.

"Sorry, sorry." Leah's low voice rolled up ahead of her. "I had this idea I'd finish two things and be right over, but—"

I opened my eyes. It didn't just feel like everyone was looking at me, they were. They knew she was coming. They all did. Then why the fuck didn't they say anything? Why didn't I think she was going to be here?

Leah stopped when I looked up. She had one gloved hand on the collar of her black wool coat. She began to slip it off her shoulder. The blue turtleneck, the dark jeans, her red glasses starting to fog.

"Oh," she said and her lips stayed there. The look flickered from surprise to something nearly wistful, to puzzlement until several forms of frustration clouded that out. It didn't end on a hard note, exactly, but I sure felt like I'd done something. "Hi," she said, more to the table than me.

I think people answered. I could only stare as she walked over to lay her coat across the back of the zebra-striped couch. She placed her gloves on top and took off a red and purple knit cap that I didn't recognize. She had three blue and green rubber bracelets on her left wrist. "Who's winning?" she asked, watching me in a wary way.

How could this be? Leah and I were in the same room. We were breathing the same molecules. She moved to the open chair opposite me. Why hadn't I noticed there was an open chair? We'd been playing all this time and I was too wrapped up in feeling good about simply sitting at the table to spot that? Phil made a bearlike, throat-clearing noise and I had a flash: I was about to be cast out of the circle.

"Look," I said, "you guys don't need, maybe I ought to—"

"Stay," Julie said.

Leah's lips came together. "No," she said. "It's—we can do this." It was Leah's practical, let's-make-a-list voice, the one that always used to reassure me.

I thought: Shit, this is how bad the future's going to feel.

"Who's with Leo?" Leah asked.

"Leo?" Hearing his name in her voice threw me. "Ah, Grace."

She frowned in a cold way that didn't seem to fit the situation.

"His aunt?" I said. "Cynthia's sister? She's been here, for a while."

The frown loosened. "Oh." She looked at Tim and back at me as if something had surprised her. I remembered that frown from the Volkswagen's rearview mirror as Grace walked Leo across the street. "Oh," she said. "Is there wine? I've been at work for a very long time."

George's chair slid back as he went to the kitchen. Somehow everyone mercifully skipped the how's-it-going stuff with Leah and started talking about *The Daily Show*. Maybe they already knew how it was going.

Tim dealt and George reappeared with a tall glass and an open bottle of white and we played for another long twenty minutes. I kept thinking, I've gotta go. Then someone would call a new game, there'd be new jokes, Phil would tell more failed action figure stories, Leah would laugh and just be Leah, and I'd throw in more chips. We kept almost looking at each other, but not. It felt like some weird therapy experiment involving enormous amounts of denial. But each time it seemed as though we might square off over a big pot, I made sure to fold.

The problem is, folding gets old after a while. We were playing seven card draw with everybody in. Tim and Jill were off on a detailed dissection of *Rocky and Bullwinkle,* as Tim had picked up a complete set of tapes at an estate sale. This spiraled into a discussion of cold war references and Sam dealt me three kings. The king of hearts showed up on the first draw. I stayed in.

In the next instant everyone folded, except Leah. It was just us and we had to look at each other, which hurt, even though it was all I wanted to do. Leah kept raising, a dollar at a time, four blue chips, then four more. That's how she plays, hand after hand of small bets followed by a big square-off, which might or might not be based on a bluff. She smiled, as if in spite of our lives being totally screwed up, or mine at least, she was enjoying this tiny drama. It made me jealous. Four kings. I had four kings. The king of hearts first, the sword in his crown. I called.

Leah's cards came down. A pair of threes. She laughed as if she knew this wasn't going anywhere from the start and that unnerved me.

I felt good about winning for maybe three seconds. And when

Leah stood to stretch I thought, she let me win. Why would she do that? Because she knows we're not going anywhere, so this was what? A gift? An eight-dollar concession?

Over on the zebra couch the cell phone in Leah's coat went off. She'd changed her ring to some perky little classical phrase that sounded like Bach. She pulled out a lime green phone. When did Leah get a new phone?

"Hey," she said. "You're still there?" Her head tipped, her hair inching down her back. She moved into the living room and turned out the lamp. The red and yellow Christmas lights across the mantel glowed. "No you don't," she said. "Stop." A laugh, tiny and intimate. "No." She glanced at me. "I'll meet you there."

My watch said ten something. Where was there?

"Twenty minutes," she said.

It's Jon, I thought. She's talking to Jon. Jon is not just work, Jon is—newly separated. I blinked extremely slowly, as if that might make her hang up.

"I lost all my money," Leah said. "Yeah, already."

By this point everyone had separated into discrete conversational groups, allowing them to talk about something else. I couldn't breathe. She's seeing Jon. Fucking Jon. How could I not even imagine that as a possibility? How can I be this devastated so quickly? How can every thought here feel so familiar?

Leah hung up. She came back under the dining room arch with the phone pressed between her palms and apologized. She had to go. Everyone said the normal see-you-soon things, but it killed me when she put on her coat. Coming here was an awful idea. I never should have left the house.

When the downstairs door rattled closed Tim picked a new deck, the one with the winged, orange Seiberling tires on the back, and everyone seemed to take a breath. I knew they only wanted to talk about Leah and if I hadn't been there they would have. It occurred to me that Card Night had never before dealt with an internal breakup. Everyone here was either half of a couple or seemingly beyond that sort of drama. My thumbs drummed the table. I felt like saying I should go, too, but then I'd catch Leah on the sidewalk and have to watch her drive off.

Julie snapped her fingers and the sound shocked me. Nobody does that anymore. "Let's cash in," she said. "I've been thinking about the Wilsons."

Tim nodded and we counted chips. With my big win I was only down a dollar-fifty. I put in two singles and took back the quarters. It always feels weird using real money at Card Night.

I lifted the last pale ale from the cooler and slid across to the zebra couch. The red and yellow lights glowed and I leaned against the spot where Leah's coat used to be. Fucking Jon. I guess it made a kind of sense. All those trips. The thrill of new projects. The excitement of professionalism. For a second I even forgot about Leo and thought: How could she dump me for him? He's her boss, sort of. He's the senior partner, or whatever they call them.

People drifted in with refreshed drinks and more food on bright red plastic plates. Julie sat next to me. She ate a piece of smoked trout and tapped my thigh. "You okay?"

I wanted to laugh. "I don't know."

"Stay," she said. "I tried to head that off but her phone wasn't on."

The projector hummed and we winced at the brilliant blank screen. I looked around at the strangely glowing faces and thought: All right, I'm here. I need these people. They're Leah's friends, too, but I need this. I took a deep breath and for a second it felt like I had something holding me up.

The slides came quickly. Intense blue-green forests from forty years ago. Hooked mountain peaks scowling over thin double yellow–line roads. Windshield shots and more windshield shots and I still felt crushed. I wanted to go home. But when would I ever get out again? Never. So I drank and watched the Wilsons' square black station wagon, now streaked in yellow mud and parked at a campsite or surrounded by trees so green they looked like part of a rain forest. Hiking shots in the mist, hiking shots at sunset. Stevie with the dark golden curls and Karen in shorts sitting on a rock with their knees bunched tight. All these family pictures with the implied dad. You know he took them, so he's always present, but not. If someone took a picture of me and Leo would you think of the implied mom? Then I saw it: Grace, Leo, and me, sitting on a fence, each of us looking distracted and grumpy in our own little ways. I tried to shake that off, only it wouldn't go away.

I still couldn't guess where in the country we were. Tim thought Washington State but Phil said British Columbia. He decided he recognized a license plate. I was about to give him a hard time. Like Phil can recognize a forty-year-old Canadian license plate? Only I didn't have the energy.

Then came the strange moment. There's always a strange moment when we're watching the Wilsons. I think that's part of the appeal. I was prepped for more windshield views but we arrived at a logging operation. Half-stripped pines were plucked from trailer trucks with a clawlike crane and pushed into the dark green river with a wide splash. The shots went on and on. It felt instructional.

"Those are going to a paper mill," Phil said. "Fifty points for me."

Once in the river the logs slid into a long corral. A boy in a red cap, standing at the wheel of what looked like a miniature tug boat, nosed them around. Then the tug disappeared and a brown-shirted guy filled the screen. He was stocky, wearing jeans and tall black boots. He moved across the bunched logs holding a white pole with a silver hook on the end. He would lean in to steer a log to a vacant slot and then reappear in the next shot, balanced atop a new log. In the last shot he wasn't there. The white pole stayed, lying diagonally across the floating logs, but the guy in the brown shirt was gone. I thought of him under water, in the cold, looking up at the logs, waiting for a pause so he could push his head into a clear space.

Tim clicked the last two slides back and forth. The brown-shirt guy kept appearing and disappearing.

"Maybe he went for lunch," Julie said.

"He left his stick thing," Rory said. "Wouldn't he lose it in the river?"

Tim ran the slides ahead. After that we were off to some new campground.

If you did fall in, how would you get back up? You couldn't push the logs apart, they were too big. All of which meant you couldn't fall off. I'm not sure why but right then I thought: I can't die. It's not as if I thought I could before, that had always been more of a Zen-like, what-happens-happens stance. But I kept seeing those Wilson kids and I thought with Leo—I can't die, at least not for a very long time. It was like finding some vista you didn't know existed.

I finished my beer and needed another. Tim flipped the slides back and forth once more, as if that might change something. If this was forty years ago then the brown-shirt guy is probably dead by now no matter what, even if he did only go for lunch. The back of my head pushed into the zebra-striped couch. I closed my eyes for a second. I knew if I stayed like that I'd never get up. The last time I was here Leah held my hand and made me promise never to ride a motorcycle without a helmet.

I t's true, you can still drive, even feeling crushed and useless. I kept watching the empty passenger seat all the way home, as if with enough glances I could force Leah to materialize. I gave that up somewhere past the strip clubs on Allen's Avenue. And when I reached the house it bugged me, anew, that I had to park on the street because Grace couldn't remember to pull all the way into the driveway.

I expected Grace would be asleep but I found her stretched across the couch, watching season four of *Sex and the City* on DVD. She wore a big purple turtleneck sweater, one I hadn't seen before, and the black sweatpants. She smiled as I unzipped my coat. I started to sit and she moved her legs at the last second. "Sorry," she said, "about before. I was being an asshole."

It seemed so long ago. "Okay," I said. "I shouldn't have fallen asleep by the tub."

Grace laughed. It sounded like a drinking laugh. She lifted a small glass of something darker than wine.

"When did you guys rent stuff?" I asked.

"After Leo's bath. He has a new Bob-the-Builder tape."

On the screen I saw a quick flash of Samantha having loud sex on a desk with an annoyed-looking stockbroker type.

"That's some picture window your neighbor has," Grace said.

"You saw that?" I laughed. How did I think no one in the house would ever notice? Leah never did. But that started after she left.

"I watched for a while," Grace said.

"You did not."

"I did. He needs curtains. You need him to have curtains."

"Leo's not that tall."

"How long does he watch?"

"Hours."

"You know this?"

"No." I smiled. It felt strange and I wasn't sure why.

"How was Card Night?"

I didn't feel like telling her about Leah. "It was—okay."

"Bet big, win big? See people?"

"Yeah. I forgot, some of them have kids. I never noticed that."

"You didn't have to." Grace took a sip. "I'm drinking all your port."

"I didn't know I had any."

"It's new. Do you want a glass?"

I couldn't decide. Another episode started with that shot of the Chrysler Building, then Carrie Bradshaw's picture on the bus.

"About before," Grace said, "you can guess, but Tom and I are not in the best spot. A lot of what's happening has to do with his reaction to Leo. I wasn't going to bring Leo back with me, ever, really, but we fought." She sipped again. "It was one of those fights about the hypothetical where you learn actual things you didn't want to know. He keeps diminishing the fact that Leo's mine, too. He won't recognize that Leo is part of the family, too. Cynthia wanted that. So—Jonah's fine. I called. He's not bothered about his thumb. You know, badge of honor." She finished her glass. "Sometimes I think we're one of those couples who will hold it together only until the kids leave. I don't know what I think about that." She rubbed her knee. "It gets harder over time, in different ways."

Over time. How in the world am I going to have enough time to find that out? "Can I have a taste?"

Grace handed down her glass. The stem between my fingers seemed silky. The lip felt cool. I like port. I always used to.

"Keep it." She went to the kitchen for a new one.

The port tasted rich. Warm in a way I didn't expect. "It's not for me to say, but," I waved around the room, "this is a lot, what's happened, Leo. You'd think Tom might cut you some slack. Any slack."

Grace settled back into the couch and filled her glass. "Thank you."

"If he's not, then being away, makes a kind of sense."

She blinked at me and didn't look at the screen and I had this sudden, amazing realization that we were going to sleep together. It didn't feel like a choice, rather a thing that would simply happen. I wasn't sure what I thought about that. I wasn't sure I wanted to figure that out.

Other episodes went by. The lamp in the corner went dark. Grace dragged the red wool blanket down from upstairs and it happened. At first tangled and heavy on the couch, then smoothly and surprisingly up in bed. She tasted smoky and new as if she had been out and I hadn't. Even through the haze it felt shockingly familiar.

NINETEEN

It was earlier than I thought: 5:42, according to the red clock radio numbers. The house smelled cold and I touched the tip of my nose to make sure. I burrowed my shoulder beneath the comforter, closer to the warmth next to me. I heard the rattle of the furnace kicking in. I closed my eyes, waiting for the radiator hiss.

Back in the dream I'm in a big platform bed with gray stumpy posts at the corners. Leah and I are floating on a deep green air mattress. We're in sleeping bags, mine red, hers yellow, and the air is cool, though it's still summer. We're high up in some kind of fort or outpost that has been built into a golden cliff. It's all faded, washed-ashore planks, blue Styrofoam and plywood, cobbled together with rusted screws. Spars spring from the corners, hung with white rope, old T-shirts, and the occasional flag. Dozens of dented and chewed orange and white lobster floats make slight thwacking noises in the breeze. The ocean is right out front, silver, broad and sparkling cleverly. The mist from the breakers threads through the beach rose, covering the gray and gold bluffs on either side of us. It's hard to move but when I finally sit up it feels like I'm looking out from the inside of a parade float. I tug at my orange T-shirt until I see the white letters that say BLOCK IS-LAND, only they're upside down. The waves get louder and I take a deep, damp breath I know I can't hold. Leah is asleep on her side. She opens one eye. It's her yeah-I-know smile, the smile we have when one of those moments you can't quite believe creeps up on you. The edge of a bright blue tarp flutters in the opening where a window might be. I hear small footsteps on the plywood roof, but I'm staring at the twirling tarp and the sunlight beyond. I'm getting closer and closer until I'm leaning through the opening and it now seems as if our fort has actually been built on top of a small dock. The water below is calm, green, and translucent, like a shallow lake or an incredibly slow river. It feels as though I should be able to touch the sandy bottom, then I'm staring at something round and white and speckled in red. It's a poker chip, a ceramic one, not like the plastic kind we use at Card Night. That deep voice behind my ear says: *You can't fold. That's the thing, you can't fold.* But the voice is calm, as if I should remember this and perhaps take it on as a mantra. My arm goes out and I follow, tipping through the opening in one smooth motion as my face enters the surprisingly warm water. Bubbles wiggle past my chin and the chip brightens when my fingertips dig around it in the sand. I feel the chip in my palm and when I look up, Leah's face flutters down from the other side. I tell myself not to breathe until I reach the surface.

I opened my eyes and saw the island-shaped water stain on the gray ceiling and the white venetian blinds. I saw the red wool blanket bunched at the end of the bed. I had on sweatpants but no shirt. My hand pressed against my chest. It took a long time to remember where I was.

You slept with Grace, the voice behind my ear said. *You slept with Cynthia's sister.*

I looked over. Grace was on her side, breathing easily in the brightening room. Her outline seemed smaller under the covers and staring made me feel both panicked and unfaithful. I slept with Grace. The panic made sense, I mean, I slept with Grace. But who had I been unfaithful to? Leah used to sleep here, and we did pick out this bed, but technically, was that still an issue? I felt the warmth from under the comforter. I closed my eyes.

The radiator hissed. The clock radio said 7:49 and Leo was still asleep. I couldn't believe it. Then he called out: "Somebody, come get me," and I closed my eyes.

Grace's arm swept back the comforter and I heard her bare feet touch the painted floor. "I've got him," she said, sliding out.

My eyes opened and I watched that brown-fringed spot on the ceiling. You slept with Grace. You slept with Grace. How could this happen? Then I realized that the how of it didn't matter. It happened. It had become a historical fact. The frightening thing? It was good. Actually, worse than that, it was great. It was startling and pent-up and restless and breathtaking and fierce in ways I never would have imagined. It was also strange and familiar in some dreamy sense that I did not want to think about. Little things, like the size of her hands or the way her head felt against my chest. You slept with Grace.

Over in Leo's room Grace said, "Yes, we can go downstairs." A drawer closed. "We can watch TV. *Peep* is on. You like *Peep*."

"I do?" Leo said. "Oh sure." They padded to the bathroom.

I slid my hand along the floor, feeling for a T-shirt. I couldn't find one so I pushed my shoulder back in against the dark sheets. I smiled. I couldn't help it. Grace. Grace is married, to Tom. What the fuck are you doing? I looked at my wrist as if I had been wearing a watch.

My eyes closed again and I saw Leah's face flickering through the pale green water. I could still feel the poker chip. Then we were back in sleeping bags, in the fort. Leah smiled and I felt that, too. I heard the thing Tim said about how all you get are moments. How it's a big stack of moments. You can't expect it to all add up, but you want the best ones you can have. Yeah, I thought. Yeah. I knew this was a moment from a dream, but I wanted it. I sat up. I wanted Leah back. It didn't matter what I had to do or how I had to do it, I wanted Leah back.

I took a long breath. The air tasted steamy and the room seemed bright. I heard Leo downstairs singing, only it stopped with a thump, and for once I didn't feel overwhelmed. I didn't even wonder what thumped. I felt clear, like I'd come around a corner or finally spun the map in the right direction so it at last made sense. I'm not trying this out, I thought. This is it. This is my life and Leah is what I want. I suddenly and precisely understood how someone could undergo a religious conversion.

I picked a purple towel up off the floor, hopped across the hall, and took a quick, surprisingly hot shower. I had bounce. I could feel it in my heels. I hadn't had bounce in so long. I opened the closet and the soft black button-down shirt I wanted came right to my hand. I went downstairs, still buttoning, as Leo sat in front of the TV watching *Bob the Builder*. "Can we fix it! Yes we can!"

At the bottom step I saw that even though Leo had red-blankie across his shoulders, he wasn't wearing clothes. His pajamas were scattered across the dining room, while the sweatpants, purple undies, and Thomas shirt sat stacked on the couch.

"Hello," Leo said. Grace emerged from the kitchen holding a piece of buttered toast between her thumb and index finger. She had on black fleece pants and my gray, long-sleeved Red Sox shirt. "You're wearing Keeper's shirt," Leo said. "Why?"

Grace laughed. "I'm not sure."

It dawned on me that I might have actually slept through the night, again. "Was he up?"

"Yup," Grace said, still chewing. "Twice."

"You got him?"

"That's because I am a good person," she said. "I'm taking a shower. He's got ten minutes before meeting."

Meeting was across the street at daycare and always at nine. I finally learned that it was the big moment of their day and the artificial deadline that shoved us out of the house. Without meeting we'd be on the couch watching PBS and eating Honey Nut Cheerios from the box until noon. Most days getting Leo ready to go was all I could handle. I'd always forget his lunch or a mitten, but that morning it seemed amazingly simple. I was in some strange, completely efficient zone. The after-effect of sex or of making an actual decision? It was hard to sort out but something had changed.

"Leo," I said, "did you eat?"

"Waffle," he said.

"Good news!"

We got dressed, made it into the red coat, found the hat, se-cured the mittens, and I remembered his lunch, which Grace had already packed. We turned off Bob and Wendy and left. The sun felt wide and extra white. Maybe it was all the ice but the entire street seemed unnaturally reflective. I got Leo through the door at the five-minute cleanup signal.

"You certainly seem to be in a bright mood," Mrs. Green told me.

"Yes, I am." I kissed Leo on the head.

"You did kiss my brain," Leo said, and went to read a book on the rug.

I waved and started back. Only the moment I stepped off the curb that big deep voice behind my ear zoomed in. *This is com-pletely quixotic,* I heard. *You can't bring people back. Once they're gone, they're gone. And Leah is gone.* I stuffed my hands in my pockets and thought: Shut up. You can too. Instead I heard: *Oh yeah, last night she didn't even say, "See you later." She didn't ask about Fred. Every time you've talked she's asked about the cat. She's moved on.* I shook my head and remembered all the bills on the counter I hadn't been opening. Most of them, the house bills, were in Leah's name. Just seeing her name on the envelope had a lot to do with my not opening them. So how long can you go not opening bills? Weeks? You can go weeks. But how many? Then again last night Leah didn't ask about her things and her things are all still here. Point for my side. After that I remembered how happy she sounded on the phone with Jon and how settled and impenetrable that felt.

By then I'd only made it to the middle of the street. I glanced up at the bedroom window. The sun bounced off the glass and Grace was probably still taking a shower. She took very long showers. So did Cynthia. I blinked and a whole new set of wor-ries began to blossom. It felt like watching the quick birth of a cloud. I mean, what did Grace think about what we'd done? Was this part of some larger plan? I guessed she knew we shouldn't have done it. That was the overtone, even though I was buzzed. And Grace is a quite attractive person, more so if you don't actually know her. Did she think this could really happen? It couldn't happen, for thousands of reasons, starting with the weirdness factor. Besides, we fundamentally don't get along. That's always been the definition of us. Or was this a thing Grace had been contemplating for some time? Stepsons. You'd have stepsons. There'd be courtrooms and Tom's visiting rights. What would Leo think? He'd be all for it. Then I kind of saw Cynthia looking at me in the middle distance with her head at an angle. I am Grace's dead sister's ex-husband, I thought. Grace slept with her dead sister's ex-husband. My hand covered my mouth.

At that point I'd been stationed on my strip of ice in the center of the street for untold minutes. Or that's how it felt. It took a polite honk from a bearded contractor in a white Econoline to inch me toward the curb.

I got stuck again on the front step. I had my hand on the knob and the knob was cold. But my hand felt light, as if by not turning the knob I could sidestep the fact that something momentous and irrevocable had happened.

The hall smelled like oatmeal. I sat on the stairs, taking off my boots. It seemed like there were all these ghosts I needed to wave away.

Grace sat at the dining room table, her fingers wrapped around a cup of coffee in a maroon checked mug. She slid the cobalt blue cereal bowl to the side without looking at it. She had on another big gray sweater. Her hair was tied back and damp and I thought, this is still a very attractive person. She glanced up from the paper and didn't seem happy or sad, more perplexed than anything.

A second cup of coffee, already laced with half-and-half, waited across from her in my white CAR TALK mug. I sat. For the longest time I wasn't sure if anybody was going to speak. We sipped. We watched each other in a surprised and pleasant way. I started getting nervous.

"We can never do that again," Grace said.

"I know," I said, as the itch of relief spread over my shoulders. Then something about that seemed almost sad. "I know."

She shook her head. "It was too good. I mean I haven't—it was also far too weird."

"For you, too?"

Grace's eyebrows did that arch thing, as if to say what-kind-of-question-was-that? "Yeah," she said, "it's like discovering something you always wondered about and being shocked that you were right."

I nodded. "Because usually when you find those things out they're complete disappointments. That always seems to be the point, that you should have just kept it all in the abstract and gone on wondering. But this." I covered my mouth. "We shouldn't have done it," I said, recognizing that while this wasn't technically an infidelity for me, it certainly was for Grace. But what does technically mean when you're still in love with someone who just isn't around? Two people, I realized, sort of.

"But we did," she said. "I think Cynthia shook things loose."

I stared. "You're right," I said. "I also think you ought to go back to Pittsburgh."

Grace laughed as if leaving were now impossible. "Oh sure, we have great sex and you're sending me back to Pennsylvania?"

"Okay, okay. I'm sorry. I didn't mean now." I had some more coffee. It tasted great. I watched the mug. "But—I'm not sorry it happened."

"Me either."

"I am a little scared by it, because, I mean this means it was there lurking all the time. Think of the damage we could have caused."

"We wouldn't have."

"Right, you're right. What was I thinking?"

She sipped. "It is sort of about you and us and wondering about it, but it's other things, too." She looked out the dining room window. "I've never been in this spot before. It feels—"

"It wasn't about me?"

Grace smiled. "Well—"

"That's it, that's the problem. You know, it turns out nothing's really about me." I'm not sure why I said that.

"Come on. I don't mean to be totally blunt, which I haven't been for a while. I've been good, but since you told me to go back to Pittsburgh . . ." She smiled. "I mean it's possible we were headed, we could have headed . . ." She shook her head. "I don't think we have to really figure that out. Do we?"

I laughed. I wasn't sure why. I thought of the fort on the cliff and sitting up in bed and finally knowing what I wanted.

Grace gave me an extended look, as if she needed that much time to piece something together. "Was Leah at Card Night?"

I nodded.

"Did you talk?"

"No. But I learned things. Like she's seeing someone. Which is why I was a little—but you know what? I've decided it doesn't matter."

"That's good. That makes sense. You still need time to get this all," Grace waved over her shoulder, "working."

"It doesn't matter because we're getting back together." The words felt clean. "I don't know how, but it's going to happen."

Grace winced. "Jimmy. If it happens, fine, but—"

I felt my head shake. "I've decided. I was completely amazed at the world when I fell in love with Cynthia. It had never happened like that before. And I know I fucked that up. I'll know that to my fucking grave. Then it amazed me again, completely, when it happened with Leah. I'm not sure it can happen that many more times. I'm not sure it can happen again at all."

"Why would you think that? It happens all the time."

"Not to me. It feels like I'm only going to get so many chances."

"It happened twice, so why not more? Jimmy, you can't just decide. It's good that you sound like yourself again, but you also sound like someone on TV talking about true love."

"Well, yeah, I'd never say that but—"

"There's nothing true about it. There never is. It's there for a while then it turns into another . . . thing."

"No, that's not what I meant." This conversation wasn't going at all where I wanted, so I took another hit of coffee. "Look, you know what the big thing is? It's you and me and Leo. I know, we're in this together for the long whatever and I didn't really get that until recently."

Grace tilted her head and looked somehow relieved.

"Like when I was off the cliff with all that despair and not calling you to say how Leo was or to ask questions, that was screwed up. But I get it now. It took a while, but I get it. Even at this advanced age I can apparently still learn stuff."

"It's always a plus to find that out."

"There are moments here, where it feels so natural, the three of us moving through this house, that—"

"It's a little frightening? Like looking down some alternate path?"

"Like walking down. Like some strange parallel world where we—"

"So," her hand turned in the air, "maybe that's why it felt—"

"That?" I pointed at the ceiling.

"That didn't feel like walking a path." Grace did a slower version of the eyebrow thing. "You're right. Leo is what we have to work out. I kept waiting to go until you were a little more ready. And to be honest, yeah, I am worried about going back to Pittsburgh, but that's different. I am going to be in Leo's life. I am going to see him regularly." She stared. It was that fierce look of Cynthia's that always made me smile and feel lost all at once. "I want him to spend time up at camp in New Hampshire. I want him to know all his cousins. I want him to understand that he's part of a large family. I have to do that, for Cynthia. It's—I miss having a kid that age. They get bigger and you lose things. You forget, about the way they dance and the bits they say. It's sad. But if this means a lot of commuting, so be it. You'll have to commute, too."

"Pittsburgh?" It takes weeks to drive to Pittsburgh. Only in the next second all my ingrown resistance somehow scattered like a cloud. "That's fine. I'll do it."

"You will?" Grace peered. "Promise?"

"Promise."

She held out her hand. Her palm was warm and soft and that small shake felt more binding, more permanent than anything I could remember.

Our fingers came apart but we kept looking at each other. A car sluiced up the street. "Don't you need to go to work?" she asked.

TWENTY

A few minutes later I stood at the bottom of the stairs, zipping my coat and feeling the cold soak through the front door, as Grace handed me a white piece of paper. It was folded in quarters and you could see where the scribbled blue and green markers had bled through. I was about to open it when she shook her head.

"It's a map," she said, "from Leo. He made me one, too, last night. We're both supposed to open ours all at once, at noon."

"Noon." I slid the folded paper into my coat pocket and felt my phone. Leo had been drawing lots of maps lately, but I could never decipher them.

"Have a day." Grace waved and sat back down with the newspaper.

It was bright out, not blinding like before, but brilliant enough. I hopped down the last two steps and slid on the ice, only I caught myself in time. I still had bounce. It felt like I was getting away with something, an entirely unfamiliar and unnerving sensation, given everything that had fallen on me.

I sat in the car picking a CD when Tim called. "Can you meet me at the house?" he asked. "There's a thing I need to move to the yard."

"What thing?"

"A couch thing. I've got the van."

"Okay," I said. "I'm backing out now." I put in that Talking

Heads greatest hits compilation and skipped to "Once in a Life-time."

At Tim's the same parking spot I had last night was open but using it seemed strange, so I made a big K turn and found a fresh one across the street. I hiked down the driveway and up the back stairs, like last night, which also felt strange. The kitchen door was unlocked and a second later I stood in the dining room, staring at Leah's seat at the table. It stung. I mean it's not like Jon was in the room, but she talked to him, right here. His voice moved through the air.

Over in the living room nobody had put away the slide projector or the screen. I heard the shower going upstairs, so I knew Tim wouldn't be down for a while. I flicked on the projector. The remote somehow made it into my hand and I flashed through half a dozen slides. It was a new carousel of the Wilsons and they seemed to be in New Mexico. I recognized a shot of Taos gorge, a long cut in the pinkish-brown landscape. How could they have covered so many miles while I slept?

I hit reverse and took out the slide. It said "NM box 5" in pencil on the white and yellow cardboard border. I don't know why I find the Wilsons so fascinating. Maybe it's the ordinariness of it or the details, this sea blue plastic camping plate, that pink short-sleeved shirt, and I start wondering where those objects are now. Or it's the mystery kick of watching someone else's apparently functioning family. I skipped ahead through shots of low red-roofed ranch buildings, a beery-looking guy and his black dog grilling steaks beside an adobe wall. Then we jumped to a small corral, with white smoke and actual cowboys wearing brown Stetsons and long-sleeved button-down shirts. They're roping and branding red-brown and white calves who pop up and run away in the next slide.

I looked over at the spot where last night Leah's coat lay across the back of the zebra-striped couch. My stomach tightened.

Tim came down in jeans and a purple, long-sleeved T-shirt with a mushroom cloud on the front, buffing his hair with a turquoise towel. He seemed surprised, but he always looks that way without his glasses. "Coffee?" He pointed. "More? You?"

"Yeah." I was stuck, still holding the remote, hung up on watching the next flipped calf about to be branded.

"No peeking into the future," Tim said.

"We need a wall map," I said. "Then we could figure out where these guys are. Do the thing with the pushpins."

"Only then Phil couldn't guess and always be wrong." Tim laughed.

"Leo's drawing maps," I said. "Except I can't read them."

Tim rubbed his temples with the towel. "That was rough, last night. I didn't know you were coming, which is why Julie did that freak-out thing in the kitchen."

"It was just a look," I said.

Tim went back through the dining room to get coffee. I turned off the projector but left the fan on to cool the bulb. "Wait, what's getting moved?"

"The zebra couch is going to the shop."

"Really? It's a fixture." I followed him into the kitchen.

Tim does this all the time, cycling through furniture the way other people retire T-shirts. He always says Julie likes coming home to find something new. That wouldn't work with Leah, too many deals to make and points of view to include before a decision could begin to break the surface.

"I'm tired of the couch," he said. "The couch is tired of being here. A big hole in the room will make us hunt for something better."

It occurred to me that only people without kids had the luxury to think about this stuff. Tim handed me a full TEXACO mug with the half-and-half already in it. "Thanks," I said. "Last night was awful, but now I know what I want."

Tim had that look, the big wince.

"I want Leah back."

"Oh." He sat on the stool, placed his coffee on the counter, picked up a balled pair of gray cotton socks and unrolled them. "Keeper, I hate to lay this out, but it's not going to happen."

The room seemed smaller. I should have been prepared but— how could Tim actually say those words? "You know this?"

"I don't, but—"

"Then don't say no."

"Look at what's happened. That's denial talking."

"Yeah, I'm turning denial into a positive force."

Tim's hand slid past like a plane taking off. "Just jump ahead. Put down some miles and drive on. You get over this by—"

"I don't want to get over."

"You've got to desensitize yourself. List two hundred things you never liked about Leah. Put them on the refrigerator and stare at it."

"There aren't two hundred."

"Fifty? Ten?"

I held up five fingers. "Four and a half, maybe."

Tim watched as if my hand happened to be on fire only I somehow hadn't noticed. "I'm serious," he said. "Apply what you've learned, write down everything that could have gone better and—"

"Shut up."

"Is it really a surprise? If she doesn't want a kid, no, if she doesn't want to raise someone else's kid, who could blame her? It's a mess and while it would make my life significantly easier if you two were back together—"

"See."

He frowned at his remaining bare foot. "Are you thinking, my life's ruined so I'm taking someone else down with me? If so, that's a fairly dark thread."

I had thought that, at one point. "I'd never think that," I said. We sipped and the twitch across my shoulders told me I'd already had too much coffee. "I'm determined," I said. "And I had this dream—"

"No."

"I did. This morning."

"Wait. I'm supposed to talk you out of doomed quests. That's my job. Do you need your life to be a quest for Leah?"

"I had a vision," I said. "Visions work for prophets." I told him about the cliff fort, the ocean, and Leah's smile, but the more I talked the more worried I got. Does explaining a dream ensure that it will never happen?

"I have a lot of dreams and they never—"

"This was different. It felt like it was already done. Like a memory. Like watching the Wilsons." My arms folded. "Leah's it. She's the one. I can't imagine a future without her."

"Have you ever said that to her?" This came with the you-might-want-to-think-about-that nod. "Like I said, I've had a lot of dreams and—"

"I had one that did. The duplex in Somerville, with Cynthia? I saw that before I knew I'd end up living there. I was sitting on the steps, waiting for someone. It wasn't Cynthia, but those were the steps."

"How come no one has these dreams when they really need them?"

"I need this now," I said.

Cars went by and after a while Tim's look began to turn, as if his will to argue had dissipated. "You can't just win someone back. In movies, but—"

I felt my shoulders lift, that or maybe it was the too-much-coffee thing kicking in. "I saw this ad for a male witch in the *Phoenix*. Casting and removal of spells, get back the one you want."

Tim put on the other sock. "You're perilously close to the 1-800 psychic phone call." He smoothed out the toe. "Or you could just challenge Jon to a duel. I'd be your second."

"You would?" I paused, until it felt like I'd already agreed to a plan. "Naw, we'd have to get him to go along. Jon's never looked like the dueling type."

"He wears glasses." Tim tapped the counter. "Well, good, we've got determination and a hopeless situation. Let's move a couch."

We were in the van, all loaded up and heading down Cypress on our way to the yard, and I still had my fingers around the TEX-ACO mug. It had maybe an inch of cold coffee left and I thought about finishing that off when I noticed that my thumb felt like it was moving, only it wasn't. Sometimes excess coffee just makes me talk faster, other times it feels like I'm out of my body. I rolled down the window and poured away the end of the cup. Then I let go of the mug, completely by accident. It bounced with a clank before it broke.

"Did you drop my Texaco mug?" Tim looked in the side mirror.

"My thumb did. I'll get you another one. Really."

He glanced over and at first I got nervous, only Tim seemed almost bubbly, as if now he couldn't stop thinking about the project at hand. "People usually analyze this stuff for months," he said, waving at the stoplight. "The endlessly vexing what-to-do-next questions, but we don't have the luxury. First, we identify the problem."

"We broke up. Or Leah disappeared, ran off, whatever."

"Plan your work, work your plan."

"Who says that? Somebody says that."

"Marv Levy. Former coach of the Bills."

I talked my hand into rolling up the window. "You know too much."

"That's it, that's the problem. All right, what would work on Leah? Every relationship has its own logic. You have to anticipate. Imagine what Leah might be thinking about this. What's her position? Then assemble a plan that negates the objections."

Her position. At first this seemed unimaginable, then it all showed up in a rush. "She's incredibly angry," I said. "She has to

be. With one move I upended our lives in a completely nonnego-
tiable way. A new house, a new yard, the expanding future, and I
blow it all up. Smithereens."

Tim frowned. We crunched across the yard's gravel lot. "You're
right," he said as the zebra couch shifted loudly in the back.

I turned on the lights while Tim went straight to the computer.

"How about change?" he shouted across the office. "Can you
change? Become what she's always wanted?"

"Nope." I drifted to the mail crate and culled the thick copies
of *Maine Antique Digest*. "I'm too old. I was just fine a couple of
weeks ago. It's like I've been abducted by aliens."

"Or the alien has attached himself to you." I heard typing.
"There's always stalking. But that'll probably get you a summons.
Bomb her with flowers? Presents? Flat-out bribery? Think about
deals. Something *like* bribery."

"Bribery is not the proper foundation for a long-term—"

"Launch a campaign to change her perception of the situation?"

"Like last summer when I tried to convince her she liked
camping? That only drove her into the office for all of July."

"Convince her that life with Leo won't be half as bad as she
thinks."

"But it will," I said. "She's already thinking drudgery."

"Make it attractive drudgery."

"It's still drudgery. But less with two of us. So she signs on for
half of a complicated life? That's as good as it gets?"

"She gets you." Tim kept typing. "A promotional video?
Scenes of future bliss. Joyful moments on the playground? A big
montage."

"And we're so good at marketing." There were no new messages on the machine. "It's hard to see with all the customers in
here."

"You didn't check e-mail and you're not helping. How about
calling up to pour your heart out?"

"Thought about it, but she's screening me. Besides, I'm better at those when I'm drunk. Then I'd have to handle Leo with a hangover—"

"Grace could."

"Ah." In the next instant I almost told Tim about what happened, but the context didn't seem right. "Grace is going back to Pittsburgh."

"Oh," he said.

I came around and watched Tim Google things like "get my girlfriend back now." I couldn't look so I went back to the mail: National Grid, Citizens Bank, twenty percent off from Bed Bath & Beyond.

"You could go to the bookstore and haunt the how-to-make-people-love-you aisle," Tim said.

"At that point we're back to the male witch."

"Maybe the male witch isn't so bad?" By then Tim had found a guy who'd put a petition up on the Web to try and guilt his girlfriend into reconsidering. "He's got eight hundred ninety-seven signatures and it still hasn't worked. E-mail campaign? Spam her back into the niche? A blog? She'd read. She's a curious girl. Think of this as a new relationship? The seduction route? Plan a night she would never expect?"

"I'd have to get her to talk to me first."

"Play to your strengths."

"Leo negates all my strengths."

"Get a makeover."

"What list are you reading?"

"Five surefire steps to get the girl? Success is an aphrodisiac. Model your successful friends, that would be me. Hire a dating coach?"

"She'd only be cute and perky and tell me to work on my issues."

"Perform community service?"

"What?"

"It's on the list." Tim got up and went out to stand under the glowing cloud of chandeliers. "If she's furious, how can we unfurious her? What does Leah love? What can she not help herself in front of?"

"Truffles."

"Secrets," Tim said. "Leah can't stand secrets. You know that. Let's go to the shop and talk to Maggie."

"Let's not," I said. "I feel bad about Maggie. I barely see her."

"You two are never in the same spot. Come on, Maggie is wise. Since you've been gone Maggie is my new favorite person. We're guys. We can't think this shit up, by definition."

Tim tossed me the van keys. "Is this going to be one of those days we spend driving around?"

"Yep," he said.

The bell on the Wickenden Street door jingled and Maggie looked up from her book, smiling as if she had been waiting. Maybe she had. And Maggie knew everything. I guess I was aware that she knew about Leo and Cynthia, but she also knew that Leah had moved out, that I was in a tailspin, and Tim's version of my role in our big business-threatening fight. I suppose that was okay, I mean, I didn't know Maggie well, except that she was sly and funny and wildly resourceful and probably a good soul. She liked the shop because as a grad student she could get work done. The desk behind the counter now looked like a library carrel, stacked with books on nineteenth-century industrial architecture. Maggie pulled up the sleeves of her bright black ribbed sweater, the same black as her chin-length straight hair, and placed both arms on the top of the display case.

"Keeper has determined that he needs Leah back," Tim said. "We need a plan."

Maggie's palm slid under her chin. "I knew it would come to this."

"You did?" I asked.

She gave me a look as if I had interrupted something. "We can come up with a plan," she said, "but there's always the problem of timing."

The "we" surprised me. I don't know why, maybe because I still couldn't get around the idea that people actually wanted to help. Then timing, the notion of it, depressed me, again. I mean the mysteries of timing are at the heart of everything. It's the giant bewildering force at the center of the universe of all human interaction. Was the window closed or open? Closed, I thought. Closed in a way that no plan could unlock.

"Timing can be overcome," Maggie said. "Only you have to work at it. You have to decide that what you want already exists. That it has already happened. Some would call that lying, but how important is it to be slightly delusional in life?"

"Delusional," I said. "I can do delusional."

"Is Leah in love with Jon?" Maggie asked. "Actually?"

I watched Tim. I didn't want to know. I wondered if he knew something more, maybe from Julie. "Have you ever met Leah?" I asked.

"No," she said. "Does it matter?"

"I guess not." We needed ideas. Did I care where they came from?

"If she is," Maggie said, "you have to solve for that."

"Solve for." I didn't like the math aspect of this. I looked at Tim. "Can Julie spy?"

"That'll cost me. She's tough with the confidentiality stuff."

Maggie appeared to be watching something across the street. "In the best-case scenario she's having a knee-jerk reaction."

Knee-jerk. The temporary response that goes away. "Really?"

"I think you have to cloud the picture," she said. "To find out for sure."

"Cloud the picture how?" Tim asked.

"Distract her. Take her attention away from Jon. Find a way to lure her in. It's a workplace romance, those never work. A boss-partner rebound thing. The odds are actually in your favor."

"They do have a lot in common," I said. "The mystery of work."

"That can work against you," Tim said.

"Mystery secret admirer?" Maggie gave us an enigmatic smile.

I felt a gap in the air. The sun and moon grandfather clock in the corner started to chime. It was noon.

"Lure her with clues," Maggie said. "Every seduction is a journey. You move from one place to another. All busy romantic girls are dying to be distracted."

Then that deep voice popped up over my shoulder and said: *Leah likes puzzles.* "Yeah," I said. "Leah loves puzzles."

"A book of indulgences?" Maggie grinned.

Tim glanced at the clock, which kept on chiming. "But we still have to convince her that the prize is a good one. You get to spend the rest of your life parenting someone else's kid."

"Don't make that the prize," Maggie said. "Mystery secret admirer."

The chiming stopped. "Sounds like lunch," Tim said.

What was I supposed to do at noon? I felt for my back pocket and pulled out Leo's map. I knew he was going to ask me if I looked at it at lunch and I didn't want to have to lie about it. I flattened the thing against the counter. It was a series of bright green spirals, almost like a topographic map, except most of the lines intersected. At some of the crossings he'd put bright red smears that looked like flames. Along the bottom he'd made a light blue shape. He'd drawn LEO at the top in dark capital letters, only the E was backwards.

Maggie hummed. "What's that?"

"A map. Grace and I were supposed to open ours at noon. Only Leo wouldn't say why."

Everyone nodded as if this made perfect sense.

I stared at the concentric circles. I could feel the parts of something nearby, only they hadn't quite knit together.

TWENTY-ONE

Upstairs everyone was asleep and over in the living room something called *Haunted Lighthouses* rolled along on the Travel Channel, as I sat at the big dining room table zeroing in on my craft project. Yeah, I know, a craft project, but not just any craft project, a craft project destined by definition to change the course of current romantic disengagements.

Before me I had a freshly trimmed place mat–sized piece of gray foam core, found in Leah's stack of architect supplies, an X-Acto knife with an array of blades, a sheet of tracing paper, a purple glue stick, colored markers, green safety scissors, and a roll of silver ribbon. I had catalogs, *Design Within Reach, Title Nine Sports,* and a bunch of others. I had a stack of paint-chip cards for room colors I once nixed but Leah liked. I had magazines, gardening and travel ones, plus a few issues of *Sports Illustrated* I found in my neighbor's recycling bin. I should have been worried that Leah might recognize some of this stuff, thereby cancelling the mystery part of the mystery-secret-admirer equation. But right then I was more concerned with my dubious tracing skills, as I had to trace the outline of our yard from a landscape plan that Leah found in the box the owners left for us the day we moved in. Leah liked the plan. I remembered that much.

A tad desperate? But what choice did I have? I had to capture Leah's attention and I had no channels. I'd left messages on every phone I could think of (cell, work, Cecilia's, cell again). I'd sent the unnaturally perky "Let's Talk!" unanswered e-mail. I almost resorted to snail mail, but I couldn't find the stamps. I actually considered standing in the brick courtyard below Cecilia's fifth-floor loft yelling, "Leah" in a two-tone *Streetcar Named Desire*–inspired wail until it echoed off the windows. So there I was, tracing the plan of this house and its future garden with a black, micro-fine Uniball pen.

How did I get there? How does anybody get anywhere? This calamity pops up, the thing you'd never expect swoops in, and you're off on an entirely different ramp. Back at the shop Maggie kept saying "mystery secret admirer" like that was it, the whole solution, while I stared at Leo's topo map, sensing there was an idea there somewhere. Eventually I put the map in my pocket and forgot about it, while we argued over how much sushi to get from down the street. But on the way to pick up Leo I remembered wanting a connect-a-dot map of the Wilsons' travels and I thought about those branding slides and how the smoke and button-down cowboys and the tied-up calf made me think of some weddings I'd been to. I couldn't stop thinking about that.

When I picked up Leo Mrs. Green seemed happy to see me, but Leo said: "I want Gracie." We found her across the street, boiling water for pasta.

"Leo, honey," Grace said, kneeling down, her arms wide. "I opened my map at lunch, just like you said."

Leo shook off his red coat and waved. "It's too steamy."

"I did, too." I pulled mine from my pocket. "What's it a map of?"

Leo wrapped his arms around Grace's shoulder. "I so tired."

"Honey," Grace said, "tell me about my map."

"Oh sure, of course." He grabbed mine and clutched it like a steering wheel. "You can figure it," he said. "It's about going round and around." He pointed to the middle. "That's a garden. You get there." Then he folded the map, tore it in thirds, and carried the pieces to the dining room table.

"Leo, why'd you do that?" Grace said, sounding more annoyed than necessary.

Leo circled to the couch. "It's a puzzle," he said.

I stood at the table, flattening the pieces. A map *and* a puzzle. I could feel the idea, right there and about to stick, but it was time to get the plates out for dinner, so I carried everything over to the chair beneath the window.

Only later, sprawled across my too-big bed and staring at the ceiling, did I get it. I needed a map to get us back together. The words felt loud in my ear. I needed a map to show Leah the future, with us, only it had to be a map that ignored the fact of Leo. No, I thought, not a map, a puzzle. The puzzle of the future. The future is always puzzled together one wrong move at a time, isn't it? Leah has never been able to help herself in front of a puzzle. The puzzle of the future of love. I sat up.

Soon I was downstairs pacing the living room, thinking: A puzzle of what? A painting? A painting of the house? The yard and garden she'll never have if she doesn't come back? I remembered the landscape plan and went to find it. This was a fine plan, as far as I could tell, lots of raised beds, a flagstone patio, shrubs I couldn't identify. Then I made the big jump—to collage. You used to be a collage all-star, I reminded myself. It was elementary school, but still. That'll be the other side. I'll add in the places we'll go, the landscapes we'll see, a compendium of all the startlingly wonderful things that will never happen if Leah stays away. This will work, I told myself, heading outside in bare feet to search for magazines in my neighbor's recycling bins.

The bird's-eye drawing of the house and the yard turned out to be smaller than the piece of foam core, but that was okay. I centered it, leaving room around the edges for more pictures. Leo had a book, *Berlioz,* about a bear with a bass violin, where they did that. The main scenes were surrounded by smaller ones showing you everything that was happening offstage. Leo has lots of books about bears. I tried to imagine how far offstage Leah was right then. Only the moment I closed my eyes I saw Jon's curly, sandy-white hair, his hand waving, pointing to nothing as he took off his black-framed glasses and stood in front of a tan couch. That couldn't be. It was one in the morning. Everybody else in Rhode Island was asleep. Leah was, too, in the spare room at Cecilia's. I could feel it.

I started in on an old copy of *Travel & Leisure,* tearing out pages with pictures of things I liked—castles in Wales, San Antonio, ribs in Memphis, the Grand Ole Opry, until I remembered that wasn't the point. They had to be things Leah liked. So I found beaches, white sand, black sand, red sand beaches, old Europe, Vienna, Prague. I cut out the words "Best Kept Secret" from the cover of *National Geographic Traveler.* I found mountains and fields and the occasional horse. I located a few art deco skyscrapers and carefully trimmed three basketballs and a clear backboard from *Sports Illus- trated.* It's hard to trim with safety scissors but I had entered a zone. I kept thinking: If I do a really amazing job here Leah will think twice. I moved on to *Fine Gardening* and found lush vistas, a hidden wall with red vines. I snipped the Yo La Tengo ticket stub from my wallet into strips and glued them down around edges. That's what I liked. You could arrange everything, foreground and back, exactly the way you wanted. Why do people stop doing art? Why did I?

I finished the border, flipped the foam core over, and did the other side. I went back to the plan of the house and yard and drew curvy lines across it with a red maker, remembering to make enough notches so the pieces could in fact lock together. I started cutting. There were ten pieces in all and I tied each with a length of silver ribbon. I put them in a green box that used to hold my hiking boots and hid it on top of the refrigerator.

It was three-something in the morning. The Travel Channel had gone from a show called *Bigfootville* to *Haunted New England.* My shoulders ached but I climbed the stairs thinking about those pieces safe in the box. This is the exact thing, I thought. It has in- trigue *and* suspense. It's unstoppable.

————

still needed more coffee when Julie called Saturday morning to invite us all over for dinner. Grace declined, which was cool. Grace and I had somehow slipped to this other place, as if Thursday night's event never quite happened, or we couldn't quite remember. She had already offered to take Leo for the day, so I could have more hours at the yard, and she decided to drive back to Pittsburgh on Monday, a decision which seemed to leave her both resigned and a little upset. I told her to come back whenever she wanted to see Leo. Just show up, I said, which was a big step for me. We agreed that it wouldn't help to tell Leo she was going until just before. Even as I glued things down last night I knew Grace's departure counted as an actual deadline. With Grace gone when would I ever have time to think up anything?

That night Leo and I went to dinner. He seemed happy enough about it, given that I had to pry him away from his trains and agree to bring some engines (Thomas, Percy, and Gordon) along for the ride. In the knapsack I put a bottle of wine (Australian, white, $12), along with a cheese stick (round food), and extra sweatpants and underwear. I also brought the first puzzle piece, a corner, sealed in a quart-sized Ziploc bag. Just touching the bag made me nervous.

When I pulled up to the vast inclined parking in front of Cecilia's loft Leo asked why I was "driving all mixie." I didn't think I was and said so. He growled.

"Why are you growling?"

"I'm a bear."

I wove through the lot until I spotted Leah's black and glistening VW bug. It was a relief to find it and I got out feeling unnaturally calm. I gently lifted the driver's side wiper and slipped the bag under. I gave the glass a "Hello" tap with my knuckle. It felt like I was returning a book or a favorite CD. I got back in and said, "Leo, why are you a bear?"

Leo growled again and I wondered if he knew that Grace was leaving. As I pulled away the backs of my knees began to twitch and when I saw the Point Street Bridge the twist in my stomach reappeared, because leaving that bag under the wiper now felt like a completely irretrievable moment, the same as clicking "Send." But the declaration was away. I couldn't reel it back. I was no longer hiking the path of least resistance and that felt strange.

"This will work," I said as Leo showed his claws in the rearview mirror. He swiped the air. How did I get here? Driving through Providence with a troubled bear in a car seat?

"That was that boy's car," Leo said. "How come he's not here?"

"You mean Leah? Leah's a girl."

"Oh yeah, sure. How come she's not here?"

"We had a disagreement."

"Why?"

"That's complicated."

"Why?"

"It just is."

"I know," he said brightly, "she doesn't want to be friends anymore. Like in the grocery store when I had the carrots? You remember? At my old school you can't say you won't be friends."

"That's a good thing to say."

"Was it because of me?"

I shook my head. "No."

Leo clawed the window. "I think so."

"Not at all. No." I tapped the steering wheel. I was good. I did not say: Yes, of course it was you. You dropped in and blew the whole thing apart! You were the catalyst! I didn't say that. Good Keeper. By then we were halfway across the bridge.

Leo only began to get wary as we climbed the back stairs at Julie and Tim's. He kept asking if there would be kids or cats? I'd say no and he'd ask about toys. "Yep," I'd say. "Tim has old toys."

"What's an old toy?"

"An antique."

"Oh. Who's that?"

The kitchen smelled like garlic and something crackled on the stove. Julie seemed unnaturally happy to see us. I wondered if she was feeling bad about the awkwardness of Card Night, but that was my fault, mainly.

"Hey." She rubbed her hands on a silver-and-white-striped apron.

"Never seen you in an apron."

"I'm pretending it's Halloween." She slid her hair behind her ears.

Leo pulled my arm. "Is there going to be a pumpkin?"

"We're having this asparagus thing I found in the newspaper," Julie said. "Leo eats pasta, right? Mini penne?"

"Leo?" I asked. "Noodles? Tubes?"

Leo dropped to all fours, growled, and pawed the floor.

"Sometimes he's a bear," I said.

The asparagus smoked in the sauté pan and Julie went to turn it. "Being a bear makes a certain kind of sense," she said, "given the circumstances."

Leo stood and swiped at my knee. "What's a circum-dance?"

I put a hand in his curls but couldn't come up with a definition, so I aimed him through the arch into the dining room, thinking a get-acquainted tour might help. Leo wandered over and ran his fingers across the spaceship end tables on either side of where the zebra-striped couch used to be. I had to pick him up so he could see what was on the shelves. He took his time, squinting at the wind-up toy trucks from the 1930s, the stuffed songbirds, the patent models.

My arms were tired when Tim came downstairs. Inside of a minute he had the wind-up trucks out on the rug and Leo dropped down next to him. I went to open the wine and set the table and from there on it all went well. Leo sat atop the Yellow Pages and didn't mind that his food wasn't on his regular Cat-In-The-Hat plate. He even tried a piece of asparagus.

By default we started talking about work. Tim had found a toy train auction house in Connecticut and sent them the Lionel Hudson locomotive, still in its wrapper, plus the boxes and the rest of the rolling stock, yet another thing I'd meant to sort out. I knew the engine, which was both rare and mint, would sell. It's strange with trains. The inner and outer boxes can be worth as much or more than the pieces themselves sometimes. Everybody's searching for that perfect original thing.

When Leo got squirmy Tim set him up with a Noddy video. I didn't know about Noddy. He left Leo on a puffy red cushion right in front of the screen. Leo seemed pleased.

Tim sat back down. "Happy camper."

"You should try him here solo sometime," Julie said. "You could leave the car seat. We could do things."

"Really?" My shoulders went back. It might have been an overreaction but Grace was leaving in a day. "You'd do that?"

"Sure." Tim rubbed his palms. "Did you come up with a plan?"

Julie squinted. "A plan for what?"

"Keeper's getting Leah back," Tim said, as though I had just finalized my decision to buy a marked-down snowblower or to learn to play the mandolin.

Julie's mouth formed a small circle. She whistled faintly.

"I've got to. Failure is not an option."

"Not an option? Are you renting war movies again?" she asked. "*Band of Brothers*? Sounds like."

Tim gave me the enabling nod, so I went on with the unveiling. His hand kept rolling, all through the parts about the puzzle and the collage. His eyes widened as I talked, like I'd been able to get a clear look at the first pitch and hit it out with one swing. "See, when Leo tore up his map," I said, "I thought it's still a map but now it's a puzzle, too. The kid might have blown us apart but the puzzle will draw us together. That it's his idea has this weird symmetry."

Tim took off his glasses. "If you didn't have a plan I was ready to resort to buying 'Bring back the one you love' spells from real Wiccans on eBay."

"You can do that?" Julie finished her wine.

"But the Ziplocs," Tim said. "I never would have thought of

that. How about, put in a little something, a gift, a little indulgence, with each piece? A coupon for something? A perfume? That Chrysler Building pencil sharpener at the yard? Truffles? The other thing is, how soon do you want her to know it's you? You have to plan the order of the pieces so she has time to think. But you don't want her to go down that whole stalker path, either. Mystery secret admirer, stalker, it's a fine line. You should also set up another e-mail account so you'll have an avenue of cloaked communication."

"Were you in the CIA and forgot to tell me?" Julie asked.

Cloaked communication. The indulgence. Why didn't I think of this? These were huge loose ends. What the fuck was I doing?

Tim tapped Julie's wrist. "She'll be flattered, right? Intrigued?"

"It might creep her out that someone's thinking about this so much."

"It could?" This also hadn't occurred to me.

"How does it end?" Tim asked. "There's this big meeting, like Leah has to go somewhere special to find the last piece, it's her favorite restaurant, you're at Al Forno, you have this jaw-dropping meal and there in the salad—"

"This is all a little gimmicky," Julie said. "Isn't it?"

Gimmicky. I thought about the word. The long sound of it. I mean she had a point. Could any craft project really have this kind of incendiary, life-changing power? Sure. People do this with paintings and songs all the time, right? It certainly seemed possible last night. That was what, a few hours ago? Persuading anybody to do anything always involves some sort of gimmick. It's sales. That's all. I sat up and put my elbows on the table.

"Come on," Tim said and tapped Julie's shoulder. "We're guys. This is how we think. The big swooshy, slightly late declaration."

"That perfectly ignores the facts of the situation." She smiled.

"In this instance," Tim said, "the facts are not our friends."

Julie filled her glass. "How are you going to know if it's working?"

Tim hummed. "We might need help. We might need status reports."

Julie punched his shoulder. "You're not going to ask me to spy. Are you going to ask me to spy? You spy. You're her friend, too."

"I'm compromised," Tim said. "She'll figure it out. We're dealing with a clever girl."

"A clever girl under stress," Julie said. "I don't want to take sides."

Tim's head went at an angle. "No?"

Julie looked straight at me. It was a strange unfolding stare, one that began as a kind of naked appraisal and then softened. Maybe she had just recognized this as a moment where she could help shape the landscape of the people in her life. Maybe that's what I wanted to think. She sipped again. "Okay," she said. "I'm not a big Jon fan as it is. I never have been."

Tim stood up. "Whew. I was afraid we were going to end up back at the male witch. Or we'd have to pull out our remote viewing techniques."

"We have those?" I asked.

"I keep them at work. That's how I find stuff."

I smiled. I felt like toasting something, even if I had a feeling it was something slightly dubious and probably harder than I imagined to pull off, but first I had to fill my glass.

TWENTY-TWO

It's a strange thing, feeling completely unencumbered. I was at the yard and the rain wouldn't stop, but inside it all seemed surprisingly bright. The chandeliers twinkled and every song on shuffle play turned out to be a good one. Grace had taken Leo on a final outing, first to the Children's Museum and then to Acme on Brook Street to rent kid videos, leaving me with acres of time to whittle away at the height of my inbox. I had hours *and* minutes. I was also painfully aware that with Grace heading to Pittsburgh the next day, a Sunday afternoon like this might never pass my way again.

So what was I doing? Scouring my mind to come up with fresh ideas for tiny indulgences that I could attach to the puzzle pieces, which would then wear down Leah's wall of resistance and lure her back. I remained in the grip of the plan. My elbows and knees felt twitchy and I bounced all over the office, as if bouncing might help me think. The trinkets I'd located so far made a small mound at the end of the long oak table beside my desk. Leah has a thing for pens and I found a Pelikan 100 from around 1938, dark green with a silver band and cap. I saw one like it on eBay go for about four hundred dollars a while back. I also had a 1940s Bakelite bracelet, cream with black polka dots, an even older Bakelite bracelet made of mahjong tiles, plus a white and gauzy celluloid rhinestone bangle, all from a tray of estate sale things that Tim never sorted through. I found a Superball shaped like a globe—you could see the earth inside through the scrim of clouds; a beach rock with a black-and-white ring around the middle; a *Gone with the Wind* postcard, the big kiss in front of the fiery sky; an antique postcard of Boldt Castle in the Thousand Islands, which is close to Leah's parents' cottage; a silver Victorian fabric tape measure, embossed with the face of a cat that looks remarkably like Fred. It felt like Christmas shopping.

Of course, there were other objects that I didn't have but thought I needed: wasabi peas, a new chutney, a coupon, maybe for something like dessert at Gracie's, where I would present Leah with the final puzzle piece and we'd sort out the remaining details. That is how it would end, with Leah smiling after a shockingly good meal at her favorite restaurant. We'd talk through the forest of the future and decide that even with Leo we could manage. We'd kiss a little awkwardly across the table, stroll into the foggy night, and head up Washington Street to her car, shyly holding hands, as if we knew this was the way it was supposed to work out all along.

I stared at the pile. Is that enough? Enough for now, I thought, and placed each indulgence in the shoe box with the remaining puzzle pieces. But should every indulgence have a special meaning? A saying? Like the ones you find on those chalky candy valentine hearts? Be mine! No, let the objects stand for themselves. E-mail, I forgot to invent an e-mail account and I needed a back channel. So I went to Yahoo and clicked my hidden self into existence: loveanddeath11@yahoo.com, all inside of a minute. Why eleven? I've always liked the way that number looks the same coming or going. Plus, it's been mine forever, from back when I was six, playing hockey, and all through soccer. I printed up a sheet of the new e-mail address on tiny labels, so Leah wouldn't recognize my handwriting, and put them in the box.

It was almost four and if I was going to make it to the chocolate shop on Hope Street, the new one run by escaped Manhattan chocolate chefs, I had to go. I shut down the office and wedged the shoe box under my arm. The rain stopped and all the way up to the East Side I kept mulling the idea of truffles. Leah loves truffles. I could leave a bunch on her windshield with the next puzzle piece, but only if it stayed cold. Then again, if someone left a truffle on your windshield, would you eat it?

It all turned out to be moot, given that it was Sunday and, of course, the chocolate shop wasn't open. I kept on sliding down Hope, aiming for the Point Street Bridge. Then I veered over to South Main and drove past Leah's office, sort of thinking I might see her car.

There it was: LZ 707, up on the right by the Cable Car Cinema, almost as if I had conjured the thing into existence. I blinked a few times and pulled into an open space half a block ahead. Okay, she drove here and there's no bag on the windshield—she must have the first piece! My stomach did a small flip. I opened the shoe box and put the Pelikan pen in the bag with the next piece. I stuck a label with the e-mail address on the bag as my windshield started to fog.

Outside the cold air helped. Leah's office is across the street and down, two floors up on the back side of the building overlooking the river, so there was no way she'd see me. Still, I kept looking around, feeling like I was about to commit some great big act of vandalism. I slid the bag under the wiper and saw the first piece on the passenger seat. Good, I thought. We have contact.

Back in the car I felt suddenly calm. Maybe because this wasn't the first time I'd done this? Maybe because I'd expanded my comfort zone? I checked the mirror and realized that I could watch Leah's car from here. I could wait and see her reaction. But did I want that much information?

My cell went off and I jumped. It was Grace, asking if I'd left the yard? I said no, because I couldn't tell her what I was doing. Even after Tim and Julie basically approved the plan, explaining it to other people seemed entirely off-limits. It's so easy to talk a thing to death.

"I think Leo knows what's up," Grace said. "That I'm leaving.

He's been bearlike ever since we got home. We'd better figure out how we're telling him."

"Oh," I said. I closed my eyes. We hung up and when I glanced at the shoe box on the other seat I felt both silly and a little shady.

On the way home, for once, I wasn't only thinking about Leah, or the lack of Leah. For a few minutes I actually worried about Leo. It's true, things had been relatively smooth since Grace showed up. We'd had a lot less crying for Mommy, which still tore me apart every time, and better sleep at night, only as I drove down Narragansett along the bay, that all began to feel very fragile. Who was I kidding? It *was* fragile. He missed his mom. I missed his mom. How can you explain that to anyone? But these last days had at least been tolerable, mainly because of Grace. I was grateful and I'd never felt that about her before.

The snow piles kept on turning to slush and the mist thickened as I stopped in front of the house. Leo will be fine, I decided. This will be a smooth transition. Tomorrow they'll hug, we'll make plans to see Grace again, and Leo and I will live happily ever after. Leo and I. My shoulders shook.

As I opened the front door Leo threw a ruby-colored cloth ball trailing a yellow streamer at me from the top of the stairs. It bounced off my ear and I made a "Whaa?" sound before looking up to see Leo scamper away. He was barefoot, in black pants and a yellow Bob-the-Builder shirt.

"Leo?" Grace called from the dining room. "Finish your French fries or I'm eating them."

"O. Kay." But he didn't come down.

I took off my jacket and thumped it into the couch.

"Kids' meals," Grace said, sounding so businesslike. She had her feet up on Leo's chair, her red socks crossed. "Wendy's seemed like the right prize before we tell him." She rubbed her palms on a yellow paper napkin.

"Fine by me," I said. Grace smiled as though she had won a point. I almost told her how glad I was that she was here, then I remembered that we'd slept together and it all got instantly confusing. "He knows? The leaving part?"

"I thought so, but now I'm not so sure. Now thinking about going has me nervous." She waved at the kitchen. "I got you a chicken thing, but you should zap it first."

My hand looped through the air, I guess signifying the act of talking to Leo. "When are we . . ."

Leo came in swinging his ruby ball by the tail. "My new bear will eat this. It's a kids' meal toy." He grabbed the brown plastic grizzly bear from the table, today's present from the Children's Museum, I surmised.

"Honey, come here." Grace reached for his shoulders and centered him before her. "Tomorrow, I'm going back to Pittsburgh," she said. "I have to go back to be with my family. You're my family, too, but I need to see my boys."

"The big kids," Leo said.

"Yeah, they're almost grown-ups. I'll come back soon and I'll miss you and you can call me anytime, okay? But I want you to know that tomorrow, when Jimmy picks you up from across the street, I'm not going to be here."

Leo nodded solemnly. "Can I watch new Thomas?"

"Sure," I said and went to find the video. I had no idea Grace was going to tell him right then. I decided I could let it bother me or not.

"Can I watch with red-blankie?"

"Of course," I said.

"I'm a thousand days' tall," Leo told me. "It said so at the museum."

I pushed in the video and Leo positioned himself with red-blankie across his knees. He looked tiny and calm and I thought, that went well. I headed to the kitchen in search of my sandwich and Grace followed. She seemed puzzled. "That went okay," I said. "Didn't it?"

Grace pushed up her dark green sleeves and folded her arms.
"I don't think he got it," she said. She asked how things went at
the yard, which prompted me to lie about my time management
techniques. I asked how things went at the Children's Museum.
"Great," she said. "He likes the water room. You should remember that."

"Are you all right about going back?" I asked. On the one
hand I wasn't sure if this was any of my business, since I did not
want to slip into the tangled world of Grace and Tom. On the
other hand Grace looked sad and I probably already was wound
up in the world of Grace and Tom. "You can stay longer."

She frowned at the floor and I had another intense moment of
missing Cynthia. My knees felt thin and I had to lean against the
counter. I finally sat down on the radiator cover. Sometimes the
feeling hovers first and I can tell it's coming. Sometimes it just appears. This was all happening in the shadow of Cynthia. All of it.
Sometimes I'd forget.

Grace went back to the table and after a minute I got up and
started moving a flock of mugs from the sink to the dishwasher. It
helps to do things.

"It's okay," Grace said, bringing over Leo's plate. "Jonah called
this afternoon to ask when I was coming back. That kind of
snapped me out."

"It's fine to be away," I said. "It is."

"You know, I thought I could come here and fix things and,
your hands are full and all, but—" I got Grace's wise it-is-what-
it-is smile. "We only don't get along because we like each other.
You know that."

"Yeah," I said. "I've always known that. I'm glad you're here."

She smiled as if something amused her. "I need music," she
said. The Matt Flinner mandolin CD I just got in the mail was already in the boom box. She turned it on. After a few seconds she
said, "Leo isn't talking about Cynthia. I asked in the car. He says
she's still away and that he'll go see her on a plane. I'd almost
worry about it, but they handle these things in bursts."

"How do you know that?"

"I had kids? I read up?"

The in-between music before another Thomas episode pranced across from the living room. "Leo," I called out, "how are you doing?" I glanced at Grace. "Leo?"

"He's probably locked in. That kid needs his downtime."

I moved to the dining room but Leo wasn't on the couch. "Leo?" I went to the bottom of the stairs. "You up there?"

I felt it, that same itchy panic, just like before the time I threw Leo into the couch. Grace appeared at the edge of the living room. A second later I heard a grunt in the far corner and we found Leo behind the wingback chair with the red-blankie over his head.

"Are you hiding?" I asked. Of course he was.

Another grunt. I moved the chair away and this produced a growl. Leo swiped at my knee and red-blankie fell to his shoulders like a cape.

Grace hummed. "Leo, are you a bear?"

He roared and we stepped back. Grace ran into the kitchen, which triggered the bear's chase response. Only Leo stopped halfway and cried.

"I'm not talking to you." He pointed. "You leave me alone."

Grace sat on the floor with her back against the arch.

Leo ran up and punched her chest. "You said you'd stay forever."

"Honey, that hurt."

"I like it when you're here regular."

Grace's hands cupped his shoulders. "I'll come back. I will."

"Calvin says you're mean. Calvin says you're a house full of squirrels." He pointed at her nose. "You stay. That's regular. I like regular."

I somehow couldn't remember who Calvin was. "Who's Calvin?"

Grace said, to me: "Calvin's not real."

"He is too," Leo shouted. "You're hurting my feelings. Just because you can't see. Calvin does things better. He can skip. You're hurting his feelings." Leo stamped his foot. "I'm a bear. You call me that." He stamped on the top of Grace's knee.

"Ow," she said. "Leo."

When the phone rang I decided it would be Leah, only it was my mom. "If you're not going to call your mother," she said, in her pretending-to-be-fed-up voice. "We had an understanding."

"Hi, Mom." She asked about the noise in the background and I explained.

"Does Leo want to talk to me?"

Leo started to twirl. "I don't think so." He stopped to jump in place, moving into the fringes of a full-fledged tantrum. I went up to my room and settled in front of the computer. Mom wanted to know how we were doing? I turned on the monitor before I gave her the outline. I always do that when she calls. I'll be emptying the dishwasher, folding laundry, a little quiet multi-tasking never hurt anybody. Leah has to sit stoically on the couch when she's talking to her mom, as if being a statue were part of the deal. With the computer booted I gave in and went to Yahoo to check my new e-mail.

"Welcome, JK! You have 2 unread messages." The first was from Yahoo, the second from: lsil222@gmail.com. My chest felt tight. Leah has a new e-mail account. Even that worried me. The subject line said: "puzzled."

Mom told me some story about Mark and a boat and one of his kids and an iguana. I opened the message.

It said: "do i know you?"

I stood. I stepped back. But I didn't drop the phone. Do I know you? The words looked the same even across the room. I went closer and backed away. I couldn't believe it. This worked! Something actually worked! I left the message up on the screen and told Mom I couldn't talk because Leo was still having a tantrum. I headed for the stairs, but glanced back at the computer, somehow certain that I could now deal with anything.

Leo finally calmed down and as the hours piled up, through bathtime, more *Teletubbies,* Thomas, and a stack of Dr. Seuss, all I could think about was: How to answer? It never occurred to me that I would have to deal with this aspect of the plan. The options felt endless. I would only be talking to Leah, I had to keep reminding myself, but the pressure, I mean what if she figured out it was me and bolted before I had a chance to give her the entire puzzle? What if some phrase gave me away? But I had to answer. I could say: You used to know me but . . . I could answer with a poem, then I'd have to find one. Answer with a link? To what? A song? I'd have to get a link and the right song. Use emoticons? Bad idea. Leah hates emoticons. Be coy but sound like yourself? Yes, only by then I wasn't sure I knew what my self still sounded like.

Around midnight this is what I came up with: "I could tell you but where's the fun in that?" I gave it one last look. I hit "Send" and immediately wondered if it sounded too stalkerlike. Maybe, but it was gone. I unplugged the computer. Insurance, so I wouldn't spend all night checking e-mail.

How could I not imagine that the next day was going to suck? This is one of the problems that comes with a history of dogged optimism. You're always surprised. Of course, Leo was up that night, he had a bad dream about the couch, he needed saltines. Of course, we were downstairs at six in the morning to catch *Teletubbies*. Calvin came, too, and I had to give him a bowl of Honey Nut Cheerios. Leo wanted to know what happened to Calvin's blankie? I said, what blankie? Calvin's yellow blankie, Leo wailed. That led to a meltdown, which I solved with an Oreo, two actually, one for Calvin, which he didn't want, so Leo ate it. All this before Grace came down at eight.

Leo stared solemnly as Grace motored through the house, stuffing her things into paper grocery bags and then throwing those into the back of the Saab. I was distracted, half of the time looking for an opening to run upstairs, plug in the computer, and see if I had a response from Leah. But I resisted. And as the front door kept not closing, it also occurred to me that certain things here would be far easier once Grace left, the smoking issue, the kitchen clutter, the new-present-for-Leo every single day. Finally, after more coffee and Cheerios for everybody, Grace couldn't find her car keys, which a few minutes before she'd left on the stairs. Leo volunteered that Calvin had hid them in the sink, which he had. Another disaster narrowly averted.

At nine Leo wanted us both to drop him across the street, so we obliged. I told Mrs. Green what was up and she seemed sympathetic enough, though with Mrs. Green it could be hard to tell. Grace kissed Leo's hands so he could put them on his cheeks and remember her if he felt sad later on. We were back on my front steps when Leo waved to us from the window. He hopped off the radiator and his face disappeared. I gave Grace a hug. "Don't worry," she said, "you have a good heart," which got to me. I sat in the car after she drove off, thinking about that and feeling like a storm had just cleared.

Yes, the instant I got to the yard, of course I checked e-mail. No word. No word again seven minutes later or twenty-three minutes after that. It went on like this for hours, until a petite woman with bright white hair, who told me she had just finished her second round of chemo and needed a prize, came in looking for an eighteenth-century mantel. Luckily we had one that was the right size. It even fit into her minivan.

At lunch I thought if Leah's not going to e-mail back, I'm putting another piece on her car right now. So I went for a drive, only I couldn't find the car. It wasn't on the streets around her office or in the lot in back and it wasn't in the lot outside Cecilia's apartment. This brought a new ridge of panic. Maybe the plan was fatally flawed after all? Maybe I needed to hide the pieces in specific places so I wouldn't have to hunt all over Providence for Leah's car?

I eventually calmed down and got myself back to work, hoping that Tim would show up to keep me focused. He didn't and as soon as I turned on the computer the phone rang.

"He's growling," Mrs. Green said. "Tell me what's up with the growling."

"Sometimes he thinks he's a bear. Or he is a bear."

She paused. "Well, he could just be sad, but bear or not, he also doesn't quite seem to be himself. I'd think about picking him up early."

I looked at the three, green pre-1800 wineglasses I had to pack and wondered if we were still out of small bubble wrap. I stared at the 1930s slide projector with two slide reels of the 1939 New York World's Fair that was going to Sweden. "Okay," I said. "I'll get him."

But I didn't. I packed, I went to UPS and Shaw's because I knew I couldn't handle navigating the grocery store later on with a sad, cranky child. How wrong was that? I did pick up one of those Boboli pizza crusts, since Grace had promised Leo they could make pizza together. I needed to prove that we could do that, too.

Leo seemed a little subdued when I got there and Mrs. Green said, "He's still not himself." Fresh sadness will do that to you, I thought. Leo made me carry him across the street and his lower lip folded in once he realized that Grace really wasn't there. The house did feel empty. It surprised me to think that it might take time to get used to this, just the two of us, again.

"When's Gracie coming back?" Leo pounded my chest. "You call her."

"I will. I will."

"When?"

Leo had no interest in making pizza, so I set him up with a Thomas video. I had the crust out on top of the stove. We had sauce, we had pepperoni, we had shredded mozzarella. "Leo, do you want to see?"

"Carry me," he said.

I plucked him from the couch and he dragged his Cat-In-The-Hat doll along by the arm. I held him over the pizza. "There," I said.

Leo hummed. He slowly brought Sleeping Cat's arm to his nose, then he lurched and threw up over the whole thing. He got my arm, both thighs, Sleeping Cat, which he wouldn't let go of, the stove, the floor.

"Ohhhhhh." I held him out with both arms and did some kind of awful dance. "Ohhhhhhh no. Stop it."

Leo threw up again.

"Aw, help," I yelled. Then I realized I was yelling to an empty house.

"Wipe me," Leo shouted.

"I will," I shouted. It felt like we were at sea in a disabled boat.

"Sleeping Cat." Leo waved it in my face. It dripped. "Fix Sleeping Cat."

"I'll wash Sleeping Cat," I yelled. I put Leo down, grabbed the paper towels, and started wiping myself off. I can't do this, I thought. I can't do this alone.

Leo's hands went up. "Pick me."

"I'm trying," I said. "I really am trying."

TWENTY-THREE

If anybody asked I'd have told them that as day five in Mission Return Leah dawned, we were exactly on track. So when I hissed through Wednesday morning's slush on the Point Street Bridge, which has never been the quickest way to the yard, I wasn't at all surprised to see Leah's black bug a thousand yards away, across the river in the pay lot behind her building. I had a sense, by then. It's true, I couldn't find her car anywhere on Monday and I missed Tuesday's delivery completely, because Leo wasn't allowed back at daycare until I could prove he hadn't thrown up for twenty-four hours, which meant the kid had a home day. But the mission remained a go.

I looped back to South Water Street, pulled in at the curb, and there it was, LZ 707, parked at an angle up by the door to the Wild Colonial. I pulled the puzzle piece with the black polka dot Bakelite bracelet from the shoe box and got out. The parking hut girl scowled at me but I didn't care. I felt like the flower delivery man or a FedEx driver. This was my new role.

Tiny steam wisps rose from Leah's tires so I guessed she had just pulled in. I slipped the bag under the driver's side wiper and saw no other puzzle pieces on the passenger seat. Good, I thought. This is working. She must have them spread out on Cecilia's big glass table. She's intrigued and wondering what's next. When I started back to the car my only real worry was that just leaving puzzle pieces on Leah's windshield wasn't interesting enough. Maybe I needed to send the clues by e-mail and go back to thinking about placing pieces at romantically significant spots around town? Maybe I needed to make this a true treasure hunt?

I had my fingers on the wagon's door handle when two helicopters came up over the Point Street Bridge. They flew low along the river, right into downtown. It was only cloudy out, but the red one in front had a searchlight going, and the following one was shiny and black. The downwash left rings on the water. It looked like a chase scene from a movie or a thing I might see later on the news. Only I no longer watched the news, since it scared Leo. The helicopters climbed over College Hill and curved out of sight.

Someone called, "James," and I turned. Leah wasn't up on the third floor at an open office window, she was down at the door. She had on a ribbed, pale blue sweater and black pants. She waved. "James. Stop."

Fight or flight? I'm so obedient. I got in and started the car and turned off the radio, as if with that small distraction vanquished I'd make better decisions.

Leah held both elbows and ran to her car. I drove back over the Point Street Bridge and up the other side of the river. When I looked across Leah's parking space was empty. Think, what's the fastest way to I-95? Past the mall? Go. I bobbed and weaved to the ramp and up on the highway I felt somehow safe. There's no way she could have followed me. She wouldn't know where I was going. My knees stopped twitching right before the Branch Avenue exit. The plan's still fine, I decided. A close call, sure, but the mission survives.

Only as I veered to the off-ramp that other deep voice came up behind my ear: *She saw you—you idiot. You left the bag on her windshield while she watched. It wasn't like you randomly stopped behind her office to stare at the helicopters. And why are you running? Wasn't contact the point of all this?* No, I thought, not yet. She isn't supposed to know it's me until later.

I took a left up North Main and headed for the yard. Eventually

I felt a little better, as if I could decide that this whole episode just hadn't happened. I made the last left a mile later, casually glancing in the rearview mirror as I rolled past a stop sign and into a hubcap-deep puddle.

A round black car, LZ 707, right behind me, with the puzzle piece still on the windshield. I watched the bag cross the glass with the wiper and come back. She didn't even stop to take it off? I looked at the street again with just enough time to swerve into the yard's empty gravel lot.

Leah pulled up beside me. We got out. We were both breathing fast. You could see it swirling away.

"What are you doing?" She pulled the bag from under the wiper and shook it. "What the fuck are you doing?" Her bangs swayed. She had on the red-framed glasses. They started to fog. She still wasn't wearing a jacket.

I stood in front of my bumper, feeling more caught than ever in my life. I couldn't think of a thing to say. She looked great. "You look great," I said.

Leah frowned. She examined the bag and put her fingers around the polka dot bracelet. Her lips pursed as her thumb pressed in on the plastic. She wasn't wearing a bracelet. I hardly ever saw Leah without a bracelet.

"James." She hugged her arms and the bag left a damp mark by her elbow. "Why are you doing this?"

"I don't know," I said. "I miss you."

"You don't have to do this. You shouldn't do this."

"It makes my stomach hurt, that's how much I miss you."

Leah's hands slid up to her shoulders and I stepped back to unlock the glass doors to the yard. The lights made that snapping sound when I turned them on. Leah kicked the slush off her boots but didn't let go of her elbows.

"How'd you know I was coming here?" I asked.

"It's your work," she said. She waved the bag and it seemed to take in the whole space. "You go to work. I've been to where you work."

I backed up a bit and Leah followed me into the office. I turned on more lights. Lights seemed like a good idea. "Why are you mad?" I asked.

"Why are you doing this to me?" She shook the bag. "I feel awful enough about everything as it is."

"I'm not doing it to make you feel awful. Wait, you knew it was me?"

"Of course I knew. The e-mail gave it away."

I must have made a face. "How?"

"Love and death? It's in the address. It's the name of the store."

"Oh." How did I not think of that?

"Plus, I know your favorite number."

"You remembered my favorite number?"

"Of course I remembered your favorite number. James, come on. At first I was flattered, then I thought it was Jon, but he wouldn't think like this, then I started to think it was some creepy-icky person, like that one time, but it's you."

"You like to be wooed."

"Yeah, but," she leaned against the long table, "and I do miss you—"

"Then, then," I felt my hands rise, "that should do it."

She shook her head. "No," she said. "That can't do it."

I couldn't look away from the wet, unopened bag. How did I imagine this would make a difference? I felt that tingle in my legs, the one edged in nausea, right before you look out over the cliff edge.

Leah flipped the puzzle piece in her hand. "What's it a plan of? I figured out the collage, but what's the plan?"

"Nope." I wasn't going to answer. As if holding on to that little secret might keep the whole thing alive.

"The backyard?"

I shook my head. Rogue stubbornness felt like the only option.

Leah closed her eyes. She took her glasses off and put them back on. "Yeah, I'm flattered. I'm stunned, but it completely ignores the situation. If you felt this why didn't you say so when we were still in the same house? When you first found out about Leo? Why didn't you think about—"

"Because I was flattened," I said. "I couldn't."

Her head angled, as if she had forgotten something.

"It still counts," I said. "Even if it's late."

"But it doesn't change anything. It can't—"

"I just want you to—" I said, only the sentence felt so naked. "I wish I had more coffee."

Leah laughed. The sound shocked me. "I didn't get any either. Is there some here?"

"Ancient instant espresso," I said. "It might be decaf."

Her head dropped in mock sorrow. "Decaf never solves anything."

"How's work?" I asked. I knew this was a delaying tactic.

She shook me off. "James, wanting me back doesn't solve the problem and the reason we're not talking about the problem is that it's insoluble."

"No it's not," I said.

"I can't do the things we'd need to do to stay together."

"How do you know? We haven't tried. We had a few bad days, some bad days in a row. Kids are a mystery. You love a mystery."

Leah shook her head as if I might have stopped making sense a while ago. "Even if they are, I can't do that now. I don't want to. This hurts me, too."

I pointed at the bag. "But I'm wooing. I'm doing the woo."

"That's not it. We wouldn't be what we used to be. It'd be a disappointment. I'm not sure I'd be good at it and I'm afraid of what I'd turn into."

"What if you like it?"

"What if I can't handle it? All the worry that never goes away? The stress?"

"You'd get used to it?"

"I'd just start bossing you around and being awful. You're not acknowledging what life would be like. On a daily basis—"

"Of course, I'm not acknowledging it," I said. "I can't acknowledge it either. I'm just trying to get through the next twelve hours. I'm just trying to find the next day."

Leah examined the plan side of the puzzle piece. She spun it ninety degrees as if that might help her see where it could fit.

"Any second thoughts?" I asked. This, too, sounded pathetic.

She took a breath and held it. It looked like if there had been second thoughts she was never going to tell me now. She reached behind and her fingers found a sheet of bubble wrap. She popped a bubble. And another.

"I don't have that much left," I said.

"I like this kind. It's the big bubbles." She finally took the bracelet out of the bag and tried it on. "I liked the pen, too. What was next?"

"You could have waited to find out."

"You know, Tuesday, when there wasn't one, I thought about it all day." She closed her eyes as if she hadn't meant to say that. "Look, when it doesn't, when it stops being, when something forces you to go, it doesn't reflect on what you had."

"Forces? Come on, I'm begging. That's my knee down there." I pointed to the floor.

"The situation is forcing it."

"So, if I had been abducted by aliens, it would be the same thing?"

"Aliens wouldn't have been so bad. They could always bring you back."

"Then the way you're imagining it, how bad it's going to be, really outweighs . . ." I felt my arms going wide, taking in the entire space, ". . . this?"

"I'm not just imagining it," Leah said. "I've realized some things in this last bit. I'm kind of happy waking up with only my own thoughts." She crossed her toes. "I miss you but, where we were isn't there. It's been washed out."

"It's there. It's underneath."

She shook her head.

"Look," I said, "I think all we get here, on this planet, are moments and I want more with you. What if later—"

"How do I say this without sounding like a bigger bitch than I already feel like I am? I'm not going to decide anything later. Okay. One more thing I worry about? I worry that you just want me back as a way of dealing with Cynthia. I worry that part of you thinks if you hadn't left her this wouldn't have happened, but now that it has I'll be your bounce-back girl. You want to put us back together so you can rebound, which leaves me stepping in as the mom in a family that isn't mine and wasn't meant to be and I'm not sure I want."

"Not true. Not true." I stamped my foot. "You can't be the bounce-back girl because you were the girl before. The only girl. The roles don't change. You—you're it." My hands kept gliding around.

Leah looked tired, not pissed off, but tired. She popped another three bubbles. Then two more. "Is Grace still staying? How is it going?"

How is it going? The sentence draped in front of me. There were other routes I could have taken. I could have lied. I didn't have to her tell everything. I could have at least sanded the edges.

"Grace left on Monday. Then Leo got sad and sick and threw up. He's better now only he turns into a bear. Leo's invisible friend Calvin is here. So I have to give Calvin tours of the house anytime we hear a scary noise, and make sure he has a plate, since he only eats Oreos. Except he never finishes them so Leo does. We also can't find Calvin's blankie. It doesn't help that I've never seen Calvin's blankie, but I hear it's yellow. So sometimes I have a kid who turns into a bear. Sometimes I have a kid who has an invisible friend who makes as many demands as the visible kid. Sometimes I have a kid who has an invisible friend and an invisible bear. Sometimes I have a bear with an invisible friend, only I don't speak bear. And when I get it wrong, there's a meltdown. Ever try to clean up invisible kid throw-up? In a grocery store? With old people watching?"

Leah looked befuddled. I could almost see the gap in the air between us. "What the fuck did I just do?" I said. "Why did I say that? I'm a fucking idiot."

She took a deep breath. "No. You said that because that's what's going on. That's what you should have told me." Something behind her voice sounded pleased but I couldn't quite read it.

"I am so painfully in the present," I said. "Rory told me that's what kids do, they strand you in the present, only she says it's a blessing."

I stared out at the constellation of chandeliers and thought about how I nearly lost it at the grocery store when I saw this old guy with a fishing hat pushing the fire truck grocery cart, the one I needed for Leo and Calvin. What are you doing? I almost yelled. Give that back. You don't have any kids!

I looked down as Leah crossed her long fingers at the tips. I've been pulled through, I thought. It's a portal and I'm in a very different place. I want to go back but I can't. We were each leaning against the edge of the same table, but the three feet between us felt canyonlike. Maybe, I thought, she really can't get across.

"I, too, am painfully in the present," Leah said.

"Okay, how about two houses." I stood up straighter. "I read something in the *Times* about couples who do this. We get back together, one house has a kid, the other house, no kid."

She seemed nearly amused. Her bangs shook. "But I don't want that."

"It's a possible solution. It is."

"We are going to have to talk about the house. We don't have to do it today, but—"

"Talk about the house?" My head went back. Then everything sprawled away, flooding off in far wider directions than I ever imagined. This is where we are. Leah isn't coming back. The long disentanglement is under way. "Oh." I put my hand back on the table and my palm slid. "Oh."

Leah quickly looked at the door and I wondered if bringing up the house frightened her, too.

"What the fuck," I said. "We might as well talk about the house."

"No, it's too much." She glanced at her wrist but there wasn't a watch. "I have to get back. I have to come and pick up my stuff. Later this week I'll get a truck. Or someone with a truck. I'll call and do it when you're here. I might just move to Cecilia's."

I stared at the spot on the table where the collection of indulgences once sat. I saw an old Monopoly board piece, the silver roadster. I forgot to add that one in.

"Okay." Leah blinked and turned and went out the door with the Ziploc still in her hand.

TWENTY-FOUR

The rest of the morning went by in a jangly cloud. Every time I slowed down or stood still I felt like throwing up. I couldn't manage e-mail or start an invoice or look stuff up or pack. I could only pace and organize. I cleaned off a set of ladder-back chairs and put the mirrors in a different order. I straightened the racks of window sash and lined up all the ends. Then I started culling the shutters, because who buys shutters anyway? None of this even dulled the edge. Leah wasn't coming back. It wasn't going to happen. I'd get used to the news, eventually, but why couldn't she even try? I mean if you give it a shot and life turns out to be a train wreck, you clean up the debris and move on. But this, this is an amputation.

Like some radio station I couldn't reset I kept thinking if I'd only given her cooler indulgences or picked up more things on the list, like the truffles, then maybe. But she loved the pen and it still didn't work. Eventually I slipped over to thinking about Leah and Gary, and how Leah beamed out just when it looked like she had signed on to drive a minivan into the deepest suburbs. But you couldn't call this a preemptive break, since I'd already brought Leo home. A defensive break? But we bought a house together. That's as good as married for a ton of people I know.

The phone kept ringing so I put some Dead on the big speakers and let the machine take all calls. Then Tim came by at noon with subs and found me still in among the shutters. He gave me this look. I was too embarrassed to tell him about Leah. Of course, the plan was doomed. Tim had it right the first time, weeks back, when he said I should let Leah go. Of course, Leo was too big a deal. Leo was the thirty-one-pound Godzilla of deal breakers. How did I expect otherwise? But I did, I expected more. I thought Leah and I could be big enough to do this. Tim winced when I finally told him. "Look," he said, "if you had to twist her arm off at the start, how long was it going to last?"

We ate and talked shop. Tim wanted to know if I'd started to find buyers for those 1920s fishing reels he got a while ago. I hadn't. After an hour he headed back to Wickenden Street, just as a couple about my age came in. The guy had a beard and looked scientific and she was short with short blond hair and a very direct stare. They had a fresh downtown loft and a need for tall objects. I steered them toward the columns and said they should search at their leisure. I know, if I'd done the actual tour I could have sold something, but at least I remembered to smile. They wandered and I slumped into the rust-colored leather couch below the office windows. Leah and I made love there, once. I heard the woman say, "Thanks." The glass door jingled and I fell asleep. You can only do so much.

I managed to wake up in time to collect Leo. And on the way to daycare it did occur to me that it might not be entirely healthy to have a job where you can go whole afternoons without talking to anybody. At pickup Leo wrapped himself around my leg as Mrs. Green handed me a knotted plastic Shaw's bag holding another set of dirty sweatpants and undies.

"We've had better days," she said. "A little too much of being a bear. We took a swipe at another kid. We had an accident, since bears don't need to use a bathroom. You know all three-year-olds here are supposed to be toilet trained. We spent some time in time out."

"We did?" My hand went to Leo's head. He looked up. "No more being a bear at school. Leo, that's the rule."

"Oh sure," Leo said. "I forgot."

Mrs. Green put her hand on my shoulder. "We need to talk."

I nodded and ducked out to collect Leo's coat from his cubby. In no way did I feel up to an appointment with Mrs. Green.

Across the street I set Leo up on the couch with a Caillou tape and started constructing a stir-fry with boneless chicken, hoisin sauce, and red peppers. It's comfort food that I can make blind-folded. I'd chop a little and think about the house. I kept running through the list of projects we would never finish, like putting up those stamped-brass light fixtures I found for the pantry but never rewired. When I felt I could stand it I looked into the living room and started to imagine where the actual holes would be once Leah took her furniture. We'd have a table but no sofa. We'd lose the gray rug and everything on the walls. But I could borrow stuff from Wickenden Street. Maybe the zebra couch? Eventually it occurred to me that I would need to find a way to buy out Leah's half of the down payment and take over the mortgage, un-less she wanted the house. She might want the house. Then Leo and I would have to move, only I just got him here. And where was I going to get that kind of money? I could barely pay to send Leo across the street as it was.

I got stuck looking at the two-inch-deep pile of bills sitting on the counter, all in Leah's name, and my stomach did another twist. Not opening those had seemed like part of the plan, a move to ensure that this would all work out fine. But how would that go? Welcome back! Want some bills? Even if Leo and I stayed I'd still have to change the name on all the accounts. For some rea-son that alone felt insurmountable. How was it that Leah and I never got married but we're still getting divorced? I put down the knife. Maybe I was never really afraid of marrying Leah in the first place. Maybe this is what had me scared.

The luminous top of Leo's head appeared at my side. He stepped back and pointed to the cluster of sliced red peppers on the cutting board, Leah's cutting board. "Calvin doesn't like those."

"Calvin doesn't have to eat those."

"Give me Mommy's book."

"Mommy's book, please?" I'd stashed Cynthia's notebook on top of the refrigerator. I wasn't sure why. Leo carried the note-book off like a plate and came back a minute later. "What does that say?"

He had his fist on a paragraph Cynthia wrote back when Leo was two. "Things I'm going to miss: Leo's happy tiptoe dance with his belly sticking out. You come, too, he says that all the time. Swinging his arms before he sets off anywhere. His yes with the hiss at the end. There's this extra person in my thoughts who wasn't here before. It is like falling in love." I paraphrased since I didn't think I could read it aloud.

"I think Mommy's not coming back from flying that plane," Leo said.

I caught his shoulder as he started to spin. "But you're okay," I said. "You have me and Gracie will be back. You have red-blankie and Sleeping Cat. You have friends across the street. Right?"

"I like Miss Nicole, my teacher. And not that boy. He's not here."

"You mean Leah?"

"Yeah."

"No." I rubbed his cheek. "You know, I think Mommy can see you when she's flying." The words didn't exactly feel like a lie.

Leo put the crook of his elbow over his mouth and took it away. "But she doesn't talk to my phone. It's not working."

"She will." He watched me and I thought, day after day, I still don't know what to do here.

In the living room the tape ran out and the trumpets for the *NewsHour* on Channel 2 startled me. "Do you want Bob the Builder?" I asked, switching tapes before Leo could answer. The gang came up singing, "Can we fix it? Yes we can!" Another cruel myth.

I heard a growl in the kitchen, then a sound like a bright

waterfall, followed by a loose plastic thud. A bear had reached up
to claw down the five-pound tub of rice. The rice skittered across
the linoleum and into the corners, all the way to the dining room.

"Uh-oh," Leo said. "It did fall."

I leaned against the arch. I closed my eyes. Why couldn't I just
fold?

That night I had a hard time sleeping and in the morning I woke
up sad. I kept dreaming about Cynthia. We're always walking
when it happens, this time through a soft orange evening along
the bottom of Wickenden Street. We're leaving the Coffee Connection and she says: This is *good* iced tea. It's *peach*. We're looking
in the antique store windows and she stops to show me a tattoo
on the inside of her arm. It's a drawing of a sad plate, complete
with arms and legs, holding a lobster but bending down to pick
up a lemon. You know, she says, I was always in the weeds. I nodded. That's restaurant speak for being overwhelmed. When I sat
up I thought, why can't you tell me more? The question depressed
me. Then I remembered Leah. I fell back and the pillow hissed as
my head pressed in.

Leo got me up a few minutes later and we had what passed for
a normal morning: Cheerios, Teletubbies, Clifford, Caillou, and
Elmo. At a quarter to nine I asked if Calvin would be coming to
school, too?

Leo squinted at the space on the couch. "Calvin has a home
day."

"Oh good," I said. "He'll like that." For a second I thought,
having two kids isn't that much more work. Then I finished my
coffee.

At drop-off Nicole and I chatted about where to get the best
frozen ravioli until Mrs. Green floated over. "We are going to
have a good day," she said.

"Right," I said, trying out my helpful-parent voice. "The bears
are at home."

"Some things are home things and some things are school things." Mrs. Green tapped Leo's shoulder. "Leo, am I right?"

Leo scanned the room as if he couldn't quite remember how this all worked. I gave him an elbow squeeze and he ran to an open easel. He looked happy enough so I slipped out.

At the yard I was more or less able to function. I started in on the e-mail and wondered why I ever picked loveanddeath11 for my Yahoo account? Love and Death, of course, Leah would get it. Tim showed up and asked how it was going? I said, shitty. He gave me a perky look and said maybe I should think of this as a chance to reinvent myself.

"That's the problem," I said. "It's already happened. I've been reinvented and I don't like it."

He left me alone and the hours trundled away. I actually pared down some lists, then at noon Mrs. Green called. "Two things," she said. "There's been a power failure, so we're asking all the parents to pick up early. By that I mean now. Second, Leo bit someone."

"He what?" My kid is not a cannibal. My kid will not be a cannibal.

"We don't condone biting."

"Me either." It sounded like a point of pride. "Was he a bear when he bit?"

"You'd have to ask," she said. "But it doesn't matter. See you soon." I wondered if Mrs. Green's cheer quotient went up every time she talked to parents of difficult kids.

When I got there the whole neighborhood was without power. And since I clearly couldn't do anything with Leo at home, I took him back to the yard. He fell asleep up on the highway so I circled, killing time, as a twenty-minute nap would be better than no nap at all. At the yard I found Tim at the computer and Julie sitting on the leather couch in a dark jacket and skirt. I never saw her in work clothes.

"I don't even get to be a spy?" She showed me her palms. "This sucks."

"For once it turns out I don't need a spy," I said. Leo hugged my neck. "Stop," I said as he squeezed tighter.

"You left Calvin home," Leo said. "Alone."

"Calvin's fine. You didn't say he was supposed to come."

"He's home in the *dark*."

"Who's Calvin?" Tim asked.

I mouthed, "Imaginary."

"I had lots of friends like that," Tim said. "A little man who was supposed to live on a boat, but mostly he lived in my pocket. Had a beard. Sailed the world."

I asked Julie: "Did you have those?"

"I don't think so. I had siblings. I hear my mom all the time when she's not here. Does that count?"

"Only if she's a friend," I said.

"We've all got invisible folks," Tim said. "I used to have an imaginary stunt double in college who shouldered the blame every time I got drunk."

Julie picked her coat up off the couch. "I've got to go so my imaginary coworkers don't stage a revolt."

I sat Leo down at my desk and unzipped his lunch bag. He started in on the carrots and I asked him to tell me who he bit? He shook his head. When I asked again he put his hand over my mouth. What's the protocol here? Apologize to the victim's parents? Send a card?

Tim went to buy more bubble wrap while I zapped last night's leftovers and found a box of very old crayons and a roll of white paper. I told Leo to draw me a picture of Calvin.

"Sure, fine," he said. "I'll draw the invisible world."

This all worked for about an hour until Joan Blain, the white-haired woman who bought a mantel from us a few days before, showed up and wanted an exchange. The first mantel had a ridge on the back and wouldn't fit the space. I offered to sand down the ridge but she declined. We usually have about sixty mantels hanging on chains down past the doors, except I didn't know if we had another one the right size and age. You can slide them out to take a look, only if somebody bumps into the one on the end they all swing like dominos.

Tim and I carried the first mantel in from Joan's minivan. I convinced Leo to hold the door, which he did with utter solemnity. But as we stood talking about a replacement, Leo wrapped his arms around my leg and bit the side of my thigh. I picked him up. "How about drawing more of the invisible world?"

"I'm a bear," he said. "I'm bored." I put him down and he crawled off to the end of the row. Joan Blain seemed to think this was amusing. I got embarrassed. She was a real customer. We barely had any real customers.

I had my hand on top of a stripped white oak mantel that I thought was eighteenth century when Leo pushed the other end of the line. The mantels clunked. I heard the wave coming. I said, "Hey," only I left the little finger on my right hand, the hand I do everything with, hanging over the edge. It got caught.

A sliver shot of pain went through my palm, up my arm and past my elbow. I pulled my hand out, but it hurt so much I couldn't make a noise. I finally yelled, "Fuck!" as half of my hand went numb. "Fuck." I shook my arm and banged the finger on the chain. "Oh fuck." My knees kind of buckled. The finger bled and I cupped it in my left hand. There was a cut on the side and the pad of the finger looked flatter. I watched the swelling start, right between the knuckles. It turned bright pink and I thought: I'm in trouble. I need to go back in time. I need to go back now.

Tim and Joan huddled over my hand. A paper towel appeared. I wrapped it around but the throbbing kept on. It felt like I had a pair of pliers attached to the end of my finger.

"Let me see," Tim said as he unwrapped the paper towel. The finger had a distinct bend to the right. It had turned pale purple. "That's broken."

knew it was broken. I had hope but even as I kept thinking, this can't happen, I knew. We wrapped it in ice and Joan Blain, very nicely, gave me a ride up the hill to Miriam, the hospital with the nearest emergency room. Leo stayed with Tim, since I knew I couldn't handle a kid, a long wait, and a broken finger. They numbed the pinky and X-rayed it and even through the swelling saw the fracture. Bob Eastlake, the lanky, balding red-haired orthopedist with long careful fingers, lined it back up, which hurt more than I can explain. I got a prescription for Tylenol with codeine, some starter pills, and a purple fiberglass splint. Bob said to make an appointment for early next week and call if the pain got worse. In a few days they would probably take off the splint and tape the pinky to my ring finger, so it could still move. "In a case like this," he said, "immobilization gets you in almost more trouble."

"More?" I asked. "How can I get in more trouble?"

He seemed bemused. "Keep the wound clean."

They set me free. I meant to call Tim and ask for a ride, only I somehow decided to walk down the hill back to the yard. It was dumb, but at least I felt like I was in control of my destination. I had a block to go when my cell phone rang. "You still up there?" Tim asked. "Did they cut it off?"

"Still got the digit," I said. When I told him I was walking he said I was nuts. "It's the drugs," I told him. "They're refining my vision. I'm almost there."

"Good, because we're at our house. You should have walked over instead of down. I took your car, since I couldn't figure out how to unbuckle the car seat. Leo got hungry and I didn't know if the power was on at your place."

I stopped. "Is Leo okay?"

"Fine. He's fine. Get the van and come up. The keys are in the place. You can drive, right?"

"Probably." I folded up the phone.

Driving the van felt strange, like I had been assigned to pilot a spacecraft except I could only steer with one hand. The novelty of this kept me from getting even more depressed, but that wore off by the time I got to Tim and Julie's. My whole hand throbbed and I kept banging it on stuff, even soft things, like the arm of my jacket. Every time it happened I thought my pinky was going to pop off.

I found Leo smiling and eating frozen peas. "A new discovery," Julie said. Apparently there were power outages all across Providence and her office over in the Armory went down at three.

Leo seemed impressed by the splint, mainly that it was purple. He wanted to know if it would be on forever. "Like how Mommy's away?"

I shook my head and watched Tim order pizza, too foggy to think about toppings. I kept looking at my hand. Even with years of playing soccer, of being a goalie, I'd never broken a finger. I broke a rib, I wrecked a shoulder, but never this.

We ate and Leo wanted to know about the slide projector, so Tim turned out the lights and we watched the Wilsons wander the southwest. Leo did a tiptoe dance every time a new sunset covered the screen. He'd never seen pictures that big. After a while Tim said, "There's something strange about this. Isn't there one less kid?"

I kept watching and he seemed to be right. We saw lots of pictures with Karen, but never Stevie. Even through the codeine this upset me. I thought if they lost a kid, how could they keep going on vacation? "We should put on a different carousel," I said.

My cell went off. It was Mrs. Green, which threw me, since by this time she had to be calling from home. I felt like I'd already done something else wrong.

"We haven't had our meeting, which is why I'm calling. Is now a good time to talk?"

I looked at my hand. "I guess."

"In light of this morning, and I've discussed this with the other teachers, we need to consider if this center is the best solution for your son."

"Consider what?"

"I can't have aggressive behavior. I can't have biting. Bears don't listen because they don't speak English and—"

"Wait." I held up my hand. "You don't know what's happened."

I heard Mrs. Green's TV in the background. It sounded like CNN. "I'm aware of some of it," she said. "His aunt said you're—relatively new to this, but, I have a center to run."

I walked to the kitchen. I didn't want Leo listening to this, but I also couldn't quite fit the parts together. "Yeah, yeah," I said, "I have a job to run, too, and I have a kid to take care of and—"

"Are you all right?"

"No, I am not all right. I have a broken bone. Can we—"

"Whether a child stays enrolled has always been at the director's discretion."

"Enrolled? You're kicking him out?"

"As of now, I think we need a change. I don't do this lightly. I only do it rarely."

"You can't. He's happy there. I'll have to make other arrangements. I just broke my finger."

"He just can't stay."

"A week, can I have a week?"

I heard the TV again. It was CNN. "Yes."

It felt like I'd won something, but I was pretty sure this would all get worse later. "Did the power come back on? We haven't been home."

"It's on in Warwick, at my house," she said brightly. "I think it came back later in the afternoon. Have a good evening."

I pushed "End" and stared at the phone. I'd been staring at a lot of phones in the last few weeks.

I came back out and watched the mountains of New Mexico pass by. The new carousel was one I'd already seen, back on the zebra couch with Leah. After a few minutes Leo said he wanted to see something else and Tim found the Noddy video. Julie came over to ask who was on the phone and I couldn't tell her. I mean my kid had just been kicked out of daycare for being a bear. How could I do this without daycare? I shook my head and felt it coming up, that stupid way I get where I decide that from now on I'll have to do everything all by myself.

At 8:08, I realized that Leo had to go to bed at some point. Then my hand started to throb. The end of my pinky felt tender, like a balloon, and I began to recognize the scope of things it was going to be impossible to do: carry Leo, find anything in my pockets, wear gloves.

We said good night and Leo kept bouncing, even in the car seat. This had been a big day for him. I also managed not to look back and say: Kid, you broke my fucking finger. Good Keeper. At home we found a tall white box on the front step with Leo's name on it. Grace had sent it overnight. It was a set of tuned bright plastic tubes that rang in different pitches when you hit things with them. Leo took an F and a C and pounded a two-note Philip Glass medley on the stairs. At the bottom of the box I found a clear inflatable ball, covered with glow-in-the-dark stars. I blew it up and we played soccer in the living room.

"In soccer you can't use your feet," Leo announced.

"You can use your feet but you can't use your hands unless you're a goalie."

"But your hand's broken."

Leo wanted to make the stars glow so we held the ball under a lamp and turned out the lights only it didn't work. He wanted to try it outside and I said sure. We walked out to the gently sloping concrete driveway.

He held the ball up to the purple sky. "It's still not working," Leo said. He handed it to me and ran down the driveway. "You kick."

I placed the ball on the wet cement and kicked harder than I needed to. The ball hooked right, beyond Leo's reach, and he spun trying to catch up. It bounced once and floated toward the sidewalk. "I'll get that," Leo said. He ran.

Headlights grazed the corner of the pale yellow house across the street. "Leo," I said, and the ball meandered drunkenly on. Leo reached the sidewalk as I saw the car, a silver Crown Victoria station wagon from the eighties. I saw Leo's silhouette. His hands rose over his head.

"Leo," I shouted.

The car stopped as if the driver had heard me. I threw my arm around Leo's middle and pulled back. "Leo." I felt like shaking him.

The driver had his window down. I smelled cigarettes but couldn't see a face. A low voice said, "Good save," and the car continued on.

"Leo, what the fuck. You can't run, you can never run into—"

"I didn't. I stopped." He hit my shoulder. It was true, he did stop.

I sat on the wet sidewalk, pulled him down, and hugged him, then harder. That was all my fault. I put the kid at the wrong end of the driveway. I didn't think. I wasn't used to thinking that way, but I didn't think.

Leo pushed at my shoulders and I wouldn't let go. "I tired," he said and I felt his arms relax around my neck.

And right then I gave up. I gave up on Leah. I pressed my nose into Leo's hair and thought: This is where I am. I can't do anything about Leah. I can't make it happen, so I have to fold. For a second it felt like falling, then I realized I was already on the ground.

TWENTY-FIVE

How could a broken finger clear my mind? Can the pain of the present really wipe out the worry of the future? That's what seemed to have happened. Or maybe it was letting go of Leah and the idea of that particular future. I don't know. I don't understand the whys of timing and how the river of events actually moves. I'm willing to think a lot of this is random, but sometimes it feels like there must be reasons, just the way you can look at a forest and never see all the math hidden in the trees.

I was still a wreck. Whenever I raised my eyes to check, the landscape looked newly lonely in a vast, future-flattening way. It appeared to be an endless plateau, one I knew I'd be walking for a long time, so it made a kind of sense to get used to the view. Then there were other moments where I felt cleaned out, taller, as if my posture had improved overnight.

Yes, the finger hurt, a ceaseless throb that produced a big zeppelin of caution every time I thought about moving my arm. It felt like I had a furniture clamp stuck to my fingernail and the ache kept me awake most of Thursday night. Leah would have made me call in for better pain drugs, but I didn't. In the morning I managed to get Leo over to daycare at the regular time and without coffee. I hadn't told him that next week would be his last. I wasn't sure when I would. At drop-off even seeing the white back of Mrs. Green's head made me want to punch something. It was a strange ferocious anger that just welled up. I got home, did some more Tylenol with codeine, and burrowed back into bed.

I emerged around noon and made my way to work. The yard stayed quiet and I pared down a few lists as the hours floated past. When I went to pick up Leo at four, Mrs. Green was gone and as far as I could tell the kid hadn't bitten anybody new. We walked to Lindsay's for milk and donuts and smoked turkey, only when we came back I found my mom's deep blue Jeep Wagoneer parked aggressively across the sidewalk.

Leo stopped at the curb. "Whose is that?"

"Your grandma's."

"That not Joan's car."

"No, your other grandma."

Leo wanted me to pick him up, only I couldn't do that and still hold the grocery bag. He stamped into a puddle so I tried to instigate a race up the steps. Mom's puffy blue coat covered the end of the couch like a cape. I spotted a white cooler on the dining room table and found her in the kitchen, leaning against the stove while she talked on the phone.

"It's Grace," she said, covering the mouthpiece. "Jimmy, your front door was open. Well, unlocked."

My mom talking to Grace. My shoulders did a little shudder. It made me nervous. I wasn't sure why.

"Gracie?" Leo ran to stand in front of Mom.

"We'll talk more later," Mom said. "You have my number. Yes, I know. Here's the little man." She gave Leo the phone.

"I'm a kid," Leo said.

It was a strange tableau, my Mom handing the phone to her grandson so he could talk to his aunt, a configuration that weeks ago was entirely unimaginable. "How come no one in this family ever calls ahead?" I asked.

"A sense of surprise in life is nice." Mom smiled. "I always quite liked Grace." She pointed as Leo ran by and passed me the phone.

Grace was only checking in, which I appreciated. I didn't tell her about giving up on Leah or about Mrs. Green, but I did tell her about my finger. When I asked how things were she said, "quiet," and sounded pleased. We didn't say much more.

"Why are you here?" I asked as I handed Mom the phone.

"Because you broke your finger," she said. "Tim called."

I stared at the purple splint as if it were a new development. I took it off and showed her the finger. I told the story, prognosis and all.

"Are you getting enough pain relief?" she asked. "Pain relief is crucial."

"I don't think there's ever enough pain relief."

"Well, I brought dinner. Several dinners actually. I thought I might stay over and tomorrow take Leo to the Children's Museum."

Leo ran back in. "I *always* go to the Children's Museum."

"Oh." Mom started opening cupboards. "How about a snack?" She handed Leo a full box of Wheat Thins.

"Mom, he won't eat those, they're square." Leo stuck his hand in and took some anyway.

Mom stared at me. It was almost a frown. "You can thaw, right?"

I really was glad to see her. "Yes," I said. "I have the capacity."

"I know you have the capacity. You have a lot of capacities. Many more than you think."

I turned to watch Leo rolling across the couch with his red-blankie as he watched Thomas, and thought, maybe I do. It wasn't a bad moment.

After dinner (a pasta casserole with meatballs and three kinds of cheese), I told Mom about Mrs. Green and the biting. Mom said the biting would stop, that there had to be other daycare centers and she could come down to cover the gaps if I needed it. This amazed me. Then every time I thought about Mrs. Green a new gust of anger would ride in. "How can I get that mad at her?" I said and got up to clear the table.

"This changes you." Mom pointed over at Leo, just as he crawled off the couch and moved his face right up to the screen. He put his hands over Thomas' eyes. "He's your kid," she said, "and someone is trying to make his life more difficult. Of course it makes you—it makes your heart bigger. It sounds strange to say but . . ."

I looked at the empty plate in my hand and thought, if that can happen to me why can't it happen to Leah? Only the idea felt dangerous, so I buried it.

Mom's advice? Talk to Mrs. Green. Tell the story. It might not work, but you'll feel better for trying. And I thought, okay.

That night I had a new dream about Cynthia. This time we're walking in a dusky pine forest from one trail to another or maybe from a campfire back to her brother's tiny cottage at the camp in New Hampshire. She's ahead of me, her hair floating a little, when she turns and brings a set of claws to her face. "Of course, he's a bear," she says. "Wouldn't you be?" She reaches out to punch my arm.

Mom slept on the couch. When I came down she and Leo were already painting and she had made pancakes. Leo went back to cutting his in half and calling them "half rounds." I hadn't even finished my coffee when Rory called to say that Leo and I were coming over on Sunday for a breakfast playdate. I stared at the phone when we were done.

"If the boy's not up for the Children's Museum," Mom said, as Leo shook his head, "I'd better get back to see what your father has to say. Though I probably already know what your father has to say."

"I'll see you again," Leo said. "We'll do that painting."

"Yes," Mom said. "Yes, yes, yes."

She left and a few minutes later Tim and Julie came by. They wanted to take Leo for the day. I couldn't quite believe that either, but Leo seemed intrigued and Julie insisted. Tim said, "You can collect him when you have dinner at our house."

"Why'd you call my mom about my finger?" I asked.

"Keeper, you wouldn't ask for help if your shirt was on fire. You'd still be standing there trying to get the buttons undone."

At that moment the house felt very full. It seemed odd. I gave up on Leah and people moved in to fill the space.

Later, on the way to Tim and Julie's, I kept worrying about Leo's nap and how bad things would be if he didn't get one, only I found him sitting happily at their dining room table, holding a paintbrush. He was surrounded by big blue paintings and had apparently been at it for a long time. There were also lots of marker drawings that might have been maps and others covered with different colors of masking tape. He seemed happy.

"We did great," Julie said. "Calvin was here for a while but he had to do errands. Leo napped on the couch. He's a portable kid."

"He's portable?" I said. "I guess."

Tim got all the way upstairs before I could make it out of my coat. They had ordered Indian food and this time I at least remembered to chip in. I kept trying to unwrap the naan with one hand when Tim said: "I have two thoughts."

Julie crumpled the black and gold plastic bag. "Only two?"

"We should close the Wickenden Street store."

I felt my eyebrows going down. "We should?"

"Yeah," Tim said. "It'd be one less rent. We could have all the stuff in the same spot. There won't be as many weekends to cover and Maggie thinks it's a great idea."

"You've decided this?"

"Well, I'm talking to you about it now."

"What about our foot traffic?"

"What foot traffic? We have a lot of footprints going past the door."

Weeks ago I would have been annoyed. Closing the store was a big decision and this wasn't the way we made those. I would have picked a fight about the process. Yet this could make my life easier. "It means reorganizing the yard," I said.

Tim nodded. "We should do it soon." And that was it.

At dinner we got stuck on the Wilsons and how now there really did seem to be one less kid. "I skipped ahead," Tim said. "It's strange. But if they lost a kid, don't you think they'd go home? Cut the vacation short?"

"I thought that, too," I said. "But if they lost a kid—it's too sad. I don't even want to think about it."

"We might be only imagining it," Julie said. "Maybe they left him with somebody. Or it's the order of the slides and that's the story we're inventing?"

"Did Leah ever call to get her stuff?" Tim asked.

"No," I said. "It'll happen when it happens. That's my new stance." The words felt funny, but true.

Julie gave Tim a sideways glance, as if she was about to say something but changed her mind. "Leo had fun today," she said. "You should bring him by tomorrow, after Rory's. I'm not doing anything. You could use the afternoon. Tim found a racetrack."

"Hot Wheels," he said. "Vintage. It was in the basement at the shop."

"Why are you guys doing this?"

They looked at each other as if they couldn't remember who was supposed to answer first. "We like your kid?" Julie said.

Tim waved his fork. "Keeper, you need help and we're your friends. He's your kid so we're your kid's friends by definition."

"I think his real friends are shorter," I said.

"He needs a bigger net," Julie said. "We can take him some on weekends, be around."

I put down the last piece of garlic naan. Of course, they were right. Of course, I needed help. Of course, I was never going to ask. "I'm really bad at asking for help, aren't I?"

They laughed and Leo came over to stand under the arch. I realized that ever since Leo appeared it felt like the world had been getting smaller and smaller and that it would simply keep on getting smaller until the day it all folded in on itself and I finally left the planet. But right then it seemed to actually be expanding.

"What's up with Mrs. Green?" Tim asked. "What are you going to do?"

"Do," I said. "I don't know. It still feels like I need to punch somebody out. I don't have time to find a new place for Leo. He's happy there."

"It's just ridiculous," Julie said. "It's ridiculous of her to do something this drastic without talking to you. It's like you had the rug pulled out."

"Talk to her," Tim said. "It's hard to imagine someone would go ahead with this if they knew the story. At the very least you can make her feel bad. Make her lose some sleep."

The sleep angle appealed to me. It was a weird moment. I had to stick up for my kid. I knew that. I had to come up with a plan, a speech. I was a different person in a very different spot.

In the car on the way home Leo kept talking about the invisible world. He told me it was blue and you could draw planes "very many ways."

"Where'd you get all the tape?" I asked. "How'd you think of that?"

"Oh sure, that boy came. We used tape. Tape holds anything together."

I wasn't paying attention. I was too busy worrying about Mrs. Green.

Of course, they were right. How could I let my kid get kicked out of daycare for being a bear? That's the sign of an authentic and active imagination. So on Monday, day one of our last week, I caught Mrs. Green at drop-off. Could we meet, I asked, and she said, "Today? At three," as if we did this all the time.

When I got to the yard I decided to have a normal day, only

that kept not happening. I couldn't stop winding myself up and polishing my armor. At three I found Mrs. Green laughing with a blond, earthy-groovy-looking mom by the front door. The mom touched Mrs. Green's arm. "Sunday?" she said. I thought, how could you touch Mrs. Green's arm? How could anybody?

Mrs. Green's expression faded when she saw me. "Oh," she said, "let's go in back." I followed her to what I always assumed was her office, but it turned out to be just a desk in a small room with a stacked washer and dryer in the corner. There were two computers and kid paintings and calendars on the walls. I took one of the two straight-backed seats across from her. It felt like I was about to open a dialogue with an astute predatory bird.

"What was it we wanted to talk about?" Mrs. Green asked.

"Leo," I said. "I fail to see how with no warning whatsoever you can decide to kick a kid, to uproot—"

Her long hands rose. "You can stop right now. Have you read the handbook?"

"I never got a handbook."

"I gave one to his aunt. I know I did."

"His aunt loses things."

"It's one of the conditions you agreed to. At the center's option . . ."

I stared at the white washer-dryer. "I'm going to tell you the other conditions," I said. "I'm going to tell the story and if you get tired of it, you can go out and do more daycare things, but I'll still be here talking."

Mrs. Green tilted her head as if she had never met someone like me. "Close the door," she said. "Please."

"I need help," I said. "I'm shitty at telling people that, but here's why I need help." I did the big download: the story of Cynthia, me and Leah, how I got Leo and lost Leah. It felt strange and naked but in the middle I realized I didn't care. All I cared about was making this one thing easier for the kid.

Mrs. Green's index finger pressed against her lips. She watched the screensaver on the nearest computer, a waving field of daisies, and sighed. "Let's start over," she said. "Can you call me Dolores? The children call me Mrs. Green, then the parents start, and, you know, it turns out to be my name."

"Some people call me Keeper," I said. "Some, Jimmy. It depends."

"I like Jimmy." The phone rang. She pushed a button and it stopped. "Jimmy, I don't think you understand. I love kids. I do. That's why I do this. It's not the money, god no. They're fascinating and—do you know what the saddest thing is? When they leave. I've seen these kids every day almost, for years, and then they go to another school and disappear out of your life. That's the hardest thing. I think you and I, you're always picking up and dropping off so quickly. At first you seemed annoyed at having to be here. I think we got off on the wrong foot."

"Maybe," I said.

She floated her hand across as if the story were still draped before us. "Now the rest of it, I never knew. I had only the barest details from—Grace?"

"Grace."

"I wish I had known. I can tell you that Leo is a very resilient child. I'm amazed at how resilient, knowing all of this. He has a tremendous vocabulary. He wants to do everything for himself, lots of kids do, but it's different with him. He gets frustrated but he bounces back. He has friends, Julian and Alex and Miranda, mostly, his favorite area is art—"

"What do you make of Calvin?"

"I don't see that much of Calvin, but Calvin makes sense. Calvin is reliable. Calvin does what you tell him to. He doesn't go away."

"Why does he want to be a bear?"

"Why do you think?"

"Because his mom died and he's pissed as hell and I moved him."

Dolores took a long breath. "Sometimes they don't want to show grief because it upsets the people around them, like you. Or

it scares them. Sometimes they think they are much more power-
ful than they really are." She stared across. I could see her coming
up to the ridge of a decision and dropping over. "Okay," she said.
"What can we do?"

The question stunned me. I took a breath. I told myself to
think, to remember the script. "What if he wears pull-ups during
the day?"

"That would help."

"The biting?" I said.

"If he bites he goes home? Would you go along with that?"

"That could work in his favor," I said. "One good chomp and
he'd be on the couch watching videos."

"Biting means no screen time?"

"Sure. The bear stuff. How about he can only be a bear before
school and at home?"

"Make it a part of the routine," she said. "Mostly he gets aggressive when he's tired or sad. If we can't head it off I'll call and
you'll get him? Right away?"

"Yes."

"There's also, and this has worked before, we can make a
mommy book and a book for his aunt, a book for you, with pictures and drawings. Or we can put them all in one book and
when Leo's feeling sad or angry he can go to the rug and look at
those."

"That sounds fine."

"I don't want to pull him out. You need to believe me. He is
part of the tribe, already, and he hasn't been here long. You're
lucky to have this child."

A strange prickle crossed my neck.

"Have you talked to his pediatrician?"

I had to swallow, twice. "His pediatrician is in Boston."

"I have names of ones here. They know counselors. It might
be—"

"A good idea," I said.

"We'll talk," she said and the phone rang.

I slipped out to find Leo. My neck and arms felt clammy, probably from having to bare the bones of my life and fuck-ups just to keep a kid in daycare. But I didn't care. I got a deal. I closed with Mrs. Green. I stopped and watched as Leo painted. More blue.

We got home and I was about to close the front door when a maroon and silver van pulled up. It was one of those conversion vans with a picture window in the side and a ladder to the roof.

The passenger door opened and I saw the paws of a very large orange cat covering the knees of a thin woman's black jeans. The cat slowly stood, as if he'd had enough driving for one day, and leapt off the woman's lap. He perched on the running board and leapt again. He scowled at me from the street and climbed the steps. I held open the storm door, like I'd done so many times before. This is Leah's dream, I thought, the one where Fred can drive, only this is the end of it.

Leo froze. "Cat, cat," he shouted and pushed past me to run upstairs.

It was Fred. Twenty-seven pounds of Fred. I couldn't stop staring. The signs in the village were still up, but by this point I didn't think it could matter. Fred regarded the space where Leo used to stand. He gave me a mildly bored look and ambled to the end of the couch. His tail switched twice and he clambered up. When I touched the top of his head he purred as if nothing had happened.

TWENTY-SIX

I couldn't find Leah. I called her cell and Cecilia's apartment and left messages. I called her office and some guy said she was supposed to go to North Carolina but didn't, so at least I knew she was still in the state. I left a message with Tim and Julie and thought who else would know? Jon. I could look up the number. No, I couldn't. Fred might have returned but I would not call Jon.

The giant orange cat stared at me from the dented couch cushion. You're supposed to forget Leah, I told myself. That's your job and forgetting takes distance. You need to find some distance. You could pretend this hasn't happened. You could call the SPCA and tell them a strange beast has wandered into the house and, given the circumstances, no one would think that badly of you. At this, Fred jumped down and head-butted the front door. I opened it. He could have gone out and never returned. I could have helped. I could have been an asshole. Instead, Fred sniffed once, climbed back to the couch, and began to snore.

Leo stayed curled up on the stairs through all of this. I finally carried him back down and he watched videos at an angle from the safety of the dining room while I invented dinner. The problem was if Leo had to go past the couch, say up to the bathroom, I had to carry him, which got old fast, given that I only had one functional hand. After dinner Fred still hadn't moved. I eventually got the kid up and into bed, only Leo made me leave a large bowl of ice cubes in front of his door, since cats hate cold water, and this would protect him from Fred.

Later I rediscovered the bags of Fred's food in the cellar. There was even a clean cat box down there. I hauled up a new bag. "Hungry?" I asked. Fred squinted as if he'd been expecting something in a can. "Big guy, cat box down there if you need it." He blinked slowly, the eternal sign of love.

That night I had a hard time sleeping. No new Cynthia dreams but I kept hearing Fred, thumping down to the floor after a fresh tour of the windowsills. The house seemed small.

The next morning at Wickenden Street I had just opened an e-mail from that toy train auction house in Connecticut explaining that the Hudson locomotive had sold for $11,200 to a collector in Manhattan. I kept rolling the syllables, eleven-thousand-two-hundred, across my tongue. Then Julie called my cell. "Leah's in the hospital," she said.

"Say again?" I put down my coffee. The light across the street, the Hard Boiled Jazz show on WRIU, just like the morning I got the call from Cynthia's mom.

"She's at Miriam."

"Why is she in the hospital?"

"Her knee. She wrecked her knee."

I heard "wreck" and thought car crash. "Is she okay? When? When did this happen?"

"Yesterday. They did the surgery last night."

"Shit. Where is she?"

"Miriam Hospital."

Julie tried to say something more but I'd already hung up.

I just went, on out Hope for maybe a mile and a left on Fifth. I didn't even turn on the radio. The I-have-a-mission stance only began to fray when I got to the front desk and asked for Leah's room. The round woman with the checked scarf whistled at her computer, wrote the number on a slip, and handed it over, waving me away in one motion.

Everything slowed as I walked the halls. How were all these women I used to love ending up in hospitals? I shook my head. This was a different thing. I stopped a few feet from Leah's open door. What if she didn't want to see me? My jaw felt strange. What's the worst she could do? Tell me to go? My knuckle tapped the metal door frame. It rang.

It's always surreal, seeing someone you know in a hospital bed. You always think: What world allows this to happen? The room felt cold. Leah had on a green hospital top and her hair was pulled back. Her eyes were closed and her face looked pink. She had a pale blue plastic ID bracelet on her right wrist. It was her left leg, up on a dull silver support, her toes sticking out at the end of a long, dark blue cast. The cast seemed to go halfway up her thigh. A green blanket covered her other leg. It was a private room. The TV was on ESPN but muted. A pair of aluminum crutches leaned against the chair's blue and yellow cushion, clearly out of reach.

My feet stopped. "Wow." It came out in a whisper.

Leah's eyes slowly opened. She tried to sit up and fell back. Her lips pressed together. Her chin wrinkled. She blinked and the look went from surprise to something wary to something I couldn't place. "I can't believe this," she said. Her voice was low. I hadn't heard it for a while.

"Me either." I slipped the crutches off the chair and sat.

"I nearly called you."

"You did? You should have." It just came out.

"How'd you find me?"

"Julie."

"Oh." She sounded almost pleased. "Cecilia had to go to Syracuse. Her mom's worse. I don't know how long she's going to be there." Leah gave me a look, as if she were still trying to place the fact that I was sitting across from her. Her head came forward. "I'm glad you came but—"

"No, stop." I pointed to the door. "That stuff is all out there. It's done. You're still you, I'm still me. What was I going to do, find out you were here and not show up?"

Leah's tongue crossed her bottom lip as if something had surprised her. She watched me again. "What's that thing on your wrist?"

I lifted the hand, remembering that I had an appointment somewhere downstairs the next day to take off the splint. "The kid did it. My pinky got caught between two mantels, last week at the yard." I didn't tell her it was right after we talked.

"Last week?" Leah winced. "Oh, Keeper."

"It's fractured. I'll live. It's not as bad as—what did you do?"

"I broke my kneecap."

A streamer of pain went up my right side. "Shit, how?"

"I don't want to tell you. It's too stupid."

"So if I run into you some summer afternoon later in the century and there's this big scar on your knee, then you'll tell me?"

"It's because of Jon."

"Jon broke your kneecap?"

"No. Jon's big fucking dog broke my kneecap. It happened yesterday. They set it and wired it together with surgical cable last night. It was in three pieces. I'm still kind of fuzzy. Do I sound fuzzy?"

"Not that much."

"It's hard keeping my eyes open."

"How long are you here for?"

"Three days? Five? I don't know. I can't imagine longer."

"So you were walking Jon's dog? Where's Jon?"

"North Carolina. He's staying all week in fucking Carolina. I shouldn't be telling you this."

"I didn't know Jon had a dog."

"He doesn't. It's his separated wife's dog. Phoebe went out of town and I don't know how I ended up taking care of the dog. This is all too embarrassing."

"Where did it happen?"

"Wayland Square. I started to trip and Sunny pulled and my knee hit this ridge in the sidewalk. He's a husky. I let go and screamed and the dog ran away, so Jon's mad about that. But I broke my knee."

"Sunny?"

"I know. I called Julie, then Seth at work to find the dog. I don't know what happened. I was walking his separated wife's dog. I played basketball all these years and never wrecked anything, even an ACL. Now look."

"How much does it hurt?"

Her fingers folded into a fist. "They come with meds when I ask. My toes itch and I can't reach them. They get prickly. I'm really fuzzy. Did I say that?"

I got up to massage her toes.

"Keeper, no, you don't have to. Okay, that feels good. I guess I'm not going to say no."

I waved the length of her leg. "How long for this?"

"Months. Two until it's healed. I might get a brace. Wait, Julie said you called? Fred came back?"

"Last night. A van pulled up and he hopped out. He's sitting on the couch right now, even as we speak."

Leah gazed out at the construction next door as if she had forgotten what she meant to say. "Really?"

"No, I invented that as a ruse to see you."

"Well." Her hand floated. "Is he okay?"

"Seems it. He hasn't lost weight. I think he found a better meal ticket somewhere and just stayed. Leo's scared to death of him."

"He is?"

I heard a knock and turned to see Bob Eastlake, the orthopedist who worked on my hand. He tilted his head and closed one eye, as if that might help him understand how I happened to be in Leah's room. Why is it such a surprise when your doctor recognizes you? "Well then." He touched his red beard. "I know that splint."

I stepped aside and went to the chair as he picked up Leah's chart. "You two?" His index finger wiggled between us.

"We just, you know—ships in the night." I wasn't sure what I meant.

Bob Eastlake smiled strangely. He asked Leah how the pain was, if she slept? "Pink toes, that's a good sign." He stared at the chart for a minute, wrote something down, clicked his pen, and turned to me. "Let's see that hand." He undid the splint and started moving the last two fingers, which were taped together. "How's this?"

"Ow," I said.

He hummed. "We're going to want to work on more movement. You're coming in? If you don't want to put the splint back, don't. Okay, everybody be good." He left.

"He's yours, too?" Leah sounded almost dubious.

"Ow," I said, still staring at my hand. "I don't like that he can just come in and make my hand hurt." The whole arm started to ache. I shook it out, gently. "Do you need stuff? Your things? You've only been here? Right?"

"Are you okay?" she asked.

"I guess."

Leah sighed. Her hand slid across her face. She closed her eyes and opened them slowly. "Can you help me get to the bathroom?"

"Yeah." She sat up. I put my hands under the cast as she eased it down. She slid around. Her arm draped across my shoulder. It felt warm and a little damp, like we did this all the time. We hopped the three steps to the bathroom.

"Thank you," she said as we made it back to the bed. "I'm so sleepy. It was like a racetrack out in the hall last night. They forget to close the door. I only got a private room because that's all they had." She laughed. "They told me not to make any big decisions for twenty-four hours." I helped get her leg back up. "Can you bring me a picture of Fred? Walking a cat never would have done this to me."

"Walking Fred might have, if you could walk a cat."

She yawned. "Julie's supposed to bring me things this afternoon. Can you find me Doritos?" Her hand did a floppy wave. "I think I have to sleep now."

Leah's head pressed into the pillow and I watched her eyes close. I turned off the muted TV and slipped out. I wasn't sure exactly what had happened, but something had.

TWENTY-SEVEN

I kept going back. It wasn't a plan and I didn't think about where it might lead, it simply felt like the thing I needed to do. At the shop I reread the e-mail about the Hudson locomotive a hundred and seven times and forwarded it to Tim. As soon as I hit "Send," the wealth effect kicked in and I decided that was enough work for one day. At home I made a brief time-and-date-stamped documentary video of Fred as he sat on the couch, then I crashed. When I woke up it was gray out and I almost drove right over to the hospital, but the idea of it felt wrong. A little too eager? I'm only helping out a friend, I told myself. I timed the trip back so I'd have about an hour before I had to leave and pick up Leo.

I found Leah asleep with her laptop balanced on her stomach. She had on a black T-shirt, which somehow made everything, the cast and the hospital bed aside, feel a little more normal. In my knapsack I brought a fleece top she'd left at the house, a bag of Cool Ranch Doritos, a bottle of Polar Orange Dry soda, and the video camera. I put the knapsack on the chair and undid the zipper.

Her eyes opened. "Oh," she said and the laptop started to slide. She seemed surprised. I caught the computer with my good hand and moved it to the chair like a waiter subduing a balky drink tray.

"It's so slow here," Leah said. "It's like I saw you days ago." She sat up and ran both hands over her ears. "Or maybe it was that long a nap. No, I had lunch, Julie came by. I'm still fuzzy, from the drugs."

I unloaded the knapsack.

"I need that whole bag of Doritos right now," she said.

I tore open the top. "Is it a sign of age or maturity that at home I've started opening these things with scissors?" I asked and Leah smiled.

"There's a hotspot here," she said, pointing to the computer. "One of the nurses told me. It's from the office behind that wall. I was wandering around on 'Art In Ruins' before I fell asleep. Do you know that? It's a blog with a lot about Providence buildings and rehabs. I found a link to Frank Lloyd Wright houses made of Lego."

I clicked the switch on the camcorder up to "Player" and re-wound the documentary. Leah brushed back her hair. "I wish I could wash my hair," she said and pressed her eye to the eyepiece. "Huh, he's the same size. Is this old footage?"

"Look at the date. Rewind too far and you'll end up with Leo."

She kept running the little clip over and over: Fred asleep, Fred opening his eyes, Fred waving one paw across his nose, Fred putting his head back down. Her smile didn't change. It was the look you get when you're watching something you're thrilled to see but can't quite trust.

"How's the pain?"

"It depends," she said. "It's okay. When Julie went to get my stuff she said the elevator in Cecilia's building is being replaced. I can't believe that." She tapped the cast.

We watched a Boston College basketball replay on NESN. It felt calm and companionable and only out in the parking lot did it finally dawn on me that even though I might have folded, things could still be in play.

The next day I got there at midmorning and Leah's room was empty. It felt like a scene from some bad movie. I backed out into the hall, just as I would have in a bad movie, and a nurse with tight dark hair and a pink floral hospital top said: "She's just moved. They know where." She arched her index finger back to the nurse's station without breaking stride.

I started walking but it turned into a run. I mean it wasn't like she'd gone to ICU and the new room was only down the hall, but Leah had a roommate.

There was something bright on the TV up in the corner above the door. "Oh," Leah said. She seemed surprised but it was different from the first time, more pleasure and less shock.

"This is Joe," Leah said. "We solve world problems."

Joe was long and thin in his late sixties, I guessed. He was mostly bald with a high pink forehead and a white ship captain's beard. Joe gave me a small open-handed salute. "Silver here and I get along fine. We'd close the curtain but how could I miss this?" They were watching cartoon pigs with the sound off.

"Cartoon Network?" I asked. It was some kid show I'd never seen before. "They have little kid shows in the morning? When did this start?"

"It's colorful," Joe said. "But they're still pigs. Silver, we're going back to ESPN as soon as I get over there to wrestle that remote from your grubby fingers."

"We're an exceptional couple," Leah said, "since they don't as a rule have mixed rooms. I said I didn't mind. Everyone gets called by their last name."

"Too much coaching," Joe announced. "High school hockey in Massachusetts and here, then I retired. Coached tennis, too. Taught social studies, driver's ed. I still play pick-up hockey, Wednesdays at the URI arena in South County. We've got a good group. They let me score pretty much whenever I want. Do you play?"

"I did as a kid. Then I went to soccer."

"Why'd you stop? It's turning into a transition sport these days, like golf. You can find a league. Lots of no-checking leagues. Just go, find one."

This hadn't occurred to me. But how could I do that with Leo? I couldn't.

"Joe broke his hip," Leah said. "Lifting a box for his sister. He's feeling pretty perky so we've decided he's getting the better drugs."

"Actually it wasn't the box, it was the ladder. I fell off the ladder."

"We both have Lanky Bob," Leah said. "I think this end of the hall is Doctor Bob's warehouse."

"Maybe I should move in," I said.

"Why?" Joe squinted.

"I have the same doc."

"What's that on your hand?" he asked.

I held up my pinky and told the story. "And I was a goalie, in soccer. I had concussions, broke a rib, but not this."

"Your three-year-old did that? Just wait. Let's hope that's the least of it," Joe said. "Look at us."

"Did you bring any more Doritos?" Leah asked. "By chance?"

I unloaded the new bag and another liter of soda from the knapsack. I rambled on about selling the Hudson locomotive and how with the rolling stock we made almost $13,000, not counting the commission. "That's all the good news this week can handle. From here on it's downhill."

"Optimist," she said.

"You sold a locomotive for thirteen thousand dollars?" Joe asked. "What kind of work are you in?" I explained and Joe said, "Oh god, I have some of those model trains somewhere. Can you find me thirteen thousand dollars? No? All right, I'm watching beach volleyball from now on. Miss, you have a visitor, switch to ESPN."

Leah handed me the remote, which I passed to Joe.

"Does it hurt?" I touched the cast. "I mean how bad does it hurt today?"

"It aches. It still feels like someone hit my knee with a hammer. And I so wish I could roll over without it being a production. Come on, distract me."

I told her about making plans to close the Wickenden Street store. I told her about the Wilsons and how Tim thinks there's one less kid.

Her eyebrows lowered a little. "Like they lost one? Like one of the kids died?"

"That's it," I said. "We don't know. It's kind of too awful to think about. But I'm thinking now that next time I want to peek at some of the later boxes, just to make sure that's not it."

Leah nodded, as if she meant to be there, too.

"Could you kids spare me a Dorito?" Joe asked. I handed him the bag. "Ah," he said.

I stayed awhile longer but I don't remember what we talked about. It had started not to matter in a way.

After dinner I was on the couch with Leo, watching a Thomas video and holding an aqua ice pack against my newly aching pinky, when we heard a knock on the door. Leo grabbed my arm. Usually at that time of night it's earnest college kids trying to sign me up for the Save Our Sky Action Coalition or Clean Water Lives Free or something, but it was Julie.

She unzipped her coat. "Hi. I'm here to put Leo to bed."

Leo nodded, as if this were part of some vast plan he had already approved. "Oh sure," he said.

"If I do that you can visit Leah."

"You know I've been there?"

She regarded me. "Of course I know."

What was I going to do, refuse? I'd learned a few things. "You're enabling," I said and put the ice pack on a plate.

"Enabling what?" Julie looked baffled. "Leah needs visitors. I am helping my friend." She almost frowned.

That night, crossing the street from the hospital parking lot and walking beside the construction fence, I got a little anxious. It might have been the strangeness of being out on my own after dark or the stack of things Leah and I weren't talking about, starting with how she was going to make it up to the fifth floor at Cecilia's without an elevator? Or drive?

I found Leah and Joe sipping beer from white squeeze bottles and watching Maine and New Hampshire play hockey on NESN. They seemed to be talking about love, or Joe was. He didn't notice as I slipped into the chair.

"Gloria," Joe said, "now she was a great love of my life. You'll notice I said *a* love of my life and not *the*. Dark hair, we used to dance so well together. But Gloria wouldn't move here from California. She had family there, lots of sisters. This was after the navy for me and I suppose I could have stayed out west. But I got mad that she wouldn't do this. I stomped out and got on a train. A big scene. It was almost a bluff. I thought of it as a bluff, only I played it out. I was young. I thought there would be someone else and there was, but it wasn't the same, not that you're ever going to tell anyone that. You know, I wouldn't have had the kids I have now, the grandkids. I'm a sticker. I usually don't give up, but that time I did."

Leah smiled faintly. "That's sad."

Joe's long hands caught his elbows. "Yes and no. Other things come along. But are they better? It's funny how you'll never know." He sipped. "Holy cow, how did he miss that? That kid has a shaky glove." He looked over. "Mr. Keeper, how'd you sneak in? Leah and I have been talking about large issues in your absence. Good to see you."

"Good to be seen," I said. "How are you doing?"

"Not out and about as much as I'd like but I'm alive. That's starting to be a consideration." He toasted me with his squeeze bottle. "It's frowned upon, this, but in our condition . . . My daughter supplied us."

"Joe, do you live alone?" I wasn't sure why I asked.

"Generally. My Kathleen is moving in for a while when I get out."

"Joe's not letting me watch basketball," Leah said. "We're going to have to have a talk. See my new walker?" She pointed with her pinky. "The nurses say I'm young for a walker. But it's easier than crutches. How's Fred?"

"Grumpy about his food, but nesting on the couch. He's Fred-like."

"Am I going to have to kidnap Fred? When I get out?"

"I don't know. Mobility is the key to any kidnapping."

This got me a wry smile. "Is Leo still frightened of him?"

Hearing his name surprised me. "He's better. He keeps his distance. It would be best if we had more than one couch."

"What's Leo painting?"

I couldn't remember. "I think they're using glue now at school. We don't have an easel. Julie does but I should get one."

"I liked the blue paintings. Tomorrow Joe and I are watching only soaps and basketball. Joe has never seen a soap."

"In between," Joe said, "soaps in between. Honey, we're lucky we get along as well as we do, but neither of us are watching that *Supernanny* show again. That's a disaster."

It took a minute then I thought: How does Leah know about Leo's paintings?

"Lanky Bob was here," she said. "He tells me he'll decide in the morning when I'm going home." She gave me an odd look, almost trolling for a reaction, but the moment forked away.

We watched hockey, I massaged Leah's toes, various nurses stopped by. Leah took her evening meds and everyone fell asleep halfway through the third period. I rinsed their squeeze bottles before I left.

It's the small futures that lead to the bigger ones. Wednesday morning I got there around eleven and Leah sighed when she saw me. It was a multipart look: sad, frustrated, and unsure of how to proceed. She leaned back against the white towel covering her pillow. Her hair was wet. "You missed Lanky Bob."

I glanced around as if Lanky Bob might be hiding. Joe appeared to be asleep. "What did he say?"

"I'm going home tomorrow afternoon." She puffed out her lips.

"You don't look as happy as I'd expect."

"I don't know if I can do it," she said. "I think it's too soon. I slipped in the shower trying to wash my hair. I didn't fall, or I sort of did, but they have handles."

I sat in the too-familiar chair and wished I could increase the caffeine levels in my system through mental imagery alone. My fingers slid under my chin. "I've been wondering how this was going to work. There's a lot we haven't been talking about. Like Cecilia's elevator?"

"We should talk about that."

"All right."

"I'm not going back to work with Jon."

My head did a little dip. "You're not?"

"I can't," she said. "It's stupid. I shouldn't have even, there's no shortage of empty mills to rehab in Rhode Island. I should have left when Jon started looking at projects in North Carolina."

"Yeah, but I thought you—"

"No." It was a no I knew. "There are things you don't know about that. I had a Jon problem before you and I met."

"You did?"

"Why do you think Tim and Julie kept working to get us in the same room? Why do you think I met you at Card Night? Jon was this bad decision that everybody knew about and I kept making. He wasn't separated then, the first time. And you and I came along and it stopped. It did and I thought finally, that's done. It was just when I started staying at Cecilia's that—I didn't want to tell you about all the stuff from before and make you worried when there wasn't anything to worry about, because there wasn't."

"Only later."

"Only just recently. I needed to go somewhere. Jon was the path of least resistance."

The next thought arrived like a billboard. You can flare up at just the mention of Jon or you can let it go. I was tired. I needed coffee. I let it go.

"I called him yesterday. He's still in North Carolina. It's all done."

"Really?" I believed her but I didn't know what to think. Then I saw Leah at work, with Jon across the room by the windows looking out over the river. "If we hadn't broken up you wouldn't have been walking that dog," I said. It sounded like this had just dawned on me. "With no Leo we wouldn't have broken up."

"That's true," Leah said.

I blinked. Then other than Leo, was there really anything wrong with us? There wasn't. I knew that. It began to occur to me, the same way you first notice a change in the landscape, that we were edging up on something.

"Don't look at me like that," Leah said. "I had second thoughts all the time. I felt awful when Jon called at Card Night. I got intensely jealous that afternoon when I saw Grace walking Leo across the street. But I didn't know who Grace was. Then I saw your car in the rearview mirror and it felt like I'd driven myself to an ambush. I don't even know what I was doing driving by. I'd make such a lousy stalker. Leo's a whole set of challenges I hadn't signed up for and didn't know if I wanted. It felt like a giant compromise."

"It is," I said. "It's one giant compromise after another. It's fucking hard. It fills your head and makes you vulnerable in ways I never imagined. But it's happened so—" Leah began to squint and that deep voice behind my ear told me to shut up.

"I was so mad at you that night in the driveway," she said. "Out in the snow, when you weren't listening and you do that, you assume that all things will work out fine. You didn't even talk to me beforehand. You sprang it on me and the monitor went off and Leo yelled and—I've never been that mad. It's like what I thought couldn't matter. Like we didn't matter."

"That's not true."

"That's the way it felt. Then I'd miss you and get mad at myself for that. It's not like I never wanted kids, but he's Cynthia's kid."

"I didn't tell you because I didn't want to blow things up. Only they blew up anyway."

"Then later I kept thinking, what do I do, stay mad and give up the love of my life?"

"You thought that?"

"Yeah, I'd never say that but, yes. If I were ten years younger, at that point you always think someone else is coming along, but with us." Her hand dropped to the green blanket. "Then I got all stubborn because I couldn't imagine it, the three of us."

"The three?"

"Yeah, see, I said it. Why is it a surprise? I told Mom what happened to my knee and you showing up and everything and she says, 'Honey, sometimes you just have to overlook a few things.' "

"There's no way to overlook Leo."

"I know. Julie said you have to imagine which is better, living with the thing you're ambivalent about or not living with any of it. I thought, what if Leo hadn't appeared and I turned out to never be ready for kids and you and I went on as before. Say we took Path A. We would have gotten bored at some point. People get dogs. They raise llamas. Become missionaries. By then I might have wanted a kid. We did talk about it."

"We only decided there never would be a good time to have a kid." I took a long breath. I began to think about what I would have to overlook. I'd have to overlook Jon. I could overlook Jon.

"Leo looks like Cynthia," Leah said. "She's still going to be in the house. I worry about how I'm going to handle that. And I feel bad about feeling that. And I don't want to stop doing what I'm doing and I don't want to turn into one of those angry moms you see piloting strollers around the mall. I don't want things to be like they are for my sister. Don't you ever get scared by who you might turn into?"

"Why didn't we ever talk about this?"

"Because you wouldn't. And because I was scared. The openness of it scares me."

"It scares me, too," I said. "All the time. The thing is, having a kid doesn't make your life better. It does not improve your life, but it does make things richer. It's a different thing. I didn't expect that."

Leah closed her eyes and nodded, as if she agreed or as if she might want to see how that felt. My breath caught. It all seemed to be opening up too fast.

"I saw Leo over the weekend," she said. "We painted at Julie's. Both days. The first time was a coincidence, but not the second. I brought all the tape. I met Calvin, but Calvin had to do errands. I've seen Leo other times, too."

"You have?"

"That time with Tim. I got curious. Tim called."

"After all those things you said at the yard? That was a complete no-fest."

"I know, I know, but it was the big campaign. Every time I found another puzzle piece it made me feel more guilty. I felt cornered. I knew Jon was a mistake." Her fingers covered her eyes. "How was it ever going to work if I only came back to stop feeling guilty?"

"Oh." I'd never thought of that.

"Now you're here and you're you, regular you. I started thinking again. Or it might have been the drugs wearing off." Leah squinted, like she was still waiting for me to catch on.

"If it was just the drugs," I said, "I'd seem different by now." Then I realized, this was always going to end with a deal. That was the way out from the beginning. "What do you want?"

"Us," she said. "If you want us, I do too. I miss it."

"Okay."

"Just okay?"

"No, I mean, yes, but how? It's Leo, too."

"I'm going to need help. We have to figure out some way to preserve a bit of you and me."

"I can do that," I said. "Grace wants visits. Tim and Julie. My mom. There are all these odd alliances."

"I don't want to be cut off from the rest of the human race."

"No," I said, "it turns out you meet different parts of the human race."

"I don't know that I can do this."

"So we try."

"Promise it won't be us alone?"

"Yes."

"Promise me, I don't want to rule out the possibility of our having a kid."

I blinked. I heard that voice behind my ear: *You can barely do one kid. How could anybody do two?* Leah kept staring. Think. All right, if I can do it most of the time with one real kid and one invisible one, if I have the capacity for that, then maybe. I've already been pulled through the portal. How much more crushed could I be? "Yup," I said. "I mean, yes."

"Promise me, I want to be married. You know that. I don't care how, I just want to be."

"I heard that." Joe's hand covered his eyes as if he couldn't bear to watch. "You get 'em."

I looked back at Leah, at that gaze, the one I missed, the one I wanted. She held out her hand. I took it and squeezed. "Okay," I said. The amazing thing was I felt completely calm.

Joe said, "Now you've done it." He chuckled.

TWENTY-EIGHT

Some things happen before they really do. It's months later, the ridge of July, and we're on Block Island: Leah, Leo, and me. We're here because friends of Julie's rented a tiny house, only they had an elderly parent emergency and couldn't stay. We're filling in like hermit crabs.

It's maybe nine in the morning on our second day. The sky is half white but it's hot already and the air clings. We're prickly with sweat as we finish climbing down the 250 wooden steps to the base of Mohegan Bluffs. I was against this, since Leah's knee is still in that Frankenstein brace, only she said go. I also wasn't sure Leo could make it back up, but he will, on my shoulders, as my calves tighten through every porchlike switchback. The sand before us is the color of a bruised peach and hard, the cliffs a darker gray, and the surf hisses, still riled from some distant tropical storm. The pale green-brown waves cut in from odd angles and people are running through it, but I wouldn't go out there. We've left behind the clutter of boogie boards and coolers and rounded a point. We're still scrambling over bowl-sized rocks when I look up and see the fort.

It's been pieced together from grayed planks and plywood scraps and sticks out from the cliff like a fantastic set of stairs. There are three flat roofs, decks, and windows, and a trail of pink stones leads up to a doorlike space on the side. Spars and poles point off in every direction and it's all draped with plastic jugs and faded-white lobster buoys. Shreds of blue and silver tarps crackle in the wind and tangle in the netting above.

I'm standing with my heels in the fine sand and my back to the ocean, which they say you should never do. I'm ignoring the rack of dark clouds off along the tip of Long Island, as the waves foam around my shins and dig the sand out beneath me. You can think you're standing still but you're always going somewhere.

Leo vanishes inside and shouts, "Yubb bubba beee," from the first room. He is louder now and demanding in fresh ways as he settles farther in. The house feels smaller than Leah and I ever could have imagined. Leah follows him up, leaning stiffly to the right with every other step. She pulls aside the yellow canvas and disappears. Rehab is slow and Leah is impatient. She hasn't found another firm yet or decided if she wants to set up her own shop. I know we're still riding the energy you get from finding a thing you once thought was lost. It is minute by minute, but in the good ones Leah will look over and say: We're okay, we just skipped a few steps.

In September, there will be a small, relieved wedding at Leah's parents' cottage in the Thousand Islands. Grace will be there, Joan, Tim and Julie, my parents (my dad using a walker after he breaks his hip), both brothers, and the destructive nephews. There will be Leah's grad-school friends, her sister and brother-in-law, her brother, and all the Providence people and their kids we can convince to make the drive. There'll be a zydeco band, coaxed up from Syracuse with their partners and spouses and kids, who we'll feed all weekend and they will become our great friends who we'll never see again. And none if it will matter in a way, because Leah and I already know, even here, that it all happened way before, when I squeezed her hand.

Only it's now, and Leo climbs higher into the fort. It worries me, even though at this point he still stops when I say so. He pops out on a porch and slaps a pink plastic buoy with both hands. He pushes and the buoy makes a slow, two-part thud against a gray post before it swings back.

"Leo," Leah calls from the big room, "there's a hammock and a bed with posts and a pretend TV."

I will go up, only for the moment this doesn't seem necessary. I know it's the room I saw in the dream months ago, after Leah left, the room I saw beforehand, as Leo would say, where Leah opened her eyes and smiled as the mist moved through, riffling the beach rose behind us on its way up the cliff. This is the fort from the dream, only it's richer and festooned in ways I could never have imagined.

"I'm here," Leo says. "Here, here, here."

"I know," Leah says, and her voice fades.

I should go up, but I'm still watching. I'm stunned that this moment even exists. I don't know for sure how long this is all going to hold together, but it might. My mom once said that people can get to good places in very strange ways and I think this must be true. I'm here, I'm holding up the sides, I'm folding in the flaps, I'm trying for saves and taking up the slack, I'm keeping my finger on the string.

1. Jimmy Keeper has an offbeat job. How does it mesh with his personality?

2. Keeper's life changes overnight. What has he lost?

3. Is Leah's reaction to Leo's arrival realistic? Does it echo anyone else's reaction to a new and disturbing situation?

4. Can you relate to Cynthia's keeping of such a secret? What role do secrets play in the book? What makes people give them up?

5. What is the fascination with the Wilsons? Would you be as intrigued if you were at Card Night?

6. Why do you think Keeper is so bad at asking for help when he needs it?

7. "It looks like life has flattened out and presto, some completely cool object pops up right in front of you." Is this in any way an analogy for the story?

8. How do Keeper's parents figure into the story? Should they have appeared earlier? Why do you think they didn't?

9. The "wooing" of Leah—Keeper's plan to get her back— does it work in any way?

10. What does the return of Fred foretell?

11. What does Keeper gain from the upheaval of his life?

12. Where do you think these characters will be in five years?

A
Reading
Group
Guide

For more reading group suggestions, visit
www.readinggroupgold.com.

St. Martin's
Griffin